MOST PRECIOUS BLOOD

Enjoy!

GUERNICA WORLD EDITIONS 2

MOST PRECIOUS BLOOD

VINCE SGAMBATI

GUERNICA
World
EDITIONS
TORONTO · BUFFALO · LANCASTER (U.K.)
2018

Michael Mirolla, editor
David Moratto, cover and interior design
Guernica Editions Inc.
1569 Heritage Way, Oakville, (ON), Canada L6M 2Z7
2250 Military Road, Tonawanda, N.Y. 14150-6000 U.S.A.
www.guernicaeditions.com

Distributors:
University of Toronto Press Distribution,
5201 Dufferin Street, Toronto (ON), Canada M3H 5T8
Gazelle Book Services, White Cross Mills
High Town, Lancaster LA1 4XS U.K.

First edition.
Printed in Canada.

Legal Deposit—First Quarter
Library of Congress Catalog Card Number: 2017955489
Library and Archives Canada Cataloguing in Publication
Sgambati, Vince, author
Most precious blood / Vince Sgambati. -- First edition.

(Guernica world editions ; 2)
Issued in print and electronic formats.
ISBN 978-1-77183-306-6 (softcover).--ISBN 978-1-77183-307-3
(EPUB).--ISBN 978-1-77183-308-0 (Kindle)

I. Title.

PS3619.G37M67 2018   813'.6   C2017-906460-6   C2017-906461-4

For Jack & Jesse

On the Upper East or West Side of Manhattan,
Lasante's would be considered
a gourmet grocery store. Its tin ceiling
and hanging cast-iron fans seen as retro.
But at the cross of 91ˢᵗ Avenue and 104ᵗʰ Street
in Glenhaven, Queens, it was a vestige for the few Italians
who remained in the neighborhood, and for
their adult children who drove in from Long Island
before holidays and special occasions
to reclaim some remote flavor of ethnicity.

1

A *babbalucci* slithered down a sack of semolina but recoiled its tentacles as Lenny plucked it from the burlap and returned it to its fellow snails. Its ambitious foot left a shimmering memory of one more failed escape. A second plodding fugitive found its way to the sawdust-covered, wood-plank floor and went unnoticed.

Lenny returned to his book. Sweat dripped from a wax-coated cheese hanging from an iron hook above his head, and he slid the book along the worn Formica counter adjacent pyramids of groceries displayed in the storefront windows, which blocked much of the natural light and made it difficult for Lenny to read the small print.

"Why did you stay so long?" It was his papa's voice.

"Why did you die?" Lenny said.

"I had no choice," Papa answered.

As usual, Lenny nodded, shrugged his shoulders and thought: *Neither did I.* He often spoke with the dead.

He closed the book and pushed it aside along with his tired regrets. Lately, he'd finish a chapter and have no recollection of what he had just read. Once he memorized Shakespeare's sonnets, but that was long ago, before Papa died, and he had to help Mama with the children and the store.

The front door swung open, and the noise from the crowded avenue followed Lenny's son into the store. Except for his mother's green eyes, Frankie was the younger version of Lenny—thick black curly hair, olive complexion, medium height, and solidly built from lifting heavy cases of canned olive oil and plum tomatoes, and from heaving weighty prosciuttos and provolones on and off iron hooks above the store counter and lining the storefront windows.

Stinking of perspiration and beer, and with his soaked t-shirt wadded up in his right hand, Frankie leaned over the counter and kissed Lenny's cheek. "Hey, Dad."

"What the hell happened to you?" Lenny said.

"The guys where throwing water balloons."

"Smells more like beer balloons." But Frankie didn't answer, and Lenny asked him if he had had his fill of Big Vinny's block party.

Frankie stretched, rubbed his t-shirt across the sweat on the back of his neck and under his arms. "Yeah, I'll help you after I wash up."

He walked down the right aisle of the store to the breezeway that connected the store to the house, but then stopped and spun around as if someone had grabbed his arm. That's when he told Lenny about the cabdriver.

"Holy Crap! I just remembered. This cabdriver tried to ram his way through the block party. Imagine doing something so stupid? But a bunch of the guys went after him. They threw bottles and stuff and scared him off. Can't imagine being so dumb. Big Vinny's face got so red I thought he was going to burst an artery."

"And you?" Lenny said. Lenny sensed the familiar tightness in his chest and jaw.

"Me? I stayed out of it. I kind of felt sorry for the guy though. He's lucky they didn't catch up with him."

More Big Vinny drama, Lenny thought, and reminded his son to stay out of trouble. "One more year, Frankie. Then you're out of this lousy neighborhood and off to college. Just keep your nose clean. That's all I'm asking."

"I know. I know," Frankie shouted and disappeared into the breezeway. "That's what I'm gonna do now. Clean my nose and my armpits while I'm at it."

Lenny shook his head and sighed. Before him stretched two narrow aisles flanked by shelves groaning with groceries.

Behind Lenny stood a chrome and glass deli case filled with a few domestic cold cuts, but mostly with imports like capicola and also freshly made cheese like ricotta, which the old timers pronounced gabagool and rigot. At one end of the deli case was an open cooler stocked with juice, soda, milk, and other prepackaged dairy products. At the other end was the checkout counter where longtime customers bragged or complained about their children, gossiped about neighbors, argued about everything, sighed about the past, and shook their heads or clicked their tongues about the present. The future was never discussed.

Frankie bounced back into the store wearing a clean t-shirt and smelling of cologne. Wet furrows shone where a comb failed to tame his hair. The avenue was busy, but the store remained quiet, just a few customers came and went, buying small items like cigarettes or gum, occasionally some produce or a roll of toilet paper.

It was dark when Frankie stood at the open doorway, and outside young men with tattooed, beefy arms, bulging from sweat-soaked t-shirts, tossed mats of fireworks onto the burning heap in the middle of the avenue. Their gold chains and pinky rings reflected the fire's flickering blues and yellows. Ash cans and cherry bombs exploded; flares and rockets careened. Lenny could hear the warnings rise from the feverish spectators to the neighbors leaning out of second or third story windows, above storefronts, or standing on fire escapes. Some adults snatched children away from the inner circle, and older children protested. Lenny had once been one of those adults. The air was thick, hot, and stunk of sulfur. Back when Giuliani was mayor there had been a crackdown on the massive sale of fireworks, but men like Big Vinny were very resourceful. His Fourth of July bash, fireworks and all, took place not three blocks from a police station. Cops patrolled from rooftops and in helicopters, but they never shut down Big Vinny's party.

Until the concrete cooled and the scrawnier fledgling thugs swept up the smoldering ash, Lenny postponed closing his store—a ploy to keep Frankie off the streets.

As he wiped down the already spotless slicing machine, the rotten-egg stink of fireworks became unbearable.

"Shut the door," he said, but he didn't mean for Frankie to step outside first. Slowly, Frankie moved away from Lenny's view until he disappeared into the crowd.

One more year, Lenny thought. *Just one more year, and you'll be out of this dead-end neighborhood.*

He pressed his hands against the Formica counter and felt its coolness through his calloused palms while his eyes scanned barrels of

olives, baskets of loose beans, legumes, figs, and the basket where another foolish snail began its escape. Behind the barrels and baskets was
a tall narrow case with glass shelves where each morning Lenny stacked
loaves of semolina bread, and once savored the aroma of the fresh warm
bread, especially on cold mornings, but that was when he recited the
sonnets from memory and thought work was noble. Now he held his
breath while he filled the shelves, for fear he might vomit.

An explosion dwarfed the sound of the fireworks and rattled the
storefront windows. Lenny jumped over the counter, ran out the front
door, and shoved his way through the chaos.

2

It was the day before Big Vinny's Fourth of July block party when Frankie and Gennaro, Big Vinny's youngest son, drove to Old Man Tucci's place in the Catskills. Cheers and applause greeted them as Gennaro steered his convertible off the curving Catskill road onto Tucci's rutted driveway, where noise from a television game show blasted through the torn screens in windows propped open with split logs. Tucci's rusted-out pickup truck was parked under a stand of cedars in front of his rusted-out house. Ragged patches of screen hung from the once screened-in porch, and the boys climbed its three rickety steps and approached the front door, where spiders disappeared behind the rotting doorjamb. Gennaro yelled a string of profanities. He was repulsed by spiders and mice and snakes—anything that scampered or slithered. Frankie laughed.

The front door was ajar so, after Gennaro finished swearing and scratching at his arms, he stuck his head into the foyer and yelled: "Mr. Tucci ... it's me ... Gennaro DiCico." No answer.

Entering the house was a risky venture given that Tucci was never too far from his loaded shotgun, but the boys inched their way through the open door and foyer, and then into the living room where Tucci snored in his green, Naugahyde recliner—more foam stuffing than Naugahyde. Next to the recliner, on a braided rug, Tucci's old bulldog, Meatball, harmonized with Tucci.

"Door number four!" yelled a couple with orange complexions and Hawaiian shirts.

"Fuck me," Gennaro whispered. "If that didn't wake him, he must be dead."

Meatball opened his eyes, looked at the boys, but after one or two feeble wags of his tail, he went back to sleep.

Gennaro lifted an envelope from a table cluttered with mail and magazines, scribbled a note, and placed it on Tucci's lap along with five dollars.

"Come on," Gennaro whispered to Frankie, "we'll check in with him later." The orange couple on television won matching snowmobiles but looked disappointed.

Back on the porch, Gennaro swatted at cobwebs and tripped over a rubber boot while Frankie chuckled. It was hot for early July, and Frankie was glad to be out of the city, despite Gennaro's complaints about spiders and cobwebs. Had they been in Glenhaven, Gennaro would bitch about the heat. He just liked to complain.

When Frankie was little, he and Lenny made regular Sunday trips to Tucci's, driving 130 miles from Queens to Purling where Rocco Tucci owned 60 acres of woods, including a 20-foot waterfall and swimming hole. They often brought Gennaro and sometimes Lena, Gennaro's younger sister. Lena was Frankie's age, and Gennaro was two years older. On occasion the older DiCico brothers, Michael and Jimmy, joined in the summer excursions to Tucci's, but Big Vinny rarely went along.

As Frankie and Gennaro walked the pine-needle path to the waterfall, Frankie imagined the sound of his father's footsteps behind them and the image of his father carrying the Sunday *New York Times*, a six pack of cream sodas, and several eggplant or sausage and pepper sandwiches wrapped in butcher paper—one sandwich Lenny would have left at the house for Tucci. Back then, Frankie's Grandma Filomena worked in the store so Lenny and he and whichever DiCico kids joined them could leave before the Major Deegan became congested with traffic.

The meld of balsam and humus must have spurred Frankie's memories of childhood visits to Tucci's, but as he and Gennaro approached the swimming hole, and Gennaro stripped off his jeans and t-shirt, childhood memories vanished.

Gennaro climbed the moss-covered rocks to the crest of the waterfall. Centuries of erosion had carved and polished the rocks beneath the cascading water into a slide that stopped about six feet above the

swimming hole. The limbs of hemlocks, white pines, and a few scrag-
gly balsams reached out from shady spaces towards Gennaro, who
beckoned Frankie with his outstretched muscular arms. "Veni qua,
Francesco!" he shouted above the fortissimo of crashing water.

Frankie removed the camcorder from his backpack, adjusted the
zoom to capture the full length of the falls, and then focused on Gennaro,
who lived to be admired, and Frankie was more than willing to oblige.

Gennaro jumped—a bronze V piercing the rainbow-colored cata-
ract. He drew up his knees and locked his fingers around his shins,
cannonballed the final six feet, and splashed into the water. In seconds,
he emerged like a young Neptune and bellowed: "Mother of God, this
is liquid ice."

Camcorder off and returned to his backpack, Frankie whipped off
his t-shirt and jeans. Not a bronze Adonis—like Gennaro—chiseled from
hours of curls, bench presses, and crunches in the neighborhood gym.
Frankie's was the brawn of a working boy on the cusp of manhood.

They dove into the swimming hole, and like two young tigers they
roared and splashed, slammed into each other, wrestled, ignored each
other's not-so-flaccid dicks, and swam toward the bank, mounted the
slippery rocks, slid down the waterfall, and crashed into the swimming
hole, over and over as if they had spent their lives in captivity and were
almost but not quite free.

Eventually, Mr. Tucci hobbled down the path, leaning on his quad
canes as if he were clawing his way to the falls. He appeared ancient.
Time, loss, and regret had eroded his energy the way the falls had
eroded the rocks. Years ago, had he declined a neighbor's offer to drive
his family to church, he might now be watching his own grandchildren swim rather than Frankie and Gennaro. When Vincenzo Lasante,
Frankie's grandfather, had first met Rocco Tucci, there was also a Mrs.
Tucci and two young children, and every August, Vincenzo, his wife
Filomena, Lenny, and his siblings drove to Purling for a three-day
holiday—the Lasante family's annual vacation, and, except for funerals
and weddings, the only days that the grocery store was closed. Back
then there was a small bungalow adjacent the Tucci's house where the
Lasantes stayed. Frankie never saw it, but Lenny spoke of it so often that
Frankie could imagine its white clapboards, green trim and shutters,

the smell of lilacs that once framed its front porch, and hear his father, aunts, and uncle share scary stories while they dared not fall asleep.

In June of 1969, when Vicenzo Lasante called Rocco Tucci to confirm what had become a routine reservation, he learned that during the winter Mrs. Tucci and the children were returning from church in a neighbor's car when it skidded off the road, rolled over a steep embankment, and all of the passengers were killed. Tucci usually drove his family to church and waited for them in his car until Mass was over. That Sunday, a neighbor had offered to save him the trip and the hour wait in a cold car.

Filomena never returned to Purling, but Vincenzo visited that summer and every summer until his own premature death. He took day trips, not to leave Filomena home alone overnight, and she sent along a box packed with home-cooked meals and baked goods. Frankie learned of this from Lenny's stories. He also knew that Gennaro's Grandpa Giacomo often joined Grandpa Vincenzo. They took turns driving Vincenzo's old black Buick with red Naugahyde bench seats and packed with Lasante and DiCico children piled on each other's laps. There were photographs in the Lasante photo albums of the old Buick crammed with many children leaning out of the open windows and making faces into the camera.

Tucci finally waved to the boys.

"That you, Frankie Lasante?" he hollered.

"Yeah, Mr. Tucci. It's me and Gennaro DiCico," Frankie said, but he knew the old man couldn't hear him above the roar of the falls.

Tucci shook his head and flicked his wrist as if he were swatting at black flies. "You come visit before you go," he yelled, and hobbled back to his house.

Early evening, the sunlight abandoned the lush understory of ferns, wild rhododendron, jack-in-the-pulpit, and the few lingering trilliums, and it shone above the orange bark of scotch pines and the wispy branches of hemlocks and dawdled in the canopies of pale green pin oaks and sugar maples. A disgruntled chipmunk scolded a pair of impudent chickadees, and again Frankie recalled past trips with his father when Lenny guilted and bribed Gennaro and him to take hikes through the woods.

"Okay, boys, enough swimming, and on the way home we'll stop for ice cream," was Lenny's most persuasive carrot, and he'd slip a small naturalist guide book out from the hip pocket of his khaki pants, while Gennaro and Frankie begrudgingly followed him into the cool of giant white pines, where the boys turned fallen branches into weapons and conquered imaginary villains, but mostly they dragged their feet through the cushion of pine needles and yawned. Frankie's yawns were spurious, a pretense to save face before Gennaro, to disguise that he actually enjoyed the woodland adventures, just as he enjoyed museums, libraries, concerts, plays, and most anything that he did with his father, though he would have never admitted this since Gennaro had very rigid rules about what boys liked and didn't like. Naming woodland wildflowers was definitely not for boys.

Gennaro yelled over the music blasting through his headphones: "Let's go visit with Tucci!" He sat up. His skin glowed bronze and his close-cropped, curly, dirty blond hair was flecked with summer gold. Frankie turned away to conceal the rise in his boxers.

After they gathered empty bags and soda cans, stuffed them into their backpacks along with their towels, headphones, and iPods, they stepped into their jeans, slipped on their t-shirts, and headed back to Tucci's house. It would have been disrespectful not to visit. On their way to the house, Frankie glanced at the remnants of the long-ago bungalow—a stone fireplace and chimney where Gennaro and he once found rusted metal matchbox trucks and cars, toys that Tucci, Lasante, and DiCico children played with years ago.

The television still blared, but they found Tucci leaning against his cluttered kitchen counter, holding an almost empty can of dog food in one palsied hand and a spoon in the other. He looked puzzled, and Gennaro rested his arm around Tucci's bird-like shoulders and shouted above the sound of the television. "It's Gennaro DiCico and Frankie Lasante. We were just swimming out back. Damn, the water's cold. Didn't you pay your heating bill?"

"I pay too many bills already," Tucci scoffed. "Now you want me to heat the waterfall. That's God's job, not mine."

"I'll take that," Gennaro said, and he took the bowl of dog food from the counter and placed it on the floor before the drooling old bulldog. He then took Tucci's elbow and escorted him back into the living room and turned down the television's volume. Gennaro flashed Frankie a grin and nodded towards an empty bottle of homemade wine and a stained glass that sat on the cluttered table next to Tucci's chair as if to say: *He's okay. It's the wine that makes him foggy.*

"So did you boys have a good swim?" Tucci asked.

"Great!" they responded simultaneously.

"And how's your father?" Tucci looked at Frankie. "Lenny's a good man—lousy luck—but a good man."

"He's doing well. I'm sure he'll drive up to see you this summer."

Tucci turned to Gennaro. "And your family? How are they? I haven't seen your father in a long time."

"They're all good. Tomorrow's my old man's big Fourth of July blowout."

"Your father should come up here sometime with Lenny. It's good to get out of the city ... too many people in the city ... too much trouble."

"You know how my old man is. He don't like to leave the neighborhood."

They visited with Tucci for over an hour—Gennaro carried most of the conversation, while Frankie washed dishes, cleared tables and kitchen counters, and emptied the wastepaper baskets from the kitchen, living room, and bathroom into a large plastic bag. Tucci told him not to bother, but this long-established Lasante ritual of trying to make life a little easier for Rocco Tucci dated back to the time of the fatal car accident. Frankie wasn't about to break tradition. Gennaro on the other hand held up the DiCico tradition of gabbing.

Toward the end of their visit, Tucci became confused, calling the boys Lenny and Vinny, although Gennaro looked nothing like his father, but they didn't correct him. Finally, Gennaro pointed to his watch and gave Frankie a look, while Frankie crammed a bunch of foul-smelling wilted flowers into the overstuffed plastic trash bag.

"Well, Mr. Tucci, it's getting late, and Martha Stewart and I have to hit the road," Gennaro said.

"Martha who?" Tucci said.

"No one special. Just a girl that has the hots for me," Gennaro said, laughing.

Frankie rolled his eyes.

They each gave Tucci a peck on the cheek and patted old Meatball, who was sleeping off dinner. He wagged his tail but barely opened his eyes.

Frankie wondered if it might be the last time they'd see Tucci, but then he always feared that. Frankie was a worrier.

As they got back into the car, Frankie shared his concern that Tucci seemed more feeble than last summer and his fear that someone might hurt the old man, but Gennaro told him to stop making something out of nothing, which was what Gennaro often told him.

"He's fine," Gennaro said. "Didn't you smell the wine on him? That's what was making him groggy. Plus he'd blow someone's head off before they had a chance to hurt him."

"He didn't blow anyone's head off when we snuck into the house. He didn't even hear us."

"So you'd feel better if he blew our heads off? Then you wouldn't have to worry about him." Gennaro twisted his mouth to the side and shook his head. "You're a trip, Francesco."

After driving a few miles they turned into the parking lot of a beat up motel—a one-story stretch of doors in dire need of fresh paint, side by side with dirty picture windows and yellowed blinds, the kind of motel where folks rented rooms for reasons other than sleeping, but the price was right. Last summer they had stayed there with another friend, Johnny Pickle, and spent half the night overhearing a man in the next room talk dirty and moan as if he were in a porn flick.

The following morning when they heard him leave his room, the three boys peeked out through the yellow broken blinds, pulling them off the window. They wrestled with the Venetian blinds as the tidy, little, balding, middle-aged man dressed in a three-piece pinstriped suit, white shirt, and red tie, carried an attaché case and leading a pug on a rhinestone-studded leash. The man adjusted his sunglasses, scooped his dog into the car, and disappeared behind the smoke-tinted windows of his SUV.

The boys roared their way home from the Catskills.

"Wow! This is the best I've ever had," Gennaro said.

"That's it, scratch me behind my ear," Johnny yelled followed by panting and howling, and rubbing his knuckles behind his own over-sized ears. Johnny was all legs and arms and ears, like a child's drawing of a stick figure.

This time Frankie remembered to pack earplugs, just in case.

Inside, the motel office smelled of Pine-Sol and stale smoke, and behind the front counter a woman with red shiny lipstick bleeding into the creases above her upper lip watched the same reality police show that, by now, Tucci was probably snoring through.

"Excuse me, Miss." Gennaro cleared his throat as the woman pointed to a coffee-stained sign on the counter that indicated the motel was full.

"There's a hot air balloon festival going on and motels are booked for miles around," she explained between drags on her cigarette. Her eyes teared from the smoke, but remained focused on the television screen.

"Hot air?" Gennaro said and flashed a smile.

The woman's eyes strayed from the television to Gennaro, first his hazel eyes framed with long lashes, and then to his shoulders, arms, and hands—broad, veiny, and pressing down hard on the top of the counter. Finally, she looked back into his eyes.

"Yeah, hot air," she said. "Something I bet you're an expert on."

Gennaro laughed and threw his arm around Frankie. "Come on, Francesco, let's get out of here. We got our reputations to consider."

Frankie rolled his eyes, inhaled the scent of Gennaro's perspiration mixed with suntan lotion, and yielded to Gennaro's tug.

After 30 miles of no vacancies, they stopped at a mom-and-pop gas station and convenience store and bought a couple of premade subs wrapped in cellophane, two cans of cream soda, and a large bag of jalapeno flavored chips.

"I guess it's for the best," Gennaro said as they walked from the store back to the car. "If we drive back tonight, I'll be home all day tomorrow to help my old man and brothers get ready for the block party. Your dad gonna keep you trapped in the store tomorrow?"

"Probably. You know how he is," Frankie said, tossing the bag with their convenience store dinners onto to the front seat.

"Help me get the top up," Gennaro said. "Funny, during the day I like the country — well, except for all those creepy crawling things — but at night there's too much sky. All these stars give me the creeps."

They secured the top of the convertible and continued their trip back to the familiar, where buildings framed patchworks of sky and streetlights replaced stars. Crossing the Tappan Zee was the last thing Frankie remembered until pulling into the DiCico's driveway where two sentinel lions guarded the DiCico's white arched wrought iron gates.

It was 2:00 a.m. and all of 104th Street was asleep, except for Mrs. Pentaro's black and white cat that lifted its face from the mangled rat under its paw and narrowed its eyes as Gennaro and Frankie stepped out of the car.

"It's late, ya wanna just sleep in the basement?" Gennaro asked. The DiCicos lived in a gentrified and expanded one-family, white elephant of a house that was once a modest two-family on a double city lot. In the basement was a second full kitchen, a game room with a bar, bedroom, and bathroom. Several neighbors on the block had a second kitchen in the basement. Their flats were for show and the basement for actual living. But the DiCicos, as with everything they did, took this ethnic idiosyncrasy to an extreme. Their basement was more posh than their neighbors' main homes. In turn, Gennaro's two older brothers and their brides had lived in the DiCico basement after they married, until Big Vinny bought the first couple a house in Howard Beach and the second a house in Broad Channel.

Frankie agreed to spend the night, claiming that he didn't want to disturb his father by coming home so late. That was the excuse he gave Gennaro and himself.

Gennaro unlatched the oversized wrought iron gates, and Frankie followed him past Big Vinny's Lincoln and through a maze of ornamental roses, evergreen topiaries, and cement statues. In the dark, the DiCico's yard resembled a cemetery. Garden lights shone on a statue of Saint Lucy baring her eyeballs on an oval platter as if she were serving escargots. In the Lasante's yard there was an arbor, heavy with purple grapes in late August, a fig tree, roses and hydrangeas, and the ubiquitous vegetable garden thick with tomatoes, zucchini, peppers, and eggplants in the fall. There was also the required statuary, but just one, a small replica of Saint Francis, Frankie's namesake—about three feet tall with a bird perched on his shoulder and a wolf resting at his feet, but the three-foot Saint Francis, despite the stigmata imprints on his hands and feet, paled in comparison to the DiCicos' life-sized Saint Lucy carrying her eyeballs. A few steps past Saint Lucy, water trickled from the dueling cement penises of twin boys peeing into an oversized cement clamshell. The sound reminded Frankie of his own engorged bladder, and in the basement, more water trickled from the filters in three fifty-five-gallon saltwater fish tanks. Frankie pushed past Gennaro, around a pool table, and into the bathroom. After relieving himself, and then a little soap and water under each armpit, two quick swipes of deodorant, and rubbing toothpaste on his teeth and gums, he joined Gennaro back in the bedroom where multiple Frankies and Gennaros appeared in a V of mirrored closet doors. Upstairs in the master bedroom were more closets, also with mirrored doors. Marie DiCico was quite the fashion maven and, outside his home, Big Vinny always dressed like a CEO. He could be flipping steaks on a grill and the most he'd remove was his jacket—never his tie. Maybe he'd loosen it.

Frankie sat on the satin bedspread and removed his sneakers while Gennaro took his turn in the bathroom, but before he had the chance to step out of his jeans, Gennaro jumped him from behind and pinned him to the bed.

"I don't know, Francesco, you're too easy," Gennaro said, then ruffled Frankie's hair, gave him a kiss on the cheek, and said something about going to sleep because tomorrow was his old man's big day.

Like a rock, Gennaro fell asleep while Frankie lay there struggling not to think, or more accurately not to feel, Gennaro's warm breath on his back. Whenever Frankie stayed at the DiCico's house he swore to himself that it would be the last—it wasn't worth the torture—that is until the next time Gennaro asked him to stay over.

3

Gennaro was 19 and Frankie 17. Frankie had long admired Gennaro's cool confident ways, but at some point — he wasn't sure when — admiration became feelings that Frankie didn't understand, until he did understand. Prayer didn't help, but that night he prayed until the morning light filtered through slits in the basement's short vertical blinds and illuminated Gennaro's silhouette. Frankie fell asleep somewhere between *Hail Mary* and *forgive us our trespasses*, while imagining Gennaro with his arms outstretched and perched as if on a pedestal atop the falls at Tucci's place.

When Frankie woke, he found a note from Gennaro taped to the mirrored doors explaining that he had gone to the Canarse Markets with his brothers to buy beer and other supplies for the party. Frankie went home, and after he showered and changed into a clean pair of jeans and a t-shirt, Grandma Filomena insisted he eat breakfast before he helped his father in the store. Frankie was anxious to see if Gennaro had returned from Canarse and was outside helping his brothers set up for the block party, but Filomena was not someone you refused. When she said eat, you ate.

"So how is Mr. Tucci?" she asked as she added two slices of mozzarella to the sizzling eggs and then covered the cast-iron skillet. She appeared taller than she actually was — her chin held high and her perfectly squared shoulders added to her stature and gave her an air of confidence and authority. She had been washing windows and was still wearing a housedress, but once her housework was done, and whether she planned to help out in the store, run errands, or sit in the house and crochet, she would change into a more presentable dress.

She lifted the cover from the skillet and folded the omelet with the precision of a star chef.

"He's good," Frankie said. "I don't know ... somehow different. Older I guess. Gennaro said he was fine."

"You're a good boy, Frankie. Gennaro's a good boy too, but too much like his father. He doesn't take the time to really see a person. All the DiCico children are too much like Big Vinny. Poor Marie. She's a good mother, but even a good mother can do only so much." Filomena lifted the omelet with a spatula, slid it onto a china plate, and then buttered two chunks of Italian toast.

Frankie removed a placemat and silverware from the drawers next to where Filomena prepared his breakfast. "I don't know, Grandma. I think Gennaro is more like his mother."

Filomena set the plate before him at the kitchen table. "He looks like her anyway," she said. "Lena and Gennaro have their mother's good looks. Michael, Jimmy, and Big Vinny look like triplets. God forbid."

Filomena made the sign of the cross, and they laughed as she poured herself a cup of coffee, and then joined Frankie at the table. A string of mozzarella stretched from the omelet to Frankie's mouth. They continued to chat while Frankie devoured his omelet, Italian toast with whipped butter, and two glasses of milk. He yawned numerous times, but neglected to mention how difficult it was for him to fall asleep when lying so close to Gennaro.

He placed his empty plate, glass, and silverware in the sink, kissed Filomena on the cheek, told her she was the best, and then dashed from the house, through the breezeway, and into the store to help Lenny, or at least he pretended to be a help—making an inventory of dry goods that needed to be shelved, while he mostly stared out the front door looking for Gennaro.

Across 91st Avenue, three old men sat on metal folding chairs around a small card table in front of Big Vinny's club—a storefront with tinted windows. Inside, the club resembled an old-time pool parlor except for the large flat screen TV and wet bar. A locked door separated Big Vinny's office from the rest of the club. The old men alternated sips of espresso with puffs on De Nobili cigars, and several of Big Vinny's sidekicks drank beer from plastic cups while Michael and Jimmy un-loaded gas grills from a van, but no sign of Gennaro.

Jimmy dropped his end of the gas grill. Michael flailed his arms, as did Jimmy, and Frankie knew they were arguing and probably shouting a litany of curse words. It didn't take much to set them off. In hushed tones, neighbors often called them Cain and Abel.

Lenny ate a salami sandwich on a Kaiser roll while Doug Turner sat on a stool across the counter from him and also ate a sandwich, but his was capicola on white bread. Doug worked in the auto-repair shop across 91st Ave., next to Big Vinny's club. Having lunch with Lenny after the noon rush was Doug's standard practice, once workers from surrounding banks, shops, several small factories, and warehouses had already descended on Lasante's during their lunch breaks and left.

In a neighborhood where nicknames were as common as flies, most folks, except for Lenny, called Doug Prosciutto. When boning a prosciutto, Lenny saved the hambone and fat for Doug, who boiled it with greens—hence his nickname. He was an upbeat, friendly man, and Lenny enjoyed his company. They had become fast friends soon after Doug began working at the auto-repair shop four years ago—maybe because they were both single dads, or because they liked talking about politics and had similar views, or because they each felt a little out of sync in the neighborhood, though for different reasons. Doug was African American.

"Great sandwich as usual," Doug said. "What do you call this ham again?"

"Capicola," Lenny said.

"Whatever it is, it's delicious." He was a tall, gangly, and animated man, and as he sat on the stool across from Lenny and ate his sandwich, he looked as if he couldn't quite figure out how to manage his arms and legs.

Lenny asked Frankie why he kept looking out the window.

"Nothing. Just being nosey," Frankie mumbled.

"From here I can see that we need a case of ziti and a case of cappolini," Lenny said.

"Leave the boy alone," Doug said. "How many boys work as hard as he does? Good student. Works in his father's store. Most kids today act like taking out the garbage is a fulltime job. You're a good kid, Frankie."

"Thanks, Mr. Turner." Frankie feigned writing on his pad.

A customer examined a red pepper as if she were a dermatologist diagnosing a carcinoma, and another customer asked Frankie to get her a roll of toilet paper. "I can't reach up that high. Your father thinks we're giants. And don't get me none of those used rolls."

"The board of health made us stop selling used toilet paper," Lenny said.

"Man, you're a piece of work." Doug shook his head and laughed.

The customer covered her toothless grin and also laughed. "You know what I mean. I don't want no smashed rolls. They don't work so good." The wannabe dermatologist nodded in agreement and both women commiserated about how hard it was to get a smashed roll of toilet paper to unroll. Frankie found her the perfect roll.

After the customers left, Lenny and Doug finished their lunches while rehashing the pros and cons from the Democratic primaries.

Lenny was impressed with the hope that Obama instilled. Doug was less enthusiastic. Not that he didn't like Obama, he just figured that white Republicans would do anything to make a black President look bad, and little would be accomplished.

"Nothing I'd like better than to see a black man in the White House. And I don't mean waiting on tables," Doug said. "But America's not ready. There are folks who would still prefer for people with my color skin to ride in the back of the bus. Obama's smooth, thoughtful ways are going to be seen as him being uppity."

But Clinton had already conceded a few weeks earlier, and both men hoped Obama would secure the election.

"Well, I bet when black folk were building the White House they never dreamed that one of their own would someday be president. In the meantime, I got some brakes to repair."

Doug went back to work. Frankie restocked the shelves and re-filled the barrels of olives while Lenny waited on customers. It was mid-afternoon when Frankie finally spotted Gennaro.

"Looks like the sun is getting strong," Frankie said—his excuse to go outside and lower the awning. Lenny nodded. He was weighing cornmeal for a customer who was revered for her gnocchi di polenta.

The avenue was closed to traffic for one block on either side of 104th Street. Young ones, most visiting their grandparents, played red light/ green light, jumped rope, tossed a football, or drew with large pieces of chalk in the middle of the avenue. Most of the adults gathered in front of Big Vinny's club. The smell of barbeque, especially grilled sausages, found its way to where Frankie turned a large iron crank and lowered the faded green and red striped canvas awning over the storefront windows. Instead of reentering the store, Frankie crossed the avenue and joined Gennaro and other friends.

"So your old man let you out?" Gennaro said, throwing his arm around Frankie's shoulder. He was shirtless and Frankie felt Gennaro's damp heat. His face was only inches from Frankie's, and his breath had that sweet stench of fermentation. He already had too much to drink.

"I fell asleep after I got back from Canarse," he said. His lips pressed against Frankie's cheek, and Frankie became aroused. Fortunately his grocer apron covered the front of his pants.

"Maybe all that country air did me in," Gennaro said. With his free hand he chugged his beer, and then held the mouth of the beer bottle up to Frankie's lips. Frankie tried to drink, but most of the beer spilled down the front of his t-shirt.

Someone yelled: "What the fuck do you think you're doing?"

A gypsy cabdriver had stepped out of his cab and moved one of the wooden horses away from blocking off the avenue. He yelled: "I got a fair to pick up on the next block," and got back into his cab and began to inch his way through the less crowded side of the avenue. Jimmy and Michael approached the cab looking as if they might pummel the intruder, and Gennaro dropped his arm from around Frankie's shoulder and followed his brothers. The cabdriver backed up and lowered his window. "My bad. Sorry man."

The three DiCico brothers stood with empty beer bottles in their hands as the driver made a U-turn, and a couple of younger neighborhood boys kicked the cab's bumper. The cabdriver extended his arm out the window, shot up his middle finger, and then sped away under a barrage of flying beer bottles while at least a half dozen guys, including the DiCico brothers, chased the cab until Big Vinny yelled: "Not now! Let the asshole go."

Gennaro fumbled with a pen, scratching something on his arm. Frankie noticed it was a short series of letters and numbers—probably the cab's license plate number. He soon became tired of hearing Gennaro bitch about how they were going to "… mess that fucker up."

"I've got to go back and help my father," Frankie said. He slipped off his wet t-shirt and headed back to the store.

Customers straggled in and out of the store for the rest of the afternoon and most of the evening making small purchases until the fireworks began, and Lenny told Frankie to shut the door to keep out the rotten-egg-stink. Frankie stepped out onto the sidewalk, kicked up the doorstop, and closed the door behind him.

A sulfur-y fog engulfed 91st Avenue, and Frankie inched his way through the crowd and the stink of sweat and beer until he finally spotted Gennaro squirting charcoal lighting fluid as if he were pissing on the mound of burning cardboard and exploding fireworks. Still shirtless, his skin shimmered behind a kaleidoscope of yellows and blues. Frankie felt light-headed—anxious. Above the cacophony of firecrackers, cherry bombs, and cheers there was the sudden, stunning boom, and Gennaro vanished behind a flash like a magician's assistant.

Everyone froze and then burst into incoherent screams, but Frankie heard one clear shriek: "It's Big Vinny's kid!"

He fought his way to where Big Vinny knelt next to Gennaro. Except for his heaving chest, Gennaro lay motionless in puddles of beer littered with plastic cups and cigarette butts with his neck twisted and his head propped against the curb. Big Vinny lifted Gennaro's shoulders, and Gennaro's head flopped over the crook of his father's right arm—a tableau of father cradling son, shrouded in smoke and waves of heat.

Out of the shadows came wailing and cursing and praying in broken English and Italian, and above the tumult, Big Vinny roared: "Call a fucking ambulance."

Jimmy yelled into his cellphone, Lena held her mother's arm while

Marie DiCico bit into her fist to keep from screaming, and Big Vinny extended his hand to Frankie, who stood there trembling—his green eyes and sunburned face shimmered with tears.

As if caught in a nightmare, Frankie drifted towards Big Vinny and Gennaro while the stench of Gennaro's burnt flesh filled his nostrils, and the word faggot seared his brain like a branding iron. It was his fault that this had happened—punishment for his burning desire and for wanting his desire to be reciprocated.

Frankie's forehead pressed against Big Vinny's as Big Vinny's mitt-like hand clinched Frankie's shoulder like a vice. They stared down at Gennaro, unblinking against smoke and tears, and willing him to live. Moments or hours passed before sirens and flashing lights subdued the havoc, and the crowd cleared a path for the paramedics. Big Vinny released his grip on Frankie's shoulder and whispered: "We gotta get him to the hospital."

The EMTs lifted Gennaro onto the stretcher while Big Vinny tossed his keys to Michael, his oldest son, and told him to get the Lincoln and drive his mother to the hospital. "I'm riding in the ambulance," he said.

Lenny took Frankie's hand as Big Vinny climbed into the back of the ambulance. The lights flashed, the siren screeched, and the ambulance left. "Just let me lock up the store and tell Grandma we're going to the hospital," Lenny said, and Frankie remained standing with Lena and Marie in the surreal stillness, like the calm after a storm had wreaked havoc. Shadows trudged past them. Some pushed brooms, others carried buckets of water, still others embraced and swayed. The mound of burning cardboard and fireworks smoldered into ash.

Michael drove up in Big Vinny's Lincoln, parked in front of Lasante's grocery store, and Frankie followed Marie and Lena into the backseat. Lenny sat in the front seat next to Michael. They drove to Saint John's Hospital to the clicking of Marie DiCico's rosary beads. Jimmy followed close behind in his Lexus with his and Michael's wives.

By the time they arrived at the hospital, Gennaro was conscious but vomiting. He had suffered a concussion, but his burns weren't serious. Only Big Vinny and Marie were allowed to see him.

Frankie recalled having seen a sign for the chapel when they entered the hospital, so once he knew that Gennaro was at least alive, he left the others in the emergency waiting room and retraced his steps to the sign.

It was a small room with a single, backlit stained glass window of a sunrise, and Frankie took a seat on one of the maple wood chairs arranged in a half circle before the simple maple wood altar. The space was austere and quiet. No crowds and cries. Prayer pamphlets representing various religions lay on the seats. One had the picture of Michelangelo's *Pietà*, and Frankie recalled Big Vinny holding Gennaro's limp body. "He'll be okay ... he'll be okay ... he'll be okay," Frankie repeated like a mantra until Lenny's voice startled him.

"Mind if I join you?" Lenny took the seat next to Frankie and placed his arm around his son's shoulder. Frankie leaned into his father, inhaled Lenny's smell of sweat and the store, and felt safe. He looked down and stared at his own t-shirt, stained with Gennaro's blood. "He'll be okay," Lenny whispered. "He'll be okay. I promise."

4

Since he was old enough to wonder, Frankie's eyes sparkled at the sight of what Lenny and his siblings jokingly called Mama's Church. On the top of Filomena's dresser, vigil candles burned before a host of saints, including the Blessed Mother and Padre Pio, a Capuchin Friar from Filomena's parents' hometown in Italy. Very young Frankie was enchanted by the glow of so many benevolent smiles, even if they were only plaster. Lenny thought little of prayer and less of religion, but Filomena insisted that Frankie attend a Catholic elementary school where, as it turned out, he relished in the nun's fanciful stories and devoured books about the lives of saints. Unlike Lenny and the Lasante men before him, Frankie was a magical thinker—choreographing elaborate funerals for deceased pet fish and spending hours listening to Pavarotti or Andrea Bocelli sing "Ave Maria." For his 12th birthday, he wanted an extreme unction crucifix, which was used by priests to perform last rites. To Lenny's credit he yielded to his son's wishes and bought him one despite his own distaste for what he considered to be a lot of hocus-pocus.

The Lasante men's ambivalence, with the exception of Frankie, regarding the Catholic Church, dated back to Leonardo Lasante—Lenny's grandfather. Leonardo had carried his mistrust of authority figures—whether political or liturgical—from Taormina, Sicily, to Little Italy in Manhattan, to Glenhaven in Queens where it was sealed.

In 1918 when Leonardo and his wife, Lucia, purchased the store and connecting house on the corner of 91st Avenue and 104th Street, the immediate neighborhood was made up of Italian immigrants, but the larger neighborhood was mostly first-and-second-generation Irish and Germans with a few of the more distant descendants of the original French and Dutch immigrants remaining.

A new basilica was under construction to accommodate the booming influx of Catholics, but once the new Most Precious Blood was open, Pastor Cunningham suggested that the Italian parishioners attend a *special* Sunday Mass, which would be held in the church basement. Leonardo took this as an insult, especially given that most of the masons and artisans who had built the new basilica were Italians.

We're good enough to build their church but not good enough to worship in it! was Leonardo's maxim, and he wasn't shy about making it known.

In the early 1900s, the more reserved and Anglicized American Catholic clergy and laity considered Italian immigrants too uninhibited and superstitious. *Wops* practiced "street religion" with their tawdry feasts and processions. Leonardo told Pastor Cunningham that he'd burn in hell before he'd attend Mass in the church basement, and added if he got to hell first, he'd save the good father a seat.

Three years after Most Precious Blood opened, when a new pastor, Father Alterisi, replaced Cunningham, not only were Italians welcome in the main church for all Masses, but each Sunday at the 11:00 a.m. Mass, Fr. Alterisi delivered the gospel and homily in Italian. But Leonardo still refused to set foot in the basilica, even when his children received the sacraments—including marriage. The first time he entered Most Precious Blood was for Lenny's father's funeral. Lucia rebuked Leonardo. "Now you go to church, when it's too late! My Vincenzo will not rise from his casket, and your grandchildren will not have their papa back. Stay home, old man. It's too late. You've already brought the *malocchio* on my son."

Leonardo didn't argue, nor did he yield to Lucia's demand for him to stay home, which he knew she halfheartedly meant. He knotted his black tie and sat at the kitchen table sipping espresso while Lucia finished dressing. At Vincenzo's funeral Mass, first Filomena and Lenny followed the casket into the church, next were Leonardo and Lucia, arm and arm, as if they had attended Mass together every Sunday for the past 50 years.

Before they had purchased what was to become Lasante's Italian American Grocery Store for three generations, Leonardo and Lucia had lived on the Lower East Side in Manhattan, where street life was a comedy of negotiations, and merchants in narrow, dank stores, or at their curbside pushcarts, bartered with savvy customers, and an eggplant or a chunk of cheese or a handful of semolina was the source of histrionic deliberation. Leonardo was one such merchant.

Lucia and he shared a three-room, cold-water flat with relatives above one of the many storefronts along Mulberry Street, where on humid, summer nights, fire escapes served as bedrooms. Such living arrangements were typical for new immigrants—cramped spaces with inadequate plumbing and poor sanitation. Tenement windows flew open to the shrill of the street sweepers' whistles, and garbage, including human waste, rained down like noxious hail onto the narrow streets. Men bent with age or boys barely out of short pants swept up the putrid refuse and carted it away.

Among the Lasante archives were postmortem daguerreotypes of Lucia's first- and second-born infants, too fragile to survive such unhealthy conditions—their tiny doll-like bodies in white dresses and framed by roses, gardenias, and rosary beads. Upon the advice of paesani, the young couple moved to Glenhaven, a rural section of Queens, New York, where they purchased a small grocery store with an attached house. Back then the area was mostly marsh and farmland with plenty of open space, salty air blowing in from nearby channels and bays, and many Italians lived there—the perfect place to raise fat, healthy bambinos.

Lasante's soon became an oasis for immigrants and first-generation Italian-Americans, attracting customers from miles away, including farmers from Long Island grateful to no longer travel into Manhattan for Italian imports. Within five years, Leonardo renovated the store, doubling its original size. A few years after that, he added a warehouse behind the store, providing ample space for him to carry enough stock to develop a modest wholesale trade where he sold to other retailers and local restaurants. Vincenzo, the first-born to Lucia and Leonardo in their new Glenhaven home and their only son, eventually took over the family business, but he did not want the grocery business to be his children's legacy. They would become professionals, and Vincenzo especially encouraged Lenny, who preferred Dante and

Voltaire to Ronzoni and Progresso to lead the way for his younger siblings. When Vincenzo clutched at his chest and collapsed onto the store's greasy, sawdust-covered, wood-plank floor, Lenny's acceptance letter to Columbia University was in Vincenzo's breast pocket.

Instead of Lenny becoming the first Lasante to attend college, he took on the role of Lasante patriarch and helped Filomena manage the store and care for his younger siblings. That's when Lenny came to be known as Hard Luck Lenny, and it may have been one of the reasons he didn't share Frankie's belief in God, at least not in a benevolent God.

5

It was the morning after Gennaro's accident, Mass had just ended, and several elderly women and men lumbered down the long center aisle, moving as slowly as the snails in Lasante's. The church's nave seemed infinite. Frankie knelt at a small side-altar before the statue of Saint Francis, slipped a dollar into a metal collection box bolted to a rack of trays holding votive candles, and pressed a dime-sized button, which triggered a flickering electric light among tidy rows of other monotonous flickering lights that paled in comparison to the elegant, tall, slender vigil candles Filomena kept lit on her dresser.

As he knelt among the electric fireflies and mumbled something about healing Gennaro, a hand reached around him, and a chubby finger with a hot-pink fingernail pressed another button.

"I'm sorry, honey, but I gotta get my son to his grandma's and go to work, and you look like you're gonna be awhile." The voice came from over Frankie's shoulder.

"Oh no, it's okay, I'm just about to leave." Frankie's attempt to stand was futile given that the woman's large protruding stomach pressed against his shoulder—she was quite pregnant. Their awkward positions and close proximity didn't prevent her from talking.

"Hey! Ain't you Lenny Lasante's son?" she asked as he shrank away from her. "Of course you don't remember me. I'm Tootsie. I used to work in Panisi's Bakery. You were a little boy when I shopped in your father's store. I moved to 123rd Street about eight years ago, but I still come here for Mass. Mostly Black churches where I live now. Baptist or something. I went a couple of times, but you gotta be prepared to make a day of it. I like the singing, but I can only take so much church."

Tootsie stepped back enough to allow Frankie to stand, but she continued talking, barely taking breaths between sentences. "Hey, wasn't that terrible what happened to Big Vinny's son? I wasn't there, but I heard he almost got himself killed. You used to play with him, didn't you? Are you two still friends? I'm telling you, kids can make you crazy. You never know what they're gonna do next. Of course, all those fools gotta mess with fire. I'm surprised one a them didn't blow themselves up long ago. I know your father wouldn't let you near those *cafones* and their fireworks. You listen to your father. He's a good man. Cute too. He still got his black, curly hair, or did he give it all to you?"

A little boy pulled at Tootsie's sleeve. At least Frankie thought it was a little boy, but he wasn't sure.

"What?" Tootsie yelled, and she shook her arm free. The boy's nails were as pink as Tootsie's. He twitched his head and shoulders and proceeded to promenade a naked Barbie doll along the marble altar railing in front of Saint Francis.

Tootsie lowered herself onto a pew. "I swear, if this baby don't come soon, I'm gonna need a backhoe to get around." She glanced at the boy, who was now stuffing the doll into a marble scroll beneath the railing.

"Tyrone, if you get Barbie's head stuck again, I'm throwing her out." Tootsie threw up her hands and turned to Frankie in desperation. "Honey, do me a favor and snatch him away from there before he breaks something."

An old nun cleaning the main altar shot Tootsie a disapproving glance while Tootsie arranged herself on the pew, and Frankie attempted to reason with Tyrone, who, if not for jamming a doll's head into an altar railing with his hot-pink fingernails and given his curly, light brown hair, amber eyes, and a golden complexion, somewhere between the color of his hair and eyes, might have been mistaken as a model for one of the church's painted cherubs peeking over clouds.

Instead of liberating the doll from the railing, Frankie accidently decapitated her, causing Tyrone to wail and the nun cleaning the altar to fume. Frankie pressed his thumb against the doll's head until the miniature blond projectile shot from the railing and landed on the tray of votive lights. He then retrieved the doll's head, shoved it back onto her torso and lifted wailing Tyrone in one fell swoop. Holding Tyrone, who was spinning Barbie like a miniature baton in a parade, and trying to ignore the nun who was now scrubbing a chalice as if she were exorcizing demons, Frankie collapsed onto the pew next to Tootsie.

"Yes, Gennaro and I are still friends," Frankie said between gasps. He was a little spent from the whole doll incident.

"Were you there when the explosion happened?"

"Yes, it was terrible, but I guess Gennaro saw the flame catch on the stream of gasoline and threw the can before it exploded. That's what he told his parents last night. Anyway, the doctor said that his burns aren't too bad. He got a concussion, but his burns aren't bad."

"DiCico luck," Tootsie said. "They fall in shit and come up smelling like roses."

Frankie was surprised and somewhat perturbed at how boldly Tootsie spoke of the DiCicos. Lenny and Filomena often criticized Big Vinny, but neighbors never bad-mouthed them — at least not openly. Only Lasantes reserved that right — like family criticizing family. Tootsie was a stranger.

"He did get a bad concussion though," Frankie said, trying to garner some sympathy for Gennaro, but Tootsie was unmoved.

"Let's hope it knocked some sense into him," she said.

At first Frankie was peeved, but Tootsie was right. After all, Gennaro was squirting lighter fluid on the fire. Earlier that morning, Filomena had actually said something similar, except she also went on and on about nothing good will come of the DiCico brothers with a father like Big Vinny. Frankie almost spoke up, but Lenny gave him one of his don't-even-think-of-contradicting-your grandmother looks.

He told Tootsie about going to the hospital last night, but that only Big Vinny and Mrs. DiCico were allowed to see Gennaro. "I'm going back today after I help my father in the store," he said.

"Good for you, honey. You're a good son and friend, and it looks like someday you'll make a good daddy, certainly better than I am a mommy."

Curled up against Frankie's chest, Tyrone cradled Barbie in his own small arms. When Frankie looked down at Tyrone, he recalled the time about 10 years earlier, when Gennaro had caught Lena and him playing with Barbie dolls. Gennaro, all of 9 years old, didn't laugh or tease him. "Frankie, you're getting too old to play with girls," was all that he said before he took Frankie's hand and led him from the yard to the driveway while poor Lena ran into the house screaming that Gennaro stole her best friend.

"See Frankie, you hold a baseball like this," Gennaro had said. "Next time my brothers take me to Shea Stadium, I'll ask them if you can come with us. Do ya like the Mets?"

Frankie didn't know who the Mets were, but he told Gennaro that he loved them.

Now, holding Tyrone and thinking of Gennaro, Frankie wondered if God was communicating through this little golden, pink-finger-nailed angel. What he felt for Gennaro wasn't right or wrong or good or bad, it just was. He thought, *What would Mary have said if she caught Jesus playing with dolls? Put that doll down, Jesus. You're going to save the world, and no one will follow a sissy. Now go play slaughtering Roman soldiers with your cousins like a good messiah.*

Frankie grinned at his own thoughts and wished he could have shared them with Tootsie or, more importantly, with Gennaro. Last night he was convinced that the explosion was a punishment for his feelings, but now he wasn't so sure.

Tootsie no longer appeared to be in a rush to get to work. Frankie wondered why she was having another baby if she didn't think that she was a good mother, but it was none of his business. After all, they had just met. He checked the time on his cell phone and told Tootsie that he had to go. "Great meeting you," he said.

"You bet, honey," she said. "Tell your father Tootsie from Panisi's said hi! Your mom was crazy to leave him."

Frankie tried not to react. First she badmouthed the DiCicos, and then she spoke of his mother as if they were best friends. Even neighbors rarely mentioned Frankie's mother. It was as if Tootsie had no filters and whatever popped into her head spilled from her mouth. Half asleep, Tyrone slid from Frankie's lap onto the pew and caressed his mother's stomach.

At the hospital that afternoon, Frankie wanted to talk about this odd but funny woman he had just met, but Gennaro was in a terrible mood. He wore sunglasses to protect his eyes from the light. He had a very painful headache. Frankie was grateful to hear Gennaro's voice, even if most of what Gennaro did was complain.

6

By the time Frankie was born, the area surrounding 91st Avenue and 104th Street was no longer the neighborhood of Leonardo, Vincenzo, or of Lenny's youth. Most of Lenny's peers had moved after graduating from high school or college. By default, those who remained became the keepers of traditions started by the old timers. One such tradition was the Feast of the Assumption, which began on the Friday before August 15 — the actual feast day — and culminated on the following Sunday with a procession, including a band and men carrying a statue of the Madonna up 104th Street, turning left onto 91st Avenue, and then continuing the five blocks to Most Precious Blood Church.

During the Feast, a bird's-eye view would show an L shape of booths running the length of 104th Street and turning onto 91st Avenue in front of Lasante's, where vendors hawked ceramic figurines; candy dishes and jewelry boxes with hand painted naked cherubs; miniature replicas of donkeys crowned with feathers and hitched to colorful carts; plaster statues of the Sacred Heart, the Madonna, Saint Francis, Saint Anthony, Saint Lucy, and the Infant of Prague decked out in a red satin dress; plastic rosary beads that glowed in the dark; holograms that morphed from portraits of President Kennedy into Pope John XXIII or Frank Sinatra into Sophia Loren. A new Italian American celebrity, Stefani Joanne Angelina Germonotta better known as Lady Gaga, had recently exploded onto the music scene, and the Feast of the Assumption acknowledged her with a hologram of Madonna (not "the") morphing into Lady Gaga.

Lenny was looking for Frankie — something he seemed to do a lot that summer — when he passed a booth where zeppole sizzled in a cauldron of bubbling oil while a woman called Angelina Zeppole (for obvious reasons) scooped up the golden orbs of deep fried dough with a large slotted ladle, tossed them onto a wood-framed mesh tray, and then shook the zeppole with powdered sugar in a small brown paper bag. Food was delicious and plentiful, but zeppole, the size of a child's fist, was the manna of Italian feasts. With the hem of her apron, Angelina Zeppole patted beads of sweat from her face, hands, and arms. Her flesh was soft and pliant like the dollops of dough that she dropped into the boiling oil.

At past feasts, late into the night, after the crowds had dispersed and canvas booth awnings had been lowered, Angelina offered Lenny more than hot zeppole. Since Frankie's mom had left, Lenny had had little interest or time for romance. One-nighters sufficed. No one got hurt. Angelina winked at Lenny and jiggled another bag of sugared zeppole. He laughed and felt the familiar stir in his groin.

"Red number 5! I win!" It was Gennaro's voice. "You pick what you want," he said to a girl with long chestnut hair and almond shaped eyes. Lenny didn't recognize the girl. Gennaro liked boasting that he could have anything or anyone he wanted. The girl picked a stuffed panda, and Gennaro handed her the prize, then kissed her full on the lips. Like a puppy, Frankie was heeled in Gennaro's shadow, and Lenny's stomach tightened. He had long surmised that Frankie was gay. Little things, like when Frankie was very young and played with Barbie Dolls with Lena. At first Lenny was glad when Gennaro intervened and Frankie appeared to be more interested in sports and playing with other boys. But by the time Frankie became a teenager, Lenny wondered if in fact he was more interested in Gennaro than baseball. However, Lenny wasn't sure, and he didn't know which concerned him more — that Frankie might be gay or that Frankie's feelings for Gennaro put him at greater risk to be drawn into a DiCico calamity.

This was the first feast since Gennaro was 12 years old that he didn't take part in the grease-pole competition, where teams of boys and young men climbed and slid and climbed again to win the basket of prizes at the top of the pole, plus the status of super virility. Gennaro's burns were almost healed, but Marie made him promise not to compete.

"Frankie!" Lenny shouted above the noise. "I need your help with customers. Hurry up! Grandma's alone in the store."

Frankie rolled his eyes. Helping Filomena was a ruse to get Frankie off the streets. He hoped that if he cut short the time Frankie hung out with Gennaro then there was less chance for Frankie to get into trouble. "One more year," he'd tell Frankie over and over, "and then you're off to college." But a lot could happen in a year to derail a life. A lot could happen in a moment, as Lenny well knew and feared.

They paused at Leo and Nina Napolitano's stand, where the elderly couple sold torrone by the pound, much tastier than the prepackaged boxes of torrone Lenny sold in-store. Leo held a wedge against the huge block of nugget candy, tapped it with a hammer, and chipped off a chunk so precise that it would be within an ounce of the customer's request. Children smacked their lips in anticipation, while adults admired Leo's skill as if the torrone were marble and Leo might uncover a masterpiece like Michelangelo's David or Moses.

The Napolitanos also sold dry ceci beans, pistachios, salted peanuts, and Jordan almonds in white wax paper packets—Frankie's favorite —the kind that a bride and groom might give as wedding favors tied with white satin ribbons in little mesh pouches and stuffed into fragile china slippers or teacups. Lenny bought a packet of the Jordan almonds and tossed it to Frankie. "Forgive me?" he said. Frankie nodded.

The Napolitano's booth stood at the curbside outside Lasante's. Next to the grocery store was the Lasante house—a narrow, two-story brick building where on either side of the front stoop sedum spilled from matching, white cement flowerpots embossed with clusters of grapes, and pink and blue hydrangeas overwhelmed the postage stamp gardens. A neighbor had made the flowerpots as a gift when Leonardo and Lucia bought the house years ago. With a little whitewash each spring, they looked as good as new.

A slip of alley, barely wide enough for small children to squeeze through during games of hide-and-seek, separated the house from Verdeschi's Italian Restaurant where Johnny Boo Boo made the best pizza in the neighborhood. Next was Romano's Funeral Parlor, Captain Beltrani's old cigar store (now empty, its windows covered with yellowed newspapers), and on the corner where 91st Avenue intersected 105th Street was Panisi's Bakery where Tootsie once worked. Every Sunday, after Masses, lines of impatient customers waited to buy fresh hard rolls and crumb cakes—two inches of crunchy butter and confectionary sugar topping a thin layer of yellow cake. The customers salted their gossip with complaints about the long line or the heat or the cold or their latest maladies, but the following Sunday, they stood in line again rehashing their gossip and complaints. On Christmas Eve and Easter morning, the line of customers extended from Panisi's, past Lasante's and around the corner, down 104th Street. For birthdays and other special occasions, Filomena ordered cassata from Panisi's, a layer cake with a hint of rum. In between the layers was cannoli cream and slivers of milk chocolate.

When Frankie and Lenny entered the store it was crowded with customers buzzing in loud, discordant Italian dialects and broken English, but Filomena handled them with the authority of a general. She stood behind the counter at the cash register, erect and square shouldered, her white hair combed into a neat bun at the nape of her neck, and her hands in constant motion, directing the customers as if they were her recruits.

Lenny slipped on his apron and stepped behind the slicing machine. "Who's next?" he said.

A man raised his hand. "I'll have two pounds of ..."

But Filomena cut him off. "No, you won't. Rosa was ahead of you. Then you go."

Frankie stepped behind the counter, next to Filomena, and bagged the groceries after Filomena rang up the prices on the register.

Once the crowd cleared, Lenny told Filomena that Frankie and he could handle the store while she rested a little before the family arrived.

A lone customer dumped change and several religious medals from a small purse onto the counter to pay for her two quarts of milk. "Yes, Filomena, you go inside and rest. Better your grandson helps his father. Keeps him out of trouble."

Filomena removed her apron and slipped the bib strap over Frankie's head. Frankie tied the apron around his waist.

"My Frankie's a good boy," Filomena said. "He knows how to stay out of trouble."

She kissed Frankie on the cheek as he counted the old woman's change.

"There's enough there? I have to buy milk for my grandchildren. My son-in-law is too busy playing the horses to remember his children." The customer made a spitting sound with her tongue.

"There's enough," Lenny said, and winked at Frankie who nodded in return and swept the coins into his hand.

Filomena went in the house to nap, and for the rest of the afternoon Frankie helped out with only an occasional grumble. They closed the store early, and by dusk the whole family gathered in the Lasante's yard to make up the annual order of hero sandwiches for the vendors at the feast. They sat around a table made of heavy plywood nailed to wooden sawhorses under an arbor thick with twisting trunks and vines and clusters of grapes that took on the glow of the colored Christmas lights strung across the arbor. A red and white checked oilcloth was fixed to the plywood table top and covered with sheets of butcher paper, and drumlins of warm Italian bread framed streams of sliced cold cuts — Genoa salami, capicola, prosciutto, mortadella, and provolone — while citronella torches repelled mosquitoes.

The aromas of the fresh bread, Italian cold cuts, and citronella — like sauce simmering on Sunday afternoons or baccalà on Christmas Eve — were pungent and familiar. The Lasante ritual commenced. Filomena sat at the head of the table while Lenny sat at the other end facing her. To Lenny's right sat his brother, Tony, his sisters' husbands, and his sisters Amelia and Irish. Irish was nicknamed for her small, turned-up nose. To Filomena's right sat Lenny's sister Angie, closest in age to Lenny, divorced, and with a penchant for politically left-leaning men. Next to her were three children. Two were Irish's and one Amelia's. Frankie sat between one of his cousins and Lenny. In total there were 12 family members at the table. Filomena would not have allowed 13 — bad luck, like the last supper.

Tony and his wife, Laura, took turns chasing their twin boys around the yard — too young and antsy to sit still. Laura took the first shift.

They all laughed, reminisced, and occasionally bickered, which Filomena immediately curbed. Years earlier, her position as hero-maker impresario had been shared with her husband, Vincenzo. He once sat where Lenny now sat. Before that, it was Leonardo and Lucia. Leonardo had been a cofounder of the annual Feast.

Filomena and Angie slid sharp knives alongside loaves of bread, beginning at the farthest end, piercing the warm golden crust, and drawing the knives toward their breasts with the grace of first and second violinists. Sesame seeds speckled the butcher paper beneath their hands.

"Careful, or a customer will get a little more than he paid for in his sandwich," Lenny warned. But as usual they ignored his bawdy humor. They handed the splayed loaves to the giggling children. Each child's responsibility was to add a cold cut or condiment. Since Frankie was the oldest, he was foreman—in charge of quality control and making sure that his younger cousins didn't remove their plastic gloves or sneeze. The remaining adults, including those who married into this culinary assembly line, cut the plump heroes into three chunks and wrapped each chunk in wax paper.

Watching Filomena and the other women fuss over the children made Lenny recall the times he had asked Frankie if he wanted to search for his mother. Frankie's pat responses, which Lenny found puzzling if not worrisome, were some variation of, "Why would I do that? I have enough family. Who needs another mother? I already have Grandma and Aunt Angie." Frankie was too content for Lenny's liking, as if the neighborhood was all that he needed or wanted.

Amelia corrected her husband on the way he wrapped the hero, and Irish told him not to listen to her. "Leave him alone. He's a doctor, not a grocer." The table went quiet until Lenny dismissed the unintended implication of his sister's remark by telling a knock-knock joke to the children. They giggled and everyone resumed talking about baseball or movies or politics. Angie had volunteered for Hillary's campaign until Obama won the primary. Now she supported Obama. Irish, Amelia, and their husbands were Republicans. Tony thought all politicians were bums.

All the siblings held fast to their opinions, and their discussion became heated until Filomena said: "American politicians are better than that jackass Silvio Berlusconi," and then told them to change the subject.

The front of the store and house faced 91st Avenue, but the yard extended across the back of the house and warehouse open to 104th Street, which gave the family a clear view of a large section of the feast, especially the makeshift stage where Netti Squalanti sang "Funiculi, Funicula." Rhinestones dangled from Netti's earlobes, peeked out from under her generous second chin, and disappeared into the cleavage between her even more generous breasts. Her twin brother, mirroring her corpulence minus the exposed cleavage, accompanied her on his accordion. The audience sat in rows of folding chairs, donated from Romano's Funeral Parlor.

A low brick wall, capped with ornamental wrought iron, separated the Lasante's yard from the sidewalk. Just outside the wall, a hedgerow of old women sat on wooden stools or metal folding chairs like sentries guarding the Lasante property. Two women wore simple housedresses; several were dressed more conspicuously, wearing brocade dresses and hand-crocheted shawls even though it was a humid August evening; some were dressed all in black, including black stockings rolled at their knees. One woman yelled: "*Veni qua*, Filomena! Come sit with us. Let the young ones do the work."

"Beh!" Filomena said as she waved her mottled hand, pursed her lips, and scrunched her shoulders—all sign language for *they'll mess up without me.*

Scrolled metal frames, strung with red, green, and white lights, arced above the street and stage, creating a Felliniesque mood. Two teenagers kissed while leaning against the low brick wall.

"Oooh!" One of the sentries shouted. "Cut it out, Theresa, or I tell you mother."

The girl blushed and pulled away from her boyfriend, but Filomena glanced over her shoulder and reprimanded Ninella for teasing the young lovers. "Mind you own business, you old buttinsky. You don't know what your own granddaughter is doing."

Another woman, Carmella Rosario, also sitting along the wall, chimed in: "If the granddaughter is anything like her grandmother was, we know exactly what she's doing."

Laughter, *"Mama mia's! Dio Mio's!"* and signs of the cross followed Carmella's jibe. Even Ninella enjoyed the fun made at her own expense.

By now, the Squalanti twins were bowing and blowing kisses from the stage to an appreciative albeit distracted and noisy audience.

Lou Romano, the MC and neighborhood undertaker, before introducing the next performer, reminded neighbors that the folding chairs they sat on were a courtesy of his funeral parlor.

Carmella poked Ninella. "Business must be slow, *grazie Dio.*" The old women giggled like naughty children.

"And now ... I know you have all been waiting for this moment." Lou took a deep breath. "Our very own Mario Lanza ... Gennaro DiCico."

Like magic, the crowd hushed. Filomena slapped the palms of her hands on the plywood table. "Now we take a break," she said, and turned her chair around to face the stage. Frankie pressed his fingers to his lips to silence his younger cousins. One cousin stuck out her tongue and climbed onto Filomena's lap. Tony exchanged places with his wife so she could enjoy Gennaro's singing, and he watched the twins. Carmella and Ninella poked a tall skinny man sitting in front of them; the man immediately removed his hat and slouched down in his seat.

From the stage, Gennaro flashed his winning smile; his teeth, eyes, and close-cropped curls reflected the colored lights. "Grazie, Signor Romano. I only hope that I can do justice to the great Mario Lanza." Gennaro's muscles flexed beneath his tight t-shirt. Lenny glanced at Frankie, whose eyes were riveted on Gennaro, and sighed.

Like Big Vinny, Gennaro was dangerous, but he was more charming than his father and as sweet a talker as he was a singer. He knew how to get his way with most anyone. He reached for the microphone, lifted it toward his parted lips, and seduced his audience with Lanza's signature Neapolitan folk songs, arias, and vintage songs from 1950s movies.

His rendition of "Torna a Surrinto" and "Paglicci: Vesti la giubba" evoked a tsunami of cheers, whistles, bravos! and applause, but when he sang "Because" and "This Is My Beloved," the audience became serene. Young lovers, husbands and wives, parents and children, and even friends held hands or embraced—some dabbed tears away from the corners of their eyes.

The crowd yelled: "Encore! Encore, Gennaro DiCico! *Bellissimo! Come un Angelo!*" Frankie more than shared in the crowd's enthusiasm.

Lenny didn't have anything against Gennaro. With a different father, who knows? Maybe he would have been another Mario Lanza, but Big Vinny was his father, and because of that Lenny feared for Gennaro, but more so for Frankie. He tried but to little avail to dismiss his suspicions about Frankie being in love with Gennaro. Regardless, he took a deep breath and joined the crowd in their applause.

7

The feast had shut down for the night, and the Lasante assembly line was replaced by Frankie, Gennaro, and Johnny Pickle playing rummy at one end of the plywood table, and Angie, Big Vinny, Bruno Scungilli (called "Scungilli" because his favorite pasta dish was spaghetti with snail sauce), and Lenny at the other end, sipping Chianti from jelly glasses and snacking on slices of ricotta salata and sliced peaches. The rest of the Lasante family had gone home, and Filomena sat with her friends near the short brick wall between the yard and 104th Street.

Except for the few vendors lowering their awnings or sweeping up, the street was dark and still. Some vendors slept on cots inside their stands, but most drove home to other sections of Queens, or to Brooklyn, Staten Island, or lower Manhattan, knowing that Big Vinny's "eyes"—including a few local cops who earned healthy tips during the Feast—would keep a close watch. You could have left your wallet bulging with cash in the middle of 104th Street and it would be safer than in a bank—one of the perks for having Big Vinny as a neighbor, although Lenny was loath to admit it.

"So, Angie, how's the house?" Big Vinny asked.

"Good. It's a nice place to live."

After her divorce, Angie bought a brownstone in Hell's Kitchen, Manhattan—a symbol of her liberation from a bad marriage, though Filomena claimed it was Angie's way of saying: *Don't expect me to move back here with you.* It turned out to be a rather lucrative symbol since property values in her neighborhood skyrocketed soon after she purchased her house.

Big Vinny complained about the Feast not being what it used to be, and Gennaro mimed sliding a bow across the strings of a violin.

"*Strunzo*, this is how Mario Lanza shows his father respect? You'll be singing *castrati* if you're not careful." Big Vinny said and downed a glass of wine.

"Too many outsiders," Big Vinny argued as he poured another glass. "No more people from the neighborhood."

"Most of the people at the Feast were from the neighborhood," Lenny said.

"You know what I mean, the old neighborhood. When we were kids maybe you had a handful a Micks, a few Polaks, two or three Jews, but it was mostly Italians."

Johnny Pickle was Jewish, but he appeared not even to hear Big Vinny's complaints. He was more focused on the card game and yelled: "Rummy!"

Lenny lifted a slice of ricotta salata between his thumb and pointer finger. "Most of the old neighbors moved, Vinny. They were smart enough to get the hell out of here." Lenny took a bite of the cheese, glanced at Angie, and shook his head as if to say *Here we go again*, and sure enough, Big Vinny persisted.

"A feast is supposed to be Italian. We knew everybody back then. Now I look around and I don't know half of the people. Too many strangers."

Scungilli clasped his hands as if he were about to pray. "Times change, Big Vinny. You want only Italians? Go to Italy. Even there, I hear they got all kinds a people now. At St. Gennaro's Feast—I went last year—they got Chinese people selling egg rolls and chop suey. What kind a feast sells Chinese food?"

Big Vinny nodded and slapped the palm of his hand on the table; jelly glasses bounced and wine spilled on the checkered oilcloth. "Exactly!" he said. "Imagine selling Chink food at a feast. Egg rolls don't go with pasta. *Minchia*, they're not even Catholic."

"Chinese people or the egg rolls aren't Catholic?" Lenny said. "And since when did you get so religious?"

Angie laughed. "Didn't Marco Polo bring the noodle back to Italy from China?" She scanned the group as if she were lecturing her university students. "Big Vinny would have scolded Marco Polo for mingling with strangers. Now where would we be without spaghetti?"

"She's got a point!" Scungilli cried. "Madonna mia, I'd be dead without my spaghetti."

Everyone laughed except for Big Vinny. Like a cartoon villain, he swelled to twice his size. "Well now." Big Vinny sucked his fingers as if they were covered with sauce. "We can always eat collard greens," he said with a smirk. "Maybe Lenny's lunch buddy Prosciutto could teach us how to make 'em." Lenny's friendship with Doug Turner had long stuck in Big Vinny's craw.

"So whaddaya think, Lenny?" Big Vinny was like a dog on a bone, he just wouldn't let it go. He swept his right hand across the table, spilling a glass of wine. "At next year's Feast, we give Prosciutto his own booth, and he'll teach us all how to cook chitlins? After all, us wops don't know nothin about cooking."

Scungilli tried to change the subject. "So, Angie, how's your writin goin?" Angie was a professor in Women's Studies at Barnard and fairly well published, but Scungilli's idea of reading material was the daily picks at Aqueduct Racetrack. His question about Angie's writing was an obvious ploy to diffuse the tension, but Big Vinny was relentless.

"Minchia!" Big Vinny shouted. "What's happening to this neighborhood? First Hard Luck Lenny is taking soul food cooking lessons, and now Bruno Scungilli is becoming a feminista. No one's happy just being who they are."

"And *you* get to decide who we are, Don DiCico?" Lenny snapped.

"Oooh, cut it out. You're gonna spoil a beautiful night," Scungilli pleaded, followed by collective pleas from the other adults, including Filomena.

But Big Vinny wasn't about to let Lenny's "Don DiCico" crack slide. "No! Better your buddy Prosciutto ... that N ..."

Lenny cut him off before he could finish. "Vinny, it's time for you to shut your big mouth and go home."

Big Vinny jumped up to take a swing at Lenny, but Scungilli stepped between them and caught a punch to his shoulder.

Filomena rushed to the table. "Two grown men—what kind of

example are you setting for these boys? Grow up, both of you!" Angie pulled her out of harm's way, although both Big Vinny and Lenny would have punched themselves before they'd hurt Filomena.

Their fists flew while the few remaining street vendors and some neighbors jumped the brick wall to break up the fight. Scungilli and two other men restrained Big Vinny. Frankie and Gennaro grabbed Lenny.

"Get your hands off of me," Big Vinny ordered. Like a human chameleon, he changed back to stoic, cool Big Vinny DiCico and smoothed his starched white shirt, straightened his tie, and ran his thick fingers through his black, patent leather hair.

"That's always been your problem, Lenny." Big Vinny's tone was flat, his mannerism perfunctory. "You put strangers before your own. Strangers don't have your back. Not the way I do, but you never understood that."

The small crowd that had gathered in the yard cleared the way for Big Vinny to leave. He paused and removed a handkerchief from his pants pocket and dabbed at his nose. Spots of blood stained the white of his handkerchief and shirt.

"Just one more thing." Big Vinny talked into the air without looking at anyone, but loud enough for everyone to hear, as if he were making a proclamation. "You're no better than us. With your fancy words and your books and your high opinions. You think you're better than us ... always have ... but you're no better than us. Tomorrow and the day after that you'll still be slicing salami." Lenny allowed Big Vinny this final blow.

Gennaro gave Angie, Filomena, and Lenny a kiss goodnight. A few moments earlier his father and Lenny had exchanged punches, but as any of the adults would have said, especially Big Vinny, *It didn't involve the kids. The kids must show respect.* Gennaro gave Frankie a hug. Their old men fighting was nothing new.

After Big Vinny left, Filomena said: "Just once, I'd like that my supper doesn't sit on my stomach like a rock. Never a dull moment." She gave each of her friends a peck on the cheek.

"Go in the house, Filomena. Let the young ones clean up," Ninella said as she waved then closed the gate to the yard.

Neighbors ambled along 104th Street, waddling arm in arm—

shapeless shadows passed under the occasional spot of a streetlight
—and up their front stoops and into their homes. Street vendors vanished under lowered awnings. Frankie, Angie, and Lenny picked up
chairs while Filomena wiped up the spilled wine with a paper towel.

"Ma, you go to bed. We'll finish cleaning up here," Lenny said.

"Lenny, you know he's *pazzo*. When he starts, just go in the house.
You can't win with him."

"Don't worry, Ma. Tomorrow Vinny will have forgotten all about
this." And for this Lenny was right. In the morning, a Lasante could
have asked Big Vinny for anything, and he would give it, no questions
or strings attached. Anyone else, he would seek revenge.

Filomena hugged Lenny and planted a kiss on his cheek. "You are
better than him, and he knows it," she said and blew a kiss to Angie
and Frankie.

"Angie, you stay here tonight. Too late to take the subway." The
swish of Filomena's navy blue taffeta dress with tiny white polka-dots
sounded like a parting whisper as she turned away from her family
and went into the house.

Soon after, Frankie and Angie also went up to bed. Lenny put-
tered around in the yard, working off some of the steam from fighting
with Big Vinny. His comment, "... you'll still be slicing salami," had
struck a nerve.

Once inside, Lenny sat in the kitchen with his elbows pressed
against the cool enamel-top table, and he drained the last few drops of
Chianti from the bottle. It was a hot night and he had removed his
shirt, packed it with ice, and held it against his eye where Big Vinny
had landed a good punch. Lenny wasn't slim, but he had the solid build
of a workingman and, except for a few gray hairs in his thick black
curls, he looked younger than his 50 years.

*You will be the first Lasante to go to college. And what a brain God has
given you. You will show the way for your sisters and brother.* Lenny remembered how his father would boast about his grades to salesmen
and customers. *No more Lasante grocers; my children will be educated.*

Lenny was so lost in the memory of his father's words that he
didn't notice Frankie until he heard the sound of the refrigerator
door. In the refrigerator's glow, Frankie's green eyes reminded Lenny

of Vi. *His mother's eyes, but more noticeable with Frankie's olive complexion,* he thought. He was tempted to say: *I know you're scared to leave home, but there's nothing here for you.* Instead, he said: "Can't you sleep?"

"Just thirsty," Frankie answered and shrugged his shoulders.

"It's hard to believe, Son, that this year you'll be a senior. Time to start thinking about college applications."

"I'm half asleep, Dad. Please don't start."

"All I'm saying, Frankie, is ..."

Frankie slammed the bottle of juice down on the kitchen table. "I don't want to talk about college again. I don't want to make any promises about not looking back. I know you lost your chance, but if you want to get out of here, go. Suppose I don't want to go to college? Leave me alone."

Lenny's brown eyes went wide and, for the first time in his life, he feared he might strike Frankie. He took a deep breath and tried to keep his voice low not to wake Filomena or Angie. "Oh, you're going to college," he said. "I'll be damned before I watch you waste your life sucking up to Gennaro the way Scungilli sucks up to Big Vinny — like a slobbering lapdog."

"I'm nobody's lapdog!" Frankie growled.

"Then stop acting like one." Lenny sniffed at his shirt in disgust and pointed to his swollen eye. "Is this what you want ... to spend your life stinking of cheese and fighting with bums?"

Frankie leaned in a little too close to Lenny, as if he were trying to threaten him. "You know, Big Vinny is right," he said. "You do think you're better than everyone."

Lenny grabbed Frankie's wrist. "No, not everyone," He fought back tears and could see Frankie was doing the same. "It's time to go to bed, Frankie, and we'll talk about this tomorrow ... Now, did you forget something?"

Frankie tried to pull away, and the veins in Lenny's hand and forearm appeared as if they were about to explode. He feared that he might very well snap Frankie's wrist in two, but Lenny wasn't going to be disrespected, especially not by his son and in defense of Big Vinny.

"You're upset, but I'm your father." Lenny's voice remained calm. "Now! Did you forget something?"

Frankie kissed Lenny on the cheek, and Lenny released his grip. Frankie spun away and left the kitchen.

Instead of dwelling on what just happened, Lenny thought of old neighborhood friends and classmates, now professionals with large homes on Long Island or upscale apartments in Manhattan. A few occasionally returned to the neighborhood to visit an aging parent, and when they did, they stopped in the grocery store, each of them expressed the same sentiment: You were the best of us, Lenny. Next he saw his father clutch at his chest on the grocery store's sawdust-covered floor and recalled the death rattle that quashed his ambitions. "No, you're not going to turn into me," he muttered, and then made a fist of the hand that had grabbed Frankie's wrist and shoved his chair away from the table, stood up, stumbled out of the kitchen into the yard, and sat at the plywood table beneath the grape arbor.

The moonlight cast ghost-like shadows along the low brick wall and the makeshift stage. It took him several seconds to steady his hand enough to light the candle, but when he finally did the smell of citronella and grapes hung in the humid night air and the light from the flame exaggerated the contrast between the hairs on his chest, the shadow of a day's beard, and his halo of curls against his sweaty flesh, making his hair blacker and his skin paler like a figure in a Caravaggio painting. Lenny removed a slip of paper from his wallet and unfolded the small, yellowed note. Above the candle's flame he read:

> *Dear Lenny,*
> *I'm sorry, but I can't do this. I know that you'll make a remarkable father and a better mother than I could ever be.*
> *Regretfully, Vi*

He read the note several times, then refolded it, returned it to his wallet, and his thoughts drifted to Angelina Zeppole and her soft, pliant flesh like the dollops of dough that she dropped into the boiling oil. He blew out the candle and stumbled out of the yard.

8

The following morning, Frankie, Angie, and Lenny sat alongside Filomena's bed, waiting for the ambulance to arrive. Earlier Angie had peeked into Filomena's room where embroidered pillowcases and sheets lay undisturbed, and Filomena's head lay peacefully against two pillows, but her chest remained still. Angie caressed Filomena's hand, but the warmth had already left, and Filomena's taffeta dress hung silent in her closet.

Well-worn rosary beads hung abandoned on Filomena's bedpost. So often had she kneaded them, while she mumbled Hail Marys and cooked or ironed or sat in the yard under the arbor, or years ago when she grieved losing Vincenzo and felt overwhelmed being left a widow to raise her children. A safety pin fastened the crucifix to the chain of crystal beads, and the crystals caught the morning light that reflected tiny rainbows on the faded, peony wallpaper.

The paramedics said that there was no sign of suffering; she slipped away peacefully and never knew what happened. Several days later, the coroner's report would state that Filomena Lasante died from a ruptured cerebral aneurysm. No one's fault, the doctor said. Regardless, Lenny added upsetting his mother on the night before she died to his list of regrets.

Within a few hours their home was filled with family. The festivities outside mocked their grief, but it was too hot to close windows. Angie and Lenny met with Lou Romano to make funeral arrangements. Irish met with Father de la Roza about the funeral Mass. Amelia and Tony made phone calls and attended to visiting neighbors.

Sauce simmered on the stove and released the sweet vapors of tomatoes with herbs cut fresh from Filomena's garden. Angie drained the al dente rigatoni. In the puff of steam, she resembled Filomena, a likeness Lenny noticed while he spooned ricotta into a large macaroni bowl, and Angie added the rigatoni to the ricotta, and then several ladles overflowing with sauce. She folded the mixture together with a wooden spoon and wiped a tear from her cheek with the back of her wrist. Sauce splattered the front of her mother's apron, and Angie pulled a tissue from its pocket and dabbed at the sauce.

The family prodded and picked at their food. Conversation was somber, and punctuated with soft weeping. No one laughed. No one argued.

Tony waved a fly away from the macaroni and cursed in Italian. Filomena would have frowned.

After clearing the barely touched plates of food, the family again gathered around the dining room table for dessert, but the little ones appeared confused while seeking a lap to climb onto — the most coveted lap was gone. The tray of pastries courtesy of Panisi's — tidy balls of baba rum surrounded by pasticiotti, sfogliatelle, and cannoli — sat undisturbed like the decorative pillows and sheets on Filomena's bed.

It was dark outside when Carmella Rosario knocked on the kitchen door and, despite Angie's protests, insisted that the family step outside. "Out of respect for your mother," Carmella pleaded tearfully.

Lenny was the last to step out into the yard. The street was crowded with silent shadows. A solitary flame glowed before a large statue of the Madonna, while a shadow ascended the stage and stood next to the statue. Upon hearing the crystal clear first note of "Ave Maria," Lenny recognized Gennaro's voice, and cool water pulsed through his veins and bled warm from his eyes. Frankie pressed his face into Lenny's chest. All of Filomena's children, their spouses, and her grandchildren wept, as did many friends. Grief flowed gently from the yard, over the low brick wall, and onto 104th Street like an evening tide and, despite a few pauses when his voice began to crack, Gennaro completed his song then joined the Lasantes in their yard and was drawn into Lenny and Frankie's embrace.

By the following evening, The Feast of the Assumption had been dismantled and trucked away, and the Madonna returned to her plinth above a side-altar at Most Precious Blood. Inside Romano's Funeral

Home, flowers, mostly wreaths and baskets, filled the largest room, and at the head of Filomena's casket stood a bleeding heart—dozens of miniature red roses formed a heart shape. Red satin ribbons bled from its center. On one of the ribbons were the words *Beloved Mother*.

Filomena was dressed in a burgundy dress with a bolero jacket that she had bought to see *La Traviata* at the Metropolitan—last year's birthday gift from Angie and Lenny. The lower half of the casket was closed (Filomena hated the look of a corpse's feet pointing straight up) and blanketed with white roses, mums, and baby's breath like a mantle of fresh snow. A ribbon curled across the blanket of flowers with the words *Beloved Grandmother*.

One floral piece dwarfed the others—an arch of flowers above two golden gates with a lifelike white dove perched atop of the arch. Lenny explained to Frankie that it represented the gates of heaven and the dove was the Holy Spirit.

"When I was a boy," Lenny said, "funeral flowers resembled miniature parade floats—a wheel with a missing spoke represented the family member lost, or a clock with its hands pointing to the deceased's hour of death. That was the world of the old-timers, your great-grandparents and, to a lesser degree, your grandparents and great-aunts and uncles. They had little use for tidy bouquets and tidy emotions. They threw themselves on the caskets and wailed and screamed in Italian. When Grandpa Vincenzo died, I had to lift Great-Grandma and Grandma off of his casket. One of Grandpa's sisters fainted at the cemetery and almost fell into the grave." Frankie grinned and Lenny chuckled. They sat in the first row of chairs facing the casket, along with Lenny's siblings.

"And it wasn't just the women," Lenny continued. "The men were just as emotional. Your Great-Uncle Cosimo, after a doctor told him that his wife had died, picked up a large statue of Saint Jude and threw it out of the hospital's third floor window. Fortunately, no one was hurt, just a mess of smashed plaster."

At that they both chuckled.

"Italians are crazy," Frankie said.

Lenny nodded and looked at Filomena's profile. Oddly still. She was never one for naps or even to put her feet up on the couch or an ottoman. Even when she watched television she sat erect with her hands in constant motion as she crocheted another afghan or mended something worn or kneaded her rosaries.

"Those old-timers grieved hard," Lenny said, "but then they moved on with their lives and did what they had to do. They didn't whimper at funerals and spend the next 20 years in therapy. Grandma acted as if the world had come to an end at Grandpa's funeral, but the next morning she got out of bed, made us all breakfast, and opened the store."

Filomena's wake, except for the occasional outbursts from her friends and the presence of the gate-of-heaven floral piece with the card *Until we are all together again, the DiCico family,* mirrored the more reserved ways of assimilated Italian-Americans — that was until Bruno Scungilli whispered in Lenny's ear, and Lenny nodded and said: "Of course."

Big Vinny approached, followed by his family. He kissed Lenny's sisters and brother, offering his condolences. When he reached Lenny, Lenny stood up and they embraced. Big Vinny collapsed into tears and caressed Lenny's face between the palms of his wide hands and lamented in Italian. He paused, brought his fingertips to the shiner he had given Lenny two evenings before, shook his head and said: "Faccia brutta. Sometimes I can be such a gabbadost."

Lenny didn't respond, and Big Vinny turned towards the casket. He leaned over it and kissed Filomena's forehead while Lenny held his shoulders as if to keep him from falling forward, and then they knelt next to each other and bowed their heads. By now, everyone in the room was in tears, and the old timers wailed unabashedly as if Big Vinny had not only given them the permission to mourn like real Italians, but demanded that they should.

Two days later, after a high funeral Mass at Most Precious Blood, a cortege of black limousines followed the hearse carrying Filomena's casket past their store and home where it paused for a final farewell, and Lenny heard the whisper of Filomena's taffeta dress. Then on to Saint John's Cemetery where each mourner dropped a rose onto Filomena's casket before leaving the gravesite, and Big Vinny drew flowers from the gate-of-heaven floral piece atop the mound of flowers next to the open grave. He placed the flowers before an adjacent tombstone where etched in pink marble was the family name DiCico. Even in death Lasantes and DiCicos were destined to be together.

9

It was 2:30 in the morning, but it felt more like noon—one of those hot summer nights when the day's heat clung to concrete and brick like a tenacious memory. The air was thick with the smell of bread from Panisi's ovens and as heavy as the six feet of dirt that weighted down Filomena's casket. No breeze passed through Frankie's bedroom window, only the cries of irritable cats and the racket of trains against steel tracks that came from the EL.

Frankie lay naked on sheets damp and musky from his sweat, sat up too quickly, and his bedroom began to spin. He stumbled while he slipped on a pair of gym shorts, a t-shirt, and sneakers, and then he inched his way quietly past Lenny's bedroom, down the stairs, and out the kitchen door. Once outside the yard he jogged down the block to Gennaro's house, a short distance, but in the heat his t-shirt clung to his back, and by the time he reached the DiCico's, his hair lay soaked and flat against his forehead.

Lightheaded, he unlatched the wrought-iron gate and meandered through the maze of statues, praying that he wouldn't become target practice for Big Vinny. He scooped up several white pebbles from the base of the dueling penises' fountain and tossed the smaller ones at the top windowpanes of Gennaro's second floor bedroom. No Gennaro, so he tried a larger pebble. *Crash* followed by, "Shit!" Gennaro appeared at the open window. "Are you fucking crazy," he whispered. "You smashed my mother's plant."

"Sorry."

Gennaro disappeared back into the house. In a few moments, the cellar door rose, and Frankie tripped down the concrete steps into the basement past Gennaro who with one hand lowered the cellar door and with the other held out the remnants of the fallen Blessed Mother planter. "Look what you did. It was my mother's favorite."

A china nose, a section of blue veil, and the praying hands. Again, Frankie apologized. Gennaro's frown slowly turned into a grin until he fell against Frankie laughing. Frankie was only too glad to follow Gennaro's lead. They pressed their fingers to each other's lips to shush their laughter.

"Aside from vandalism what brings you out so late?" Gennaro said.

The mood turned somber when Frankie explained that no matter how hard he tried he couldn't stop thinking about his grandmother.

"That sucks," Gennaro said.

"It's like I'm not paying close enough attention. Like she's there but I keep missing her, like I didn't look quick enough. I hate it. I know she's not in that damn casket, but she has to be some place. Maybe heaven? I don't know. That's what she would say, but I don't want her to be in heaven. I want her to be here with us." Frankie leaned against the pool table. It was dark except for the lights from the fish tanks. This was the first time since the accident that Frankie had seen Gennaro shirtless and without bandages. Gennaro's burns had healed, leaving a slight topography of knolls and streams further defining his sculptured pectorals and the underside of his biceps.

Gennaro placed his hands on Frankie's shoulders, and Frankie brought his fingertips to Gennaro's chest and lightly traced the sinuous map of scars. "Does it still hurt?" he asked.

"Na, it's a lot better. I could have climbed that stupid grease pole last week, but my mother worries too much."

Frankie's eyes met Gennaro's. "That was a terrible night," Frankie said.

Gennaro's hands slid from Frankie's shoulders down to his chest and stomach, and then pulled at Frankie's t-shirt. "You're soaked," Gennaro said. Frankie's breaths quickened, and he stretched up his arms as Gennaro lifted the t-shirt until its thin, drenched cotton tore free from Frankie's shoulders.

The fluorescents over the fish tanks cast a surreal glow, and the aerators and filters murmured a bubbling hum. Gennaro dropped his boxers and Frankie did the same with his gym shorts. Denial had been so much a part their friendship that despite their naked bodies and full erections, Frankie half expected Gennaro to laugh and say this was all a joke, but then Gennaro took Frankie's hand and led him away from the glow and the bubbling hum and into the darker, quieter bedroom where the V of mirrors reflected their awkward passion. Their shadows rose and fell, expanded and contrasted along with their muffled moans until they lay still, but for only a moment, and then Gennaro rolled away from Frankie, shifted himself to the edge of the bed and sat up with his feet planted on the floor.

Frankie lay there staring at the shadow of Gennaro's back. He didn't ask what was wrong. He knew that they had just slipped back into denial, as they had done over the years when they wrestled but never acknowledged that they were engaged in anything but wrestling even though their bodies told them otherwise. Words unspoken had long been a part of Lasante-DiCico relationships, but Frankie and Gennaro brought it to another level. Frankie knew this was how they would deal with love making, or more accurately not deal with it. It wasn't Frankie's choice, but he knew better than to force Gennaro to acknowledge something he wasn't ready to acknowledge.

After that night Gennaro moved his bedroom to the basement, and Frankie stayed over more frequently with the unspoken pledge of what happened during the dark hours in the DiCico basement stayed in the basement while during the day they acted as if nothing had changed, and Gennaro continued to play out his role of Casanova, flirting with but no longer seducing every new girl he came across.

Come September, Lenny ruled that Frankie had to be home on school nights, but that didn't keep Frankie from occasionally sneaking out for an hour or so after Lenny was asleep.

10

School had been in session for several weeks, and the Democratic Party was promising America its first African-American president, while 91st Avenue was transformed into what resembled an on-location set for a crime show. Police officers, unmarked cars, detectives, federal agents, TV news vans, and crews converged upon 91st Avenue and the sidewalk before Big Vinny's club. Yellow crime-scene barricade tape blocked pedestrians from passing. But unlike a movie set, no adoring fans crowded behind cameras waiting for celebrities to appear. Instead, neighbors kept their eyes lowered and their mouths shut.

Doug Turner and Lenny glanced out of the front store windows through the fine drizzle, but neither of them acknowledged that anything out of the ordinary was taking place across the avenue.

In between bites of lunch, they spoke of the vice presidential debate.

"Can you imagine Sarah Palin being a heartbeat away from the presidency? Lord help us if that happens."

Lenny nodded, but he was distracted by the two plain-clothes detectives who had just left Big Vinny's club. They held newspapers over their heads to stay dry as they crossed 91st Avenue and approached the store. The younger of the two opened the door and allowed the older detective to enter the store first. The senior detective—a balding man with a bulbous nose—inhaled and smiled as if recalling a long-lost olfactory memory.

"You make heroes here?"

"Yes," Lenny answered.

"You got mortadella?"

"Yes."

"Make me a mortadella and provolone hero." He scooped up a

handful of dry fava beans and let them fall through his stubby fingers back into the burlap sack. "You don't see these kind-a stores no more except in lower Manhattan. Even there, things are changing. Chinatown has just about wiped out Little Italy."

Lenny thought it ironic that this detective shared Big Vinny's nostalgia for intact Italian neighborhoods, especially if he was the one who at 6:30 this morning had escorted Big Vinny in handcuffs from his house to a police car.

The chatty older detective pointed to the hanging provolones and prosciuttos. "When I was a kid, we had a lot of these kinda stores in Brooklyn. Now you got all these shitty convenience stores and dollar stores. I don't know why they call them dollar stores. You can't buy nothing in them for a dollar, even though nothing they sell is worth more than 50 cents." He leaned toward his younger partner. "Ain't you getting nothing?"

"Do you have hamburgers?" the younger detective asked. He resembled the Howdy Doody puppet Lenny once rode on the back of his Radio Flyer tricycle.

"No, sorry," Lenny answered, and glanced at Doug who swallowed the last of his sandwich.

"Hamburgers!" the older detective roared. "That's all kids today know how to eat. Look at all the good stuff in that case. And you order a goddamn hamburger. Does this look like a fucking McDonalds to you?"

"Alright," the younger detective said, blushing, "give me a ham on white."

"Knock yourself out, kid!" The older detective said, laughing.

Lenny forced a smile.

The older detective eyed Doug. "You live around here?"

"Not too far. I work in the auto-repair shop across the street."

"No shit." The detective nodded. "You don't see too many coloreds, I mean African Americans, in this neighborhood."

Doug's jaw tightened, but Lenny hoped he'd let that comment go. The less said the better. While making the sandwiches Lenny thought of the money Big Vinny had asked him to store away last Christmas. Lenny had put it in his safe and forgotten about it. *I guess this is one of those rainy days that Big Vinny had worried about,* Lenny thought as he wrapped the sandwiches in wax paper, slipped them into a paper bag, and placed the bag on the counter.

"DiCico a friend of yours?" the older detective said.

"I know him," Lenny answered.

"Yeah, well be careful who you make friends with. By the way, seems that there was a block party here back in July, and there was a fight between some thugs and a cabdriver. Either one of you guys know anything about it?"

Lenny's stomach tightened. "I was working in the store all day," he said.

"How about you?" The detective turned to Doug.

"Sorry, I was working at the garage, and then I left work early and went right home."

"Hmm ... such hard working guys," the detective said, and took the bag of sandwiches and left the store without paying. His sidekick followed close behind the way Scungilli followed Big Vinny.

"Nice guy. Free lunch. Maybe I should have made a citizen's arrest for petty larceny," Doug said.

"It takes all kinds," Lenny said.

Doug stood and tossed a crumbled ball of wax paper into the trashcan. "I get there are certain things that ain't discussed around here, and it's none of my business, but I know you're probably worried. Just saying, that's all." Doug stretched his arm across the counter and gave Lenny one pat on his shoulder.

"Thanks," Lenny said, but broke eye contact with Doug. He didn't want their conversation to continue.

Once Doug left the store, Lenny clicked the remote for the small portable television that sat on the counter next to the cash register.

Officers wearing blue jackets with patches reading FBI Police or Police Department City of New York flanked a line of at least a dozen men shackled with handcuffs. Tomorrow's newspaper would show a photo of this scene above the caption, *Reputed Mob Figures Escorted Out of Manhattan FBI Office To Waiting Police Vans.*

Lenny spotted Scungilli and a glimpse of Big Vinny's sons, Michael and Jimmy. Finally there was a close up of Big Vinny with an agent on either side of him and one behind him. The corners of his mouth were turned down and his nostrils flared like a trapped bull about to attack.

The scene cut to the U.S. Attorney and the Queens County District Attorney standing behind a podium. They took turns listing the federal and state indictments, including racketeering, conspiracy, extortion, theft of union benefits, mail fraud, false statements, loan sharking, embezzlement of union funds, securities fraud, money laundering, illegal gambling, and conspiracy to distribute cocaine and marijuana.

Next, New York State Attorney General Andrew Cuomo stepped up to the podium and said: "We will not rest until organized crime is a distant memory in New York, and we will not rest until every member of organized crime is caught and convicted. Period."

The news location shifted from New York to Sicily, where a similar sweep had taken place.

Across the street several police officers wore plastic slickers, and one agent held a large black umbrella while his partner made checks on a note pad. The drizzle had turned to a steady rain. Until watching the news on television, all Lenny knew since earlier this morning, when he found Frankie sitting with Gennaro at the kitchen table, was that Big Vinny had been arrested. Gennaro was in tears. "Those fucking pigs arrested my old man," he cried.

After the last police officer snapped shut a newly installed padlock on the front door of Big Vinny's club and got in his car and drove away, neighbors appeared in Lenny's store like meerkats sensing that the jackals had left. They shook wet umbrellas and patted their faces dry with handkerchiefs. They had always assumed that Lenny knew more than them about Big Vinny's schemes, but Big Vinny was as tight-lipped with Lenny as he was with anyone on the block. All he ever said about his source of income was that he was a silent partner in several diners and bars. No names. No locations. No one believed him.

Even with Big Vinny in custody, the folks in the store were careful not to speak of more than what had been reported on television for fear that boasting about some privileged information, no matter how insignificant, might get back to the police, or worse, to Big Vinny. Remarks were more sympathetic than critical. Had Filomena been alive there would have been at least one renegade voice: *It's not enough that he brought disgrace on his parents. Now he has to shame his wife and children.*

Sharp Nick, once the neighborhood arrontino (knife grinder), stood across the counter from Lenny. He was a shrunken man with hearing aids in each ear and lips so sunken that his mouth appeared to be a small round hole under his beak of a nose. His toothless hole expanded and he yelled that he had seen Frankie with Gennaro this morning. *Implying what?* Lenny thought. The neighbors looked from Sharp Nick to Lenny.

Worry gripped Lenny's chest. He recalled Frankie's comment about the cabdriver on the day of the block party and the detective's question, and his forehead and armpits grew damp, his thinking became clouded, and everything went flat as if the neighbors became cardboard cutouts against the backdrop of a grocery store. Panic attacks were his doctor's diagnosis. They started soon after his father died, then disappeared for years, but occasionally surfaced as if to remind Lenny that tragedy was a sly and untiring predator.

He heard his voice, but had no sense of speaking. "If you're buying something please pay now. Otherwise please leave."

A few neighbors set their items back on shelves, most paid and left, and an old woman as shrunken as Sharp Nick and dressed all in black—her stockings rolled down to her ankles and a plastic rain cap atop her sparse, white hair—told Lenny not to listen to the old fool. "His brain is smaller than his hearing aids." She looked familiar, but Lenny couldn't place her.

After the last customer left, Lenny checked to make sure that all was quiet in front of Big Vinny's club, and then he locked the front door and flipped over the sign to read CLOSED. If someone asked why the store was closed in the middle of the day, he could say that he had to use the bathroom and no one was around to keep an eye on things. A few minutes, that's all he needed.

He walked up the three rickety steps, through the dark breezeway that connected the store to the house, stumbled around crates of returned soda bottles, and up three more steps to the windowless office where a battered oak desk, swivel chair, safe, and wooden file cabinets lined the walls, leaving only enough wall space for the three doors—one connecting the breezeway to the cluttered office, one from the office to the house, and one from the office to a tiny bathroom—and barely enough floor space to walk from one door to the other. On walls that Lenny had no memory of ever having a fresh coat of paint were sepia portraits and daguerreotypes of Leonardo and Lucia with Vincenzo and Lenny's aunts as children, Vincenzo and Filomena's wedding portrait, and professional photographs of relatives who remained in Sicily—probably long dead. The pictures were framed in heavy carved wood and plaster. Lenny sat at the desk, glanced at the safe, then pulled a wad of tissues from a box on the desk, wiped the perspiration from his brow and neck, glanced back at the safe, but this time his gaze lingered, and he recalled what had happened last Christmas Eve.

It was very late, and Lenny had just locked the door when he heard rapping at the storefront window and assumed it was a customer wanting baccalá or anchovies or sardines to complete the spread of seven fishes for Christmas Eve dinner. It was Big Vinny, but Marie had already shopped several times. By now her baccalá salad would have been chilled with steamed cauliflower, olives, sweet vinegar peppers, and a touch of lemon. She would fry the remaining codfish after the DiCico family finished their linguini smothered with calamari sauce that had simmered over a low flame, the way her mother-in-law and Filomena had taught her years earlier, making the calamari tender enough to cut with the edge of a fork. Big Vinny wasn't there to shop. A line of snow traced the black of his broad square shoulders and the brim of his fedora. Lenny unlocked the door.

"Buon Natale." Big Vinny shook the snow from his hat.

"Merry Christmas," Lenny said.

"I saw you locking the door when I was leaving the club so I thought I'd stop by. I can only stay a few minutes."

Without Scungilli or some other sidekick in tow, Big Vinny was like a comic without his straight man. An awkward silence hung over them until Lenny asked him if he was okay.

"Minchia, of course I'm okay," he said. "Am I keeping you from dinner or something?"

"No. Mama, Frankie, and Angie are at midnight mass."

Big Vinny removed his black kid gloves, folded them into his hat which he had already removed and loosened his cashmere scarf. He had a taste for nice things.

"It's warmer in the house. How about we go in and have a cup of coffee or a drink?" Lenny said.

"No, I can't stay long. Marie's waiting for me to get home so she can throw the macaroni in. The boys are here for Christmas Eve dinner with their wives. Did you hear that Michael's wife is gonna have a baby?"

"No. Congratulations," Lenny said. "Here sit down." He moved a stool closer to Big Vinny.

"But just for a minute," Big Vinny said. "Marie is waiting. The boys are here. Lena's got her boyfriend coming over too. Boyfriend, my ass. She's a junior in high school. I met him once. He looks Irish, but she said he's a WASP. Whatever the hell that means. She said I better be nice or she'll poison my vino. My daughter's got some temper and mouth on her."

"I wonder who she takes after?" Lenny smiled.

"Yeah, you're right, but you're always right."

Big Vinny shifted his weight on the stool, reminiscent of elementary school days, when the nuns made him sit on a stool in the corner of the classroom, under a statue of the Blessed Mother crushing the serpent's head with her tiny bare feet. Even back then, Big Vinny was too big for the stool and had a hard time sitting still.

"Imagine, I'm gonna be a grandpa," Big Vinny said. "It feels like yesterday that I knocked up Marie. Now my oldest is gonna be a father. Marie's knitting all this blue baby stuff."

"A boy?"

"Yeah, I guess they did one of those sonograms. Ya know where they can see if the baby's got a prick. Imagine?"

"Yes, pretty amazing."

Big Vinny cleared his throat. "Lenny, I need a favor from you. You never know when something might happen. Something crazy. Who knows? You know maybe something happens to me, and for some reason Marie can't draw money out of our bank accounts. You know how crazy things happen. I mean like what happened to your old man. My mother had just left your store, and ten minutes later your father is dead. She hadn't even put the groceries away. My old man yells in the door, 'There's an ambulance in front of Lasante's.' My mother dropped the capicola your father had just sliced all over the kitchen floor and ran out of the house. Minchia, what a terrible day that was. A hundred years ago, but it feels like yesterday. You never know what's coming next, Lenny. And it's not only dying you gotta worry about. Who knows all the crazy things that can happen? If something happens to me, I need to know that my family isn't going to wind up in the street. You know, until I can get things settled. Some things take time."

Big Vinny removed a bulky brown envelope from the inside breast pocket of his coat and Lenny heard Vincenzo's gasps, the blare of sirens, and a jumble of discordant voices: *He's not to be trusted ... But he's like family ... He's always up to no good ... He'd risk his life for you and Frankie ... He'll pull his family and yours down with him.* The last voice sounded like Big Vinny's father.

Big Vinny's eyes were small and dark and hard to read. "I just thought of your father," Lenny said.

"My father? Why the hell are you bringing him up?"

"I don't know. The holidays? And you mentioned my father so it got me thinking."

"You think too much. That's always been your problem." Big Vinny began rambling again, but this time about his father, which gave Lenny time to think up excuses for not accepting the envelope.

"That's one of the things I hate about Christmas. It makes people think too much. After my brother got himself killed in Nam, my old man was no good. If it wasn't for my mother—may they all rest in peace—I think he would have gone back to Sicily. You know what he said to me once? This was after I dropped out of high school and started paying my own way. I even offered him money. Ya know, to pay for my room and board—tried to make his life a little easier. He said to me: 'Keep your blood money. I left Sicily to get away from scum like you'."

Lenny knew this story. Filomena had told him years ago. Big Vinny's mother had told her.

"Blood money?" Big Vinny was on a roll. "My old man didn't know shit about me, and it was his own fucking fault that he barely had a pot to piss in. He had passed up every chance his bosses gave him for advancement. Why? So he could be a big fucking union hero while my mother pinched pennies, and then after all his being pro-union he even got on the outs with the them. Said they had become more corrupt than management. Remember, he got on that soapbox about the union not helping coloreds. What the hell did that have to do with him? He lost a lot of overtime over that fight. All my old man knew how to do was make enemies. By the end I was sneaking my mother money, or they wouldn't have had nothin. And he knew it, but he would have choked before he'd admit it was my blood money that ... For Christ's sake, what the hell are we talking about this crap for? It was a hundred years ago."

Big Vinny fidgeted as if he were still sitting under the statue of the Blessed Mother. "Sit still, Vincent," the nuns would scold. But expecting him to be still was as useless as expecting the plaster statue of Mary to dance.

"I know, I know. You were always on his side." Big Vinny laughed. "You ate up his goddamn stories about the oppressed. When I was a kid, I even found old copies of that Commie paper, the *Daily Worker,* on his bookshelves. I was looking for girlie magazines like my brother Sal used to hide under his mattress. My mother caught me reading my father's *Daily Worker* newspapers, and she threw them out. I remember they had a big fight over that. Remember how the nuns used to make us read that Catholic kids' magazine with all the stuff about the evil Communists? One time in confession I told the priest that my old man was a Communist. The priest said that Communists would burn in hell. I told my father and he said that there wasn't enough room in hell with all the priests down there."

"Sounds like my grandfather." Lenny laughed.

"Yeah, well after that, I had nightmares that these giant priests and cops would break into my house and arrest my old man."

They both laughed.

"Forget all that shit," Big Vinny said. "I know one thing. If you ain't there for your own family, then you're no good for no one."

"You're right," Lenny said.

"What do you mean I'm right?" Big Vinny looked stunned.

"Your father was rarely there for you, or your brother, and after Sal was killed in Vietnam, you're father wasn't there for you at all. You know I admired your father. He was a good man ... but maybe not such a good father."

"Yeah, well, I wasn't such an easy son either."

"You're right again." Finally, Lenny pointed to the envelope. Big Vinny had a circuitous way of persuading. "I think you wanted me to keep that in the safe for you," Lenny said.

Big Vinny wrinkled his brow, as if he had forgotten about the envelope, but then he handed it to Lenny. "You don't have to worry about it being traced. It's clean money."

And how you made this money? Was that clean? Lenny wanted to ask, but instead he just nodded.

"We don't always agree, Lenny. Maybe we hardly ever agree, but I know that you think taking care of family is important, and I can trust you. The money is for an emergency. Maybe Marie needs it to pay bills, or somebody gets sick. Whatever. Hopefully you'll never have to use it. Who knows? Crazy things happen. Without warning it can be a rainy day."

Sitting at his desk and staring at the safe where last Christmas Eve he stashed Big Vinny's brown envelope, Lenny thought: *This must be that rainy day.* As if the safe were sitting on his chest, Lenny struggled through several deep breaths before he returned to the store, popped a valium, swallowed it with spit, unlocked the front door, and turned the sign to read OPEN.

Later that evening, in the DiCicos' kitchen, Lenny learned that Big Vinny had been charged with racketeering, conspiracy, and theft of union benefits. *He finally took his revenge on the unions for taking his father away from him,* Lenny thought.

"And my boys were charged with murder," Marie cried.

This shocked Lenny. There had been no mention of murder charges on the news.

"Remember that cabbie that drove through my father's block party," Lena explained, "the one who was stupid enough to flip us the finger. Who the hell cared about him? We had other things to worry about that night after Gennaro got burned. Anyway, the police found his body in a bay near Howard Beach. At least what was left of it. How are the cops gonna link him being dead to my brothers? No one knew who the hell he was. Just another cabbie. Nobody laid a fucking finger on him. The pussy drove away."

"Lena! Watch your language," Marie said, weeping.

Now Lenny understood why the detective had asked about the cabdriver. As usual, his stomach tightened.

Frankie and Gennaro appeared with pizzas from Johnny Boo Boo's, while Lena babbled on about why the judge would not release any of them on bail.

"Some nonsense about priors and risk of leaving the country," she said. "Where the hell are they gonna go? Sicily? The lousy cops are arresting people there too, and they're more crooked than the people they're arresting." She tossed paper plates and napkins on the kitchen table as if she were dealing cards in a casino. Since the boys seemed unfazed by what Lena was saying, Lenny assumed that they already knew about the murder accusations and that all four men, including Scungilli, were being held without bail. Gennaro took sodas from the refrigerator and Frankie grabbed paper cups from a cupboard as comfortably as if he were in his own kitchen.

Two pizzas sat on the table. One cheese, the other anchovy. Lena and Gennaro griped that their brothers and father had been unjustly arrested. *The only thing unjust was that they hadn't been arrested before they could cause so much harm*, Lenny thought. He took a slice of the anchovy pizza and stared at it.

"My mother wouldn't eat Johnny's pizza," Lenny said. His voice sounded distant. "She complained that Johnny's mother used to change his diapers on the same counter where the dough rose. Mama turned up her nose every time I reminded her that it had been years since Johnny wore diapers." Everyone around the table stared at Lenny, and he realized that his comments about Filomena must have seemed odd given everyone's immediate concerns about the arrests, but he couldn't bear listening to Lena and Gennaro whine about justice.

"Ma, eat something," Lena said, and placed a slice of pizza on a paper plate.

Marie pushed it away. "I can't."

Lena was a younger version of Marie, the way Frankie was a younger version of Lenny, but she acted more like Big Vinny than any of her brothers. She sat there chewing her pizza and badmouthing the police without missing a beat, then briefly held the paper cup of soda between her teeth, ran her fingers through her long blond hair (same box ash blond as Marie's), twisted it up in a scrunchie, and mumbled: "Those pig cops have no problem accepting tips from Big Vinny." She mumbled this without spilling a drop of soda. When talking to her father, Lena called him Pops, but when talking about him, she often called him Big Vinny, as if it were a title of honor.

"You got that right," Gennaro said.

Frankie ate his pizza and drank his soda without saying a word.

"Lenny, take another slice," Marie said.

"No, I'm done. Thank you." Lenny stood and carried his plate and cup to the trash container.

"Leave it, Lenny. I'll clean up when the kids are done," Marie said.

Lenny bent and gave Marie a kiss on the cheek. "I'm sorry you're going through this."

"Too much, Lenny. Too much." Marie took a tissue from her sleeve and wiped her tears.

Lenny looked at Frankie. "You ready?"

"I'll walk you out to the yard, Dad," Frankie said, and Lenny could taste the anchovy repeat on him and the slight plume of acid in his throat.

Next to the dueling penises fountain, Frankie told Lenny that Gennaro was having a hard time and he was going to spend the night.

"I don't like this, Frankie. Not with everything that's going on. Don't you think it might be better to give the DiCicos a little space?"

"Better for who?" Frankie said.

"Better for everyone," Lenny answered and stuffed his hands into his pockets so Frankie wouldn't see them shaking.

Frankie kissed Lenny on the cheek, told him that he'd be home in the morning, and went back into the house.

That night in the DiCicos' basement, Gennaro no longer assumed his post-orgasm detachment, but instead, he spoke of Big Vinny, Michael, and Jimmy, and he even cried and told Frankie that he loved him and that he didn't know what he would do without him.

Another time, under different circumstances, Frankie would have been ecstatic to hear Gennaro say this.

"I can be a real jerk sometimes. I wish things were different," Gennaro said, and soon fell asleep, his naked body clutching Frankie's.

Frankie didn't ask Gennaro what he meant by different. He just lay there until Gennaro's breaths turned rhythmic, and then he slid out from under Gennaro's arm and leg, got out of bed, and sat in a leather chair facing one of the fish tanks in the game room. The leather felt cool against his bare skin. He didn't know the names of the kinds of fish in the tank, but their colors were a brilliant Day-Glo fluorescent. Profiles of fluorescent yellows, blues, and greens darted from one end of the tank to the other, over and over, until the fish blurred into a memory of the cabdriver speeding away, and Gennaro writing the cab's license plate number on his arm.

The glow from the tank reflected Frankie's green eyes, their color made more brilliant by his tears. He climbed back into bed, and Gennaro stirred. Frankie pressed his lips to Gennaro's, his hand clutched the moist soft of Gennaro's groin, which immediately grew hard, and everything beyond their entwined bodies vanished.

The following morning brought the usual last minute Sunday dinner shoppers into Lasante's—a steady flow of customers after each Mass. No one mentioned Big Vinny or the arrest. News about Lenny's behavior yesterday had traveled up and down 104th Street, which was fine with Lenny, and promptly at 2:00, he closed the store—the usual Sunday closing time. Not a minute earlier for fear of drawing attention.

Lenny sat at his desk in the office staring at the glow from his computer and stewing over Frankie not being home yet from the DiCicos'. He opened his email and typed in Dr. Violetta Geski. Vi's work email address appeared. She had once been a flowerchild wannabe who had missed Woodstock by about 20 years—at least that was Angie's assessment of Vi. Tony had been a little less harsh. He thought she was pretty enough. "For a chubby girl," he said. But to Lenny she was his beautiful alter ego. She had been Carmen to Lenny's Don Jose. He was 11 years her senior, but lifting cases of olive oil and canned tomatoes had kept him in good form. His full head of curly hair was jet black, and his jaw was strong. Vi drifted into the store and his life wearing a low-cut blouse and long skirt, sheer and crinkly like tissue paper, and there were silver bangles, including tiny bells strung through her toes and around her ankles. She had recently dumped her California boyfriend, was staying with friends in Glenhaven, and was in want of a little distraction. Lenny became her distraction, and given that his youngest sibling, Tony, was soon leaving for college, which meant the beginning countdown for Lenny's own liberation, he was more than ready to celebrate.

It began with her smile as he handed her change. Her eyes held his until Lenny blushed like a 32-year-old teenager. An hour later she returned to the store for something or other that she had forgotten to buy. She returned again when Lenny was alone in the store boning a prosciutto, and this time she said that she was in search of keys that she claimed to have dropped while shopping earlier. He handed her a thin slice of the salty ham. "Just a taste," she said, and as she licked the salt from her fingers, Lenny asked her if she wanted more.

That night, after Filomena and Tony were asleep, Lenny met Vi at the back door of the warehouse where she giggled as he fumbled with the keys. The warehouse was dark and smelled of olives in brine and aged imported cheeses, but as he drew Violetta close and inhaled her citrus cologne, the cool of the warehouse turned warm then hot, and Lenny took Vi on a bed of risotto in 50-pound bags. So began their clandestine romance. Being secretive was their aphrodisiac, as if the danger of discovery made sex that much more intoxicating and addicting, and Vi gave Lenny a crash course in the college social life he had missed, while funny smoke and much moaning ascended the citadel of the warehouse's dry goods.

Filomena pursed her lips whenever Lenny said that he had to make space for another delivery. She found his sudden preoccupation with the warehouse curious—that was until the hapless deliveryman exposed Vi and Lenny.

The Ronzoni deliveryman had interrupted Filomena while she was talking to her friend Rosa: "Excuse me, Mrs. Lasante, but I have 50 cases of macaroni your son ordered." Filomena handed him the padlock key for the warehouse's overhead door and waved him out of the store as if he had interrupted a summit conference.

He left the store, turned the corner and walked down 104th Street where his truck was parked at the driveway to the warehouse. After he unlocked and raised the door, a flash of sunlight illuminated the contents of the previously dark warehouse, including Lenny's bare buttocks and Vi's bejeweled toes. The stunned lovers fumbled to hide themselves amid the surrounding cases of confectionaries, which came tumbling down and framed them in cardboard stamped *Fragile* and *Imported*.

Dumbfounded, the deliveryman stammered: "I'm s-sorry to disturb you, M-Mr. Lasante, but where would y-y-you like the macaroni?"

Lenny mumbled something while he stood, pulled up his pants, and tried to block the Ronzoni deliveryman's clear view of Vi.

"Italian Stallion" had almost replaced "Hard Luck Lenny," but then Vi missed her period and Hard Luck Lenny became permanent. Wedding photographs taken in the Lasante's yard showed Violetta barefoot—a plump wood nymph draped in cream-colored layers of gauze, her hair crowned with miniature violets and baby's breath. Lenny was also barefoot, by Vi's design, and dressed in a tan linen suit, but in the photographs he looked more proletarian than mythical. His black eyes, thick blue-black curls and olive complexion contrasted Violetta's green eyes, straight blond hair, and creamy complexion. Under an arbor heavy with ripe grapes—the fruit of the seedlings Leonardo had planted years earlier—Vi and Lenny were married.

Six months later, long after the grapes had been picked and pressed into wine, Lenny coached Vi through her labor and Frankie's birth, but the following morning, when Lenny returned to the hospital to bring his family home, a nurse handed him a note that she had found pinned to Vi's pillow. Violetta was gone.

Lenny hadn't expected that his lust for Vi would become love, but neither had he expected to take over the family business years before or help his mother raise his siblings. After Vi said that she was pregnant and finally agreed not to abort, Lenny allowed himself to hope that his luck had finally changed and that he'd make a new life with Vi beyond the store. Once his brother graduated from college—the last of his siblings to graduate—he would have fulfilled his father's wishes, and he'd be free to leave. His family could have sold the business or paid someone else to work it. Or they could have burned it down for all Lenny cared. He promised Vi he would leave. Only three more years, and then he'd go wherever she wanted to go. Anywhere, he promised, but he didn't blame her or begrudge her leaving. In fact, he wasn't even surprised when the nurse handed him the note.

Within three months, he received divorce papers from a lawyer in San Francisco. He signed and returned them to the lawyer's address. There was no mention of child custody or visitation rights, and Lenny wondered if the lawyer even knew that there was a baby.

Frankie was about to graduate from elementary school when

Lenny first searched the Internet for information about Vi and came upon Dr. Violetta Vitkus, professor of religious studies at UCLA. She was teaching courses with titles like Religious Ethics in Comparative Perspective, Love and Its Critics, and Modern Roman Catholic Ethics. Lenny found her chosen profession and the titles of coursework amusing, especially Love and Its Critics, but he also thought that Frankie's obsession with religion may have been influenced by more than Filomena's brainwashing. Maybe he inherited more than his green eyes from Violetta.

Since discovering Vi's address, Lenny had written and deleted countless emails to her, and that morning after Big Vinny's arrest, Lenny began another email—rehashing his concern about Frankie's attachment to the DiCicos, especially to Gennaro—with every intention of deleting it:

> *Last night I left Frankie at the DiCicos. He's still not home. Maybe I should have dragged him out of there. Frankie's an excellent student, Vi, and could get into most any college, but I'm afraid that something terrible is going to happen to him before he has the chance to get away from here, especially from Big Vinny's youngest son, Gennaro. Vi, I'm sure this email comes as a shock, but I've tried writing to you hundreds of times. He's a good kid, Vi. I'm sure you'd be proud of him. No hard feelings about us, Vi. I'm just running out of steam. I don't want Frankie to wind up like me, or worse.*

Lenny read and reread the email until he was startled by a rap at the dining-room door behind him.

"Sorry, Mr. Lasante, I knocked so we wouldn't scare you," Gennaro said.

Lenny closed his laptop, forced a smile, ignored Gennaro's comment, and looked at Frankie. "Is everything alright, Son?"

Frankie shrugged his shoulders and Gennaro answered, "No, nothing. I just wanted to ask you something and Frankie came along."

Lenny stood and followed the boys into the dining room.

"I've got to get something from my room," Frankie said, but Lenny knew that Frankie didn't need anything from his room. He was just following DiCico orders.

With Frankie gone, and Gennaro leaning against the back of a dining room chair, Lenny felt as if he were on DiCico turf rather than in his own home, despite the familiar picture of the Last Supper over the credenza that his brother, Tony, had scratched his name into its frame, or the oriental jardinière near the window with the sansevieria that Lucia had rooted from a cutting, or the knickknacks in the corner curio, favors from Lasante family weddings. Pictures, plants, and knick-knacks yielded to Gennaro's presence, as if to say, *Listen up, a DiCico is about to talk.*

"Sit down, Gennaro," Lenny said and pulled a chair away from the table.

Gennaro placed a small white envelope on the table. On the front was Lenny's name written in Big Vinny's third-grade script.

"This was on my pillow," Gennaro said. "I'm not sure how it got there, but a lot of my old man's friends have been in and out of the house all day. I don't know who left it. Maybe my old man had put it there when he saw the police coming. I don't know."

Lenny glared at Gennaro. "You don't know how it got there?" It was a rhetorical question and said with sarcasm. Lenny surmised that Gennaro knew more than he admitted. After all, he was Big Vinny's son. Lenny picked up the envelope. "Does Frankie know about this?"

"No. I swear. Last night, me and him slept in the basement. I just found this upstairs in my bedroom. Frankie didn't see it. I just told him I wanted to ask you something. I don't even know what's in it myself."

"You just happened to go in your bedroom?"

"Yeah. I had to get something."

Lenny's hands shook as he opened the envelope. The note was also written in Big Vinny's script:

It's that rainy day. Sunday night at 9:00 p.m., last stop, Lefferts Blvd. Station.

He placed the note face down on the table, and the ragged edge of a callus on his pinky caught on a thread of the embroidered tablecloth.

Without warning it can be a rainy day. Lenny heard Big Vinny's words from last Christmas Eve.

"I don't mean to be rude, Mr. Lasante, but are you going to do it?" Gennaro asked.

"Do what? You said you don't know what's in the envelope."

"No, no. Of course I don't."

Gennaro wasn't as convincing a liar as his father. Lenny thought that it was careless of Big Vinny to have involved a 19-year-old in this, even if Gennaro was family.

"It's just that I figured, since there was a note, my old man must want you to do something," Gennaro said.

"Well you figured wrong, so I guess we're done talking here, except for one thing. Frankie is to know nothing about what you claim you don't know. Nothing."

"Sure, Mr. Lasante. Whatever you say."

Lenny pushed his chair away from the table, slipped the note into his pocket, stood, walked into the living room, and called up the stairs. "Frankie, no need to look for whatever it is you're pretending to look for. Gennaro and I are done."

Lenny stared at Frankie as he walked down the stairs, but Frankie kept his eyes lowered, and Lenny worried, that like Gennaro, Frankie was concealing what he knew. Back in the dining room, Frankie and Lenny found Gennaro admiring his reflection in the glass-covered picture of the Last Supper, like Narcissus gazing at his reflection in the pond. "We got one of these pictures in our dining room too," Gennaro said. "I think my grandma gave this to your mother, Mr. Lasante. Isn't that right?"

"I don't remember," Lenny said. Now it was his turn to lie.

"Our families got a lot of history."

Lenny was out of patience.

"I always thought it was a weird picture to hang in a dining room," Gennaro said.

"Why's that?" Frankie asked.

"I don't know. It's kind of like when you're sitting at the dinner table and you look at the picture, you wonder if someone is trying to tell you something. You know like bad news or something. You know like there might be a Judas at the table."

Lenny had all the DiCico drama he could handle for one day. "I'm going upstairs for a nap," he said and asked Frankie what he was doing even though he knew he'd be leaving with Gennaro. He reminded Frankie that tomorrow was school and that he wanted him home early, then he left the boys and went upstairs to his bedroom.

After he heard the front door close, he pulled Big Vinny's note from his pocket and crushed it into a ball while his eyes scanned the photographs on his dresser. First, a studio portrait of his parents, siblings, and himself, where Filomena held baby Tony on her lap, Lenny stood next to Vincenzo, and Angie, Irish, and Amelia stood in front of them. Next, Lenny looked at the photograph of Vi and him taken on their wedding day. After Vi had left, Filomena told Lenny to burn the photograph, but that wasn't his way. Keep the facts open, simple, and real. If nothing else, Frankie always knew what his mother looked like, plus he grew up hearing Lenny tell stories about Vi as candidly as he shared other family stories. Finally, he looked at the snapshot of a rearview shadowy silhouette of him holding Frankie on his shoulders, while the surf splashed at their feet, and the Atlantic met a violet sky.

With one hand Lenny held Big Vinny's crumbled note; with the other, he lifted the cardboard-framed photograph from his dresser. A few golden ditalini and tubetti clung to dry patches of paste like remnants of gilded rococo plaster. Frankie had been such an easygoing little boy, unlike his Uncle Tony, who played hooky more often than he went to school, started smoking at 12 years old, experimented with alcohol and drugs, and finished high school and college by the skin of his teeth with constant bribes and threats from Lenny. Lenny's sisters were no easier. They questioned his authority on everything: clothes, makeup, boys, curfews. In vain, they attempted to circumvent his rules by appealing to Filomena, who never contradicted Lenny in front of his siblings, at least not when they were little. But Frankie had been a piece of cake compared to his uncle and aunts, at least when he was young enough and small enough for Lenny to lift onto his shoulders. Angie had taken the photograph as she followed them onto the beach after a day of Coney Island rides, Nathan's hotdogs, knishes, and chocolate egg creams. The photo had been placed in a family album with hundreds of other photographs and soon forgotten until Frankie was in

kindergarten and made a Mother's Day frame in school with an as-
sortment of miniature macaroni pasted on cardboard and sprayed
gold. After Filomena unwrapped Frankie's gift to her—a bottle of Jean
Nate—he handed Lenny the gilded macaroni frame containing the
Coney Island picture. At first Lenny didn't recognize the photograph,
but then he remembered. They had just eaten hotdogs, and the fronts
of their t-shirts were covered with mustard. "Good thing your aunt
took the picture from behind. I'm told it's my better side anyway,"
Lenny said as he gave Frankie a hug. "This is the best Mother's Day
gift a dad could ask for."

When he asked Frankie why he had selected this photo, kinder-
gartner Frankie answered simply: "Daddy is strong."

Lenny placed the picture back on the dresser not feeling very strong
and hating himself for having agreed to keep Big Vinny's money for
him. He sat at the edge of his bed. The money was supposed to be for
Marie to pay bills in an emergency, not *Next Sunday night at 9:00 pm,
last stop, Lefferts Blvd.* Lenny would have never agreed to be a courier
for Big Vinny's bagman. His chest tightened. *It's not that kind of pain,*
he thought. Nothing sharp. Not like his father's pain. Just another panic attack.

Lenny took the bottle of Valium from his pocket, swallowed a pill
without water, and lay back on his bed. With the shades drawn and
his room dark, it was easy for him to imagine the warehouse behind
the store on a warm evening over 18 years ago, and his anxiety turned
to longing for Vi. So many years had passed, and yet she was still his
Carmen. Even when he made love to other women, he imagined Vi.
Had she stayed, maybe time would have eased his passion for her. Maybe
he would have imagined others when their lovemaking became routine. But she left, and to Lenny she remained the young, impulsive,
and exciting woman he made love to in the warehouse behind the store.
In the dark of his bedroom, though at first it was easy for Lenny to
rise to memories of Vi, they were only memories and couldn't compete
with his angst over being trapped in one of Big Vinny's schemes. Only
a real woman, not a memory, might have provided some respite. Lenny thought of Angelina Zeppole, but the Feast of the Assumption was
long over.

The following week dragged. Lunches with Doug felt burdensome, and Frankie spent far too much time at the DiCicos. Lenny lived on Valium until the following Sunday came, and again he closed the store at the usual time, allowing customers who attended noon Mass enough time for last-minute dinner shopping, but, more importantly, to avoid the questions that closing early would have invited.

Having left the smell of the store at the bottom of the clothes hamper, Lenny showered, shaved, splashed on Old Spice, and dressed in clean clothes. He shut himself in his office and opened the safe where Big Vinny's money hid beneath three generations of Lasante archives —certificates of citizenship, births, baptisms, communion, confirmation, marriages and deaths, deeds, wills, and a stack of photographs. He removed two brown envelopes from the safe and tossed them on his desk. Under the desk light he could see that one envelope was old and worn. The other was new. He lifted the newer one, opened the flap and saw that it contained cash. He didn't remember it being so heavy. Big Vinny must have been thinking more hurricane than rainy day. And of course he was correct.

The flap of the older envelope was torn, exposing the top of a photograph, which caught Lenny's eye. There were several photographs in it—all had been taken in Sicily—and letters that he hadn't seen since years earlier when Leonardo had told him the names of the people in the pictures and had explained that the letters were correspondence between himself and Big Vinny's Grandfather Salvatore about Big Vinny's father, Giacomo, coming to live in America.

The Lasante-DiCico connection went back to a small town outside of Taormina, Sicily, where Leonardo Lasante and Salvatore DiCico had been childhood friends. After Mussolini gained power in Italy, Salvatore's older son went underground to join the anti-fascist resistance, and though Giacomo was only 13 at the time, he was also strongly anti-fascist like his older brother. Lenny's family had already been established in America, and after Leonardo learned that Giacomo had been found in a pigsty, beaten and bloodied, he not only paid for the boy's passage to America, but also raised him as a second son. From their early teens, Vincenzo and Giacomo grew up under the same roof as brothers.

Lenny long felt it was ironic that the once highly moralistic, anti-fascist Giacomo fathered a son like Big Vinny, but he also thought it ironic that Leonardo's generosity had the unforeseen, dangerous consequences of putting Lenny in the position he now found himself.

Behind the letters were more pictures that Lenny didn't recognize —very stylized professional photographs, some were of nude teenage boys taken by the photographer Wilhelm von Gloeden. Curious photos, but at the time Lenny had more pressing matters on his mind, and he tossed the older envelope including the photos and letters back into the safe.

He didn't know the specifics, but he surmised that there was a link between the money and Big Vinny getting out of jail. If there were crooked politicians or judges to be bought, Big Vinny would sniff them out, and Lenny wondered if Big Vinny had money stashed elsewhere and how many stooges he was dragging into his scheme.

The faces on the old family portraits surrounding Lenny appeared more disapproving than usual, especially his parents' wedding portrait. Vincenzo, much younger than Lenny remembered him, but with the same determined eyes, and Filomena slimmer and with black hair, but even as a bride, dressed in satin and lace, she looked as if she could smell bullshit a mile away.

"You think I don't know that something can go wrong," Lenny mumbled. "I'm not doing this for Vinny. He can rot in jail for all I care, but there's his family to think of and Frankie. Whether we like it or not, what affects Gennaro affects Frankie."

"Enough!" Lenny shouted and stood, wedged the envelope with money in the inside pocket of his sports jacket and babbled: "I'm sitting here arguing with dead people? You're dead. Stay dead. This is my decision."

Frankie's voice came from the dining room. "Who are you talking to?"

"Myself," Lenny snapped. "When did you get home?"

Frankie stepped into the office. "It sounded like you were arguing."

"Yeah, well sometimes I don't get along with me. You think that you're the only one I give a hard time? I'm fine. In fact, I'm so fine that I'm going out today. I think I'll take in a movie. Maybe I'll take the subway into Manhattan and see a play. You're on your own for supper. Okay?"

Lenny grabbed Frankie's arm and directed him from the office back into the house.

"Are you sure you're okay?" Frankie said. "Maybe I should go with you."

"I'm fine."

Frankie, looking unconvinced, followed Lenny to the front door. Lenny gave Frankie a hug, pulled the front door closed behind him, and walked to the train station.

13

They sat cross-legged on the threadbare oriental carpet and shone flashlights into the open safe while Frankie removed jars of silver dollars and Indian-head pennies, and Gennaro said: "I hope my old man's not planning to buy his way out of prison with that." Earlier Gennaro had let himself into the Lasante's house after he knocked and no one answered the door.

"That's what you get for leaving the front door unlocked. You never know what kind of pervert will sneak up on you," Gennaro said when he startled Frankie. He leaned over Frankie's shoulder. "What are you doing?"

"College stuff. My father won't leave me alone until all these applications are in."

Listening was not Gennaro's strength, but he seemed even more distracted than usual. He slipped a wet finger in Frankie's ear, then flopped back on Frankie's bed. "So where did your old man go?"

"Who said he went anywhere?"

"Come on, Francesco ... you know that you can't fart on this block without someone smelling it."

"Meaning the DiCicos know everything," Frankie said.

"Now you sound like your old man." Gennaro got up and walked to Frankie's bedroom window, which overlooked Big Vinny's club. His jaw pulsed. "Those pricks are snooping around again," he said. "They've been asking neighbors about that fucking cabbie."

Frankie joined Gennaro at the window. Across 91st Avenue, one plain-clothes officer sat in a parked black sedan while two others unlocked the padlocks and entered the club.

"They weren't there when my father left for Manhattan," Frankie said.

"So your old man did go out."

Less than an hour passed since Frankie had come upon Lenny arguing with himself in the office. He had sensed something was up, but now he was convinced of it.

"Since when do you care about where my father goes?"

"Look, I didn't come here to argue with you." Gennaro gave Frankie's crotch a squeeze, but Frankie pushed his hand away.

"Guess all this college stuff is making you cranky." Then Gennaro threw his arm around Frankie's shoulder and asked real sweet if Frankie happened to know the combination to the safe in Lenny's office.

Again, Frankie pushed him away, but this time he told Gennaro to either tell him what's going on or go home and squeeze his own damn crotch.

"I promised your old man that I wouldn't say anything to you, but I don't have time for games. My old man gave Lenny an envelope some time ago. I don't know when. He said that Lenny put it in the safe. I have to make sure that it's not there."

"Why don't you want it to be where he put it?" This made no sense to Frankie. He went back to his laptop and pressed save.

Gennaro tightened his lips and rolled his eyes as if Frankie were a complete idiot. He yanked the shade down on Frankie's window, but instead it snapped and rolled back up to the top. "Because Lenny is supposed to give it to someone tonight. That's why."

"That's crazy," Frankie said. "You know my father would never do anything like that."

"Exactly." This time Gennaro lowered the shade carefully. "That's what's been eating at me. That's why I need to see if he took the envelope with him."

"Why do you keep messing with that damn shade?"

"Because I don't want to see those fuckers going in and out of my old man's club?"

"Then stop looking out of the damn window."

"I'm not looking out the window. Do you know the combination to the safe or not?"

Frankie sighed. "When is my father supposed to make this drop?"

Gennaro rolled his eyes again. "No one said anything about a drop. If you don't want to be treated like a fucking kid, then stop asking silly questions. I just want to see if he took the envelope with him. That's all." Gennaro went from the window to the door and stepped out into the hallway.

Frankie grabbed a hoodie from the pile of dirty laundry spilling out of his closet, pulled it over his head, and brushed past Gennaro.

"Come on. I think I can remember it."

Now as they sat on the floor in the office and sorted through stacks of papers under flashlights, the only envelopes they came across were relics held together with yellow tape and rubber bands. "My father must have taken it with him," Frankie said.

"I should have trusted that your old man would come through for us. Our families got a lot of history. Your old man can get all uppity, but when it comes down to it we're like blood, better than blood." This time when Gennaro reached for Frankie's crotch and slipped his other hand under his hoodie, Frankie not only let him, but reciprocated, and right there atop Lasante archives, with the old safe agape, and under the disapproving stares of ancestors, Frankie and Gennaro made love.

Afterwards they gathered papers strewn across the rug. Gennaro picked up a marriage certificate stained with a drop of seamen. "Well I guess our marriage has been consummated," Gennaro said.

"Give me that, you jackass," Frankie said, and he wiped the certificate with a tissue and added it to the pile of documents he was about to return to the safe. He picked up some photographs that had spilled from an old torn brown envelope. Some were caught in the folds of Frankie and Gennaro's clothes, which were also strewn across the carpet.

"Must be relatives from Sicily," Frankie said, while Gennaro stood naked in the glow of his cell phone. "Johnny Pickle texted me. He wants to know where we are. Should I tell him we're butt naked rolling around in your old man's office?"

Frankie ignored Gennaro's comment and kept skimming through the photographs. "Probably some DiCicos too," Frankie said.

Gennaro looked up from his phone.

"Some of the photographs are printed on cardboard. This one is of a young girl with big eyes like those Keane paintings we studied in art."

"You mean, you studied," Gennaro said.

The girl sat on stone steps against a stone building. Her bare toes peeked out beneath the frayed edge of her checkered skirt, and her fingertips rested along the neck of a water vessel. Frankie handed the postcard to Gennaro. "Beautiful, isn't she?"

"Pretty enough to be a DiCico," Gennaro said. "Although she probably borrowed those raggedy clothes from a Lasante."

Frankie examined another photograph under the flashlight, a close up of a girl whose black eyes were even larger and more enigmatic than the girl's in the previous picture. She held a basket of figs, and a translucent shawl was draped over her shoulders. "These pictures must have been taken by a professional photographer, probably an artist. They look like something from a museum," Frankie said.

"Like you. A regular David, except better hung," Gennaro said as he reached for Frankie's crotch, but Frankie pulled away.

"David is a sculpture not a picture," Frankie answered, and continued to thumb through the photos, but slowed down when he came to the photographs of boys no older than Gennaro and he—several looked younger. Some wore togas, some wore wreaths in their hair, some had leaves covering their private parts, but some were completely nude. All of the photographs were sepia and seductive.

"Holy crap," Frankie said. "This photographer must have been some kind of a porn artist ... or pervert ... or both."

Several scenes were distant, the subjects' features unclear, but there were also close-ups of solitary subjects or pairs or threesomes. In one picture, a boy stared dreamily, his head slightly askew, while a blossom dangled from his pouted lips. An open robe fell from his lightly muscled shoulders. In another, a boy sat on a rock outcropping bracketed with cacti. Two diminutive horns poked out from his thick curly mane. Frankie shifted the flashlight back and forth between the two photographs.

"Look at these," he said, and shoved the pictures into Gennaro's hands. Frankie stood and pulled the chain hanging from the bare light bulb above them, and the harsh light from the bare bulb turned what had been their soft and shadowy nakedness into patches of pimples, blemishes, and rug burns, not to mention Gennaro's scars from the explosion. "Who do these guys look like?"

"Like two wops, one with horns and one with ... hey the guy eating the flower looks like you."

"And look a little closer at the guy with the horns," Frankie said.

"Holy crap!"

"Exactly, these guys could be our twins."

Frankie took the photo of the dreamy-eyed boy from out of Gennaro's hand and held it up next to a portrait of his great-grandparents, Leonardo and Lucia, taken upon their arrival to Ellis Island. "This kid must be my great-grandfather when he was a teenager, and I bet the guy with the horns is your great-grandfather."

"Makes sense that my great-grandfather was the horny guy," Gennaro said and he squeezed Frankie's butt. "But I look like my mother's side of the family."

"Maybe just your coloring, lighter hair and eyes." Frankie scanned the still shadowy walls with his searchlight. "There. There's a picture of our great-grandfathers in Taormina. Probably taken just before my great-grandparents came to America."

The men in the photographs were slightly older than the boys in the picture and their pose was sterner, like so many old photographs. They stood beneath what looked like a lemon tree.

Gennaro placed the photo of the boy with the diminutive horns next to the great grandfathers' picture. Frankie shined the flashlight on both of them.

"Yep! The same guy and the spitting image of me," Gennaro said.

"More like you're the spitting image of him," Frankie said.

"Whatever."

Across the back of the photos, written in elegant script were the words *cartolina postale* and the name *Wilhelm von Gloeden*. "This must be the photographer, probably a German or Dutch guy. Look on the back of your picture," Frankie said.

The remaining cartoline postale lay on the carpet like a minigallery of von Gloeden's photographs. In two photographs, the boys they assumed to be Leonardo and Salvatore posed together. In one they were standing on a beach and in the other they sat on a rock outcropping in a grotto.

"I didn't know they did this kind of stuff back then," Gennaro said.

"What kind of stuff? Took pictures?"

"Yeah, but these aren't exactly your welcome to Ellis Island snapshots."

Frankie pulled the overhead string and turned out the light bulb. In the dimmed lighting Gennaro's resemblance to the boy in the sepia photographs was unmistakable.

"Italy is loaded with nude artwork," Frankie said, trying to act as if he was cool with the pictures when in fact he was as surprised as Gennaro.

"But those are statues and paintings," Gennaro said, laughing. "Like the ones in the Sistine Chapel of big guys with little dicks, as if the Pope told Michelangelo it's okay to paint dirty pictures on the ceiling as long as you give Adam a baby dick. These are photographs, and these guys don't have baby dicks." Again Gennaro reached for Frankie's crotch, but Frankie jumped back.

"You know what they say, Francesco, the apple, or in this case the zucchini, doesn't fall far from the tree."

Frankie reminded Gennaro that zucchini doesn't grow on trees, but Gennaro was laughing too hard at his own joke to hear, so Frankie left him to enjoy his raunchy humor, sat at Lenny's desk, and opened the laptop to check the web for von Gloeden. Instead he saw the email addressed to Dr. Violetta Vitkus.

"I don't believe this," Frankie said, and Gennaro pressed his cheek against Frankie's. They stared at the computer screen for several silent moments, as if trying to make sense of a paper on quantum physics.

"Isn't that your mom's name?"

Frankie nodded. Gennaro squeezed next to Frankie on the chair, their bare skin pressed together. They smelled of sex.

"I didn't know that your old man kept in touch with her."

"Neither did I."

"Are you okay?"

Frankie didn't know what to say, except that he felt weird, as if reading her name and email address suddenly meant that she was a real person. "I've never searched the Internet for her," Frankie said. "You'd think I would have, but I didn't. I really never thought much about her. When I had questions, I asked my father, and he told me everything he knew. At least, I thought he had told me everything."

"He's right," Gennaro said.

"Who's right?"

"Your old man ... about getting away from me and my family and going to college."

Until Gennaro mentioned that Lenny was right, Frankie hadn't even thought to read the email: ... *I'm afraid that something terrible is going to happen to him before he has the chance to get away from the DiCicos, especially from Gennaro.*

"You know how my father is," Frankie said, feeling a little embarrassed.

"Yea, I know how he is, but he's also right."

"He was probably mad at Big Vinny or you or me for some reason. He's been mad a lot lately. Point is he didn't even send it."

"Maybe he should have." Gennaro ran his fingers through Frankie's hair. "Beautiful curls, just like the guy in the photo."

Gennaro kissed Frankie gently on the lips and told him that he had to make visiting hours at the jail and asked that Frankie walk him to the door.

They were both erect again when they dressed, but Gennaro had to leave. Gennaro sniffed himself. "I think I have cologne in the car. Not sure it's safe to walk into a jail smelling like this. I don't want to be some big old ugly guy's bitch."

At the front door, Gennaro searched his jacket pockets. "Must have left my keys in the office," he said. "They probably fell out of my pocket when you couldn't keep your hands off of me. I'll be right back."

Frankie's thoughts swirled like the cigar smoke that rose from two octogenarians shuffling past the stoop. Exhaust belched from a bus stopped at the corner light. First Frankie had learned that Lenny was delivering money for Big Vinny, next he found the nude photos of the great-grandfathers, and then he came upon the email to Vi. Earlier, Frankie tried to make sense of an online college application. Now nothing made sense.

"Found them!" Gennaro held his keys up in front of Frankie and gave him a hug. "Ya doing okay, Francesco?"

"Guess so," Frankie said. Gennaro greeted the two cigar-smoking octogenarians and told them that smoking will stunt their growth. He winked at Frankie, jumped into his convertible, and beeped the horn as his car peeled away from the curb.

Back in the office, Frankie gathered the cartoline postale from the carpet and stacked them on the desk. The computer screen had gone blank, and he struggled to prioritize his thoughts. Check Lenny's inbox to see if there had been emails from Vi? Or search the web for the photographer Wilhelm von Gloeden? Frankie pressed the spacebar and Lenny's email page came up, but the email to Vi was gone. Frankie clicked drafts. Nothing. He clicked sent email, and there was Dr. Violetta Vitkus at 4:23 p.m. He knew that he hadn't pressed send. He was sure of it. Then he remembered: *Must have left my keys in the office.* Gennaro must have pressed send. There was no other explanation. Misplacing his keys was a ruse—a classic DiCico stunt. Frankie thought, *Gennaro figured that my dad was right about me needing to get away from him, or he was angry with my father and this was his way of getting even.* He thought to call Gennaro on his cell, but Gennaro would deny everything.

He googled Dr. Violetta Vitkus. Several links came up, most having to do with UCLA, a few regarding publications and conferences. All of the links were in purple, showing that Lenny had already opened them. Frankie clicked the first link, which included a photograph. Vi's blond hair was cut short and spiked. Her face was thinner than in the wedding picture on Lenny's dresser, making her cheekbones more pronounced. The color of her eyes matched Frankie's. The picture depicted a mature, professional woman, someone quite capable of choices —the choice to pursue an education, including a Ph.D., and the choice to abandon her baby.

Abandon? This was the first time that Frankie considered that Vi had abandoned him. He had never felt abandoned. He was always among family. Until now, the only photograph that he had seen of Vi was of a girl wearing layers of cream-colored gauze and with miniature violets and baby's breath in her hair—more a fairytale princess who mysteriously vanished than a real woman choosing to leave her baby and move on with her life. Regardless, he was too confused and overwhelmed to dwell on this or the email or his father delivering Big Vinny's money, or that he had seen Gennaro write the murdered cab driver's license plate number on his arm, which he had been obsessing about since learning that the cabdriver had been murdered. As if he were playing whack-a-mole at the Feast of The Assumption, every time Frankie dismissed one concern another popped up. It was all too big, too beyond his control.

He took several slow, deep breaths and spread the stack of cartoline postale across the desk. He imagined fanciful stories inspired by the long ago sepia photographs and found some peace in his musings. Had the great-grandfathers been inseparable, like Gennaro and he? What were they like as boys? Did they discover that they were more than friends? Did they ever make love on a hot summer night? Not in a basement in Glenhaven, but in some ancient ruin in Taormina.

Frankie googled the photographer Wilhelm von Gloeden and discovered several links including images of his photographs and articles. One article began with a brief biography:

> Baron Wilhelm von Gloeden (September 16, 1856 — February 16, 1931) was a German photographer who worked mainly in Sicily. He is mostly known for his pastoral nude photographs of Sicilian boys with props such as wreaths or amphorae suggesting a setting in Greece or Italy of antiquity.

Another article included critiques and perceptions over time of von Gloeden's work, which became widely known, if not notorious. In total, the Baron took over 3,000 images and turned an impoverished Sicilian seaside town into a vacation destination for writers, artists, European aristocrats, and American industrialists. The article also mentioned that von Gloeden was a favorite among the art collectors of the fin de siècle, and it discussed his photographic techniques, his homosexuality, his personal and romantic exploits, his artistic demise under Fascism, and the resurging interest in his work during the sexual revolution in the late 1960s and early 1970s.

Frankie had grown up on Lasante-DiCico stories. Meals were like dinner theater where family history played out, including varied interpretations and revivals. He knew that Leonardo and Salvatore had been childhood friends in Sicily and that Salvatore's son, Giacomo, had come to America as a boy to live with the Lasantes—like a brother to his Grandfather Vincenzo, but nothing had been said about the Baron Wilhelm von Gloeden or his photographs. That part of the Lasante-DiCico script had been cut, intentionally or not, and Frankie wondered if his imaginings about the great-grandfathers were more discovery than creation, as if the cartoline postale's sepia tranquility had sparked a cosmic memory within him of a time long before the dreamy-eyed Sicilian boy became his great-grandfather—bent, shriveled, and hallow-eyed. What memories stirred behind the old man's vacant expression? Frankie was barely nine years old when his great-grandfather passed away.

Though Frankie couldn't read the letters that had also been in the envelope with the pictures, it was comforting to think about what they might say. He returned most of the pictures to their envelope and locked them in the safe, but the cartoline postale and the letters he brought upstairs to his bedroom, and musing about what might have happened helped him to forget the more disturbing matters at hand —at least for the time being.

That evening, after finishing his college essay, he dozed in front of the television, but then woke to his cell phone ringing. It was Lenny calling to say that he'd be home late and not to worry. "Are you sure you're okay?" Frankie said, but despite Lenny's reassurance, Frankie couldn't help but worry that something had gone wrong with the drop.

He remembered Lenny leaving the house and feared he might never see him again. "Stupid!" he told himself. "He'll be home soon." Then he thought of Vi and wondered why she had left Lenny. "He's a good guy. Not bad looking," he told himself. "What the fuck made her so special?" Finally, Frankie lifted one of the cartolena postales from the nightstand next to his bed. The image was the one that most closely resembled Gennaro and, for a moment, he forgot about fearing for Lenny's safety and hating Vi.

That moment passed, and he again struggled to suppress one worry after another—again and again—like an emotional calliope, until he fell into a fitful sleep fractured by sepia images of long-ago Sicilian youth that morphed into images of Gennaro and him like the holograms at the Feast of the Assumption.

14

The train bumped and rocked—first above then below the ground—and each time Lenny looked up from his newspaper, he briefly made eye contact with two or three subway riders, as if they knew that the bulge in his black leather jacket was Big Vinny's blood money. It never crossed Lenny's mind that the fleeting glances from mostly women, but also a few men, might have been admiration. Clean-shaven and wearing a navy blue crewneck sweater under his black leather jacket, creased jeans, and polished loafers, Lenny might have been on his way to audition for a remake of *On The Waterfront*. He had the look of spruced up middle-aged prizefighter or dockworker—an archetype out of vintage photographs of Manhattan laborers from the first-half of the twentieth century. His brushed back black and silver hair that sprung back to curls as it dried enhanced the look and his appeal. The bulge in his jacket might have been a rolled up script that he would soon read from before some bigwig director.

Having read the same editorial numerous times and not recalling a word of it, Lenny folded his *New York Times*, contemplated the bulk of the envelope, and considered giving the cash to a man curled up behind a pushcart crammed with plastic bags and newspapers at the far corner of the subway car. Then there was the blind man with his seeing-eye dog, the young woman with three kids and another on the way, and the old couple who leaned into each other and exited the train so slowly that the subway doors almost closed on them. Any number of folks might have put the money to more honorable use than Big Vinny would have. Or maybe Lenny might get mugged and *9:00 pm, last stop Lefferts Blvd* would become moot. But at 42nd Street, Lenny left the train with the envelope's bulk still weighing on him.

He climbed the steps out of the subway and walked to 45th Street between Broadway and Eighth Avenue, where the names of Broadway plays were spelled out on a billboard in tiny rapidly changing red lights like a thespian speed-reading exercise. Hundreds of folks waited to purchase discount tickets, reminding Lenny of the wintry Sundays when Vincenzo and he stood for hours in a line that snaked around wooden horses, waiting to buy tickets for the Radio City Music Hall Christmas shows. Filomena and Lenny's younger siblings sat in an automat, sipping hot chocolate and reading or drawing until Lenny came to collect them. "Papa said to hurry. It's our turn to see the show," Lenny would say as if life on Earth depended upon everyone rushing to meet Vincenzo. Angie took charge of the younger sisters while Filomena carried Tony. In Filomena's bag were sandwiches and chunks of chocolate to eat during the show.

Matinees had already begun and an evening play would conflict with what Lenny had to do at 9:00 pm, which was just as well, as he didn't have the patience to wait in line or to sit in a theater. Instead, he shoved his hands into his pockets, edged his way through the crowds up Broadway, and walked east to Central Park.

It was sunny and cool—a perfect fall day for strolling, and the autumn colors were near peak. Two men, not much younger than Lenny, played with their daughter in one of the many Central Park playgrounds. She called to one of the men, slightly balding with a full beard. "Daddy! Watch me jump." Then she called to the other man, darker, resembling Lenny. "Poppy, catch me." The world was changing, except on 104th Street.

"Your daughter is beautiful," Lenny called out. And she was beautiful, with her beaded braids, café au lait complexion, and the light of a child adored glowing from her large almond shaped eyes.

"Thank you," the darker father responded—the one she had called Poppy. And for a brief moment Poppy and Lenny connected the way strangers sometimes do, and Lenny hoped that all would go well with their family, and then he remembered when Frankie was little and how Frankie and he often spent Sunday afternoons in Central Park. They entered the park at 59th Street and walked uptown, stopping every several blocks so Frankie could discover another playground and meet children of every imaginable background, some speaking very little English or no English at all, some with nannies and some with moms who were barely teenagers. A walk through Central Park was like traveling the world.

Lenny bought a hot dog from a street vendor not far from the larger than life bronze sculpture of Alice in Wonderland sitting atop a giant mushroom, and remembered Frankie chomping down on his first NYC hot dog. They were on the West Side, across from Central Park, in front of the Museum of Natural History, and they sat on the sun-warmed concrete steps below the Equestrian Statue of Teddy Roosevelt. Frankie went on and on about the dioramas they had just seen in the museum. Between chattering and munching on his hot dog, he paused and stared wide-eyed towards the woods across the avenue, as if expecting an Alaskan brown bear or African buffalo to break through Central Park's lush foliage. As usual, after a busy day in the city, Lenny carried Frankie back to the subway. How Lenny wished that it was Frankie's small torso pressing against his heart rather than Big Vinny's bribe-stuffed envelope.

It was still several hours before he had to meet Big Vinny's bagman at the Lefferts Blvd. Station, so Lenny walked back downtown to Saint John the Baptist, one of Filomena's favorite churches. She had several. This one was smaller than Most Precious Blood, and like with so many old buildings in Manhattan, New York City had grown up around it, dwarfing its 160-year-old façade — drab and spindly, but inside were vestiges of opulence. On either side of the slender nave, ornate chandeliers illuminated the 14 child-size statues representing the Stations of the Cross. Between Station 11, where Roman Soldiers hammered nails through the palms of a bleeding Christ, and Station 12, where the two Marys and Saint John wept at the feet of the crucified Christ, was a bust of Padre Pio, flanked by small iron and leaded glass coffers containing the padre's relics — a glove and sock, blood-stained from his stigmata.

Filomena had been especially devoted to Saint Padre Pio, who was also from her parents' hometown of Pietreclina. She spoke of smelling flowers when she prayed to the saint, meaning that her prayers were being heard. "Another Jean Nate miracle," was Lenny's usual response, but Frankie was in awe of his grandmother's devotion and ate up her stories of Padre Pio's visible signs of Christ's wounds that would bleed spontaneously.

Lenny lit candles before the Padre Pio shrine. "For you, Ma," he whispered. A choir circled a piano near the front of the church, practicing hymns in Latin. Their collective voices ascended the faded mauve colored walls and pink marble pillars to rows of pealing buttresses and circles of Plexiglas that had long replaced the damaged stained glass windows. Lenny examined the bust of Pio—the bushy eyebrows, scruffy beard, and mischievous expression made the padre more reminiscent of a naughty gnome than a pious saint. Lenny slipped his hand inside his jacket and glanced at the coffer containing Padre Pio's stained glove. What better place to leave Big Vinny's blood money than before the image of the Padre known for stigmata. He removed the envelope from his pocket and laid it before the bust of the saint. *If there is a God let him decide who's to have this money,* he thought, *but there isn't a God, so it's a foolish exercise.* Lenny slipped a hundred-dollar bill from the envelope, stuffed it into the slot below the bust, returned the envelope to his pocket, and left the church. He thought about surprising Angie, who lived fairly close, but instead walked to Penn Station to catch the Eighth Avenue subway back to Queens and to do Big Vinny's dirty work.

It was 8:47 pm when Lenny stepped from the train onto the empty platform of the Lefferts Blvd. Station and took a seat on the nearest bench. He pulled his collar up around his neck. It was colder than it had been when he left Manhattan. There was the sound of footsteps on the metal steps below the platform, and Lenny shivered and focused on his trembling hands. Someone sat next to him.

"Mr. Lasante?" Lenny didn't answer or look up. If it was a plainclothes detective, he wouldn't know by looking at him, and if it was Big Vinny's bagman, he didn't want to see him.

"Mr. Lasante?" It was a young unfamiliar male voice, someone who should go home, do his homework, and change his life while he still had the chance. Lenny reached into his jacket pocket, removed the envelope and placed it between them on the bench. There was the crinkle of paper, and then the sound of footsteps descending the metal

steps. In the distance a train approached the station, its single headlight dilated in the dark like an accusing eye, and the blurred letter A
above the light sharpened as the station trembled to the deafening
pitch of steel grating against steel.

Lenny struggled against the undertow of another panic attack. The
train screeched to a stop, and a wall of double doors swished open. A
woman stepped from the train. Lenny squinted into the blinding light
that framed her and thought she looked familiar, but the setting was
wrong—no ornate murals and chandeliers, gold leaf and a curving
staircase, a fountain with enormous gold fish, and a black sky framed
by silhouettes of Moroccan turrets, towers and arches and speckled
with thousands of stars. And she was younger than Lenny, which was
impossible. He was only a boy when they had first met. She danced
on the screen at the Valencia Movie Theater. Saraghina the beach
whore in *Fellini's 8 1/2* who seduced horny pubescent boys. But this
train-station Saraghina appeared more angelic than diabolic. The train
left the station, and, through graffitied windows, Leonardo, Lucia,
Vincenzo, and Filomena waved to Lenny.

"Are you alright?" Her voice was light and genial.

"Yes," Lenny mumbled.

"You're Hard Luck Lenny," she said.

Lenny nodded and examined her face more closely. *A customer*, he
thought. *Someone I haven't seen in a while.*

"You don't remember me." She pouted and sounded disappointed.
"I used to work at Panisi's Bakery. Margherita Cartoloni, but everyone
calls me Tootsie. I know your son—although I haven't seen him in
church for a while. You look like you can use a cup of coffee or maybe
something stronger."

Yes, the girl from the bakery, Lenny thought, *an infectious laugh and
big personality.*

"Coffee sounds good," Lenny said. "Guess I got a little woozy."

Tootsie helped him stand and took his arm, but immediately Lenny regretted that he accepted her invitation. He wanted to be home,
in his own bed, and asleep. The stilettos on her backless, open toed
shoes tapped down the iron steps and across the few feet of sidewalk
to the diner at the corner of Lefferts Boulevard and Liberty Avenue,

where a police officer sipping coffee from a steaming Styrofoam cup held the door open for them and smiled at Tootsie. Lenny worried that the officer had been Big Vinny's bagman and that somehow Tootsie was also involved—a backup, in case Lenny hadn't turned over the money.

The diner was crowded, bright, and noisy.

"Wherever you find a clean table," a waitress said to Tootsie. She balanced a tray piled high with plates of breakfast foods.

"Is this okay?" Tootsie said as she slid into the booth. Lenny sat on the bench seat across from her, still wishing he were home in bed.

"Are you feeling better?" she said.

"Yes. Thank you. I'm fine now." Tootsie's expression suggested that she wasn't convinced, so Lenny offered more of an explanation. "I had spent the day in the city, and I did a lot of walking. I must have dozed on the train ride home and missed my stop. I was going to walk home from Lefferts Boulevard, but I felt dizzy. Maybe something I ate in the city, but I'm fine now."

"I bet you got a touch of food poisoning. Did you feel like you were gonna throw up?" Tootsie said this as she pressed her fist up under her ample breasts, rubbing her stomach, which exaggerated the swell of her bosom above her low cut sweater and deepened her cleavage.

"I really feel much better now," Lenny said. And he did feel better and no longer suspicious. It might have been her breasts that persuaded him. She wasn't a stooge for Big Vinny, just a flirty Good Samaritan.

Lenny found Tootsie comical but seductive. He had long been impressed by full-figured women, from his boyhood days when Captain Beltrani sat outside his then-vacant cigar store a few doors down from Lasante's and showed the neighborhood boys photos of nude Rubenesque models stretched out on fancy davenports. Victorian looking photos—some on lacey fans. Lenny didn't know where Beltrani got them. Probably the same place the old man bought his white suits and captain's caps. His outfits were the reason folks called him Captain. Tootsie could have easily passed for one of the Captain's sirens.

"Well that's good. Food poisoning can be lousy."

"So you know my son from church?" Lenny said.

"Yeah, but I haven't seen him in a while."

"That's good. Not that you haven't seen him. Sorry, I didn't mean that. I just don't share his feelings about church. That was his grand-mother's doing."

"Well, I'm not exactly the Pope's sister," Tootsie said laughing. "But Frankie's a good boy. You did a good job. It ain't easy raising a kid by yourself."

"I had a lot of help."

"Yeah, but most guys wouldn't have done what you done. At least most straight guys. I remember when you and Vi got married, that's when I worked in Panisi's. She was crazy to leave. A lot of us girls thought that."

A blush crept up from Lenny's collar until he felt his ears turn warm.

Tootsie shrugged her shoulders and continued. "True, she was pretty and smart. Not too smart though. Right? She left you. But col-lege can do that. Sometimes I think too much education can make people stupid about the important things."

"Now you sound like Frankie," Lenny said.

"About Vi?"

"No, about college."

They ordered coffee and pie and talked about Frankie and college and even a little about Vi with the ease of old friends reminiscing. Lenny thought: *There's a pretty woman under the makeup,* and Tootsie displayed a candor among her more obvious attributes, which Lenny appreciated, especially that evening.

The waitress refilled their coffee cups and Tootsie spoke of her son, her mother, a cosmetology class she was interested in, even a little about her rotten luck with men, and then Lenny remembered that Frankie had told him about a woman he had met in church the mor-ning after Gennaro's accident and about her little boy with pink nail polish. Lenny realized that it was probably Tootsie, but Frankie had also mentioned that she was very pregnant. Tootsie was no longer pregnant, and with all that she said, she never mentioned a baby. Of course Lenny didn't ask. He didn't even mention that Frankie had told him about her.

The hour passed quickly, and Lenny offered to walk Tootsie home. After several blocks, Tootsie pointed to a two-family house with blue vinyl siding and first floor window grates decorated with white wrought iron balusters.

"This is where I live," she said.

"Do you know Doug Turner?" Lenny recognized the block from occasionally driving Doug home.

"Sure. Just to say hello. Seems like a nice guy. He a friend of yours?"

"Yes, he works in the garage across from my store."

"Well, birds of a feather. You know ... you're both nice guys.

Lenny smiled. "Your son must be sleeping," he said.

"He better be, but he ain't here. He's at his grandma's house."

"That's nice ... I mean that your mom helps out."

Tootsie fished through her purse for her keys, and Lenny ogled the jiggle of her breasts under the streetlight.

"Look, honey, as I said before, I ain't the Pope's sister, and I still think that Vi was nuts to leave you." Tootsie removed the key from her purse. "No strings, really, but you're welcome to come in if you'd like."

"Yes, I would like that," Lenny said.

15

On the Wednesday after Lenny handed over an envelope stuffed with cash to a stranger at the Lefferts Boulevard Station, Big Vinny and Scungilli were released on bail. One neighbor washing windows, another sweeping the sidewalk, and two others just leaning against a wrought-iron gate and talking about nothing in particular spotted Big Vinny's Lincoln. Scungilli was driving, and Big Vinny sat next to him. In the back seat were Marie, Lena, and Gennaro. The Lincoln turned into the DiCicos' driveway and, without a wave or smile, they got out of the car and disappeared into the house. At least that's how the general story went, though each version had its own enhancement. By evening everyone on 104th Street knew that Big Vinny was home and that something was very wrong.

After school Frankie went right to the DiCicos' house. He stayed for supper. Lenny had just closed the store and was in the kitchen reheating leftovers when Frankie came home.

"I assume you already ate," Lenny said, and spooned greens, browned with bread crumbs, sausage, and diced cherry peppers from a frying pan into a bowl.

Frankie nodded. Lenny brought his food to the table, sat, and poured himself a glass of wine.

"Aren't you even going to ask about Big Vinny?" Frankie said.

Lenny scooped up some greens with a chunk of Italian bread. "You'll tell me when you want to."

Frankie paced around the kitchen. He snatched a chair away from the kitchen table and sat down.

"Big Vinny's a mess."

"You won't get an argument from me." Lenny tore off another chunk of bread.

"Never mind," Frankie grumbled. He jumped up and pushed his chair back under the table.

Lenny ignored him, dunked the chunk of bread in his wine and popped it into his mouth. "Body and blood of Christ," Lenny said. He knew he was acting like an ass, but the last thing he wanted was to commiserate with Frankie about Big Vinny's problems. Big Vinny was the problem as far as Lenny was concerned.

Frankie stormed out of the kitchen, but within seconds he returned, took a half-gallon of milk from the refrigerator, opened it, and sniffed.

"It's fresh. I brought it in from the store last night," Lenny said, and finished his wine while Frankie drank milk from the opened container.

"Better not let Grandma catch you doing that." Lenny realized his error as soon as the words left his mouth. Frankie's eyes widened and filled with tears.

"Alright, Frankie. I'm ready to listen. No more wisecracks. Tell me what happened. All day, neighbors have been in and out of the store gossiping about what this one or that one saw. One said Marie was crying when she got out of the car. Another said that Big Vinny looked as if he had just returned from a funeral. So what's going on?"

Frankie chewed his lower lip, and his eyes darted from left to right. He joined his father at the table. "I guess Big Vinny didn't want to get out. I mean of course he did, but ... well I guess the judge released Big Vinny and Scungilli on bail, but not Michael and Jimmy. You know with them being accused of murdering that cabdriver."

Big Vinny would never make a deal that didn't include his sons, Lenny thought. *The con man was conned*. The backroom bribes had backfired and bought Big Vinny less than he had anticipated.

"I didn't even see Big Vinny. Lena brought his supper upstairs. All Mrs. DiCico did was cry. After she made supper, she went in the living room and sat in front of the television. She didn't eat anything. Even Gennaro was kind of quiet. Lena was the only one talking—mostly swearing. So it's all kind of a mess. But Lena said that the important thing is that her father can do more for her brothers now that he's out of jail."

It was hard for Lenny not to make a snide comment, but he had promised to listen. Frankie paused, stood up, shoved his hands deep into his jean pockets, and leaned against the sink. "You don't think that the DiCicos had anything to do with that cab driver being murdered, do you?" Frankie said.

Lenny's jaw clinched and his stomach knotted. Frankie knew better than to ask such questions, even in the privacy of their own kitchen. "We don't know anything about what happened, so I don't think anything about it and neither should you ... you don't know anything either, do you?"

Frankie took too long to answer, and Lenny felt his heart begin to race.

"Do you!" Lenny repeated, sounding more like a command than a question.

"No, I don't know anything," Frankie said.

"Then there's nothing to think about. We don't know what happened. And should anyone ask, that's our answer. If you are questioned by anyone, keep your answers short and simple. The day of the arrest, a detective asked Mr. Turner and me if we knew anything about a fight with a cabdriver."

"What did you say?"

"That I was working."

"But I told you what happened."

"Did you hear me say keep your answers simple? No hearsay. I didn't see anything. And if asked, you say only what you saw, which wasn't much. Now, since you went to see Gennaro right after school, I assume that you have homework to do."

Frankie nodded. "A little reading. Yes, some reading. If I can read. I mean if I can get my mind off of what's going on."

"You stewing over Big Vinny's problems won't change anything."

"But they're not just Big Vinny's problems. I mean ... I don't know what I mean, but it's got me all mixed up."

Lenny stood, approached Frankie, and put his arm around him. "One step at a time, Frankie. Worrying won't accomplish anything."

Lenny was amused by his own advice. His telling someone else not to worry was like a stone in water telling another stone not to sink. He tried to change the subject. "Maybe now Gennaro will go back to school."

Gennaro hadn't been to school since the arrest. His excuse was that, if someone made a wisecrack, he'd get in a fight and be thrown out anyway.

"No, he hasn't said anything. Maybe Big Vinny will make him go back now." Frankie kissed Lenny on the cheek. "Guess I'm kind of okay now. I'll go up and read."

Lenny remained leaning against the sink. His empty glass and bowl of unfinished greens sat on the table, and he listened to the floorboards creek above him. *At least Frankie is home safe*, he thought and wished that there was a way he could keep Frankie away from the DiCicos—away from their drama and their poison, but he knew it was impossible.

Better than blood, Big Vinny's father often told Lenny when he was a boy. *Your grandparents treated me like a son from the moment they came to pick me up at Ellis Island. And your father welcomed me like a brother.* The unsaid expectation was that Big Vinny and Lenny should also be better than blood, but they were too different. As a boy, Big Vinny was restless and short-tempered. School was like torture for him; he was often truant until he was old enough to drop out. Regardless, Lenny kept trying to be a brother, even after Big Vinny's father told him it wasn't worth it, even after Big Vinny's brother, Sal, was killed in Nam. After that, Lenny tried even harder.

Lenny was in school when the DiCicos received the news about Sal, but he'd heard the story so many times that it felt like a memory, beginning with the neighbor who had pushed her way through the line of customers and screamed: "Filomena, there's a soldier. He just rang Rosa's doorbell."

Filomena's eyes darted from the slicing machine to Vincenzo. "Go!" Vincenzo said. "I'm okay here."

Rosa DiCico's screams were heard up and down 104th Street. By the time Filomena reached the DiCicos' house—her apron splattered with blood from the roast beef she had been slicing—the car with

military plates was already pulling away from the curb. Rosa, surrounded by women from the block, had collapsed on a chair. Before
her on the kitchen table sat a lone colander of fresh string beans atop
a newspaper. The tips of the snapped string beans covered some letters
of words such as casualties and Cambodia and Laos.

Rosa wailed when she saw Filomena. "Filomena, they killed my
son. Those bastards killed my son. Mother of God, they killed my
son." Filomena pressed Rosa's head to her breast as the women swayed
and their cries rose from out of the open windows as if the house itself
were lamenting the tragic loss of the good son who had once played
stoopball on her front steps, sprayed stenciled Santas and snowmen on
her windowpanes, and dropped tiny celluloid paratroopers attached
to wispy plastic parachutes from her attic windows. The good son who
had never given anyone any trouble was dead.

Big Vinny and Lenny learned of Sal's death from Vincenzo who
sat waiting for them in the principal's office. As soon as Vincenzo
spoke of Sal's death the room reeked of Big Vinny's vomit, and there
was the sound of broken glass as Big Vinny punched his fist through
the principal's door and ran cursing from the school, leaving a trail of
blood from the gash in his forearm.

Vincenzo grabbed Lenny's hand to keep him from following Big
Vinny. The principal shook his head and sighed. His eyes met Vincenzo's. "Please extend my condolences to Mr. and Mrs. DiCico. Sal
was a good student and always a gentleman—always respectful and
considerate of others."

Vincenzo apologized for Big Vinny's behavior and offered to clean
up the vomit and to pay for the broken pane of glass. The principal
thanked him, but politely refused.

Then there was the trip to Tucci's the following spring, after Sal's
remains came home in a coffin, after the funeral, after Big Vinny's
first arrest. It was early spring, and Big Vinny loved the waterfall's
force. He was quieter and calmer than Lenny had ever seen him. He
said that he understood the water's anger. He mentioned his father and
how they barely spoke to each other, and that one night he heard his
parents talking through the bedroom wall. Giacomo said that he had
read in the newspaper that nine American boys and two American

girls were killed in Vietnam that day and that on the news they showed a Cambodian woman in rags carrying her dead daughter—the girls' arms looked like breadsticks. Rosa cried and said that at least that mother got to hold her child. After Big Vinny told Lenny all this he stared at the falls for the longest time and finally said: "So much for being the good son."

Things only got worse for Big Vinny—more problems with the police, arrests, and though he didn't have a job, he always had money. Eventually Lenny no longer sought common ground to keep the two of them connected. There was none. They had history but nothing else.

Lenny scraped the remaining greens into the garbage and rinsed his bowl and fork. He poured another glass of wine and sat at the table. *Big Vinny has always been full of shit,* Lenny thought. *Always turning reasons into excuses. Sure, his brother was killed in Vietnam. And my father died when I was a kid. Shit happens.* Lenny tore a small chunk of bread from the loaf and dunked it in his wine. "Better than blood," he said sarcastically and popped the wine-soaked bread into his mouth. He fretted over the thought of Frankie being questioned. *Whatever Frankie saw, dozens of others also saw,* he thought. But he didn't know that Frankie had seen Gennaro write the cabdriver's license plate number on his arm.

16

Gennaro surprised Frankie by suggesting that they drive to the Rockaways. Lately, anytime Frankie suggested that they do something other than stare at the television in the DiCico basement, Gennaro snapped or grunted. It was November and cool but sunny, and Frankie hoped that a walk on the beach might lift Gennaro's spirits.

He had stopped accusing Gennaro of having sent Lenny's email to Vi, which Gennaro denied anyway and told Frankie to grow up or fuck off whenever he mentioned it, although these words were Gennaro's response to most anything since Big Vinny got out of jail.

Elderly, sun-shriveled couples dressed for a blizzard strolled along the boardwalk, and an occasional cyclist rolled by, while kids with droopy jeans and gaudy bling shot hoops on a basketball court adjacent the boardwalk. Except for irritable seagulls scavenging bits of hotdog and pizza crust, the beach was deserted. No packs of teenagers poured from trains and buses to find their way to patchworks of towels and beach blankets where they would talk, text, watch YouTube, and occasionally swim. The off-season whispers of summer friendships and romances ebbed and flowed with the tide as the boys sat on the bottom step, which led down from the boardwalk to the sand and removed their sneakers and socks.

"Damn, I forgot the fucking Frisbee in the car," Gennaro grumbled.

"That's okay. I feel like jogging anyway," Frankie said, stuffing his socks into his sneakers and hiding them behind the steps under the boardwalk where lines of light streaked the dark sand. They raced to the shoreline and then slowed to a jog. Seagulls scattered. Their squawking was softened by the sound of the breaking surf. The sounds of the gulls, the surf, even of Gennaro's voice were distant-like memories.

"I'm glad we're here." Gennaro spoke between breaths. "I'm sick of watching my old man grow mold in front of the fucking television while he stares at stupid game shows and reality shows ... It's like he brought prison home with him ... All he needs is an orange jumpsuit and ankle cuffs shackling him to the fucking recliner."

Lately, Frankie felt the same way about Gennaro. His whining blended with the seagulls' squawking like some irritating but inconsequential noise. Frankie dismissed the noise and focused on the rhythmic breaths of the ocean lapping at the sand until the cool salty air turned hot, and the boardwalk and basketball courts gave way to rocky seaside cliffs of Taormina, Sicily—the setting of the cartoline postale that Frankie had googled obsessively, reading everything he could about Taormina, including Mt. Etna, the bay of Naxos, and Taormina's Greek-Roman theater, which had been the backdrop for many of von Gloeden's photographs. And when Frankie became overwhelmed by worry, he withdrew to the hot Sicilian coastline, as if Taormina and its bordering cliffs and beaches existed within him rather than an ocean away, like an oasis at the center of his being.

In bursts, Gennaro muttered despairingly about Big Vinny, but his complaints were no more than ambient noise. Maybe half an hour had passed when they slowed their pace, and high on endorphins and salty air, Frankie waded in the Ionian Sea with its picturesque bays, rocky coves, and pebbled beaches. He paused and looked at Gennaro who stood several yards away from him, ankle deep in surf, with his jacket tied around his waist and baggy jeans rolled up to below his knees. No wreath in his hair or blossom dangling from his lips, but his beauty rivaled Ganymede's, and had von Gloeden been there with his camera, Gennaro would have been his star subject.

"I hate him," Gennaro said.

Von Gloeden? Frankie thought, but then remembered they were at the Rockaways, wading in the Atlantic, not the Ionian Sea. Gennaro tilted his head and gave Frankie an odd look, but Frankie dared not mention what he had been thinking. Gennaro had no patience for his musings about their great-grandfathers and Taormina. The last time that Frankie mentioned the cartoline postale and that their great-grandfathers might have been more than friends, Gennaro exploded.

"Here we go again. Who the fuck cares if our great-grandfathers posed for those pictures? It looks like half the teenage boys in Taormina posed in the buff. Were they all in love with each other? They were dirt poor. They probably would have sucked that German pansy's cock for a plate of spaghetti."

"But why did those pictures appear now? And right after we were … well you know," Frankie argued.

And Gennaro snapped. "They didn't just appear. We were looking in the fucking safe. They didn't just jump out at us. They were on the floor with wills. Does that mean we're dead. And deeds. Does that make me a house? Everything has to have some big meaning to you. I liked it better when you went to church. At least you got this crap out of your system, praying and lighting candles and babbling novenas like an old lady. You should go back to church with that other nut job, Tootsie. She probably thinks she's fucking Mary Magdalene. You two make a good pair."

Gennaro's tirade ended with him slamming his foot down on the brakes and telling Frankie to get the fuck out of the car. Fortunately they were only about a half-mile from 104th Street. Given that the Rockaways were a lot further, Frankie didn't want to risk another argument, so he simply walked towards Gennaro and draped his arm around his shoulder.

Despite the cool air, they were hot and sweaty from running. Gennaro kissed Frankie full on the mouth and took Frankie's hand and casually turned around to walk back as if kissing and walking hand-in-hand in public was the way they always behaved. Since the night of the arrest, Gennaro had softened to the idea that Frankie and he were lovers. He no longer shut down after sex, and he was much more affectionate afterwards. In fact, it was when they were alone in the basement, making love or just embracing that Gennaro was not irritable, but a kiss and holding hands in public shocked Frankie. However, Frankie played along. As usual, the DiCicos called the shots.

"I've been doing a lot of thinking since my old man came home," Gennaro said. "I don't know how to explain this, but I'm feeling like I've got to do something, like I can't sit around and watch my old man turn into … I don't even know how to say it. I just know if I don't do something

I might explode. I'm not like Lena. She's so damn sure—like my old man and brothers are being framed, and they're going to get out of this. Like they're some kind of dago folk heroes. I'm not so sure. There are things I can't say. Things I've known, but didn't know. It's like I can't pretend anymore. Remember that fairy tale your father used to read to us when we were kids? You know, the one about the emperor not having any clothes. It's like I've always known stuff about my old man and brothers, but I didn't admit that I knew it. I'm probably not making sense."

Gennaro's rambling reminded Frankie of the many times that Lenny spoke in circles when talking about Big Vinny. As far back as Frankie could remember, Lenny had spun cryptic warnings about the DiCicos, as if he were simultaneously warning Frankie not to get too involved, while trying to protect him from knowing why. Until now, Gennaro had been either tight lipped or he outright denied rumors about his family as gossip and nonsense. Gennaro's attempt at honesty made Frankie think of his own silence about having seen him write on his arm what Frankie thought was the cabdriver's license plate number.

"I'm dropping out of school," Gennaro said.

This didn't surprise Frankie. Gennaro hadn't gone back to school since the arrests. He should have graduated two years earlier, but, like all the DiCicos, except for Lena, Gennaro had a long history of spending more time in the principal's office than the classroom. Big Vinny and his sons just couldn't sit in a classroom long enough to listen to someone else. It was as if they were constantly distracted. Lena was as tough as her father and brothers, much more than Gennaro, but she already had the patience and cunning that it took Big Vinny years to acquire.

"I'll turn 20 in a few weeks," Gennaro said. "I never thought about my future. It was like things would just work out."

"And things will work out better without a high school diploma?" Frankie said, sounding very much like Lenny.

"School's your road, Francesco, not mine. I'm gonna enlist. Maybe the Marines, if they'll take."

Frankie thought, *Without a high school diploma?* But he didn't mention this to Gennaro. They paused, leaning into each other to watch the sunset. A white orb slipped from the ashen sky into the slate-colored ocean while the incoming tide erased their footsteps.

"I warned you not to expect too much from me," Gennaro said. "I love you, Francesco, but I'll never be who you want me to be. I'm not gay."

"You could have fooled me." Frankie was sick of this tired silly argument.

"You know what I mean. I'm not like those kids in school with their rainbow pins and their protests. I don't even know what GLBTQI ... LMNOP stand for, and I don't give a shit."

"You're willing to blow yourself up in some desert to prove you're not gay?" Frankie flexed his biceps. "Mr. Tough DiCico."

"You got it all wrong," Gennaro said. "The last thing I want is to prove I'm a DiCico." Gennaro spit as if he were trying to expel something sour. He shrugged his shoulders and sighed. "Anyway, you're the first to know."

They resumed walking. The sand felt cooler.

"When are you going to tell your parents?" Frankie thought the whole conversation was ridiculous, given that Gennaro didn't have a diploma or a GED and wouldn't be accepted, especially not in the marines, but he knew that if he mentioned this Gennaro would tell him that he didn't know what the fuck he was talking about, and Frankie might lose his ride home.

"I figure, at some point my mother will get tired of asking me about school. My old man's too busy doing nothing to notice. As far as enlisting, I'll tell them when I tell them—after I enlist. So you need to keep this all quiet."

They reached the section of boardwalk where they had left their sneakers and socks. They were damp, but they put them on anyway. Maybe it was because Frankie was tired of secrets and of DiCico drama, or maybe he was sick of Gennaro always having all the power, but he finally sucked in his breath and said: "Did you give your brothers the cabdriver's license plate number?"

They were alone on the boardwalk. It was dark and the silhouette that was Gennaro seemed to swell. Frankie expected the usual DiCico rage like the night of the Feast of the Assumption when Big Vinny took a swing at Lenny, but Gennaro just took Frankie's hand.

"It's getting late, Francesco. Let's walk back to the car," was all Gennaro said.

They drove home in silence, and when Gennaro parked in front of Frankie's house, Frankie told him that he would keep his secret. Gennaro stared ahead as if he were seeing something that Frankie couldn't. "Which one?" Gennaro asked. But before Frankie had a chance to answer, Gennaro leaned over, kissed Frankie on the cheek, and pressed his finger against Frankie's lips. "Goodnight Francesco," he said, and Frankie got out of the car.

                17

Frankie hadn't been to Mass since Filomena's funeral, but musing about the cartoline postale and long-ago Taormina ceased to be enough of a distraction to stop him from worrying about Gennaro's potential involvement in the cabdriver's murder. He returned to church.

As Father de la Roza lifted the chalice and said: "... This is the cup of my blood, the blood of the new and everlasting covenant," Frankie also heard: "Psst, Frankie ... Pssst."

An old woman kneeling in the row before Frankie turned around —her head barely cleared the top of the pew—and pressed an arthritic finger to her puckered lips. "Shhhh!"

Frankie followed her glare and spotted Tootsie a few rows behind him, waving as if she were fighting off killer bees.

"Wait for me," she mouthed, pointing to the doors.

Given what Gennaro and Frankie had been up to, Frankie stayed put during communion. Tootsie on the other hand, floated up to the altar as if she were Mother Teresa.

After Mass, they met at one of the marble holy water founts adjacent the main entrance to the church. Tootsie dipped her fingertips in the water and made an abbreviated sign of the cross and a half-hearted attempt to genuflect. Frankie laughed and was struck by how much he had missed her.

"So does Tyrone have a sister or brother?" Frankie said.

Tootsie flashed a broad smile and embraced him. "How are you, honey? It's been forever. I figured the devil had got you in his clutches."

If by devil you mean Gennaro, Frankie thought, but again he just laughed. The old woman with the arthritic fingers inched past them and glared at Tootsie, reminding Frankie of the nun cleaning the altar

when he first met Tootsie and Tyrone. As usual, Tootsie seemed oblivi-
ous to critical attention. She opened the heavy church door for the old
woman and, as the woman left, she kept eyeing Tootsie as if she expected her to push her down the church steps. Finally her pinched
frown turned into a smile and Tootsie said: "Now you have a nice day,
honey."

Frankie couldn't tell if Tootsie was being sarcastic, but she sounded sincere. Again, he asked her if Tyrone had a baby sister or brother.

"It was a little girl, but never mind that," Tootsie said. "I want to
hear all about you. How about breakfast? Tyrone's in school and I don't
have to be in work until 11:00. Imagine ... I'm working in a bakery
again. And my doctor wants me to lose weight. Of course, he's fatter
than me, and he smokes like a chimney, but that don't count 'cause
he's a doctor."

Nut job or not—Gennaro's opinion of Tootsie, she was fun to be
with, and since Big Vinny's arrest, Gennaro had been anything but fun.
Frankie's first class would begin in 15 minutes, but given that he was
a senior, and he had never cut a class in his life—something Gennaro
constantly ribbed him about, he figured he was long overdue for cutting at least one class before graduation, and he needed to smile.

"Sure! Breakfast sounds great," Frankie said.

It was a cold morning so they walked quickly, postponing conversation until they sat across from each other in a booth with red vinyl
seats on either side of a white Formica table that smelled of bleach. A
waitress stood over them pressing the stub of a pencil against a pad.
Her swollen ankles tested the elastic in her shoes. "Do you two need
a menu or do you know what you want?"

Tootsie took a few moments to catch her breath. "I'm fine ... Do
you know what you want, honey?"

Frankie nodded, and Tootsie looked back at the waitress.

"I'll have a frittata ... Make sure the potatoes are well done ... And
Italian toast with just a thimble full of butter ... and coffee." Tootsie
fingered the packets of sugar in a small white bowl. "I think you're
out of artificial sweeteners, honey. Can you bring me some?"

Frankie waited for the waitress to finish writing. "I'll just have a
large glass of orange juice, thank you."

"No wonder you're so skinny. Don't Lenny feed you none? You gotta eat something or I'll feel like a pig eating in front of you."

Tootsie reached for the waitress who had just turned to leave. "Bring me another plate, honey. He'll eat some of my eggs."

"So how's Gennaro?" Tootsie asked.

Frankie remained silent for a few moments, and then finally shrugged his shoulders. "He's okay."

"Any scars? Ya know, from the explosion."

"No, he was lucky. Just little ones under his arms and on his chest." Frankie felt the heat rise in his neck and wondered if Tootsie had ulterior motives for asking this question—as if she had surmised why he would be familiar with Gennaro's scars. He jumped to the sound of silverware hitting the floor behind him.

"Well he's lucky, but those DiCicos have a way of falling in shit and coming up smelling like roses. Although maybe their luck is running a little thin after all. I heard about the arrests—saw it on television. Big Vinny got out on bail, but last I heard his sons are still in jail. Murder charges. We'll see how they get out of this mess."

The waitress brought their drinks and Tootsie emptied three packets of sweetener and two packets of artificial creamer into her coffee while Frankie sipped his orange juice and thought of ways to change the subject. "How's Tyrone?"

"Still don't talk much," she said. "But he gets speech therapy in school, not that he don't know how to talk. He just don't want to. I don't think they know what to do with him, so they give him speech therapy. I don't blame them. I don't know what to do with him either. I figure, when he wants to talk he will. Kind of like that book I read in high school by that black poet. You know the one about a bird singing in a cage. Maya Angelou, that was her name. Remember she wrote a poem when Clinton was inaugurated? Oh, you don't remember that. You were a little kid. Anyway, she had stopped talking for a long time when she was a little girl, after she was raped. When she was ready, she started talking again. Sometimes folks just do things in their own time."

Frankie recalled Angelou's book *I Know Why the Caged Bird Sings* and her poem *Morning*. Lenny recited it along with other poems when Frankie was in elementary school. But Frankie wondered what

Angelou's book and the reason she didn't speak for awhile had to do with Tyrone.

"They're saying that he has Asperger's," Tootsie said chuckling. "Leave it to teachers and psychologists to come up with a name like that."

Tootsie explained that Tyrone was given a slew of tests and that she had to attend too many school meetings where everyone talked to her like she was an idiot. "Whatever," she said. "They wrote down Asperger's, and he's in what they call an inclusion classroom with a teacher and two aides. One of the aides is this pretty little thing, and Tyrone loves to brush her hair. If nothing else, he's learning to be a beautician. That's more than I ever got out of school."

Despite the name, Frankie was more comfortable with the Asperger's diagnosis than the Angelou comparison. "Sooo, you said Tyrone has a little sister," Frankie said.

"No, Honey. I said the baby was a girl."

Frankie sat back and looked as if his orange juice went down the wrong pipe, and Tootsie finally sighed and said, "Okay, honey, guess you're not gonna let up, so here goes ... I don't even know why I'm telling you this, but it's like for some reason I trust you. In fact, it was seeing you hold Tyrone in church that time when we first met that helped me make up my mind. Ya know like sometimes you're just supposed to meet someone. I've been telling people that the baby is living with my cousin in Jersey, but that's only half true. She lives in Jersey, but with her parents."

"You mean with her father?"

"Hell no. Not that jackass. I mean with her parents. She was adopted."

"Frittata, Italian toast, and an extra plate." The waitress just about dropped the plates on the table, but Frankie welcomed the distraction, as it gave him time to absorb what Tootsie had said.

"It feels good to tell someone aside from my mother, who just cries and says her rosary. Anyway, she's a lucky little girl. I got to meet her daddies, and ..."

"Daddies?" Frankie interrupted.

"Yeah these gay guys adopted her."

Now Frankie's orange juice really did go down the wrong pipe.

"Careful, honey. You okay?"

He nodded.

"Well like I was saying, when I saw you holding Tyrone in church, I made up my mind. Like it was a sign. Like some kind of fate. You know what I mean?"

Tootsie scraped some of her frittata onto the extra plate while Frankie sat there slack-jawed and stuck on, *These gay guys adopted her*, not to mention that he had also thought of him holding Tyrone as a sign. He knew exactly what Tootsie meant about their meeting being fate. Gennaro was right when he said that Tootsie and Frankie made a good pair.

"Honey, you can close your mouth. It's not like I gave her to Martians. I knew that the baby's father wasn't going to hang around. And I didn't want her to be around any other jerks that I might hookup with. I'm a magnet for bad boys ... except maybe for recently, but we'll see how that turns out. Anyways, mostly bad boys. Tyrone's father was the worst. He tried to come back once, but I threw his ass out of the house after he near killed Tyrone. He said that Tyrone was nothing but a little faggot and he was gonna beat the sissy out of him. Can you imagine? I swear that it was because of that beating that Tyrone stopped talking. Never mind Asperger's. Tyrone's father was the biggest ass burger going. And Sarah's father ain't much better. Those gay guys named her Sarah. Isn't that pretty? It's kind of biblical. Leave it to gays to come up with a pretty name. I think one of them is Jewish, but I don't know. Maybe Arab. He's cute whatever he is. They both are."

Tootsie barely took a breath between chewing and swallowing and talking. "Ain't you going to eat them eggs, honey? They'll get cold. Nothing worse than cold eggs."

Frankie stared at his plate. He had just learned that Tyrone's father beat him for being a faggot and gay men had adopted Tootsie's baby. *And by the way,* he thought, *I'm in love with Gennaro, and I think our great-grandfathers were also lovers. I can show you their nude photos.* It seemed like the thing to say, but Frankie couldn't bring himself to do it. *Oh, and my father made a drop for Big Vinny, and Gennaro may have been involved with the cabdriver's murder.* Instead of saying anything, he just looked back at Tootsie and held his chin in the palm of his hand to keep his head from spinning off his shoulders.

"Well, as I was saying, I haven't seen Sarah's father since I told him I was pregnant. He's probably in jail. When I watched you holding Tyrone in church, I thought this baby is gonna grow up around decent men. And as I said the chance of me hooking up with a decent man ain't too good. Then I went to this adoption agency and saw this photo album from these two guys looking to become daddies. They wrote a beautiful letter. It made me cry. So I thought I could finally do something good. She'll have two daddies to love her. I told them she was meant to be their baby. The Lord just had her come into this world through my body. But she was meant for them. After all, neither one of them has a uterus and all. Believe me, I wish I could give them mine for all the trouble it gets me into. Nice guys. But you know what they say. All the good ones are either married or gay. Well I don't know about the married part."

"You're okay with gay men adopting her?"

"Honey, please." Tootsie dabbed a spot of egg at the corner of her mouth with a napkin and wiped crumbs from off the top of her sweater. "Look at me dining on the upper terrace as usual." Tootsie chuckled. "Now what did you ask me? Oh, yeah—about gay daddies. I've known enough straight men that should have had their nuts cut off, starting with my own father. Them being gay is a plus as far as I'm concerned. Are you gonna eat those eggs or not?"

Frankie had enough trouble swallowing Tootsie's story, never mind the eggs, but Tootsie devoured her breakfast as if she hadn't eaten in days.

"By the way, speaking of the few decent straight guys, I ran into your father awhile ago. Now there's a nice guy, and he's still awfully cute. Did he say anything about me? I told him that I used to see you in church."

"My father?"

"More coffee?" The waitress stood over Tootsie with a full Silex coffee pot.

"Sure, honey, just a mouth full. Yeah. I ran into Lenny getting off the train on Lefferts Blvd."

Lefferts Blvd? Frankie thought. *That's four stops past ours. What was he doing there, and when did he have the time to take a train?* Frankie remembered Big Vinny's envelope and Lenny's trip to Manhattan. He also recalled his email to Violetta, and though Tootsie's lips continued to move, he couldn't make out her words. He felt nauseated and their plates, the counter, the stools, the waitresses refilling Tootsie's coffee cup all went fuzzy. He brought the cool glass of orange juice to his forehead and held it there until he understood Tootsie saying. "Are you okay, honey?"

Next he heard himself say: "Yes, I'm fine ... just got a little dizzy for a minute."

"That's funny, so was Lenny when I got off the train—dizzy I mean. Maybe it's some kind of family thing, like you both got low blood sugar or something. Eat your eggs, it will help. So, Lenny didn't mention that he saw me?"

"No, I don't think so." Frankie took a sip of the orange juice and looked over his glass at a woman buckling a squirming baby into a high chair at the table behind Tootsie. When his vision cleared, he looked back at Tootsie and told her that his father had gone into the city that day, but that he was asleep when Lenny came home. "I never asked him about what he did," Frankie said.

"Oh, sure, I understand." But Tootsie seemed disappointed that Lenny hadn't mentioned her. "Anyways," she said, "we just said hi and he got back on the train. He must have missed his stop. You know maybe he fell asleep or something."

It was the "or something" that concerned Frankie, but he didn't mention anything to Tootsie about Big Vinny's envelope.

Later that day, when Frankie came home from school, he also didn't mention to Lenny that he had skipped his first two classes, but he did mention that he saw Tootsie at church and that she said that she had run into him at the Lefferts Blvd. Station.

Lenny tapped a roll of quarters on the edge of the counter and dropped the freed coins into the register draw. "That was the day I went into the city. On the way home, I fell asleep and missed my stop."

"That's what she said."

Lenny nodded and closed the draw. He walked out from behind

the counter, removed a razor from his pocket, and sliced open the top of a case of olive oil. He glanced up and met Frankie's stare. "Any homework?" he said.

Frankie nodded, grabbed a package of cupcakes and a quart of milk. "By the way, Dad, you never mentioned what you did that night."

"What night?"

"The night you went to Manhattan."

Lenny pressed the razor into the top of another case of olive oil. "A lot of walking. Dinner. A late movie. Nothing special." He positioned the last few gallon cans atop the pyramid display. "You have homework, yes?"

"It's just that I thought ..."

"And I thought you had homework to do. If not there are cases of coffee in the warehouse that need to be shelved."

It was clear to Frankie that Lenny was done talking about whatever happened that night. He wasn't going to tell Frankie about the envelope or what he did with it, so Frankie finally left him to his olive oil.

As he walked through the office, Frankie glanced at the safe and wondered if he should have been more open with Tootsie. After learning about the baby's daddies, he knew she would be fine with him being gay. In fact, she probably had surmised as much, but there was her opinion of Gennaro to consider. *He's bad news*, he imagined her saying. *Go find yourself a nice gay boy. Maybe Sarah's daddies know someone they could introduce you to.* Frankie shrugged his shoulders, walked through the dining room, into the kitchen, ate the cupcakes, downed the quart of milk in several gulps, tossed the empty milk container and cupcake wrapper in the trash, and headed up to his room. *But Tootsie wouldn't lecture me about Gennaro*, he thought, *considering all the jerks she said she hooked up with? I guess being attracted to bad boys was something else we have in common.*

Once in his bedroom and sitting at his desk, he wondered what it had been like when his dad and Uncle Tony shared this room, and before that, his Grandpa Vincenzo, and Gennaro's Grandfather? He imagined the grandfathers as teenagers discussing adolescent angsts and hopes, and Gennaro's Grandfather Giacomo talking about Sicily, poverty, and Fascism. And Frankie's Great-Grandma Lucia overhearing their conversation and telling them to leave all those bad memories in the Old Country where they belonged and to wash up for supper. *But not all that took place in the Old Country was bad,* Frankie thought. *Like before my Great-Grandparents had come to America, before they had married, when Great-Grandpa Leonardo and Gennaro's Great-Grandfather Salvatore were friends, maybe more than friends. Maybe those were good moments, even if they were never spoken of.*

Frankie opened his social studies book and read about Mussolini and Hitler and World War II, but his thoughts drifted to stories he had heard about Giacomo DiCico returning to Europe as an American soldier and welcoming the opportunity to destroy Fascism once and for all. And stories of Gennaro's Uncle Sal, the war hero killed in Vietnam, Big Vinny's older brother. *The good one.* Frankie had never met either man, but they were a part of Lasante-DiCico lore. He had learned about them the way he had learned about so many others, through stories shared at the kitchen or dining room table, extended with three leaves, or at the plywood table, under Leonardo's grape arbor. *But some stories weren't shared at tables—in kitchens or dining rooms or outside under arbors,* Frankie thought. Some stories may have remained underground like the roots of Leonardo's grape vine.

18

Angels and saints wearing snowy caps and epaulettes watched silently as Lenny and Frankie stepped from the just-plowed and salted road onto graves blanketed in feathery white. If the dead could exhale they would have sent each snowflake whirling and twirling like dandelion seeds on a breezy day. Lenny positioned an evergreen wreath before the Lasante gravestone and pressed down on its wire prongs until they pierced the frost. A red plastic ribbon across the middle of the wreath read: "Christmas in Heaven." This was their first Christmas without Filomena, and they'd miss the aroma of Christmas cookies baking and of pizza di scarola, a mixture of escarole, olives, capers, anchovies, pignoli, walnuts, raisins, and a touch of chocolate shavings baked between two layers of pizza dough. Lenny called the meld of bitters, sweets, and salts food for the gods, and he told himself: *Maybe that's who she'll be baking it for this Christmas Eve.*

Christmas had long been difficult for Lenny—the time when childhood friends returned to the old neighborhood to visit their parents on 104th Street and made the perfunctory Lasante stop and spouted their tired accolades: *You were the best of us, Lenny ... If only your father hadn't died ... If only you didn't have to drop out of high school ... Hard Luck ... Lenny.* Christmas had long been the season of *if-only.*

"Buon Natale," he whispered after securing the Christmas wreath. Frankie blew snow from the statue of Mary holding the baby Jesus atop the Lasante gravestone where chiseled letters formed the names Leonardo, Lucia, Vincenzo, Filomena under the surname Lasante, and numbers told the dates of their births and deaths, but said nothing of all that had happened in between those dates. Two fingers on Mary's right hand, which had once pointed to heaven, were missing.

"I should have it fixed, but I kind of like her the way she is," Lenny said. "As if she's holding up the Black Panther's Fist of Glory."

Frankie didn't respond to Lenny's hackneyed comment about Mary's hand. He said the same thing every time he and Frankie went to the cemetery.

Frankie nodded towards the DiCico family grave boasting a wreath at least four times the size of the one they just brought. "Big Vinny must have been here," Frankie said.

"I guess he wants to make sure that his parents can see it from heaven."

"I thought you don't believe in heaven."

"It was a joke, Frankie."

"Why do you come here?"

"I don't know. Tradition, maybe."

"But I just heard you wish someone a Merry Christmas. Who were you talking to?"

"I don't know that I was talking to anyone. At least not the way I'm talking to you."

"Maybe it was like a prayer?" Frankie said.

"Are we having some kind of epiphany here, Frankie?"

Frankie shrugged, turned and walked away, but before he reached the car, Lenny pelted him with snowballs and Frankie quickly reciprocated. Snowballs flew as father and son bobbed up and down behind tombstones like graveyard Whac-A-Moles. Frankie yelled: "Truce! You win ... you win! Grandma would have been mad at us for disrespecting the dead."

"My guess is a lot of these folks had some pretty good snowball fights in their day," Lenny said.

For most of the ride home their banter was light and playful, until Frankie began texting Gennaro, and the gray day turned grayer. Lenny reflected upon how the drive from the store to the cemetery, like stocking shelves or bagging groceries, just about summed up his life. Once home, the sound of steam banging in the radiators and the warmth that followed felt more stifling than comforting.

Lenny hung his jacket in the entry closet next to the carved mahogany pipe stand—a mother bear surrounded by her cubs, lifting her paws above her head and balancing the tray of hand-carved pipes. Several hinges formed a crease at the nape her neck, where her head tipped back to expose a humidor. No Lasante had ever smoked a pipe, but the bear and her cubs guarded the front door for as long as Lenny could remember. Frankie tossed his jacket on the rolled arm of the Queen Anne couch.

"I don't think so," Lenny said and handed Frankie a hanger for his jacket.

Their house was furnished with heavily lacquered, mostly European, ornate antiques. This wasn't intentional, but beginning with Leonardo and Lucia, furniture was a Lasante afterthought purchased in secondhand stores or from relatives and friends who wanted to Americanize and modernize their homes. Filomena had considered refurnishing the living room or dining room or maybe the master bedroom after Angie was born and Leonardo and Lucia moved into a small apartment around the corner, but Vincenzo was adamant that every penny be saved for the children's education. Three children later, making five, Vincenzo was even more frugal, and after his early death, leaving Filomena with the business to run and, except for Lenny, children to care for, redecorating was the furthest thing from her mind.

The elaborately carved wooden pieces were sinuous and dark, inlaid with contrasting types of wood or hand-painted scenes, while table lamps were replete with naked cherubs and floor lamps were just as elaborate. Glazed jardinières on matching stands occupied corners in the living room and dining room. Museum-like scenes or portraits with gilded frames hung from the walls, and bisque and porcelain figurines posed on the credenza, corner shelves, and end tables. A breakfront and a corner curio held crystal glasses and Havilland china with fine spidery veins just below the yellowed glaze. The furniture upholstery was intact due to Lucia then Filomena's seasonal slipcover use. You would never think that so many children grew up in this house, but they had the yard and sidewalk and street for playing—when they weren't working in the store. All in all, the Lasante furnishings were a collector's paradise, but to Lenny it was a lot of oppressive old junk, and had he the energy or interest in buying new furniture, he would have called Goodwill to cart it all away.

"How about a cup of hot chocolate?" he asked.

They worked in tandem. Lenny placed a kettle of cold water on the stove, Frankie removed two mugs from the cupboard; Lenny took two packets of hot chocolate from a box in the pantry and handed them to Frankie, Frankie emptied the contents of each packet into the mugs; Lenny poured the hot water, and Frankie handed him a teaspoon. Since Filomena passed, most meals and chores around the house were handled like this. Lenny paid a neighbor to clean the house, and Angie helped out on most weekends, but Frankie and Lenny carried out the day-to-day household chores like an Olympic tag team.

They sat at the enamel-top kitchen table and blew steam off the mugs of hot chocolate.

"I've been thinking a lot lately," Lenny said.

"More than usual? Is that possible?" Frankie responded.

"Funny. Seriously ... I've been thinking about you taking the final semester off from high school. You already have enough credits to graduate. Give yourself a break before college begins."

Frankie sipped his hot chocolate.

"Why not travel?" Lenny asked.

Frankie glanced at the clock above the window over the sink, a plastic chef with a chef's hat, apron, and handlebar mustache. The clock's face sat on the chef's large belly. Lenny asked Frankie if he was listening to him.

"Yes, I'm listening. You want me to travel," Frankie said.

"I didn't say that I want you to travel. I was just thinking the next few months offer you an opportunity to do something that you won't be able to do once you start college."

"Nope. Finishing high school feels like the right thing to do," Frankie said between sips.

"You've already finished high school." Lenny struggled to remain calm. "It's not just traveling I've been thinking about. I was thinking that this might be the perfect time to ... well, to get to know your mother."

Frankie choked and spit hot chocolate across the table into Lenny's cup and onto his white shirt. Lenny jumped back and reached for the roll of paper towels next to the sink. "We've talked about this before. I just thought that ..."

"No," Frankie said, interrupting. "What you've always said is that meeting Violetta would be my decision. When—more like if—I want to meet her, you would help me. That's what you said. The last thing I need right now is another parent." Frankie downed the rest of his hot chocolate. "I told Gennaro that I'd stop by after we got home from the cemetery."

"I know where she is," Lenny said, hoping to shock Frankie into listening.

"No shit! So do I. You're not the only one who knows how to use the Internet. If I wanted to contact her, I could have done it years ago. She's a professor at UCLA, but I don't want to contact her. I don't want to travel. What I want is for everything to stay the same."

If Lenny were drinking, it would have been his turn to choke. Not that he was surprised by what Frankie said, but hearing the words spoken aloud made his fears as real as Vincenzo once grabbing his chest and falling to the sawdust-covered wood-planked floor. The words *stay the same!* along with the sound of Vincenzo's death rattle echoed within Lenny's skull.

"Go ... go see Gennaro." Lenny's voice was small, as if he were defeated.

Frankie placed his empty cup in the sink and kissed Lenny on the cheek. "I'm sorry, but I like it here, and you're the only parent that I want. I don't owe Violetta anything and neither do you."

"You don't owe the DiCicos anything either," Lenny said.

Frankie paused at the kitchen door to the yard. "At least they've been here, which is more than I can say for Violetta." The tone of his voice was more matter of fact than accusatory, and Lenny didn't have a comeback. How could he? Frankie was right. For better or worse, the DiCicos were always there for Frankie.

After the kitchen door closed, Lenny heard Filomena's whisper. *He loves you. Is that so bad?*

"You know it's not that," Lenny said.

He's a good boy. No drugs, no alcohol, does well in school, and he even goes to church.

"Church! Don't remind me."

Okay, I won't remind you. Maybe he knows something that his smart father never figured out.

Filomena's voice became clearer, and Lenny caught fleeting glimpses of her sitting across from him at the kitchen table. First hints of her white hair, next the small gold hoops that clung to her earlobes, finally her warm brown eyes beneath the sparkle of her glasses.

"You know, every day Angie looks more and more like you."

Lenny left Filomena sitting at the table and walked through the dining room, opened the French door to the dark office, ignored the disapproving glares from the portraits and daguerreotypes crowding the walls, sat at the desk, turned on his computer, clicked the email icon, and scanned the short list of incoming emails until his eyes locked on the name of Dr. Violetta Vitkus. The already cramped room turned claustrophobic as if every photograph were leaning over his shoulder to view what he was staring at in shock. He clicked the email and read the text:

> Dear Lenny,
> What a wonderful surprise. Sorry I didn't respond sooner, but—well, I guess I have a lot to be sorry about. Entering Frankie's life (btw, I like his name) at this point might be too little too late, but if you really think I can help, I'm more than willing. It's the least I can do. I'll be in New York for Christmas. We can connect then. Think about it.
> Vi

Think about it! As if Lenny hadn't been thinking of and hoping for this moment everyday for the past 18 years. He reread the email at least a dozen times before he scrolled down to read the email that Vi had responded to.

He remembered writing her, but then the boys startled him and he closed the computer, probably without turning it off, and then Gennaro gave him Big Vinny's letter, and who the hell could think of anything else after that. He traced and retraced what had taken place since writing the email: the boys surprising him in the office, closing the computer, getting the note from Gennaro, giving the envelope to a stranger on the train station, meeting Tootsie, and Big Vinny getting released on bail, but not Michael or Jimmy. A few moments earlier Frankie said that he didn't owe Violetta anything, he didn't want to contact her, and he wanted everything to stay the same. But everything staying the same was exactly what Lenny couldn't allow.

"I'll be in New York for Christmas," she wrote. *She might already be here*, Lenny thought and pressed reply.

"Call me when you're in town," he typed, added his cellphone number, and pressed send. How simple it was. What he couldn't bring himself to do for almost eighteen years, he did in a second, without even thinking about it. "Call me ...," he typed as if they had just seen each other.

The weight of Filomena's hand pressed down on Lenny's shoulder. *She walked out on you, Lenny. She also left her son. A good mother doesn't leave her son.*

"What's worse," Lenny said, "a mother who left her son, or a mother who won't ever let her son go?"

The weight lifted.

That night, Lenny's sleep was fitful. *Had Vi checked her email? Was she already on a plane heading East for Christmas? Maybe she was already in New York.*

The next morning, Lenny dressed, ate breakfast, and opened the store with the movements of an automaton. The warm loves of Italian bread did little to take the chill out of the cold December morning. Instead, the heat and the aroma of the fresh baked bread soured his stomach, and everything about the store—the two long, narrow aisles piled to the tin ceiling with groceries and paper goods; the frayed burlap bags of dried beans and grain; the temperamental sliding glass doors on the display cases of cold cuts behind the counter; even the Christmas lights—irritated him, as did the thought of the hectic days ahead. Aside from the regulars there would be the once-a-year Christmas customers looking for special items they could find only at Lasante's— or so they said. It was as if Christmastime, especially the Eve, pulled at the roots of even the most assimilated Italians, and shopping in Lasante's made them feel as if they were coming home. But for Lenny it meant long, tiresome days and *home* did not have the glow of nostalgia that it did for those who had moved on.

Lenny filled the bread case and thought it curious that Vi was coming East for Christmas. She didn't have family here, at least that's what Lenny thought.

19

With Filomena gone, Lenny's two youngest sisters spent Christmas with their in-laws, but since Lenny was the only father Tony knew, and Tony's wife, Laura, didn't have any family to speak of, they drove the bumper-to-bumper traffic with their twin sons from Central Islip to spend Christmas with Frankie, Angie, and Lenny. For the sake of the twins, the adults did their best to make it as festive as possible, but there was no ignoring Filomena's absence. During Christmas dinner the twins voiced what everyone was feeling—"We miss Grandma … It doesn't feel like Christmas without her … Will we ever see her again?" And it was Frankie who took them on his lap and soothed them, as if Filomena were channeling her love for her youngest grandsons through her oldest grandson.

The day passed with forced smiles and teary eyes. The little ones seemed relieved when Tony said that it was time to hit the road.

Angie and Lenny helped Tony carry gifts from the house to the car while Frankie helped Laura dress the two squirming boys in boots, coats, hats, scarves, and gloves. Laura was a petite, pretty woman with endless patience, not only for her twin boys, but also for Tony, who had been spoiled by Filomena and his siblings. He was the baby of the family, and his sisters carried him around as if he was one of their dolls, even after he was long able to walk on his own.

"Okay boys, I think that Mommy has you dressed for a nor'easter," Tony said. "You look like helium balloons in the Macy's Parade. Should I tie you to the top of the car?"

"Hey, big fellas, give Grandpa Lenny a hug," Lenny said, and his nephews jumped on him. They were husky little guys with tons of energy, and they nearly knocked him over.

"Wow! Careful, boys, Grandpa Lenny's not as young as me," Tony said. "Come to mention it, he's not as strong or good looking either."

"I'm still strong enough to knock your dad down to size," Lenny said, chuckling, and wrestled his nephews into the car.

As the car pulled away from the curb, Angie and Lenny blew kisses to the boys, and Frankie disappeared into the house. Angie took Lenny's arm and they climbed up the brick stoop between snow-filled cement flowerpots. The color lights strung round the windows looked harsh, as did the large Santa Claus face despite his sympathetic smile. Lenny missed the sedum's small star-shaped blooms and the more showy hydrangeas in the gardens.

Inside the house, Frankie sat in the living room checking his cell-phone and thumbing through books that Angie had given him for Christmas, while Angie wiped the few remaining crumbs from the dining room tablecloth. She was a handsome woman. Not as pretty as her younger sisters, but elegant in a casual way—like royalty on a day off. Eyeing the occasional strands of silver in her otherwise dark brown hair gave Lenny a fleeting sense of sadness. Since Angie's divorce, she'd had no one special in her life. And her former husband, who Amelia and Irish called Mr. Feminist, had been special only in that he couldn't keep his hands off his coeds. Since their divorce there had been a few guys who sounded good politically, but, like her ex, proved to be empty barrels.

She had met the last man she dated at a lecture on global warming. He lambasted the organizers of the event for holding the lecture in a third-floor walkup that wasn't accessible to people in wheelchairs, and of course Angie was immediately attracted to him—also his thick, wavy hair and bedroom eyes didn't hurt. On their third date, he invited her to dinner at his place in Park Slope. He lived in the basement apartment of a brownstone, but he didn't own a shovel and hadn't cleared the snow from the steep steps down to his apartment; Angie slipped and twisted her ankle. So much for accessibility.

Lenny chuckled at the memory of Angie telling him this story.

"What's so funny?" Angie said.

"Oh nothing. The snow outside just reminded me of one of your Mr. Sensitives."

"Which one?"

"Umm ... have you ever thought about dating a Republican?"

"It's Christmas, Lenny. Let's change the subject. Do you want more coffee?"

Through the archway into the kitchen, Angie appeared and disappeared from view—a taller, less animated, and younger Filomena.

"Sure, coffee sounds good."

"How about you, Frankie?" she called from the kitchen. "Do you want anything?"

"No, I'm good. I'm thinking of walking down to Gennaro's for a little bit. If that's okay."

"If what's okay?" Lenny said, though he had heard Frankie.

"If I go down to Gennaro's for a while. I didn't give him his gift yet."

Angie set out two demitasse cups of espresso, and Lenny took a seat at the dining room table while Frankie charged up to his bedroom, and then back down to the front door. "Oops! Almost forgot his gift," Frankie said and grabbed a box from under the tree.

The house shook when he slammed the front door.

Angie stirred sugar into her espresso. "What's gotten into him?"

"Maybe he got a text from a secret admirer."

"Don't tell me it's Lena."

"You're warm."

"Spare me the games, Lenny. Who's the girl?"

Lenny added a drop of anisette to his espresso. "Gennaro."

Two bayberry scented candles burned down almost to their candleholders—a pair of bisque Mr. and Mrs. Santa Claus Vincenzo had bought for Filomena years ago in Little Italy at a shop on Mott Street. Tongues of fire floated above the jolly couple's heads while Angie's eyes widened, and Lenny selected a sfogiatelle from the few pastries left on the red and green platter. He tapped some powdered sugar off the pastry, pressed his free hand against his full stomach, and returned the pastry to the platter.

"Frankie told you this?" Angie said.

"Not in so many words, but it's something I've surmised for a long time. Guess I've been trying not to think about it, but last night, when

I came downstairs to turn off the Christmas tree lights, they were curled up together like two spoons, asleep on the couch."

Angie rolled her eyes and took a sip of her espresso. "Is that all? You know how Gennaro is. He's like a big puppy."

"Angie ..."

"This is speculation, Lenny!"

Lenny took a deep breath and sighed. "Look, Angie, if Frankie is gay, he's gay. Not a damn thing we can do about it. As I said, I've thought this for a long time, so it's no shock. I didn't say I love the idea. Life is hard enough, but things are changing. At least they're changing beyond 104th Street. I saw these guys a few months ago in Central Park. Two guys with their little girl." Lenny shook his head and threw up his hands as if he were trying to make sense of his own words. "Regardless, what I'm really worried about is that Frankie's feelings for Gennaro are another reason for him not to leave this lousy neighborhood and another reason not to go to college."

"You're so obsessed with Frankie going college that you're imagining things."

"I didn't imagine last night when I overheard Frankie tell Gennaro that he didn't want to leave him. Fortunately, Gennaro's not encouraging him to stay. He told Frankie that he should go. In fact, Gennaro might enlist in the Marines."

"From this you figured out that Frankie is gay, and he's in love with Gennaro?"

"You've never wondered why Frankie, a good looking, friendly kid never had a girlfriend?"

"Well, I didn't say ..." Angie looked away from Lenny and ran the palms of her hands against the tablecloth as if smoothing out problems.

"All right then." For a few moments they sat quietly and drank their espressos. Lenny cracked his knuckles. Angie picked lint from her sleeve. The steam radiators hissed followed by several bangs.

"Well, as you said, times are changing. The important thing is that he knows we love him."

"No, the important thing is that he gets the hell out of here. Times will never change on 104th Street."

Angie nodded. Lenny told her that he'd been thinking about selling the store and the house, and that that's what he really wanted to talk to her about, not whether or not Frankie is gay or how they could be supportive. "The best thing we can do for Frankie right now is make sure he gets as far away from 104th Street and the DiCicos as possible. If a bird doesn't have a nest then it has to fly."

"Frankie being the bird?" Angie said.

"Exactly!"

"Nice metaphor, Lenny, but . . ." Angie ran her thumb along the rim of the demitasse saucer. "Let's begin with the fact that you're 50, and the store has been your life."

"The store has been the means, but not my life," Lenny said. "My life has been raising all of you, getting you through college, and then raising Frankie." He tried to say this without sounding resentful. It was a simple and, he thought, obvious fact. However, Angie took offense.

"You didn't *exactly* raise Frankie by yourself."

Angie was right, but Lenny had taken umbrage at her comment about the store being his life. He tried to backtrack. "Yes, you've been great. I couldn't have raised Frankie with out Mama and you. I didn't mean to make it sound as if I had done it alone. I'm sorry."

The hissing radiators filled the silence, and Lenny wondered if Angie not remarrying had to do with Frankie and him. If not for them, might she have tried harder to make it work with someone? Lenny wasn't the only one who had made sacrifices.

"It's strange without Mama here," Angie said. "All day I've been hearing her skirt rustle in the kitchen, hearing her fuss over the twins or respond to comments that were made, and even smelling her Jean Nate. I should have made pizza di scarola, but it takes so much time and patience. I don't have Mama's patience. I don't know how she did what she did after Papa died." Angie brought her fingertips to her eyes. "Maybe the thought of selling the store feels like another loss—at least right now."

Lenny leaned forward and held Angie's hand, but there was no retreating from what he had already said or what he was about to say. "I've also been thinking about Vi. Thinking about contacting her."

"Now I know you're overreacting." Angie pulled her hand away and sat erect.

"You know I don't make rash decisions," Lenny said

"Not usually. Though where Vi is concerned ..."

"Where Vi is concerned ... what? Did I chase after her, or even try to contact her when she first left? Angie, I have one goal and that's to do anything I must to make sure that Frankie doesn't make the mistake of staying here. He'll regret it for the rest of his life."

Angie stiffened, as if she had been splashed with ice water. "You mean like his father?"

"I didn't say that." Lenny took a deep breath, licked his fingertips and extinguished the candles before they burned into the holders. Smoke rose above Mr. and Mrs. Claus. "Life happened, and I accepted it. I'm not crying about that, and I'm not crying about having had to raise Frankie, but I'll burn the store down before I watch Frankie live my life."

Angie stood and gathered the demitasse cups and spoons. She paused before leaving the table. "What do you want me to do?" The cups rattled on their saucers.

"Just support me when I talk to the others about selling." Lenny leaned back in his chair so his voice would follow Angie into the kitchen. "The Pulumbo brothers have been after me to sell the store and house to them for about a year now. You might not know them. They moved here from the old country about three years ago. Nice guys. They want to do more cooked food—you know, for takeout."

Angie returned to the dining room and nodded. She had the expression of a disapproving teacher. "And Vi?" Angie asked.

"What about Vi?"

"How can I help there?"

"I don't know. I haven't figured that out yet. You know this is right for Frankie. Even Gennaro knows I'm right. I heard him tell Frankie that in a year or two Frankie would regret it if he didn't go away to college, that he'd wind up hating Gennaro and me if he stayed here. You didn't come back, Angie. Even after your divorce. Mama thought you should come home, but I told her to leave you alone. I was glad when you bought your own house."

Angie's jaw went tense and her chest rose as she sucked in a deep breath. "I have one question. Then I'll shut up and support whatever you want to do about the store, the house, and Vi."

"Okay, shoot," Lenny said.

"Do you regret that you didn't follow her to California?"

Lenny tried to hide his irritation, but he was tired of Angie making this about him or her or the past. "Come on, Angie. How could I have done that?"

"That's not what I asked you, but I think you answered my question anyway."

Angie placed the cups, saucers, and spoons in the dishwasher. After she went up to bed, Lenny sat in the shadowy living room staring at the lights on the Christmas tree. He hadn't been completely honest with Angie about Vi. He hadn't mentioned the emails or that she was in New York, but he didn't want to talk about Vi at length with Angie. He had long learned not to discuss Vi with his family, especially Filomena or his sisters, who always made it sound as if, when it came to Vi, Lenny thought with his dick. But so what if he did? Did he regret not following her to California? Lately he was plagued with regrets. Not following Vi was only one in a long list.

He put his feet up on the ottoman and drifted in and out of sleep until he woke to the shrill of someone leaning on the doorbell and a pounding in his chest.

20

Clear lights twinkled through white, iridescent, plastic pine needles and reflected in the folds of plastic slipcovers on white recliners where Big Vinny and Marie DiCico sat. Before them was an immense flat-screen television. Big Vinny snored while Ebenezer Scrooge trembled in the presence of the Ghost of Christmas Yet To Come. "I fear you more than any specter I have seen," a colorized Alastair Sim stammered. Gennaro tore the wrapping from his gift.

"Shh!" Marie hissed. She tapped the platinum band of her engagement ring against a glass of Pepsi with ice and fiddled with the ring, pressing her thumb against its four-carat diamond.

"How does the sound of this paper annoy you when you're sitting next to a human chainsaw?" Gennaro said.

"I'm used to Big Vinny's snoring. Now quiet! I want to watch this."

"For the ten-millionth time," Gennaro whispered to Frankie. "Great sweater, Francesco."

Gennaro had already given Frankie his gift last night on Christmas Eve. After Lenny and Angie had gone upstairs, Gennaro pounced on Frankie and whispered: "I didn't give you your gift yet." But Frankie pushed him away, and pointed towards the ceiling—sign language for you're going to wake up my father and aunt.

Unfazed, Gennaro flew off the couch, bunched up fistfuls of his baggy sweatshirt, and gyrated his hips. His red reindeer boxers showed above his sagging jeans and his washboard stomach above his boxers. A line of hair beginning at his navel disappeared under a reindeer's antler.

"Very cute," Frankie said.

"I really did get you something." Gennaro sat on the ottoman in front of Frankie, grinning as he slipped a small box, wrapped in gold foil paper, from his hip pocket onto Frankie's knee. The glow of the Christmas-tree lights formed a halo around Gennaro's silhouette.

"It's not going to open itself, Francesco."

Frankie unwrapped the gift and lifted the cover off the box. In the dimly lit room, all he could make out was a small gold medal at the end of a chain.

"Bring it closer to the tree lights," Gennaro said.

Like toddlers waiting for Christmas magic to appear, they pressed close to each other. Frankie inhaled the sent of balsam and Gennaro.

"It's a medal of Saint Francis. I know how you're into all this religious stuff. I mean, I don't know a bunch about the guy except that he was kind and loving and, of course, Italian." Gennaro laughed. "Maybe he was a lot like you. And since you have the same name as him ..."

Under the lights, the gold medal and chain were luminous, and the impression of Saint Francis reflected in a shiny ornament—elongated and indigo as if painted by El Greco. Frankie kissed Gennaro. "I know I must be crazy, but I love you."

"You are crazy."

"I don't want to leave you. My father wants me to go away to college, but I don't want to."

Gennaro pressed his fingertips against Frankie's lips.

"Don't make me your excuse, Francesco." Gennaro moved away from him. "Your old man is right. You need to get out of here and go away to college. You don't belong here. And if you stay, I give it a year or two before you'll regret it, before you hate your old man and before you hate me." Gennaro inched his way onto the couch. "Plus, remember, I'm joining the Army, maybe the Marines. We both need to get away from 104th Street. Maybe for different reasons, but we both need to go."

Frankie slipped on the Saint Francis medal, let the matter drop, and joined Gennaro on the couch. It was too beautiful a moment to ruin with an argument. They lay together—fitting like two spoons, and they talked about little things and even laughed.

"This is gonna sound corny," Gennaro said, "but when you stay at my house, my favorite time is when we lie like this and we're just about to fall asleep. It's as if, except for us, the whole fucking world disappears."

"Wish we could sleep together every night," Frankie said.

Gennaro changed the subject. They talked about Angie's linguini with calamari and Lenny's baccalà salad. "Not like my Grandma's, but pretty good." Frankie said.

They talked about Johnny Pickle having a crush on Lena and how she barely talked to him, and about other friends, and about music, but they didn't talk about Gennaro's brothers, or jail, or the cab driver or anything sad. They hadn't meant to fall asleep, and later, when Frankie woke in the dark, he realized that someone had unplugged the tree lights—probably Lenny.

Now watching Gennaro's muscles flex as he pulled on his new sweater and how its royal blue color brought out the magic in Gennaro's eyes, Frankie thought of waking last night and wondered what Lenny had thought about finding them curled up on the couch—not that Frankie was concerned; he just wondered. He thought: *How could Dad not know how much I love Gennaro? How could anyone not know?*

"The sweater fits great, Francesco," Gennaro said. "Let's get out of here. I've had enough of Scrooge and this creepy ghost."

Outside, elderly neighbors called goodnight from front stoops to their children and grandchildren; car engines revved and children laughed as they threw snowballs; their parents yelled for them to hurry up and get in the car. Voices and sounds were muffled by the falling snow, which crushed beneath the boys' sneakers as they shuffled up 104th Street.

They turned left onto 91st Avenue, past Lasante's, and onto where storefronts reflected the change in the neighborhood's ethnic tapestry. When Lenny was a boy, there were Italian grocery stores and fruit stands; German butchers and bakeries; Eastern-European Jewish candy stores, clothing stores, and jewelers; as well as Chinese drycleaners. Of course there were exceptions, but this was enough of the rule to create the perception of businesses mapping out ethnic turf. Now, though the stores on either side of 91st Avenue, between 101st and 105th Streets were Italian-owned, beyond 105th Street was an entrepreneurial mix of the more recent immigrant influx to the neighborhood: Korean fruit stands, Guyanese bakeries, Puerto Rican restaurants, and East Indian convenience stores, but Glenhaven was still a neighborhood of immigrants with an ethic for hard work and a commitment to extended family. As in Leonardo and Lucia's time, siblings purchased a business or piece of property together. The difference now was that the surnames on deeds had changed from names like Marconi or Cohen to Taneja or Menendez.

They bought hot chocolates in a convenience store—the only store they found opened so late on Christmas night. A man whose complexion was the color of their drinks and who was wearing a burgundy turban wished them a Merry Christmas and counted out their change. As they left the store, Frankie noticed a kid who was checking out the display of chips, but also eying Gennaro.

"Do you know that guy?" Frankie whispered.

Gennaro shrugged. "I know a lot of guys."

The full moon illuminated their blue-gray footprints, which trailed after them in the fresh fallen snow. Frankie looked back several times and tried to shake the eerie feeling he had from seeing that boy stare at Gennaro. "I don't like the way that kid looked. Something wasn't right. When he saw that I noticed him staring at you, he looked away, but his brow was all crunched up as if he were struggling to figure something out," Frankie said.

Gennaro asked if Frankie wanted him to go back and knock the guy out. Frankie laughed, but continued to glance back over his shoulder every now and then.

They sipped their hot chocolates, and their warm breath mixed with the steam from their drinks. They talked about driving to Tucci's place. Neither of them had ever been there in winter. They also spoke of driving to the Carolinas or Florida. It was over a week before school would start again, and Frankie recalled his conversation with Lenny about not going back for the spring semester since he already had all the credits he needed to graduate. He had a fleeting thought of Gennaro and him walking the beaches near Taormina.

"The world is bigger than 104th Street," Gennaro said, sounding very much like Lenny.

Frankie was about to suggest that they take an extended trip when a rat scurried out from under a snow sculpture of torn trash bags, and Gennaro shuddered and spilled chocolate on his jacket. "Shit, I hate those fucking things," he said.

Frankie laughed, and reminded Gennaro of another time that a rat had startled him. They were waiting for a subway at the Canal Street Station on their way home from the San Gennaro Feast in Little Italy. A rat darted across Gennaro's brand-new and very expensive sneakers. "Remember, you threw up, kicked off your sneakers without touching them, and left them on the train platform." By now, Frankie was laughing so hard that tears froze on his cheeks, and he forgot about Taormina and traveling. "You rode the train home without shoes. Remember?"

"Very funny. Probably some homeless guy got a free pair of sneakers. I was just being charitable."

"Yeah, you're a regular Good Samaritan."

"Don't Tootsie live around here?" Gennaro asked.

Frankie glanced up at the street sign. "Wow, I guess we've walked pretty far."

"Maybe we should stop in for a visit."

"It's too late. Besides, I don't know her address."

"She's probably tired anyway, after giving birth to Baby Jesus."

"Boy, you're full of it tonight," Frankie said.

Gennaro's cellphone rang. "Yep, be there in about 20 or 30 minutes, maybe less." He turned to Frankie. "I have one last Christmas gift for you. Come on. I'll race you."

Be where? Frankie thought as they gulped what was left of their lukewarm chocolate, wedged the empty cups into a full trashcan, and jogged several blocks until they had to stop and catch their breaths, belching chocolate steam into the icy night. They resumed jogging but with more frequent breaks. They approached Most Precious Blood.

"Let's turn in here, I have something to show you," Gennaro said, panting.

Frankie was puzzled, but followed Gennaro into the parking lot and down the concrete steps, curving below the Basilica's stone foundation. As kids they scared each other with stories about the gargoyles that lived beneath the church—more like Gennaro scared Frankie.

"What are we doing here?" Frankie whispered, as if being within the bowels of the church warranted hushed voices.

"You'll see." Gennaro pressed the latch on a heavy wooden door. It opened. "Hey, Mr. Rodriguez! You in there?"

"Merry Christmas, Gennaro. Sorry to call you, but I didn't know if you were still coming." Rodriguez was the main custodian for Most Precious Blood. His hands were large and gnarled. Like the statue of Mary on the Lasante grave, two fingers on his left hand were missing. His breath smelled of cigars and whiskey.

"I kind a lost track of time," Gennaro said. "This is my friend Frankie Lasante."

Mr. Rodriguez extended his right hand. "I see you in church a lot, no?"

Before Frankie could speak, Gennaro answered for him. "Yeah, that's why I thought he'd like some quiet time in church. He's kind of a saint. You know how saints get all holy around Christmas."

Rodriguez eyed Frankie and made the sign of the cross. "Go ahead upstairs. I left small lights on, but don't turn on no big lights. I still got about an hour's work to do, so take your time." He smiled at Frankie. "Maybe you can say a prayer for my Isabel? Her arthritis has been bad lately. Too much cold weather."

"Sure, he loves praying," Gennaro said. "Sometimes I can't get him up off his knees."

Gennaro pushed Frankie towards the stairs to the Sanctuary. Rodriguez lit the stub of cigar hanging from the downturned corner of his mouth and picked up a broom.

"Your saint stuff was real funny. And the part about me being on my knees ..." Frankie grumbled as he felt his way up the dark steps, and Gennaro felt his way between Frankie's legs.

"Cut it out." Frankie pushed Gennaro's hand away. "I can't believe that man has to clean a church on Christmas night."

"Yeah. Remember the bumper sticker we saw: Catholic School Teacher. The Pay Is Lousy, But The Tips Are Out of This World. I guess things are even worse for custodians. My grandfather would have started a union, but the Pope would have expelled him."

"You're a riot. What are we doing here anyway?"

"I want to show you something. Remember I said that I had another present for you?"

"How did you get him to let us in here?"

"Hey, I'm still a DiCico, ain't I? For better or worse. Now stop with all the questions and keep walking."

They walked past what was once the main altar—before Vatican II and before priests faced their congregation to say Mass—down marble steps to what Filomena had called the stage. At the center of the stage was the main altar, not as grand as its predecessor. It was made of wood instead of marble, and the sides and legs of the altar showed an in-progress relief of hand-carved lilies, mixed with penciled outlines —templates for future carvings. The unfinished carvings gave the altar a this-too-will-pass appearance despite sitting in the middle of the church for more than 30 years. Filomena complained that after Vatican II priests went to acting school instead of the seminary. One of her many complaints about change in the Church, even though she never missed Mass. Not that she listened to the priests. She was too busy praying the rosary.

Frankie glanced around the immense stone cave of shadows and squinted towards the smaller grottos, which brought to mind the images on the cartoline postale. Flickering jelly jars, several wall sconces, and a small spotlight shining on the nativity scene to their left were the only lights lit in the church. There was the faint sent of balsam and frankincense.

The night before, when Angie and Frankie had attended Christmas Eve Mass, the church was packed, and Frankie found himself looking from face to face until he realized that he was hoping to spot his grandmother sitting in one of the pews, mumbling her prayers and ignoring the priests.

Gennaro slid his hands under Frankie's open jacket and drew him close. "Now for the Christmas gift I was telling you about," he said. He kissed Frankie long, hard, and slow in front of God the Father, Son, and Holy Spirit; in front of the Virgin Mary; in front of a host of angels, saints, shepherds, the Magi, and beasts of burden.

"Notice anything, Francesco?"

"You mean aside from the fact that a crazy person just kissed me in a church?"

"No ... I mean that I kissed you, and the church is still standing. Five months ago, a jackass squirted lighting fluid into a fire, blew up the can he was holding, and thought that he was being punished for loving you."

Frankie recalled the explosion and remembered pleading with God for Gennaro to live and promised to change how he felt about Gennaro. He had no idea that Gennaro was feeling the same conflicts. *So much time wasted*, Frankie thought.

"God didn't punish me for loving you, Frankie. I punished myself," Gennaro said. "Don't expect too much from me; you'll be disappointed, but I love you. I do."

Frankie stepped back just a little so he could look into Gennaro's eyes. "Do you know what you just said next to an altar in church?"

"I do," Gennaro said. "Guess it's permanent now." They both laughed.

Frankie felt the cool of the Saint Francis medal against his chest. He pointed towards the far end of the nave. "There's a statue of Saint Francis over there. I spent hours in front of that statue praying for you after the explosion." He touched the medal through his shirt. "Funny that you bought me this."

Again, Gennaro drew Frankie close. They embraced and Frankie closed his eyes. He felt the stubble on Gennaro's cheek and the rise of their desire. Their breaths coalesced—one body, one blood.

"What about Rodriguez?" Frankie said.

"What about him," Gennaro said. "I'm beginning to get what you like about this place."

Shouting came from the sacristy—a mix of English and Spanish. Rodriguez's voice, but the second voice was unfamiliar, younger, higher, but also with a heavy accent. The tone of each word became shriller, until it was punctuated by the sound of a gunshot, then silence.

Frankie tried to speak, but Gennaro pressed the palm of his hand against Frankie's mouth. Over Gennaro's shoulder, Frankie saw someone enter the church through the door from the sacristy. It was the boy from the convenience store, the one who stared at Gennaro, and like the Dickens Ghost of Christmas Yet To Come, he pointed a shadowy, accusatory finger, but the finger glinted dark and ominous, and as Frankie struggled to scream "No!" more gunshots rang out like death knells, and Gennaro slumped against him, his fingers like vices tearing into Frankie's shoulders. Two more gunshots, and Frankie felt a sharp burning in his neck and thigh. Gennaro's grip loosened. His body peeled away from Frankie like a shedding skin, and the surrounding icons looked on in mournful horror—their necks twisted, lips contorted, and eyes glistening with tears.

"Noooo ..." A primal scream vibrated in Frankie's throat and echoed through the Basilica, until he lost his breath and his knees crashed onto the marble floor. "You can't do this," he screamed. "What kind of a monster are you?"

Blood, a deeper red and more precious than the wounds and stigmata painted on plaster statues, rushed from Gennaro's quivering body. Frankie collapsed onto him, embraced him, and cupped his hands beneath Gennaro to stem the blood's flow.

"Don't go." Frankie's voice grew small, barely audible. "Please don't go. This isn't real." The pain in his thigh and neck clouded his thoughts, but he managed to press his blood-drenched palms against Gennaro's back. Gennaro's life oozed through Frankie's fingers. "Don't go. Please don't leave me ... Please ... please ... plea ..." Frankie mouthed, until he lost consciousness.

"**A**re you Mr. Lasante?"

Not fully awake, Lenny shivered at the cold and asked the young police officer to step inside. He wondered if this was about Big Vinny's bribe money, and expected to hear, *You have the right to remain silent,* but instead the officer, looking more like a boy in a Halloween costume than a real police officer, cleared his throat, removed his cap, and asked: "Are you Frankie Lasante's father?" After he said that there had been a shooting at Most Precious Blood and explained what the police discovered when they entered the church, Lenny stepped back and stumbled over the mother bear and her cubs, and Angie grabbed his arm.

With one hand Angie clutched at her chenille robe, and with the other she held onto Lenny as he tried to balance himself. Had Big Vinny been in the room, Lenny might have killed him. He didn't know how, but he was sure that this horror was connected to Big Vinny—a vendetta. Angie's grip was the anchor that moored Lenny and kept him from telling the young officer that the real killer lived down the block.

Angie quickly changed out of her nightclothes and the young officer drove them to the hospital where they learned that, when the police had arrived at Most Precious Blood, it was too late for Mr. Rodriguez and Gennaro, but Frankie, though unconscious, was alive. Had Mrs. Rodriguez not called the police when her husband didn't answer his cellphone, Frankie would have bled to death.

He was in surgery having two bullets removed, one in his neck, just missing the carotid artery and one in his thigh. A plain-clothes officer questioned Lenny, but Lenny shook so violently that she called a nurse. After a shot of Valium, he was at least able to tell the officer that he had no idea why anyone would harm Gennaro or Frankie, but the officer persisted, including questions about Big Vinny, Michael, and Jimmy, and all of Lenny's answers were some version of sorry all I know is what was in the paper or on television. The next morning the police learned all they needed to know, or at least most of it. The convenience store proprietor saw the news on television and called the police about a teenager who on Christmas night had asked him if one of the boys he saw leaving the store was a DiCico. The police arrested the teenager who turned out to be the murdered cabdriver's son.

Several hours after surgery, as the dark hospital windows faded to a pale lavender, Frankie lay in bed semiconscious, Angie and Lenny sat next to him staring at multiple monitors and machines with blinking lights, and Lenny received a text message from Vi: *Just heard the news on the radio. This is terrible. I will do whatever you want me to do.*

Too late for that, Lenny thought and slipped his cellphone back into his pocket without mentioning the text to Angie. But throughout the day, Vi continued to text and left voicemails until Lenny finally responded and agreed to meet her for coffee in the hospital cafeteria. His only stipulation was that they wait until Frankie's condition stabilized. For several days Frankie slipped in and out of consciousness, and Lenny left his bedside only to use the toilet and shower. Lenny's sisters and brother brought food, which he barely touched. They offered to stay with Frankie while Lenny went home to rest, but he refused.

Angie made an appearance at Gennaro's wake, standing for hours in the line of mourners, which meandered at a snail's pace through Romano's Funeral Home. The mourners wept, and some said that Gennaro looked like a sleeping Prince Charming. The old timers compared him to Valentino. Big Vinny, Marie, and Lena were inconsolable, especially when four police officers escorted Michael and Jimmy into the funeral parlor in orange prison garb and their ankles and wrists shackled.

Angie apologized for Lenny's absence, explaining that he wouldn't leave Frankie while his condition was still serious. Marie said she understood. At the High Funeral Mass, Gennaro's casket, ebony with enough gilt to rival a pharaoh's sarcophagus, lay only a few feet from where he had died. The church was more crowded than it had been on Christmas Eve. People stood around the parameter of the nave and poured out into the vestibules.

As Angie explained the details of Gennaro's wake and funeral to Lenny, he felt some compassion, but mostly rage for the DiCicos, especially for Big Vinny. The same rage he had felt when the detectives questioned him on and off for hours about possible suspects and motives. What could he have told them? That years ago his grandfather should never have welcomed a DiCico into his home; that after his father died he should have left—if not for college then for anywhere far from 104th Street; that he should have followed Vi to California. Or should he have told them that knowing the DiCicos meant you would do things you would otherwise never do, like give an envelope stuffed with cash to a stranger in a train station or get shot in a church on Christmas night?

22

Fleeting images—of machines and wires; of family members, especially Lenny; of strangers wearing white or pastel colored jackets, their expressions doleful and frozen like cemetery statuary—appeared then vanished. But for the most part, Frankie floated on dreamlike waves, euphoric images of times and places distant, where shepherds, fishermen, artisans, and water bearers posed against a backdrop of sea cliffs and idyllic beaches that gave way to the Ionian Sea.

Gennaro, with dirt-encrusted fingernails, tattered dress, and a mane of curls as wild as medusa's, stood before the crumbling Greek theater and smoking Mount Etna. He took Frankie's hand. Their hands were chafed and calloused. They led a donkey along rocky cliffs and down a dirt road, where they paused and shot stones from the precipice. Above them were buildings thirsting for whitewash and stacked like children's blocks, precariously clinging to a lush, sun-bathed mountainside. One tremble and they'd come tumbling down.

They resumed their walk until they came upon a fork in the road and bore left, away from the cliffs and down a steep slope where they entered the shade of a citrus grove, thick with the heady fragrance of lemon and orange blossoms.

Gennaro tethered the donkey to a tree and removed a burlap sack from the donkey's back. On the earth beneath wizened limbs, Gennaro spread a modest feast of bread, cheese, olives, and a bottle of wine. They leaned against the trunk of a lemon tree, their shoulders kissed, and they ate, drank, and spoke in soft fatalistic intonations: *Do this in memory of me.* In this faraway place, to the distant, mythical sound of Pan's flute, Gennaro's tattered rags fell away, exposing scars and bruises and his glistening bronze.

There were many dreams like this one, but there were also night-mares—a speeding taxicab, fire works gone mad, Big Vinny cradling Gennaro's limp body, gargoyles spiriting Gennaro out of Big Vinny's arms and dropping him onto a bloodied altar.

On the third day, Frankie's dreams and nightmares ebbed long enough for him to learn of what had happened on Christmas night.

"And Gennaro?" Frankie asked, but Lenny's expression was all the answer that he needed, and gagging on his own tears, he returned to the salty tranquility of the Ionian Sea.

Medications were decreased, and Frankie's flashbacks of what had happened Christmas night increased. Gennaro's gasping for air, his eyes unfocused and shifting up away from Frankie, his lips contorted. Frankie's own screams filled his ears, and he didn't know if they were memories of Christmas night or if he were in fact screaming, but it didn't matter. No one heard him. They propped his pillows, washed him, and fed him as if he were to recover, though recovering was the last thing that Frankie wanted.

23

It was New Year's Eve when Vi and Lenny finally met in the crowded and noisy hospital cafeteria—the same hospital where they were last together almost 18 years ago. Lenny raised his hand, but didn't wave —just held it above his head, fingers cupped, like a child trying to get his teacher's attention without the other students noticing. She smiled and approached the table. She was thinner and her style more sophisticated than when they had first met.

It was an unremarkable reunion, and Lenny believed it would prove to be pointless, as if the abyss between then and now—the girl Vi and the woman and the Lenny before being awakened by a police officer and Lenny now—was insurmountable. Lenny remembered their lovemaking, but he couldn't feel it. He felt nothing.

"Hello," she said.

Simple enough, and Lenny responded in kind, stood, and pulled a chair from the table for her to take a seat. No hug. No handshake. He just stood, with his hand clutching the back of the hard, plastic chair.

"Thank you," she said. She sat erect, placed her purse on the table, crossed her legs, and rested her hands on her lap with her fingers laced together. She was no longer Lenny's uninhibited Carmen, but what difference did that make.

"I was glad when you called me this morning. Glad to hear that Frankie's condition is stable and that the doctors are so optimistic."

Listening to Vi, Lenny recalled something Frankie had once said years ago while watching the movie *Peter Pan* on television. "Too bad Wendy had to grow up."

Now Lenny felt as if he were Peter Pan, and he resented Vi. Not so much for leaving him or for leaving Frankie, but for moving on with her life. She reminded him of his childhood friends who stopped in the store whenever they visited the old neighborhood. In her eyes, like in theirs, he saw pity and the tone of her voice sounded patronizing.

"He's still on a lot of pain medication," Lenny said. "Mostly he sleeps. When he's awake he cries. He knows Gennaro's dead. I wanted to wait to tell him, but he kept asking."

Vi pulled her chair closer to the table and took Lenny's hand. She seemed smug, and he wanted to smack her. "Hopefully the pain medication is also dulling the emotional pain, but time's the ultimate healer, Lenny."

Really, he thought, *you're going to lecture me about time and healing.* He looked at her hand—the small softness barely covered the spread of his knuckles. They might have been any parents waiting and worrying about their son's recovery, but they weren't, and Lenny pulled his hand away, slipped it into his pocket, and glanced around the cafeteria. There was something macabre about the white jackets, stethoscopes, and Happy New Year party hats. He drank the last of his coffee and met Vi's eyes—Frankie's eyes. "Maybe I'll get another coffee. Can I get you something?"

"No thank you." She smiled.

"Yes, I guess you're right. I mean I've also had enough," he said. Lenny clinched his fists and then stretched out his fingers. "All this caffeine is making me jumpy."

"I read that the police have a suspect in custody," Vi said.

"Yes. Yes, they do. They showed Frankie the mug shot. He was able to identify him."

"I'm sure that was difficult."

Lenny didn't respond.

"So what do we do now?"

She sounded sensible. *What do we do? There's no "we" making decisions here*, Lenny thought, but he just stared at her until his brow felt tight.

"I mean, should you tell Frankie that I'm here? Should I visit him? Might this be too much for him, especially considering what he's going through? Do you think he wants to see me?"

"He has your eyes," Lenny said.

Vi blushed.

"And your thing for religion," Lenny added. "I mean, given some of the courses you teach." He smiled, but his cheek gave a subversive twitch.

Vi also smiled. She was still very pretty. No bangles and bells or flowing skirts, and no longer coquettish, but still very pretty.

"I'll explain the situation to the doctor and get her advice."

"One more thing, Lenny." Vi paused and folded her fingers as if she were about to recite *here's the church, here's the steeple* ... She took a slow, deep breath. "You see ... I have a child."

You mean another child, Lenny thought. He wasn't surprised. In fact, he had assumed that Vi might have remarried and had a family even though her surname was still the same. However, she didn't mention anything about a husband, and Lenny didn't ask.

"A little girl," Vi said.

"How old is she?"

Vi fished through her bag and took out a wallet. She opened it and handed it to Lenny. "Just turned seven,"

The chubby little girl in the photo more closely resembled the Vi who once shopped in Lasante's than the staid academic who sat across from Lenny now.

"So you're not upset?" Vi asked, but there was no short answer to this question. "After I finished my Ph.D., I thought to contact you, to see if in some small way I could be a part of Frankie's life, but then I thought better of it. I didn't know what to do so I didn't do anything."

Lenny heard little after Ph.D. Instead, he wondered if having a sister might be of some small consolation to Frankie, like a window opening after a door had shut. "What's her name?" Lenny returned Vi's wallet.

"Oh ... Ina, after my mother."

"Your mother?" Vi had never spoken to Lenny of family except to say that her parents had died and that other relatives lived in Lithuania. That had been her excuse for not inviting her family to their wedding.

"Ina's at my parents' apartment now in Rego Park. It's where we spent Christmas."

"I thought your parents were dead."

Vi shook her head. "Is that what I told you? We were estranged for years. In case you hadn't figured it out yet, I was a bit of a mess back then."

Lenny's attention shifted to the noisy cafeteria, the cacophony of chairs scraping on tile, competing conversations, plastic trays hitting metal tables. All these years, Frankie had grandparents who lived about a dozen miles away, and Vi visited them regularly with Frankie's sister. They probably didn't know about him. This was too much for Lenny to absorb. He was startled by the sound of a toy noisemaker and noticed a woman scolding a child. "I should get back to Frankie."

Vi nodded and gathered her purse while Lenny stood and waited. He extended his hand as if to say you go first, and they left the cafeteria.

At the elevator they crossed paths with Tootsie, who visited Frankie regularly, as had Doug Turner and other friends and neighbors, and of course Lenny's brother, sisters, and their kids often spilled from Frankie's room into the hallway. Tootsie glanced at Vi. Lenny skipped introductions, but from Tootsie's smirk, he knew that she recognized her.

"Thank you, Lenny," Vi said as she pressed her fingers against the side of his arm. "Whatever you decide, please just let me know."

"I will," he said. "After I talk with the doctor, I'll call you."

Tootsie stepped into an open elevator. "Going up. Should I hold the door for you?"

Vi released Lenny's arm and smiled at Tootsie. "I think you're being summoned," she whispered.

"She's changed," Tootsie said, once the elevator doors closed.

"I guess."

"Oh, you guess," Tootsie said, laughing.

"Frankie doesn't know that she's here. Please don't say anything."

"Honey, you of all people should know that I'm good at keeping secrets," Tootsie said, but Lenny ignored her innuendo.

Frankie was awake when they peeked in his room, and Lenny stepped aside to let Tootsie enter alone. "I'll give you guys some time to visit," he said and walked past the nurses' station with the flashing Christmas tree and Chanukah candles and into the small lounge where cutouts of Santa's sled chased dreidels across green walls. He entertained thoughts of going home to rest, but couldn't bring himself to leave Frankie on New Year's Eve. So he sat down, rested his head against the back of the chair, closed his eyes, and saw Vi stepping away from the elevator. His had not been the only gaze that followed Vi through the lobby.

He was exhausted, and despite thoughts of Vi and sitting in an uncomfortable chair, he fell asleep. The next thing he knew Angie was sitting next to him reading.

She removed her glasses. "Happy New Year."

"What time is it?" The kink in Lenny's neck and back told him that he must have slept for quite a while.

"After 1:00. You missed the festivities. A few nurses blew noise-makers ... not too loudly. Most of the patients were sleeping."

"Frankie?"

"Yes, he slept through it."

"Did Tootsie leave?"

"Hours ago. Not long after I got here. Nice woman. I think she has a crush on you."

Angie tried to persuade Lenny to go home and rest. "Tomorrow night," he said and walked Angie to the elevator, gave her a New Year's peck on the cheek, and then headed back towards Frankie's room.

On the recliner next to Frankie's bed were a few folded clean clothes that Angie had left. He moved them and sat down. The room was dark except for the dim nightlight above Frankie, casting shadows and exaggerating the stubble on his chin.

Tomorrow I'll shave him again, Lenny thought. These were the mo-ments—in the dark, watching Frankie's chest peacefully rise and fall, noticing something as mundane as the shadow of a beard—that Len-ny's heart broke over and over again, and his eyes filled for Gennaro and the DiCicos, including Big Vinny. Lenny knew that Big Vinny would have taken those bullets for Gennaro and for Frankie in a heart-beat. Instead, Big Vinny was left with a wound that would never heal —like a stigmata of the heart. It might scab over, but the slightest re-minder—a picture of Gennaro, a song on the radio that Gennaro once sung, seeing Frankie, Johnny Pickle or any of the other boys—would cause Big Vinny's heart to bleed all over again. It was hard to hate Big Vinny for too long, but just as hard to love him. Feeling sorry for him was the most Lenny could do.

24

The doctor didn't foresee any problems with telling Frankie about Vi. In fact, she thought that meeting his mother might provide a much-needed distraction, but Frankie barely responded to Lenny's news. As it turned out, Lenny was the one who was stunned when he learned that Frankie already knew about Lenny's email to Vi, that Gennaro had sent the email, and that Frankie also knew about Big Vinny's envelope. Frankie was more interested in discussing the cartoline postale he had found in the safe than anything Lenny had to say about Vi.

Lenny positioned the shaving mirror while Frankie moved the electric shaver along his chin.

"Okay, so you found pictures," Lenny said, "but what do you think about Vi coming to see you?"

Frankie turned off the shaver, slumped back into his pillows, and shrugged his shoulders. "Whatever."

"So I'll take that to mean ...?"

Frankie said, interrupting: "I guess Great-Grandpa Leonardo and Gennaro's great-grandfather were pretty close friends.

Lenny let the matter of Vi's visit drop, at least for the time being. "Yes, you already knew they were friends in Sicily before Great-Grandpa and Great-Grandma came to America. I think since they were kids."

"That must have been hard to leave such a good friend. I mean they must have been close since he sent his kid here to live with our family. I mean, who sends their kid thousands of miles away to be raised by someone else unless it's by someone you really trust."

"They were difficult times, requiring difficult choices," Lenny said.

"Yeah, I know the stuff about Mussolini. But still. I mean, he was only a kid, right?"

This was the most interest Frankie had shown in anything and the longest that he had sustained a conversation without collapsing into tears since learning of Gennaro's death, so Lenny continued talking. He pushed the shaving mirror to the side and cleaned the electric razor with a small brush over the trashcan.

"Yes, he was only a kid, but he was in a lot of danger. The first time I heard Mr. DiCico tell the story about why his father sent him to America, he was sitting with Grandpa under the grape arbor. It was sometime after Big Vinny's brother had been killed in Vietnam. I was sitting with the two old men. Old? They were probably the age I am now." Lenny tapped the razor against the side of the trashcan.

Frankie didn't roll his eyes as if to say *I've heard this a million times*, so Lenny continued. "Who knew where Big Vinny was. He was already running with a tough crowd, always getting into trouble, even with the police. Not that he didn't get into trouble before, but after his brother was killed things got worse. Anyway, Mr. DiCico was reminiscing about Taormina. He did that a lot."

"From the pictures it looks beautiful," Frankie said.

"Pictures?"

"Yes, in the safe. The cartoline postale."

"Of course, the cartoline postale," Lenny said. "Anyway, Mr. DiCico talked about the morning he woke up and his older brother was gone."

"This was his communist brother?"

"I don't know if he was a communist, but I guess he was always talking about revolution and he hated fascism and Mussolini. So Mr. DiCico said that when he saw that his brother's side of the bed was empty, he went to tell his father, and he found his father sitting on a small stool in some kind of barn or chicken coop, placing torn bits of paper on his tongue—chewing, swallowing, and crying."

"Like hosts at Mass," Frankie said.

"Mr. DiCico thought that it was a note his older brother had written, telling his father that he had joined the underground resistance, and his father didn't want the note falling into the wrong hands, so he ate it. The Italian solution for most anything."

Frankie actually smiled at Lenny's little joke, and Lenny's eyes filled at the sight of his son's smile. He took a breath and continued talking. "Then, Mr. DiCico said that, like his older brother, he also began speaking out against fascism and Mussolini. He also criticized the Mafiosi for killing labor organizers and breaking up peasant cooperatives. He was barely a teenager, but he took up his brother's cause. Too bad you never met him. An honorable man. So after the fascist police beat him up and left him unconscious in a pigsty, his father wrote to Great-Grandpa Leonardo. And Great-Grandpa said: 'Yes, send him to America.' The rest you know. Your grandpa and Gennaro's grandpa grew up together as brothers. Big Vinny and I also grew up together, though I wouldn't call us brothers. And you and ...'" Frankie's eyes widened, and Lenny stopped talking when he realized what he was about to say. He took Frankie's hand. "I'm sorry."

A nurse came in the room carrying a cup with three pills, and Frankie frowned. He downed the pills quickly as the nurse took his vitals. Lenny thought of the three generations of DiCicos who had all lost sons to violence—be it at the hand of a distraught cabdriver's son, a war, or fascism—Big Vinny, his father, and his grandfather had each lost a son. He didn't tell Frankie all of what was said that day at the plywood table under the arbor. He didn't mention that Giacomo DiCico had said that Vietnam took his good son but left him with the hoodlum son. Lenny also didn't mention how Big Vinny's mother had wailed for her murdered son, as Lenny imagined Marie DiCico must have done when she learned that Gennaro had been murdered.

Once the nurse left, Frankie yawned and rubbed his eyes, but his questions continued. "So Great-Grandpa and Gennaro's great-grand-father must have been very close, right? I mean to raise someone else's kid, especially when you have your own kids to raise."

"Yes, I imagine that they had been very good friends in Sicily."

"It must have been real hard for Great-Grandpa to leave him."

"I imagine it was." Frankie acted annoyed with Lenny's brief and matter-of-fact answers. He continued to press for more information, but Lenny didn't know what else to say. Frankie suggested that two of the boys in the cartoline postale might have been the great-grand-fathers when they were young, but Lenny didn't know if that was true. He didn't remember having seen the pictures before coming across them when he looked for Big Vinny's envelope, and even then he barely looked at them. At the time, he had more pressing matters to be concerned about. Given the subject matter, he should have remembered if he had seen them before, but maybe not. Captain Beltrani's photos of nude women he remembered, but maybe the von Gloeden's nudes had not impressed him as much as Beltrani's. He was no help to Frankie, who seemed much more knowledgeable about the cartoline postale than Lenny was. Frankie explained where he had hid them in his room, along with some letters. Lenny agreed that he would go home that night, find the pictures and the letters, and bring them to the hospital.

"One more thing," Lenny said. "So are you okay with Vi coming to visit?"

"Yes, if she wants." Frankie yawned as his medication kicked in, and his eyes glazed over. Soon he was asleep. He mumbled something about Gennaro and cartoline postale.

The rest of the day was less eventful. Frankie alternated between sleep and staring at the television. Tony visited briefly and, later, while Frankie pushed his supper around on its plastic tray, Angie arrived with homemade lasagna. That's when Lenny left, but not without Frankie again reminding him to bring in the cartoline postale and the letters.

This was the first that Lenny had been home since Christmas, and the longest that Lasante's had ever been closed—at least that Lenny could remember. He didn't turn on the store lights. The last thing he wanted was to attract attention and have customers bang on the front door or windows for something they suddenly couldn't do without.

Angie had given away perishables like milk and eggs and fresh ricotta, so he wasn't concerned about food spoiling, but he checked refrigerators and freezers to make sure that they were working properly. The two, long, dark cavernous aisles seemed narrower, and he inched his way down the right aisle, up the steps, through the breezeway, and ignored the disapproving murmurs coming from the pictures hanging in the office. Once in the house, with the door shut between the dining room and office, he no longer heard the grumbling. He heated the lasagna that Angie had left for him and poured himself a glass of wine.

The kitchen radiator hissed, and Lenny responded: "Frankie's going

to be okay." He repeated this aloud several times between bites of lasagna and sips of wine. He also whispered an occasional "Thank God."
When done, he rinsed his dish and wine glass and picked up the mail
Angie had stacked on the counter. It felt good to busy himself with
what was ordinary and familiar.

Angie had taken down the tree and all the Christmas decorations
and packed them away—no reminders of the night the police officer
came to the door. Lenny wondered if Ina might someday be there for
Frankie the way Angie was always there for him. Might Frankie and Ina
become family? They were young enough to create a history together.
The thought of Frankie having a sister comforted Lenny as he climbed
the stairs, went to his bedroom, dropped the mail on his bed, and then
went to Frankie's room.

Everything was just as Frankie had left it—an unmade bed, open
books, the closet door open with dirty clothes spilling out of it into
his room, and under his mattress were the letters and cartoline postale, just as he said.

The letters were correspondence between Leonardo and Salvatore
DiCico regarding travel arrangements for Salvatore's son Giacomo to
come to America and live with the Lasantes. Nothing Frankie didn't
already know, but the cartoline postale were impressive. Lenny was
taken back, if not slightly embarrassed, by Frankie and Gennaro's likeness to two of the boys in the photos. Frankie was right, they probably
were pictures of Leonardo and Salvatore when they were teenagers.
Lenny looked through all of the cartoline postale, but still didn't recall
having seen them before a few months ago when looking for Big
Vinny's envelope. However, he was grateful that they gave Frankie
something else to dwell on aside from what had taken place Christmas
night and grieving for Gennaro.

Lenny lumbered back to his room and undressed. A hot shower
relaxed the kinks in his neck and back, and he stood under the shower
long enough to rid his mind of *What ifs* and for the water to run tepid.
He turned off the water, stepped from the tub, and rubbed himself
dry with a bath sheet Frankie had given him years ago for Father's
Day. Running diagonally across the middle of the bath sheet were the
words World's Best Dad.

Slowly the steam cleared, and Lenny caught his reflection in a full-length mirror hanging from the back of the bathroom door. He wondered what Vi had thought when she saw him. For 50, he wasn't bad, but she was 39 and looked great. His body responded to thoughts of Vi. *No fool like an old fool!* he thought. One of Filomena's many sayings.

The clean, crisp sheets and the weight of several blankets felt like a lullaby. *If only Frankie were asleep down the hall,* Lenny thought, and he dismissed thoughts of Gennaro because he could, because no matter how terrible it was that Gennaro was gone, Frankie would be home soon, and Lenny's relief in knowing that surpassed his grief. He slept an unbroken sleep, the first since he woke to the shrill of the doorbell on Christmas night, and he didn't wake until light framed the blinds in his bedroom. He dressed, drank several cups of strong coffee, and then called Vi and told her the number of Frankie's room.

"Did you remember the letters?" was the first thing that Frankie asked. A breakfast tray sat on the table reaching across Frankie's bed. The glass of juice was empty, everything else was untouched. Frankie's hair was wet. He smelled of soap and lotion.

"Good morning. Nice to see you, too." Trying small talk was a waste of time. It was clear that Frankie was anxious to see the pictures and hear about the letters.

Lenny pushed the table aside and sat on the edge of Frankie's bed. He read the letters slowly, translating each word carefully. Some lines Frankie asked him to reread over and over, especially Salvatore's words: "I miss our walks along the Ionian sea. We were young, and life was simple."

Lenny now understood that Frankie was hoping to discover an intimacy in the letters that might suggest the great-grandfathers shared more than a platonic friendship, akin to the feelings that had existed between Gennaro and him, or at least, Lenny thought, the feelings that Frankie had for Gennaro. Frankie's hanging on every word and wanting them repeated reminded Lenny of overhearing Frankie and Gennaro's conversation on Christmas Eve. Clearly Frankie was gay, and he didn't just love Gennaro, he was in love with him, but now was not the time to broach the subject, and what difference would it have made? Lenny reread the letters to Frankie, agreed to write them over in English, and listened to Frankie muse aloud about the cartoline postale, especially the ones of the great-grandfathers.

Frankie fanned out the cartoline postale on the sheet before him. He lifted the occasional photo, held it up to Lenny, and commented on the likenesses between Leonardo and him and between Salvatore and Gennaro, and Lenny understood that Frankie was longing to discover something in these photos just as he was longing to discover something in the letters, something that a bullet or even death can't erase.

Vi stood in the doorway. She appeared small and timid, not the solicitous academic who sat across from Lenny in the hospital cafeteria yesterday or the coquettish free spirit who breezed into his store some 19 years earlier. Frankie was focused on one of the photographs, and Lenny whispered to him that Vi was here. Frankie looked up, first at Lenny. His eyes shifted towards Vi. He appeared puzzled as if he were trying to understand the implications of what was about to take place.

25

The warm sepia of the cartoline postale against the harsh white of the hospital bed sheets and the emptiness of Lenny's answers were of little comfort to Frankie. Everything—a friend visiting him or a new song on the radio—reminded Frankie that Gennaro was in the past, and as he looked from Lenny to Vi standing in the doorway of his hospital room, he thought: *Here's something else that I'll never be able to tell Gennaro.*

Gennaro was the one who had set this in motion, but he'd never know how it played out. Frankie surrendered with a weak hello—a greeting that sounded loath to accept the future. Was she older or younger or larger or smaller than Frankie had imagined her? But he hadn't imagined her, or at least he didn't remember. She looked like her photograph, the one on the computer, not the one on Lenny's dresser.

Lenny stood as she entered the room. The last time they had been together had been in this hospital, but of course Frankie had no memory of that. No memory of her holding him, of the taste of her milk, or her kissing him goodbye before she handed him back to the nurse. But it was Gennaro's arms and nipples and lips he missed. Not hers.

"Hello," she said.

Lenny mumbled some excuse to leave them alone and brushed past Vi. She stood there, looking at Frankie, half smiling. Her eyes appeared moist, but it might have been the way the green of her iris reflected the light, the same green as Frankie's, but there was no revelation here. Frankie already knew that they had the same color eyes. Lenny had often said so, as if to establish some connection between son and mother, and Frankie had seen the single resemblance in the picture on Lenny's dresser and again in the picture on the computer.

The discomfort in his neck and thigh where bullets had pierced, the fan of pictures across his sheets, the longing for Gennaro were much realer and more relevant to Frankie than this petite, tailored woman with short blond hair wearing an olive-colored gauze pant suit and the kind of jewelry one might find at a trendy craft show. She just happened to be his long-lost mother, and he just happened to have her eyes. Meeting her, Frankie felt neither happy nor angry, nor even sad. At that moment, she was the least of his concerns — so he told himself. But then a person can absorb only so much change.

"I'm sorry, Frankie."

About what? he thought. This is how life will be—meaningless small talk with new and meaningless people.

"Do you remember, Gennaro?" he said. "He was about two when you left."

"Well, yes, I think ..."

"You think?" he said. This is what will happen with new people I meet. They'll never know how special Gennaro was. They'll never hear his beautiful tenor voice or see the way his hair and eyes caught the light as if he had been born to shine. Like a shooting star.

Knowing that every second that passed brought him further away from Gennaro washed over Frankie like a wave, and he feared that he might sob, but didn't want Vi to think that he was sobbing for her. He tried to stifle his thoughts of Gennaro and time passing by gathering the cartoline postale strewn across his lap, and he stacked them face down on his nightstand.

Vi spoke very slowly, as if she were contemplating every word before she said it. "That was a long time ago, Frankie ... But I remember that Marie had children. In fact, she was pregnant when, well, when I had you.

"That was Lena," Frankie said.

"Yes, so Gennaro was a toddler then."

"But do you remember him?" Frankie repeated as if he needed her to remember, as if that was the only chance she had to really be his mother. If she couldn't tell him something he didn't know about Gennaro, about how she saw him take his first steps, or how his tiny hand felt against hers, then Frankie had no use for her. She may as well leave.

"Well, I think so." Vi pulled a chair close to the bed. "Do you mind if I sit. I'm feeling a little queasy."

"Maybe you should call my father," Frankie said.

"No, I'll be okay, unless you'd rather I call him."

"Yes, I think you should." Frankie was startled by his own abruptness, but before he had the chance to apologize, Vi left the room. When she and Lenny returned, he pretended to be asleep.

Lenny apologized to Vi. He blamed the medication. She said that she understood. They spoke in hushed tones like parents concerned for their ailing child, and for the briefest moment, Frankie thought to open his eyes, but it was easier not to.

He heard them leave and soon he did fall asleep and, when he woke, the shades were drawn and the room was dark except for the glow of a small pen flashlight that Lenny shone on the pages of the book he was reading.

"You're still here," Frankie said.

Lenny closed his book and switched on the nightlight above Frankie's bed. "It's not that late," he said. "They're just bringing the trays around for lunch."

"Guess I woke up too early." They both chuckled as the smell of hospital food wafted into the room.

"So what did you think?" Lenny asked.

Frankie figured he was talking about Vi. "To be honest, I didn't think much about her."

"You said that it was okay for her to visit you."

"And I'm still okay that she visited. I just don't care. I didn't have much to say to her. She said that she was sorry. Okay, she's sorry. What else is there? We're all sorry about something."

Lenny didn't respond. He smiled and nodded as a food service worker entered the room. Her bubbly voice filled the quiet. She cranked up Frankie's bed and said that Frankie was looking better every day and that if only she were 20 years younger. She placed the food tray on the portable table that stretched across Frankie's lap. When she removed the tray's cover she announced "Spaghetti!" as if she were performing a magic trick.

Frankie was tempted to respond *If you say so*, but instead he just smiled and said: "Thank you." She vanished as quickly as she had appeared.

Lenny opened his book again and alternated between reading and glancing at Frankie as Frankie ate the Jell-O, sipped milk through a straw, but passed on the spaghetti.

"You know the doctors say that you can leave soon … probably tomorrow," Lenny said. "No more hospital food."

"Have you opened the store yet?"

"Not yet. I've been here, remember?"

"Oh, that's right," Frankie said. "Guess I won't be going back to school for the last semester after all. Remember you had mentioned that I had all my credits and there was no need to go back. You were right. No need. I can help you in the store." Frankie picked at a small cup of sherbet.

"You know, Frankie, Vi cancelled her flight back to California so you two could try again."

"I didn't ask her to do that."

"I know, but I was just wondering if I should tell her to come visit again or …"

"Are you still in love with Vi?" Frankie surprised himself with this question. He had been thinking that the smell of the spaghetti was turning his stomach, and suddenly the words just spilled out like vomit.

"This isn't about me, Frankie."

"It isn't about me either." He felt as if he might explode, dropped his spoon, and grabbed the stack of cartoline postale. "This is about me, but you want to talk about Vi. I don't give a fuck about Vi." By now Frankie was sobbing. "They loved each other as much as Gennaro and I loved each other. We were their second chance. Now there's no chance, no chance for anything."

Lenny turned the table away, sat on the bed, held Frankie and rocked him back and forth as the screaming in Frankie's head continued to pour from his mouth.

"I don't give a fuck about Vi … no one shot her … she left … it's Gennaro I want back, not Vi … it's Gennaro … please … it's Gennaro I want."

A nurse rushed into the room, but Lenny held up his hand.

"But the other patients," she said.

"Just close the door," Lenny pleaded with the nurse. "I promise he'll be calm in a minute." Lenny kicked off his shoes, pushed the tray away from the bed, lay down next to Frankie, and slipped his arm under Frankie's shoulder. He dimmed the nightlight. Frankie's sobs subsided while they lay next to each other in the shadows, like when Frankie was a small boy and Lenny rescued him from nightmares, but there was no waking up from this nightmare.

"I loved him," Frankie said.

"I know," Lenny responded.

"I mean I really loved him."

"I know," Lenny repeated.

26

It was one of those icy cold winter days when everything felt as if it were about to shatter. Lenny parked the car in front of their house while Angie clutched at her heavy sweater, descended the front stoop, crossed the sidewalk, and opened the car door on the front passenger side. Her "Welcome home, Frankie," condensed on the frigid air.

Neighbors hidden under winter bulk rushed in and out of Johnny Boo-Boo's and Panisi's. Mourners in black huddled in front of Romano's. What was once Captain Beltrani's store was being renovated into a betting parlor, and men carried sheetrock through the new front entrance. Only Lasante's was quiet. A CLOSED sign hung in the front door.

Angie helped Frankie out of the car, and, just as he feared, a neighbor passed as they approached the front stoop. The old woman grabbed Frankie's arms, almost knocking the cane out of his hand, and kissed him. A sharp pain stabbed at his neck. She rambled on in Italian—something about the Madonna—without noticing that Frankie winced. Angie intervened, also in Italian, and the woman nodded, kissed Frankie again, this time more gently, and shuffled around the corner, clutching a mesh shopping bag with a pastry box from Panisi's.

"Are you alright?" Angie asked.

Frankie nodded.

Inside, the house smelled of sauce—a welcome change from the stench of hospital mush in hot plastic trays. It would just be the three of them at the dinner table—Frankie's request—no other family members to celebrate his homecoming.

As he lay on the living room couch gazing through the archway into the dining room, he recalled the days after Filomena's death and the many family and friends who spilled from the kitchen and dining

room into the living room. The routines of life had been interrupted
—people traveled from great distances to mourn and pay their respects at the wake, funeral, and round-the-clock meals, which marked
Filomena's passing. Watching Angie set the dining room table for three
seemed too run-of-the-mill—as if Gennaro's death had changed nothing, though in fact, for Frankie, everything had changed.

He had missed the ways that Gennaro's death had interrupted life.
He knew the personal grief, the constant dull ache that without warning escalated into excruciating pain, and he knew only too well the
details of Gennaro's death, but what he didn't know were the details of
how his death had, if only for a few days, cast a pall over 104th Street.

Angie swept from the dining room into the living room, gathered
her apron between her hands to wipe them, reminding Frankie of Filomena. "As soon as your father comes in we'll eat," she said and turned
back towards the kitchen.

Frankie called to her from the couch, and she paused and looked
at him through the kitchen and dining room archways.

"Please tell me about Gennaro's wake." She frowned, and Frankie
feared she might refuse, but she stepped into the dining room, removed her apron, draped it over the back of a dinning room chair, and
sat on the rug next to Frankie.

This is how Lenny found them when he entered the house. Angie
sitting on the oriental carpet next to the couch, her legs curled up
under her, and her hand holding Frankie's while he lay on the couch.
Lenny removed his coat and sat quietly without interrupting.

At some point the three of them moved into the dining room
where Lenny served dinner, starting with antipasto, and Angie continued to speak of Gennaro's wake and funeral—how handsome he
had looked, all the people who were there, the eulogies, the music, the
flowers. And Frankie asked her many questions, more than she could
possibly answer accurately, but she answered nonetheless, weaving
what might have been yarns about the many ways that Gennaro's
death had interrupted life on 104th Street. Frankie saw the crowds and
heard the choir. He smelled the overwhelming fragrance of the scores
of floral arrangements and felt the press of many hands against his,
but he couldn't, or wouldn't, see Gennaro—not in a casket, no matter
how beautiful he might have looked.

27

Being home, back in the familiar, there was no ignoring Gennaro's absence, even during Frankie's most private moments—especially in those private moments—when he inhaled the musk of his own body, but yearned for Gennaro's scent, or when he touched himself pretending it was Gennaro's touch and closed his eyes to see whom he could no longer see with his eyes open. Sometimes his fantasies were so vivid that he'd smile and forget for the briefest moment that it was his own hand giving him relief, *pleasure* was too strong a word. A sudden stab in his neck or thigh reminded him that pleasure had its price.

And often thoughts of Gennaro's body also ushered memories of Christmas night. In sleep, Frankie no longer walked the beaches of Taormina, but woke to the sound of gunshots and lay alone in the incredible void that had replaced Gennaro.

On his laptop, he watched videos of Gennaro over and over, and on his cellphone he listened to Gennaro's saved messages, but when the pain of remembering became too strong, he no longer watched or listened, until the missing outweighed the pain of remembering. Grief was a war between missing and remembering, but there was no comfort in forgetting. That time would help him forget was a terrifying thought, more terrifying than the memory of gunshots.

He placed the cartoline postale against photos and videos on his laptop, their warm sepia looked incongruous against the laptop's cold titanium, as incongruous as his life without Gennaro. And the visits from well-meaning family and friends only reminded him more of Gennaro's absence. Another conversation without Gennaro's voice. "Not everything needs to turn into such a production," was Gennaro's standard retort. Now everything felt as if it mattered too much, but also didn't matter at all, as if life had become a chain of contradictions.

One night, Angie mentioned that the spring semester would soon begin, and that she would have to spend most nights back at her place in Manhattan. She stared at the television. Frankie thought of Vi, which surprised him. He hadn't thought of her at all since he came home.

"I guess Vi will also start teaching soon," he said. Since Angie simply nodded, Frankie assumed that she knew about Vi's visit. Lenny looked up from reading the newspaper.

"You know, I wasn't asleep when you and Vi came back in the room," Frankie said. "I just didn't feel like talking. I didn't know what else to say."

Lenny put down the newspaper and examined the palms of his hands. "A couple of weeks out of the store and my hands have gone soft. Guess they just have to toughen up again."

"Did you miss the store?" Frankie asked.

"Not at all."

"Have you ever thought of selling it?"

"Do you want an honest answer?"

Frankie nodded.

"There've been times when that's all I've thought about."

Frankie didn't respond. On the carpet next to the piano a single strip of Christmas tree tinsel caught Frankie's eye. From where he sat, he could also see the picture of the Last Supper hanging above the credenza in the dining room, where less than two months ago Gennaro admired his own reflection in the glass. "Like an omen," Gennaro had said about the picture. Now only the chandelier lights reflected in the glass.

"Yes, Vi will have to leave soon for California," Lenny said.

"Makes sense to me, or she'll have to talk very loud so her students can hear her," Frankie said.

Lenny told Frankie to stop being such a smartass, followed by Angie suggesting that the apple doesn't fall far from the tree. The three of them chuckled and looked back at the television where talking heads discussed the upcoming inauguration of the first African American President.

"Pretty remarkable," Angie said, but for Frankie it was just another reminder of how life would continue to change without Gennaro. When the news went to a commercial, Lenny again returned to the topic of Vi, and Frankie released a loud sigh.

"I get it," Lenny said, "but you brought her up and maybe there's a reason for that ..." Frankie tried to interrupt, but Lenny held up his hand as he did to the nurse in the hospital when Frankie became so upset. "Just let me get this out. After that it's up to you. I promise. You see, there's someone else you might want to meet before Vi returns to California." Lenny leaned forward and the folded newspaper slipped from his lap onto the carpet. "You have a sister."

28

Marie was peeling eggplants when she noticed Lenny through the glass of the kitchen door. She grabbed the counter. Lena opened the door and Lenny rushed to Marie to keep her from collapsing onto the floor. He led her to a chair while she sobbed. "Our boys, Lenny, our beautiful boys. Gennaro is gone. What will we do? What can we do?" Like her mother-in-law had done years ago and only a few houses away, Marie cried for a son lost to the violence of vindictive men.

Lenny hadn't seen Big Vinny since he was arrested. Neither Big Vinny nor Marie came to visit Frankie in the hospital or at home. Either they had surmised that Lenny blamed Big Vinny for what had happened, or given their greater loss, they expected Lenny to pay his respects first. Whatever their reason for not visiting Frankie, it was time for Lenny to break the ice, if in fact there was ice to be broken. Marie clasped her hands around Lenny's and apologized for not coming to see Frankie.

"I couldn't," she said. "I knew I would fall apart and just upset him. Please tell him I love him. You know he's a son to me, especially now that my beautiful Gennaro is gone."

Lenny remained silent for fear of crying himself and wondered if Big Vinny was home. Where else would he be? Since he was released from prison, few neighbors had seen him about, with the exception of attending Gennaro's wake and funeral. Since the funeral, neighbors sometimes spotted him sitting in the passenger seat of his Lincoln, while Scungilli drove. Lenny assumed that he was home and heard Marie, but that he had become numb to her crying.

Like an old Italian woman, Marie pulled a tissue from her sleeve and wiped her tears, and she wore all black. Before Christmas night,

Lenny would have found her dress to be an irritating example of how neighbors stubbornly clung to old ways, but now he was moved and oddly comforted by her appearance—the black mourning clothes, including dark stockings, even the knot of tear-soaked tissue under her sleeve. It was familiar and predictable when little else was. As a girl, Marie was a livewire, a good match for Big Vinny—not only in style, but also in temperament. She never let him boss her around. It broke Lenny's heart to see her like this, but it also felt right, as if her appearance was an open window into her misery. No sense pretending that everything was fine when it wasn't. There was a simple honesty in her attire that before now Lenny wouldn't have appreciated. Marie regained her composure, sighed, and sat erect. With her blond hair brushed back into a bun, she resembled the clichéd image of Eva Perón.

"Coffee?" Marie said. Without waiting for Lenny's reply, she told Lena to make a fresh pot of coffee and to get the pastries out of the refrigerator.

Lena buzzed about the kitchen. She had Big Vinny's mannerisms and his personality, but she had her mother's features, something Frankie once thought was also true about Gennaro, until he saw the cartoline.

"This will take a few minutes," Lena said. "If you want to see my father, he's upstairs." Like Big Vinny, Lena's suggestions sounded like orders. Marie's hands stiffened on Lenny's when Lena mentioned Big Vinny, and she pulled them away as if she were giving Lenny permission to leave.

"I'll be right back," Lenny said.

Marie shrugged her shoulders and frowned. Lena sighed and rolled her eyes.

"Stop it, Ma," Lena said.

"Mind your own business," Marie responded.

The bedroom door was ajar. Big Vinny's bulk overwhelmed a chair next to a heavily laced bay of windows while he pressed a cellphone to his ear, and his black eyes flashed towards Lenny. It was a spacious bedroom, white with pink and gold accents and an alcove sitting area—much larger, brighter, and more airy than any of the rooms in Lenny's house—and the furniture looked too dainty and fragile to contain Big Vinny. Lenny had been in this room once before, years ago, after Big Vinny had had the house renovated and invited the Lasantes over for dinner and the grand tour. Angie had whispered to Lenny that the house looked like a bordello, but Filomena overheard her and gave them both a sharp look.

Big Vinny was a comical contrast to the otherwise delicate scene. He motioned for Lenny to enter the room as if summoning an employee who was late for a meeting, and he continued to shout into his phone. "No need. I'll call the wives. I'll call you back later about the time." He slipped his phone into his pants pocket and pointed towards an empty chair. "Sit. You won't be comfortable, but it's better than standing. You know women's taste—all about show."

Despite having been mostly housebound since he left prison, and then losing his son—the son that he made no bones about calling his favorite—Big Vinny acted unruffled. However, there were telltale changes in his appearance. He was thinner; there were patches of missed stubble under his chin; and his hair wasn't slicked back.

"That was my lawyer. The judge finally came to his senses and granted that my boys be released on bail. I'll have them home by tonight. No trial date yet, but they'll be home where they belong. They'll never hang that cabbie's murder on them anyway, and everything else, even the stuff they're trying to pin on me is a bunch of crap. Their evidence has more holes in it than the Swiss cheese you sell. We'll see. We'll just see. They claim that they got someone who heard my boys talk about getting that fucking cabdriver, but I don't believe it. The cops have been questioning people, but if someone squealed I'd know about it. The cops are full of shit. They got nothing because there's nothing to get."

Lenny's jaw went tense. He had no patience for Big Vinny's bravado.

"I'm sorry about Gennaro," he said, keeping his condolence brief despite or because of the many words that pressed against his tongue —words that would serve no other purpose than to punish Big Vinny. The cabdriver had paid dearly for disrupting Big Vinny's block party, and in turn so had Gennaro and Frankie, but so did Big Vinny. *Despite all his bullshit, he doesn't need me to make things worse*, Lenny thought, so he bit his tongue.

Sunlight shone through the lace curtains and betrayed Big Vinny's stony, tough-guy charade—his tired eyes, untrimmed nails, misaligned buttons on his shirt—all minor details, but, if nothing else, Big Vinny was always about the details and appearance.

"Lena said Frankie is doing better," he said.

"Yes, physically he is."

They both nodded and, after a long awkward silence, they exchanged small talk about Lenny's siblings. Lena called them down for coffee just as Big Vinny mentioned that he had heard about VI's visit.

Lenny welcomed Lena's interruption.

The kitchen table was set for two—no sign of Marie or Lena. "Marie won't join us," Big Vinny said. "She blames me."

Big Vinny poured the espresso into demitasse cups, offered Lenny a pastry, added a few drops of anisette to his coffee, and stirred it. "She put up a good front at the wake and funeral to save face, but otherwise she hasn't spoken to me. Mothers have to blame someone." Big Vinny blew across the top of his coffee and took a sip. "Like when my brother was killed in Nam. My room was right next to my parents' room, and I could hear them arguing. My mother acted like it was my old man's fault that my brother was killed, like a father can protect his children from everything."

Bullshit, Lenny thought. There was no comparison to be made between Big Vinny's brother's death and Gennaro's. Marie had every right to blame Big Vinny. That she could live in the same house with him after Gennaro's murder amazed Lenny. He had already given his condolences, now all he wanted was to leave. Unfortunately, his coffee was too hot to down.

"I don't blame Marie, a father should protect his family," Big Vinny said. "Don't worry, Lenny, that little bastard won't get away with this."

At first Lenny was confused by Big Vinny's comment, but then he realized that Big Vinny was talking about the cabdriver's son. That kid was as good as dead.

"Not just for Gennaro, but for Frankie," Big Vinny said. "Even if we had lost Frankie instead of Gennaro, I'd still make sure that that little fuck would pay. You know that, but you didn't hear me say this. Eat a pastry." Big Vinny pushed the plate towards Lenny.

"Enough talking about that little prick!" Big Vinny announced as

if someone else had been forcing him to speak. He downed his espresso. "By the way, have you heard about old man Tucci?"

Lenny was relieved to change the subject, but before he had the
chance to answer, Big Vinny added: "He's in a nursing home. Alz-
heimer's, his sister said."

"Tucci's sister called to tell you this?" Lenny was surprised that
she had contacted him.

Big Vinny poured himself another cup of espresso and added a
few drops of anisette. "More?" he said.

Lenny raised his hand and shook his head. The sound of a television came from another room.

"I guess she mostly called about the house," Big Vinny said. "No
need to get into the details, but awhile ago Tucci had some money
problems. You remember. Unpaid taxes and some other things. You
know he liked his liquor, not to talk bad about the old man. We all got
our weaknesses. Anyway, as his sister said, she's moved him to a nursing home. He's in pretty bad shape. It's to the point that he forgets a
lot of shit. Anyway, now that he can't live there anymore, there's no
sense in keeping it."

"Keeping what?" Lenny said.

"The house. The property. What else would I be talking about?

"You mean you own it?" Lenny placed the demitasse in its saucer.

"You knew that," Big Vinny said, which was more bullshit. This
was a typical Big Vinny DiCico move. Act as if someone should know
something when he knew damn well that he had never mentioned anything about whatever the subject might be, in this case Tucci's house.

He shrugged his shoulders, blew across the top of his espresso and
took a sip. He looked as comical pinching the handle of the demitasse
cup between his large thumb and pointer finger as he had sitting on
the little chair in the bedroom.

"The Lasantes were not the only family to help the old man. What
else could I do? As I said, he had money problems. This was years ago.
You probably forgot. We got a lot of history there. And our kids liked
the place, especially Genna ..." Big Vinny sucked in a deep breath and
cleared his throat. "You know how Frankie and him loved going there.
Maybe ..."

He finished his espresso, put down the demitasse, and waved his hand as if shooing away thoughts. "No matter. That's water under the bridge. As I said, there's no need to keep it now. Maybe you and Frankie want to go up one more time before I sell it. No rush. Gotta have work done on it anyway. Tucci wasn't exactly a Mister Fixit."

There were pieces of this story that Lenny didn't understand, but he was used to that with Big Vinny. He searched for a response. "Maybe we can all go," spilled out before he realized that with Gennaro gone "all" was the wrong word.

Big Vinny frowned and shook his head. "I don't think so."

"I'm sorry, Vinny. I meant ..."

"Forget it, Lenny. I know what you meant. I haven't been there in a long time. I don't like the country."

They reminisced about Tucci, and for a while Lenny forgot how much he had wanted to leave. Finally, it was Big Vinny who cut short their conversation by mentioning that he had to call his daughters-in-law and give them the good news about Michael and Jimmy. "I have to tell Marie and Lena too, or at least Lena and she'll tell Marie. Life is too short for this nonsense. As if Marie's the only one who misses Gennaro." Big Vinny shook his head and pulled a rumpled handkerchief from his pocket and blew his nose, reminding Lenny of the knot of tissue in Marie's sleeve.

"Thank you for stopping by, Lenny. And there's no rush for you and Frankie to go to Tucci's. Whenever. Just let me know after you've said goodbye to the old place."

Lenny nodded, and they shook hands. "Frankie will be okay," Big Vinny said. "He's young ... he's smart, like you ... he'll be okay ... you'll see. We survive, Lenny. That's what our grandfathers and fathers did. And that's what we do. What other choice is there? Life ain't no fucking fiesta. We both know that."

Lenny's eyes swelled with tears. Big Vinny released his hand. "Say goodbye to Marie before you leave. It's good for her to talk. This is a lousy thing. My mother went through it. Now Marie. I guess my grandmother also went through it. Bad enough that these women married DiCico men, but they also lost DiCico sons. Too much, but I can't do a fucking thing about it."

Marie sat knitting and half watching a soap opera. She held up the almost finished baby blanket. "For my grandson," she said. "Although, he needs another baby blanket like he needs another head. But I have to keep busy." Her voice cracked. They talked about Gennaro until the hint of light that found its way through the heavily draped windows had all but faded.

Outside was cold, and Lenny pulled his jacket collar up around his neck, shoved his hands into his pockets, and thought of Rocco Tucci. Had Big Vinny helped Tucci out of kindness, or did he steal an old, vulnerable man's house and land out from under him? *Who knows and who cares?* Lenny told himself, except he did care, but he wasn't sure if it was about Tucci or Big Vinny or if it was just one more loss to grieve.

Along 104th Street, lit windows looked out from what were once open porches but had long been renovated into an extra bedroom or TV room or office. Lenny could list the names of every family who lived in every house and how long they had lived there and, in many cases, who had lived there before them. Like Marie's black dress, this was oddly comforting. And focusing on who lived where distracted Lenny from dwelling on the question that Frankie had asked him in the hospital—*Are you still in love with Vi?*—which had nagged at him ever since like a leaky faucet that refused to be shut. While reading or watching television or talking to a customer, it was drip by drip: *Are you ... still in love ... with Vi?*

Lenny knew that he once loved her, and he missed loving her. That was the closest he could come to an answer, but the question persisted as if unsatisfied with such a measured response.

Walking next to the low brick wall that separated the sidewalk from the Lasantes' yard, Lenny saw the shadows and heard the murmurs of summer ghosts. From under the arbor came the smell of cigar smoke, where Leonardo, Vincenzo, and Giacomo sat playing cards and talking about baseball, and from an open kitchen window came the smell of sauce and the sound of Lucia, Filomena, and Rosa's laughter. Tony sat on a blanket near the hydrangeas while Amelia and Irish tried to coax him to eat his baby food. Angie wore long thick braids and sat on the stoop outside the kitchen door with her nose in a book while Big Vinny called up to Lenny's bedroom window. "Aren't you done with your homework yet? My brother Sal is gonna take us for lemon ice."

"In a minute. I'll be right down." Lenny's young voice, filled with hope and anticipation, burst through the screen of the second story window.

As Lenny neared the warehouse, he heard Vi's giggle and the sound of keys. He paused and looked back over the yard at other memories, including baptisms, first communions, confirmations, graduations, and of course the day Vi and he married. She looked beautiful. Nothing could change that. And on the day of Frankie's baptism, it was Filomena, Angie, and Marie who took turns holding Frankie, while Big Vinny, Michael, Jimmy, and Tony set up the tables and chairs for the party. Gennaro hobbled around the yard. "Vinny, watch out for Gennaro," Marie said, and Big Vinny lifted Gennaro and blew raspberries into his exposed belly. Gennaro shrieked with joy.

As soon as Lenny stepped into the yard, the summer ghosts vanished and, through the kitchen window, he saw Frankie sitting at the table. No longer an infant, or a boy, but a young man who had survived a nightmare. Frankie looked up when Lenny entered the kitchen. He held an open book and next to the book were several cartoline.

"Interesting book?" Lenny said. He removed his jacket.

"Kind of. It's about Wilhelm von Gloeden. I ordered it online. Great-Grandpa is famous." Frankie held out the open book to a page with a photograph identical to the cartolina postale they assumed to be of Leonardo. Under the photograph were the words *Sicilian Youth*.

Lenny's cellphone vibrated. It was a text from Vi, and he showed it to Frankie: "Since our last conversation, I explained everything to Ina. She's very excited about meeting Frankie. Time? Remember our return flight is Tuesday morning."

"So what do you think?" Lenny said. "Tomorrow night? Dinner?"

Frankie shrugged his shoulders and placed the open book back on the table in front of him. He turned to the next page. "Tomorrow night is fine."

"Any other pictures like the ones we have?" Lenny asked.

"Maybe."

"Maybe you'll show me later."

Frankie didn't answer, and Lenny left him at the table, reading and probably angry for interrupting his comments about the cartoline postale with Vi's text. *I should have waited and listened to what he had to say*, Lenny thought.

He paused on his way up the stairs and considered telling Frankie about Rocco Tucci, but decided not to, at least not now.

The next day, early afternoon, Frankie managed the store alone while Lenny prepared sauce for dinner. First Lenny mixed chop meat, milk, eggs, breadcrumbs, raisins, and seasoning for the meatballs. He rolled each meatball and placed it on a platter while his thoughts drifted to earlier that morning, when he had hurt Tootsie's feelings. He flattened slices of beef and pork with a mallet, topped each slice with a paste made from parsley, chopped garlic, pignoli, and raisins moistened with olive oil, then rolled the braciole, tied each one with white thread, added them to the platter with meatballs, and berated himself for having been so careless with Tootsie's feelings. He browned the meatballs, braciole, and a few sausages in a large cast-iron frying pan, and pictured Mrs. Greco, so bent over that she arched her neck like a turtle to look up at him, when Tootsie breezed into the store. The way Tootsie held his gaze made Lenny think of the first time that he met Vi, and the way he stared back may have given her the wrong impression. Lenny turned the browning gravy meat with a fork. He certainly couldn't have told Tootsie that he was thinking about Vi. Mrs. Greco rapped on the counter with her gnarled fingers, and Lenny stopped staring at Tootsie and handed the old woman the bag containing a half-pound of fresh ricotta wrapped in wax paper. She eyed Tootsie.

"I used to buy my ricotta at Pentaro's," she said, "but I can't cross the avenue so fast no more. My daughter, she buys me that lousy ricotta in the plastic containers. Beh! It tastes like wallpaper paste no matter how much sugar you put on it."

Tootsie gave Mrs. Greco a puckered smile and a nod as if she were forcing empathy through a sphincter.

"Hey, ain't you that girl who used to work in Panisi's? But you used to be fatter."

At this Tootsie laughed, but Lenny was embarrassed and suggested to Mrs. Greco that she go home to refrigerate the ricotta before it spoiled.

Tootsie in fact had lost weight and she wore less makeup. She had also begun classes in cosmetology. *Maybe she was practicing on herself,* Lenny thought.

She held the door opened for Mrs. Greco, who paused again and for the second time stared at her. "I see you at Mass. You held the door open for me there, too."

Mrs. Greco turned to Lenny. "Nice girl. You could do worse."

Finally the old woman left.

"Smarter than she looks," Tootsie said and chuckled.

Lenny cleared his throat and asked about Tyrone. Tootsie often brought him with her to visit Frankie, and Lenny had grown fond of the boy.

"I dropped him off early at school," Tootsie said. "They got one of those before school programs. I just came from Mass and thought maybe Frankie might be in the store."

She often stopped at the store after Mass even though Lenny told her each time that Frankie slept late. So again, Lenny repeated: "He's still sleeping, but he'll be down soon to help out. He's been working a lot in the store. Nights are still hard for him, so he sleeps in. He has his days and nights mixed up a little."

"Baby steps," Tootsie said. "Well, I just thought I'd stop by. I've got to get to work. How about Tyrone and me come over to see Frankie tonight?"

"Sure. Why don't you come for ..." Lenny remembered that Vi was coming for dinner, and he tried to explain, but Tootsie cut him short.

"Another time," she said, and left before Lenny had the chance to apologize.

He regretted not calling her back or chasing after her, though what would he have said? The truth was he looked forward to Vi coming for dinner—more than he was willing to admit to himself, never mind admit to Tootsie, but he still regretted having hurt her feelings.

He added the browned gravy meat to a saucepot where garlic

browned·in olive oil, and he berated himself again for not inviting
Tootsie to dinner. But how would that have worked? *Ina! Don't forget this
is the first time we're meeting Ina*, he thought as he opened three large cans
of plum tomatoes, poured the contents into a blender, pressed high for
a few seconds, and poured the pulp into the mill propped over the
saucepot. The juice showered upon the golden garlic and gravy meat
and the kitchen sizzled with his parents' and grandparents' whispers
about him making excuses for hurting Tootsie's feelings and chatter
about little things, like preparing sauce and not overcooking the macaroni. Once the sauce bubbled, he reduced the flame and their voices
became more subdued. He added parsley and basil, a touch of oregano,
and a pinch of sugar. He left the sauce, his parents and grandparents
mumbling, and his guilt to simmer.

In the store, Doug Turner and Frankie were just finishing lunch.

"There's the boss," Doug said. "Frankie told me you're preparing
a feast for tonight."

"Not exactly," Lenny said.

"What's the occasion?"

"Just someone we haven't seen in a while."

Frankie removed his apron and excused himself. "Nice talking
with you, Mr. Turner. I have to go in the house for a few minutes."

"Sure, Frankie, I'll see you later, and you make a mean hero. Better than your father."

Frankie smiled and walked towards the steps to the breezeway.

"He's looking good," Doug said, "real good. He's going to be fine
—you'll see. Smart, just like his father."

"You sound like Big Vinny," Lenny said.

"Shit. That can't be good."

Lenny wiped the grease from the slicing machine. Traces of prosciutto clung to the blade. "It's Frankie's mom who's coming for dinner
tonight. She's bringing his half sister. He's never met his sister—neither have I. I just found out about her myself, and when I told Frankie,
he seemed to take the news okay."

"Wow!" Doug stroked stubble on his chin. His hands were large,
calloused, and stained with grease. Like Lenny's, they were a workingman's hands. "And you?" Doug said. "How are you doing with all this?"

"Hey, if Obama can survive the Republicans, I can deal with having dinner with my ex-wife." They both laughed, but Lenny had never called Vi his ex-wife until now, and the words felt odd on his tongue.

"To this day, when I see my ex-wife," Doug said, "I still get a pain. Like a doctor taking a scalpel to my wallet without using anesthesia."

They laughed again, but Lenny was stuck on the word ex-wife. For so long he had referred to Vi as Frankie's mother, or when talking to Frankie, as *your mother*—ex-wife felt more personal.

"Seems to me you got a lot of women trouble going on," Doug said.

"What do you mean?"

"Your ex is coming for a fancy dinner, and I've told you plenty of times that Tootsie has a thing for you."

Lenny again thought of Tootsie storming out of the store this morning. He feigned laughter. "And I told you, you're imagining things."

"Ahh ..." Deep creases formed around Doug's frown.

"And it's not a feast."

"If you say so, Brother." Doug nodded and raised his thumb as he left the store. "I'll catch you tomorrow, and you can tell me all about it."

For the rest of the afternoon Lenny and Frankie took turns working in the store so Lenny could check on the sauce. At 5:00, Lenny locked the front door and turned the sign to read CLOSED—no explanation. He was sure to face the wrath of customers the next day.

29

Frankie showered while Lenny set the dining room table with Filomena's good china and Lucia's silverware and crystal stemware. Despite the number of times Filomena and Angie had told him on which side of the plate to place forks and knives, he never remembered, so he guessed, but then rearranged them. He found cloth napkins with embroidered edges in the credenza, but the embroidery on the napkins didn't match the embroidery on the tablecloth. He searched for matching napkins until the whole thing struck him as ridiculous. *We used to screw in a warehouse not at the Waldorf*, he thought, and removed the silverware, set out the napkins with embroidery that didn't match the tablecloth, and rearranged the silverware again.

"Are you going to propose?" Frankie stood under the arch between the living and dining rooms. His hair was wet and he wore jeans and a t-shirt. "Looks like I'm underdressed."

"The only proposal I'm making tonight is that you be polite. And you look fine."

"Don't worry. I'll be a good boy, but you might want to shower and change. Smelling like provolone doesn't go well with crystal."

Lenny ruffled Frankie's wet mop of curls. "Is this a good idea, Frankie?"

"We'll see," Frankie said. "What's the worse that could happen? I've already been shot."

Lenny was stunned, but Frankie just shrugged his shoulders and walked into the kitchen.

Frankie's comment lingered as Lenny undressed. *Frankie was right. Whatever happens tonight will seem trivial compared to what Frankie survived.* But as Lenny stepped under the hot shower and was enveloped in steam, he couldn't shake his anxiety. He knew he was as anxious for himself as he was for Frankie.

Vincenzo's sudden death not only changed the course of Lenny's life from scholar to surrogate father and grocer, but it fettered his youth, especially young romance, or at least placed it on hiatus until Vi entered the store and his life.

Lenny may have been her senior by 11 years, but she was the experienced woman, and he was the neophyte who enjoyed being impulsive, secretive, and sexual. Although brief, their relationship had been intense. Maybe it was that intensity rather than Vi that he missed. Maybe he had become addicted to their secret encounters in the warehouse. Or maybe it was more than that. Once they were discovered by the Ronzoni deliveryman, and even after they were married, Lenny's passion for Vi only intensified. Sure, their romps in the warehouse were exciting, but on their wedding night, with friends and family knowing that Vi and he were a couple, he found her even more desirable. His lust for Vi never waned, it just also became love.

After Lenny showered and shaved he studied the grays in his hair and the lines in his face in the bathroom mirror, and he ran his fingers over the veins in his arms. He had the look of a workingman, someone who had spent his life lifting, slicing, and bagging rather than sitting behind a desk or standing at a podium. No matter how thoroughly he scrubbed out the smell of the store or how closely he shaved or how carefully he brushed his hair, and whether he wore a grocer's apron or a three-piece suit, he'd still be Hard Luck Lenny. A few weeks earlier such thoughts would have depressed him, maybe triggered a full-blown anxiety attack, but now he dismissed them with a sigh and a shrug, even a chuckle, and his anxiety dissipated like early morning fog yielding to a new day. Frankie was right about having been shot, and Lenny almost lost him, but didn't. This was nothing compared to that.

Lenny stared at his nakedness in the mirror. *I'm still not so bad,* Lenny thought. The night he walked Tootsie home from the train station there was no pity in her eyes when she invited him up to her apartment. She wanted him for who he was, not for who he might have been. And truth was it had been Vi who kept returning to the store with phony excuses that first day they met. She had pursued him. Sure that was over eighteen years ago, but there was some consolation in remembering that. Lenny dressed, and as he buttoned his button down white shirt and tucked his shirttails in his creased black slacks, he thought that for better or worse tonight would eventually become last night. *This too shall pass.*

Dinner preparations went smoothly. Lenny made the salad, Frankie sliced the bread and placed the pot of water on the stove to boil. After Vi and Ina arrived, Frankie attended to the macaroni, and after he drained it and poured it into a bowl, Lenny added the sauce and ricotta, and Frankie poured the extra sauce into another bowl.

They arrived promptly at 7. Except for her hazel eyes, Ina was a seven-year-old version of Vi. She removed her coat and boots without any help and, when Lenny told her that Frankie was in the kitchen, she went off looking for him.

"Bashful, isn't she?" Vi said, chuckling.

Lenny helped Vi off with her coat. She sat on the ottoman, skewed her legs to one side, removed her boots, slipped on a pair of high heels and, as she stretched the back straps of her shoes over the heel of each foot, her calves flexed under dark hose. She wore a simple, long sleeve, slim fitting, black dress, and Lenny thought that maybe he should have looked for the napkins that matched the tablecloth. Many women on 104th Street wore black dresses, *but they didn't look like Vi*, Lenny sighed.

In the hospital he had been too distracted, too concerned about Frankie to really appreciate that Vi was still a very pretty woman — slimmer than she once was but still round where it counted, according to Lenny, given his imprinting from Captain Beltrani's long-ago pictures of nude Rubenesque beauties. His eyes followed the curve of Vi's legs to the hem of her dress. As her eyes examined the living room, his eyes examined her.

"Nothing's changed," Lenny said, but immediately regretted his words. Vi didn't answer. He followed her into the dining room where Ina was holding a water glass for Frankie to fill.

"Guess there's no need for me to introduce the two of you," Vi said.

"No, Mommy. I already told Frankie who I am."

Frankie smiled. He approached Vi and kissed her cheek. "Sorry for being a jerk in the hospital." Before Vi had the chance to respond, Frankie turned back to Ina. "Okay, let's see if the water is boiling for the macaroni." Ina followed him back to the kitchen.

Given that she was a bit plump and had long blond hair, Ina more closely resembled the Vi Lenny had first met than the Vi who now ran her fingers along the dining room table cloth with the mismatched napkins.

"Well, I guess that's going well." Vi's voice was small and quivering. Her eyes were moist, as were Lenny's. "As if they've always known each other," she said. Lenny nodded.

Frozen behind the dining room chairs, they stood still as they exchanged polite small talk. Lenny never spoke without moving his hands, but he clutched the back of a dining room chair, and the veins in his hands swelled as if he were doing isometrics. Lenny explained that Filomena had passed in August, that Angie had divorced, that Tony was married and had twin boys, and that Irish and Amelia also had children. They were already married when Vi first met them.

"Please sit," Lenny finally said. "I don't know why we're standing here. I'm just going to check on things in the kitchen."

Frankie poured the macaroni into a colander while Ina stood next to him, and a burst of steam rose around them adding magic to the moment. Lenny wiped away a tear and took the large, shallow bowl from the kitchen table and placed it on the counter next to Frankie.

"Italian food is my favorite," Ina said, "except for sushi."

Ina possessed Vi's once uninhibited sparkle, and she livened the otherwise banal dinner conversation with stories about her pretty second-grade teacher, misbehaving classmates, funny piano teacher, and strict dance teacher. She was the precocious only child of a doting academic and as voracious an eater as she was a talker.

Lenny tried not to watch the way Vi's fork pierced the rigatoni, the way she brought the fork to her lips, and how her tongue found the dab of sauce at the corner of her mouth. He envied the dab of sauce. Each time she glanced at him, he'd look away for a moment and then returned his gaze.

"Are you going to eat?" Frankie said to Lenny, and Lenny cleared his throat, smiled, nodded, and scooped up a forkful of macaroni.

"Everything is delicious," Vi said. "Filomena taught you well. I remember she was an excellent cook."

"Who is Filomena?" Ina said.

"She was my grandma."

Ina scrunched up her face as if confused. "Did she die?"

Frankie talked a bit about Filomena, but Lenny remained quiet and finished eating. "I'll get the gravy meat," he said.

In the kitchen, Lenny ladled the meat from the remaining sauce simmering on the stove. He cut the threads on the braciole and returned to the dining room with the platter of sausage, braciole, and meatballs.

"Wow! You people eat a lot," Ina said. Everyone laughed, including Lenny, and Ina continued to entertain them with her stories.

After dinner Frankie stood to help Lenny clear the table, but Vi suggested that she help instead, and Ina asked to see the store. "Mommy told me all about it."

Frankie nodded and led her from dining room, through the open French door, and into the office, while Vi and Lenny gathered plates.

"She's a great kid," Lenny said.

"Thank you. Frankie is everything I knew he would be."

Lenny scraped the plates, placed them in the dishwasher, and watched Vi as she walked back towards the dining room. Before she returned he shifted his gaze to the dishwasher. "Speaking of how Frankie turned out," Vi said, "I was right about one thing."

"What's that?"

"You are a remarkable father and a better mother than I could have been—at least at the time."

Maybe it was because she had just spoken the words that she had written years ago, but Lenny took out his wallet, removed the yellowed slip of paper, and handed it to Vi. They sat at the kitchen table and she unfolded the note and placed it on the table between them. Her eyes were moist.

He didn't show her the note out of malice. It was as if he was returning something important that she had misplaced. She stared at it for some time before she slid it back across the enamel-top table.

"Ina's father treated me as poorly as I treated you. He disappeared a week before she was born."

"Karma's a bitch," Lenny said. "I read that somewhere."

They both laughed. In fact, Lenny couldn't remember the last time he had laughed that hard, but slowly their laughter settled into an awkward silence. Silence competed with words and often won out.

"She likes Frankie and you. I can tell. But what's not to like?"

They held each other's gaze until Vi looked away and fiddled with her thin silver bracelet. Lenny folded the yellow note and slipped it back into his wallet.

"Does Frankie have anyone special in his life?"

Lenny thought of Gennaro and almost corrected her with *had*. "Frankie's gay," Lenny said, which really didn't answer her question, but it seemed like an opportunity to get that out of the way.

Vi smiled and nodded. She ran her finger along the bottom of her right earlobe and gave her earing a gentle tug. "Before the fiasco with Ina's father, I lived with a woman for 6 years. Guess Frankie inherited more than my green eyes." She smiled, and for the first time since their meeting in the hospital cafeteria, Lenny saw glimmers of the girl with the bangles and long blond hair. Their conversation turned to Ina, and it was clear that Vi adored her. Lenny listened as Vi went on and on. She had turned out to be a devoted mother after all.

30

Unlike the forlorn children pining over absent mothers in those ubiquitous orphan and foundling, young-adult books and movies, Frankie had never missed Vi, and he was rarely curious about her, at least not until he saw her photo on the computer. However, when he kissed her cheek, ripples of emotion surfaced—mostly feelings of betraying Filomena and Angie—they were the mothers who had always been there for him, not Vi. Maybe there were other feelings, a primal connection, a memory from before a severed umbilical cord, but Frankie already had more than he could be expected to deal with.

Opening himself up to Ina was less complicated. She was a child. It was a stretch for Frankie to think that they shared the same mother —similar DNA, but not the same mother. They also shared not knowing, and that idea of them having gone about their lives unaware of the each other's existence intrigued Frankie. He was a bit thrown by Ina's barrage of comments and questions and by the way she stared at him as if she were trying to decide if in fact it was true that they were siblings, albeit half siblings, but he appreciated her energy and yielded to her persistence when she didn't accept his shrugs or one-word answers. The subtext of all Ina said seemed to be: *I'm here now so pay attention.* And he did. During supper and then some, Frankie didn't think of Gennaro or the cartoline postale. This was quite remarkable since Gennaro or anything related to Gennaro was all that he thought about since his stay in the hospital.

While Lenny and Vi cleared the table, Frankie showed Ina the store. He explained that they should not turn on the overhead lights because customers would appear like moths tapping on the lit windows. He flapped his arms as if he were a giant moth. Ina giggled. "You're like the man in Kafka's book."

"What?" Frankie said. He was stunned.

"Oh some crazy story Mommy read to me. She's always reading me crazy stories."

"Yes, I know the story," Frankie said. "My Dad read to me a lot, too. He also recited poetry." Lenny found this similarity between Lenny and Vi curious but also sad.

"Oh, Mommy recited poetry, too." Ina took Frankie's hand as they walked down the shadowy aisle towards the front of the store where light came from the deli display case, the corner streetlight, and the strobe of passing cars.

"What are those things hanging from the ceiling?" Ina asked, pressing herself against Frankie.

"Customers who didn't pay their bills on time," Frankie whispered. But as he felt Ina's hand tighten he told her that he was kidding. "They're just cheeses and lunchmeats. You want to taste some?"

"Sure," Ina said, but she kept close to Frankie. He feared that he might trip over her feet as he took several hams and salamis from the cooler. She jumped and let out a little gasp when he turned on the slicing machine.

"Do you like thin slices?"

"I don't know," Ina said above the buzz of the spinning blade.

"We'll make them kind of thin since you just had supper, plus they taste better that way. At least the ham does. I'll slice the salami a little thicker."

"Good. That's the way I like it."

Headlights blinked through rain dappled windows like a game of hide and seek, and Ina stood on her toes and stretched her neck to get a clear view as slices of prosciutto, capicola, sopressata, and Sicilian and Genoa salamis fell from the spinning blade onto a sheet of wax paper forming a patchwork of cold cuts.

"They smell good," Ina said.

"Here, taste the prosciutto first.

Ina took a bite. "Mmm."

Next she tasted the capicola and rubbed her tummy.

"Delicious!" she said and sucked the tips of her fingers. "But I think I'll save the rest for later. I ate a lot of pasta. How come you call pasta macaroni?"

"I don't know. We just do. Like sometimes we call sauce gravy. Maybe it depends if it has meat in it or not, but I'm not sure if that's the reason."

Frankie dropped a few boxes of torrone and some chocolates into a small paper bag and handed them to Ina. "Save these for later, too," he said. For some reason, being with Ina reminded him that Lenny had been his age when Vincenzo died, and Lenny had to leave school, help Filomena raise small children, plus help run the store. Frankie wondered if it would have been worse to lose Lenny instead of Gennaro. He didn't have an answer, but shuddered at the thought of losing Lenny.

"Thank you," Ina said. She folded the sheet of wax paper around the few remaining slices of cold cuts. "I'll save this for Mommy ... I don't mind if you call her Mommy too."

Frankie ignored her comment and asked her if she had ever held a snail.

"Eew ... that's disgusting."

"Nah ... it's cool," he said.

They walked out from behind the deli counter. She seemed less fearful and followed him across the front of the store to the barrels of olives, baskets and burlap sacks of dried beans, and the lone basket of snails. Several had crawled out of the basket. Frankie picked one up. It retracted into its shell until he flattened out the palm of his hand. Gradually the snail emerged. First, its soft muscular foot, next its head, and finally its curious tentacles stretched out, making it resemble a miniature extraterrestrial. Another headlight flashed. Ina's eyes widened when the snail slithered ever so slowly towards Frankie's wrist.

"Why do you sell snails?" she asked.

"People cook them in sauce or with olive oil and garlic."

This time Ina let out a much more unequivocal, "Eewww."

Frankie laughed, retrieved all the escaped snails, and returned them to the basket. "Come on, one last place to see. I'll show you the warehouse. That was my favorite hideout when I was your age."

Again, Ina took Frankie's hand as they walked to the darker end of the store. In her other hand she held the folded sheet of wax paper and the bag of candy. Lenny unlatched the door to the warehouse and switched on the bright fluorescents. Like magic, cardboard mountains appeared, stenciled with names like Ronzoni, Contadina, and Progresso —some cases reached up into the rafters and touched the 15-foot ceiling.

While explaining to Ina that he used to climb on these cases and pretended that he was a pirate on a ship or a knight in a fortresses, he recalled the many times that Gennaro and he nestled against each other in this cardboard sanctuary and read comics or spoke in hushed tones of their hopes, complaints, and fears, or teased each other, which inevitably turned into wrestling, and several lighter boxes of dry goods would tumble onto them. He remembered Gennaro's solidness, their limbs entwined, and the scent of boys more interested in playing than bathing. But then he felt a slight jostling of his hand and looked down to find Ina staring up at him.

"You have Mommy's eyes," she said. "Not just the color. Sometimes her eyes look sad too." The warehouse air was biting and a puff of steam followed Ina's words. "I wish my eyes were green. Mommy said that mine are hazel, but I don't like them."

Hazel, Frankie thought. *Like Gennaro's.*

Ina's voice quivered, probably from the cold.

"We better go back in the house," Frankie said.

"Are you mad at me?"

"No, I'm not mad at you. It's just cold in here."

"Okay, but next time I visit you, we'll make our own fortress like you and Gennaro did."

"What did you say?"

"A fortress. You said that you and Gennaro used to ..."

Frankie turned off the light and led Ina out of the warehouse, back into the store, up the steps into the breezeway and office while Ina spoke of things about Gennaro that Frankie had no recollection of mentioning, as if memories had spilled from his lips without him knowing.

In the office, surrounded by the old photographs, next to the safe that once concealed the cartoline postale, and the computer where Lenny typed his emails to Vi, Ina asked Frankie who Gennaro was. Frankie's hand froze on the doorknob to the dining room. He hadn't expected this to happen so soon, that someone who had never known and would never know Gennaro would ask him to explain. *Call him on my cell*, Frankie thought, *and ask him to come down to my house, tell him that there's someone I want him to meet, tell Ina that he'll be right over, and she could see for herself who Gennaro is. Or was.* But of course, Frankie couldn't do that. And even if he was unwilling or unable to wrap his head or heart around that fact, it was a fact nonetheless, and there wasn't a thing he could do about it.

"Gennaro was ..." Frankie began, and by linking those two words, Gennaro became as remote as the boys in the cartoline postale. So what if he had died only a few weeks ago. Frankie could no sooner embrace him than he could embrace Filomena or the great-grand-fathers. *Death isn't gradual, it's abrupt and final*, he thought. *One moment someone is here, the next moment they're not. Whether someone has been dead five minutes or five years or fifty years, it's all the same.*

"Gennaro was my friend," he finally said, and the words felt like broken glass in his throat. If at that moment he were to spit, his saliva would have been streaked with blood, as red as the blood that had spilled from Gennaro's quivering body.

"Did something happen to him?" Ina asked.

Frankie bent down, facing Ina. "Yes, he died." And Ina hugged him. He dismissed the slight ache where her small hands clasped over the place where a bullet had pierced his neck, another sign of time passing and healing—at least physically.

"What's that?" Ina said.

"Just a scar. Nothing important."

Her hair fell soft against Frankie's cheek, and her torso pressed against his heart. He returned her embrace, but instead of yielding to his own grief he felt protective of Ina. *Please, no more questions*, he thought, *it's all too sad for you to hear about.* Ina clung to Frankie, and he managed to lift her up despite the pain. From the dining room, they heard Lenny and Vi's voices.

"They're talking about me," Ina whispered.

"Must mean you're pretty special."

Ina and Frankie stood under the archway between the dining room and kitchen. "What a great store! Kind of spooky though," Ina said. She was quite animated. "There are all kinds of pasta piled all the way to the ceiling and cheese and meat as big as me hanging from hooks and more kinds of olives than I've ever seen. Even snails! But I didn't hold one."

She climbed onto Vi's lap, making Frankie think of Filomena holding his little cousins.

"Frankie gave me the most delicious food I've ever tasted." Ina held out a ball of crushed wax paper. "It's called prosciutto. Then we went in the warehouse and when I come back to visit again, Frankie and I are going to make a fortress there. It will be a fun place to play. Have you ever been in the warehouse, Mommy?"

Lenny glanced at the floor.

"Yes, I think so," Vi said.

During dessert, Vi and Ina spoke about their life in Los Angeles. Ina said that she wanted to be a ballerina or a spy when she grew up, which made every one chuckle. Frankie spoke about the colleges he had applied to. Lenny mostly listened or encouraged others to speak about themselves with comments like: "Interesting ... tell me more ... Wow, that's something." He cracked a few jokes, but was mostly quiet. The tone of the evening went full circle, and by the time the four of them stood at the front door saying goodbye, awkwardness returned.

Frankie gave Vi a perfunctory kiss on the cheek. All that had been left unsaid loomed until Ina broke the tension. "I always wanted a sister, but I'm glad you're my brother." Her simple acknowledgment brought levity to their goodbyes.

Frankie smiled and gave her a hug and kiss.

When Lenny hugged Ina, she whispered, but loud enough for everyone to hear her: "I wish you were *my* daddy too."

Until now, Frankie hadn't considered the fact that Ina had also grown up without one of her parents—something else that they shared.

Lenny's eyes filled with tears.

Vi took Lenny's hand. Neither of them spoke until Lenny finally said: "I'll give the three of you a few moments," as if he were a polite outsider and didn't want to intrude, but Frankie had nothing more to say. Ina filled the silence, and then Frankie stood at the top of the stoop, watched them get into Vi's rental car, and waved goodbye as they pulled away.

31

Their flight back to Los Angeles left early the next morning, and Frankie spent much of the day thinking of Ina. When he sliced cold cuts or scooped snails to be weighed or brought stock out from the warehouse, he felt Ina's small hand press into his or felt the knot of her grasp against the nape of his neck or her heart beating against his, and it amazed him how much he cared and that he thought of someone other than Gennaro.

That evening, after they closed the store, Frankie was the one who initiated a conversation with Lenny about Vi and Ina, and, throughout the week, they discussed Vi and Ina's visit in small bites as if they were slowly digesting what had taken place. Frankie also discussed the visit with Tootsie, mentioning that he wasn't sure about Vi, but that Ina was a great kid, and it was strange but kind of fun to suddenly have a little sister. The more he thought and talked about them, especially Ina, the less he longed for Gennaro, but there were also moments when thoughts of the three of them merged. After all, it was Gennaro who had sent Lenny's email to Vi. If not for the classic DiCico meddling in other people's lives, Frankie may never have met Ina, at least not now — as if Frankie reuniting with Vi and meeting Ina was a farewell gift that Gennaro had set into motion.

He shared with Tootsie this idea of an unforeseen fate or destiny behind Gennaro's press of a button, and she not only agreed, but also added her own anecdotes to support his belief about destiny, including their first meeting. "Honey, I know meeting you that time lighting those candles was no accident," Tootsie said.

Frankie remembered how holding pink-finger-nailed Tyrone made him feel peaceful and for the first time he had believed that his feelings

for Gennaro weren't sinful. They just were. Although he again suffered feelings of guilt and God's retribution, given that moments after
Gennaro kissed him at the altar he lay bleeding in Frankie's arms.

"When people pay attention, honey, they know that things happen
for a reason," Tootsie said.

Tootsie's comment didn't help. "But what reason could there have
been for Gennaro to die?" he asked.

"I don't know, honey. I didn't say I knew the reasons. If I did, people
would be praying to me, and you know what's gonna freeze over before there's a Saint Tootsie."

Late nights were the hardest times, and trying to distract himself
with thoughts of having a new little sister went only so far. Sleep didn't
come easily. Frankie stared at reruns of old television shows on his
computer until 1, 2, sometimes 3 in the morning.

Lenny would have already put in several hours of work before Frankie stumbled into the store, but Lenny always smiled and asked how
Frankie slept as Frankie yawned, mumbled something incoherent, and
downed a quart of orange juice or milk. On weekdays, Doug Turner
joined them for lunch and Frankie ate quietly while Lenny and Doug
salted their lunch with talk of politics. Lenny would try to draw Frankie into the conversation, but Frankie mostly responded with a shrug
and another bite of his sandwich.

Customers gossiped about seeing Big Vinny's sons in the neighborhood, trying to no avail to get Lenny to divulge what he might know
about why Michael and Jimmy were suddenly released on bail or information about the pending trials. Some neighbors spoke of Big Vinny
leaving his house daily with Scungilli. Yellow tape across the front door
of Big Vinny's club was a constant reminder that prison was still a very
real threat for the DiCico men.

In the evenings, Lenny and Frankie took turns eating supper alone
in the kitchen while the other worked the store, and except for Sundays
they closed the store every night around 9 pm, and Lenny fell asleep
while reading the newspaper or watching television, and Frankie closed
himself in his bedroom, turned on his computer, and watched videos
of Gennaro, or spread out the cartoline postale like tarot cards across
his bed, and according to their arrangement, he concocted elaborate

fantasies, conflating his relationship with Gennaro with the great-grand-fathers' relationship. But he also responded to friends' messages and texts, and watched YouTube or searched random sites on his computer. He even began to read books again, though after a few pages, his concentration drifted and it was back to reruns of old television shows on his computer until he was able to fall asleep.

Since meeting Ina, Frankie felt a gentle but persistent tug, as if he were being lifted up from a very deep well, but it would be a long, arduous ascent. Given the way Lenny had looked at Vi across the dinner table, Frankie knew that letting go and moving on did not come easily for Lasantes.

Close to a month passed since Vi and Ina had returned to California when Frankie received a card from Ina. He often thought to write to her or send her an email through Vi's address, but each time he began he felt foolish. He couldn't write of his relationship with Gennaro or of how Gennaro died, or tell Ina that she was a gift in an otherwise grief-stricken time. That was a lot to put on a young child. The envelope was addressed in large bold printing. Inside was a birthday card with a picture of a boy playing baseball and the words *Brother* scripted across the top, reminding Frankie of how patient Gennaro had been when he taught him how to throw and catch or hit a ball with a bat. Inside the card was a clichéd jingle about brothers, but Ina had also printed her own thoughts:

> *Dear Frankie,*
> *I miss you. Mommy said that we have to give you time.*
> *She said that you went through a lot. She said that maybe you*
> *are mad at her because of what she did. But I didn't do anything.*
> *Please don't be mad at me too. I asked Mommy if you could come*
> *visit us. She said that you could. Here is a picture of Mommy*
> *and me at the beach. I love you.*
> *Your Sister,*
> *Ina*
> *OXOXOXOXOX*

The photograph reminded Frankie of the one he had given to Lenny years ago in the Mother's Day frame he had once made in school, and

the floor creaked under his feet as he walked to Lenny's room and
then placed the two photographs side by side. In one, Frankie was
straddling Lenny's shoulders, looking out on the Atlantic. In the other,
Ina embraced Vi with the Pacific as their background. Frankie stuffed
Ina's card and photograph in his back pocket, raked the back of his
hand across his tears, and headed to the store where he found Lenny
talking to Doug—a newspaper lay open on the counter between them.
They looked up from the paper while Lenny wore a weak, thin-lipped
smile.

"I'll see you later, Lenny," Doug said and left the store. *What now?*
Frankie thought as he neared the counter where Lenny stood over the
newspaper. The headline read "Distraught Son Confesses." Lenny explained that the cabdriver's son had been in the cab the day of Big
Vinny's block party, and he saw Gennaro staring at the cab's license
plate number and write something on his arm. Frankie skimmed the
article. After the police had found a gun with the boy's fingerprints in
a dumpster not far from Most Precious Blood, he confessed, and given
that he was a juvenile and under severe duress from his father's murder, his attorney was able to plea bargain for a reduced sentence. The
newsprint blurred. Gunshots rang out, and Frankie felt Gennaro's
weight press against him.

"Are you okay?" Lenny pushed a stool next to Frankie and helped
him to lean against it.

"There's one small consolation in his confessing," Lenny said. "No
trial. No need for anyone to testify."

"He's not the only one," Frankie said.

"What do you mean?"

"Not the only one to see Gennaro write something on his arm. I
also saw him do that." Frankie covered his face with his hands and
sobbed. "But I didn't know they were going to kill that poor cabdriver.
He didn't do anything to them. Why would they kill him?"

Lenny ran to the front door, locked it, turned over the sign to read
CLOSED, and grabbed Frankie, almost dragging him away from the
front of the store.

"Listen to me." He took hold of both of Frankie's arms. "You don't
know anything about who killed that cabdriver. All you saw was Gennaro write something on his arm, and the police already have that

information. You don't know anything else. Have you ever mentioned what you just told me to anyone else?"

"Only Gennaro," Frankie said. He was startled by the rage in Lenny's voice and the sharp pains where Lenny's fingers pressed like vices into his forearms, which reminded him of how Gennaro clung to him Christmas night.

"And did Gennaro ever mention anything to you about the cabdriver?"

"No. He didn't say anything, even after I told him that I saw what he did."

"You don't know that he did anything," Lenny said.

"I mean …" But Frankie lost his train of thought. Someone knocked on the storefront window.

"Okay, we're done with this conversation for now, Frankie. Remember you don't know anything that the police don't already know. You didn't see anything. You didn't talk to Gennaro about this. There was a lot of confusion at the block party. You didn't see anything. Now I have to open the store. You go inside for the rest of the day. Your stomach is off and you have to rest."

"But …"

"Do what I'm telling you to do!" Lenny's face was red. He lifted his apron and wiped the sweat from his brow.

Frankie felt confused, as if he had done something wrong, but he followed Lenny's orders and, as he climbed the steps up to the breezeway, he heard Lenny tell someone that he had locked the door because he had to take a quick leak.

Frankie spent the rest of the day in Lenny's room, curled up on his father's bed, staring at one television show after another. Eventually the daylight shining through the slats of blinds dimmed and disappeared, and the only light in the bedroom came from the small television. He reread Ina's card numerous times and stared at the photograph. He didn't know how long he had been asleep when Lenny finally woke him.

32

The salesman looked from the open newspaper on the counter to Lenny's shaking hands.

"Are you okay, Lenny?"

Lenny stuffed his hands into his pockets. "Just a little jumpy," he said and nodded towards the newspaper. "Whenever something comes up about this, it brings that whole night back again." In Lenny's peripheral vision the store darkened and went flat and he heard a faint grumbling. He struggled to focus on the salesman.

"I read that article this morning," the salesman said as he pulled at the knot of his tie, which appeared to be girdling his thick neck. His face was flushed from the cold, and he brushed snow from his leather binder and placed it on the counter. "If you ask me the punk is getting off easy."

"At least there won't be a trial. I'm thankful for that." Lenny closed the newspaper and pushed it aside. "Now what bargains do you have for me? I know I'm low on olive oil."

Despite the steady flow of customers throughout the rest of the day, it was impossible for Lenny to stop thinking about what Frankie had said. In the hum of the slicing machine he heard *What else might Frankie be concealing?* And in the customers' faces he saw *Lasantes always know more than they let on about the DiCicos.* Nine months had passed since Big Vinny's block party and seven months since the arrests, but this was the first time that Frankie had mentioned anything to Lenny about seeing Gennaro write the cabdriver's license plate number. *There will no longer be a trial regarding Christmas night. Frankie won't be questioned.* Lenny thought these words over and over like a mantra, but it was a small consolation, given that Michael and Jimmy would eventually be brought to trial for the cabdriver's murder, and maybe even Big Vinny. Frankie might be called to testify at that trial or at least questioned. Lenny spent the day dropping groceries, miscounting change, asking customers the same questions over and over. More than a few customers asked him if he was okay. Some mentioned that they had read the newspaper article. They shook their heads, clicked their tongues, made signs of the cross, and Lenny took long, slow breaths and told himself *Frankie won't be questioned.*

The day dragged. At 9 p.m. Lenny locked the door and turned out the lights. The kitchen was undisturbed, so he assumed that Frankie hadn't eaten. He heated leftover minestrone soup, cut several chunks of Italian bread, and brought the tray of food upstairs to Frankie. The sound of the television came from his bedroom. He placed the tray on his dresser, lit a lamp on the nightstand next to the bed, and turned off the television. Frankie woke as Lenny rolled a small area rug out of the way and pushed an easy chair across the hardwood floor.

Frankie propped himself up against the pillows, stretched, and yawned. "Guess I fell asleep."

They ate in silence, blowing steam from their spoons, until Frankie drank the remaining soup from his mug, placed the mug on the nightstand, and handed Lenny the picture of Vi and Ina. "I got this in the mail today."

Lenny held the picture under the lamplight. "Did Vi send it to you?"

"No, Ina. And she sent me a birthday card."

"You made quite an impression on that little girl."

Frankie opened the card and held it out to Lenny. "You can read it."

"Smart kid. Quite a letter for such a little one." Lenny's anxiety lifted and his breaths came easier. He could hear Filomena say that when God closes a door he opens a window, or something like that. Whether it was God's doing or not, Lenny was thankful for Ina. She gave Frankie a window to the future.

"Funny how things work out," Frankie said.

"How's that?" Lenny said. He dunked a chunk of bread in his soup.

"I was just thinking about when you said that you wanted me to go visit Vi instead of finishing out the school year."

Frankie's voice had a slight edge. Lenny felt Frankie was being unfair, as if he were to blame for what had happened to Gennaro or at least glad that it had happened, but he was too tired to be defensive.

Frankie slipped the card into his pocket. He stood and gathered the empty dishes. "I'll bring the tray downstairs. I know I've been sleeping on and off all day, but I'm still tired. Since we're going to Tucci's early in the morning, I'll read a little and try to get back to sleep."

Though Lenny wanted to, he didn't suggest that Frankie accept Ina's invitation. He remained quiet as Frankie left the room. Sometimes the best a father can do, especially with a teenager, is to just shut up and wait.

Lenny looked at the picture of Vi and Ina and briefly wondered if a friend or a new lover had taken the picture, but he dismissed these thoughts, tossed the picture on the nightstand and undressed for bed. In the morning, they planned to drive to the Catskills. He had told Frankie earlier in the week about Tucci moving to a nursing home and that Big Vinny was going sell the house and land. Frankie was sad to learn of Tucci's decline and surprised that Big Vinny owned Tucci's place. Gennaro had never mentioned this to him. "Maybe Gennaro didn't know," he said. "Or maybe he half knew. Seems like there was a lot of half knowing about stuff, even among the DiCicos." Lenny didn't respond.

Rather than open the store Sunday morning, they left early to avoid heavy traffic. They had hoped to visit with Tucci at the nursing home, but his sister discouraged them from doing so. She explained that her brother wouldn't know who they were, and she was concerned that Frankie had already been through enough. "Better to remember Rocco as he was," she said on the phone.

The morning was cold but clear. Frankie wore his headphones and slept for most of the drive, while Lenny nursed a thermos of strong coffee, and his thoughts vacillated between concerns about Frankie and recalling his last visit with Tucci. It was the Sunday before Filomena died. The old man had repeated himself a little, but otherwise he seemed healthy and his memory, at least when he reminisced about old times, was sharp. He had looked disheveled and the inside of his house was a mess, but no more than usual. The outside of the house was also in disrepair, but Lenny was still shocked when he and Frankie turned into Tucci's driveway. The doors and windows on the first floor were boarded up. The porch roof was flecked with shards of glass as if tears had been shed from the shattered second story windowpanes. Tiny cedars grew from lose gutters and moss coated much of what was left of the worn siding. Nature seemed anxious to reclaim what Tucci had borrowed. Frankie stretched and removed his headphones.

"Holy crap!"

Tucci's absence made the already forlorn house appear wretched. Without an open door or window, or Meatball barking, or Tucci sitting on the porch, it was just an old broken down shell, like a deserted car on the side of the road, except instead of rusted metal, Tucci's house was a heap of rotting wood.

"Should we just go home?" Lenny asked.

Frankie ignored the comment and got out of the car. He zipped up his jacket, turned away from the house and headed down the path to the falls. Lenny followed him under the skeletal branches of deciduous trees where ferns lay brittle and brown against rocks and soil, but the spruce and hemlock were green, and Lenny remembered Frankie and Gennaro playing in the woods, turning fallen tree limbs into swords. Gennaro was the king and Frankie his knight—of course. Lenny saw them dart among the trees—Arthur and Lancelot without Guinevere, and now Lancelot was without Arthur. Whatever Gennaro may have felt for Frankie, Lenny believed that Gennaro would have married, fathered a brood of little DiCicos, and Frankie would have become another DiCico secret. It was true that Lenny had wanted Gennaro out of Frankie's life, but not like this.

When they finally reached the falls, it was as dazzling as the house was depressing, a luminous life force framed by snow and ice sculptures behind a screen of mist.

"It's beautiful," Frankie said.

The last time Lenny had seen such an expression on Frankie's face was the night of the Feast of the Assumption when Gennaro sang Mario Lanza's songs on the stage across from their yard.

Frankie eyes were locked on the falls while he raised his voice so Lenny could hear him above the crashing water. "Gennaro and I didn't come back here last summer—I mean after the explosion. We were here the day before, but we never came back. I wonder if he knew that his father bought the place. Maybe. Guess there was a lot I didn't know. Maybe a lot Gennaro didn't know too, or at least he pretended not to know. He told me something like that once when we walked on the beach."

It was difficult to understand all of Frankie's words above the fall's thunder, but Lenny felt his stomach tighten with talk about knowing but not knowing regarding Big Vinny's involvements. He didn't interrupt.

"Gennaro wanted to get away. Join the Army or something. I was afraid that he'd get himself blown up again ... you know like he did the night of Big Vinny's block party. Only this time it would be for good. I don't have to worry about that now."

A mini double rainbow arced across the falls' icy spray, and Frankie took Lenny's hand, and the feel of it so overwhelmed Lenny with emotion that he feared if he allowed one tear to escape there'd be no stopping them.

Boulders and rocks can handle a winter thaw. They erode slowly over hundreds of years, but people can survive only so many tears. He inhaled, and the air smelled of winter's reluctant yielding to spring. Before such a force of nature, Lenny's regrets and worries suddenly felt minuscule. Right now Frankie was safe like the little Frankie who once held Lenny's hand as they crossed the winding roads in Central Park from one playground to another. The past couldn't be changed, and worrying about the future was futile.

Almost an hour had passed when Frankie squeezed and then released Lenny's hand, and Lenny turned from the falls and watched Frankie disappear back into the woods. He followed him, and as Tucci's house came into view, so did Lenny's concerns.

The falls gave Lenny only a brief respite, but once in the car, he mentioned that maybe this trip wasn't such a good idea.

"No, it was good," Frankie said. "Remember how I said that I didn't want anything for my birthday?"

"Did you change your mind?" Lenny said. He turned the key in the ignition.

"Yes. What do you think of a plane ticket to L.A.?"

"If it's what you want ..." Lenny backed out of Tucci's driveway and tried to sound nonchalant.

"Really?" Frankie twisted his lips and rolled his eyes.

"Okay," Lenny said. "I admit it. It's the best news I've heard in a long time."

Maybe something about the falls had motivated Frankie to give Los Angeles a chance. Whatever the reason, Lenny was grateful, almost giddy, and he struggled to keep the smile from his face, as if being too happy might jinx Frankie's sudden change of heart.

After two hours of driving to the soothing monotony of wind-shield wipers clearing mist, he asked Frankie if he was hungry.

"No, I'll eat when we get home."

Again they fell into silence, except for the swish of the wipers. There was much that Lenny wanted to say, but again he feared that if he showed too much enthusiasm Frankie might change his mind about Los Angeles. As they approached the Tappan Zee, Lenny said: "So you're doing okay? I mean with seeing Tucci's place and all." He turned the heat down in the car.

"I'm good," Frankie said, but he stumbled over his words, and his voice cracked. "I know this sounds weird, but I wish I had gone to Gennaro's funeral. Not that it would change anything." He paused for a few moments, looked out the window. "Being at Tucci's kind of felt like a funeral. You know like saying goodbye to someone or something, but seeing the waterfall didn't feel like an end kind of goodbye. Good-bye is too permanent a word. I know I'm getting too weird for you. Gennaro would tell me to stop reading into everything, which is kind of funny because while I looked at the falls I felt as if Gennaro gave me some kind of permission, even though I don't know what he was giving me permission to do."

"Maybe to go on living?" Lenny said. Frankie stared at Lenny, and from the corner of his eye, Lenny caught Frankie's expression turn light, dark, then light again from the headlights of passing cars.

"Maybe," Frankie said. "I hadn't thought of that. Now you're the one reading into stuff." Frankie put on his headphones and rolled his jacket up under his head. "You see a lot of sky from this bridge. Gennaro didn't like the night sky, especially in the country. I hope he likes it now." Frankie continued to speak of Gennaro in a dream-like distant tone. His eyes closed and his voice drifted. The headlights grew brighter and more frequent. Frankie punctuated his words with yawns until he fell asleep.

Once home, Lenny called Vi. She was more than willing to have Frankie visit. She would turn her office into a bedroom for him. There was a couch that opened into a bed and closet space and good ventilation and Ina would be thrilled. Lenny was touched by Vi's enthusiasm. "Just don't paint Disney characters on the walls," he said. "Remember he's turning 18 in a few days."

Vi chuckled, but then her tone turned serious. "His birthdays were always difficult for me, especially after Ina was born."

"Well, that's all changed now," Lenny said.

"We'll see. I have a lot to make up for."

Lenny didn't console her, or tell her that all would be okay, though for Frankie's sake he hoped that it would. He said that he'd check into flights and get back to her.

"Thank you, Lenny."

"Don't thank me. Thank the waterfall," he said and pressed end before Vi could respond.

33

Soon Frankie would leave for California, so he no longer put off paying his respects to the DiCicos. He declined Lenny's offer to go with him, but while at the florist buying tulips for Marie, then walking down 104th Street, unlatching the gate to the DiCicos' yard, and even while meandering through the topiaries and garden statues, he thought to nix the idea of a visit and go home.

He held out the bouquet of red tulips when Marie answered the door, but she didn't seem to notice. Instead of taking the flowers, she hugged him and pulled him into the kitchen towards a kitchen chair. There was the familiar smell of strong, fresh-brewed coffee. Marie was a chain coffee drinker, especially since she quit being a chain smoker.

"Sit, sit," she said, and she sat next to him and petted his arms as if to assure herself that Frankie was real. Her eyes were filled with tears, but she didn't cry.

"Look at you," she said. She let go of his hands, pulled a tissue from her sleeve, and blew her nose. "Lena told me how good you were healing. I wanted to see for myself, but I ... and no cane. She said you were walking with a cane, but no more."

"I only used the cane for a few days after I first came home," Frankie said. "My leg doesn't even hurt." Frankie didn't mention the persistent tingling and numbness. He removed his jacket and let it drape over the back of his chair.

Marie pressed her fist against her lips, reminding him of the night of the fireworks explosion. He placed the slightly mangled red tulips on the glass-top kitchen table, and thought to take her hand, but he felt too embarrassed. She took a deep breath, lowered her fist, and spread out her fingers to gather the tulips. She smiled and her eyes widened as if the flowers had miraculously appeared.

"How beautiful." She stood. With one hand she clutched the flowers, with the other she opened a kitchen cabinet and removed a red glass vase. Her posture stiffened, and Frankie's stomach tightened as Big Vinny entered the kitchen. Frankie tried to stand, but Big Vinny pressed his hand down on Frankie's shoulder.

"Don't get up." Big Vinny kneaded Frankie's shoulder, and Frankie resisted his urge to retract.

Marie pushed the vase aside and took three cups and saucers from another cabinet. She filled each one with coffee and placed them on the table without looking at Big Vinny.

"So you're feeling good enough to take a little vacation. That's good. That's very good," Big Vinny said, and he took a seat next to Frankie.

At first Frankie was surprised that Big Vinny knew about his trip to California, but then he remembered: *He's Big Vinny.*

"Yes, just a short visit."

"Maybe. Maybe not," Big Vinny said.

Frankie didn't answer. Marie placed a plate of cookies on the table and joined them. "Soon I'll call Goodwill to take Gennaro's clothes," she said. "But first I'll let you pick out what you want. I'm not ready yet, but I'll let you know when I am. Probably when you come back from your trip."

"Maybe you should let him pick out what he wants before he leaves," Big Vinny said, but Marie didn't answer.

"There's nothing ..." Frankie said. Then he paused and looked down at their reflections in the glass tabletop. "Maybe his leather jacket," he whispered, but as soon as the words left his mouth, he remembered that Gennaro was wearing it Christmas night. Surely it had been ruined. No one spoke, just the sound of cups against saucers.

"Marie, are you just going to leave those flowers die on the counter?"

She jumped up from the table and, while she filled the vase with water and cut each stem with a paring knife, she spoke of Gennaro's funeral. Some of the details Frankie had already heard from Angie, but he was glad to hear them again. Her voice was wistful as if she were simply thinking aloud, and it mattered little whether or not they heard her. Big Vinny and Frankie were merely the excuse for her to remember.

Twice Big Vinny interrupted her. "Frankie doesn't want to hear about all that."

Marie ignored him, and when he interrupted her a third time, Frankie spoke up. "Please go on, Mrs. DiCico. For some reason I like hearing about the funeral, and you're remembering some things that my aunt didn't tell me."

"Oh, I remember *everything*," Marie said, and her comment sounded like an indictment, most likely directed at Big Vinny. Frankie wondered if *everything* included enough to put Big Vinny away for a very long time. He recalled Gennaro's words from that November day when he and Gennaro walked along the beach at the Rockaways. "Things I've known, but didn't know ... It's like I've always known stuff about my old man and brothers, but I didn't admit that I knew it."

After she finished arranging the flowers in the vase, she brought the coffee pot to the table and filled Big Vinny's cup without asking him if he wanted more.

"No thank you," Frankie said when she looked at him.

Since Frankie had mentioned that he wanted to hear about the funeral, Big Vinny remained uncharacteristically quiet, and the few times he spoke, Marie pursed her lips and stared at her jittery hands. She didn't once look at him, at least not that Frankie noticed; however, Frankie's attention was spotty. The swinging jalousie doors between the kitchen and dining room were a constant distraction, as if at any moment Gennaro might push through them. He'd be shirtless, his jeans drooping below his boxers, and he'd yawn and stretch, exposing the line of hair beneath his navel. The kitchen light would exaggerate the faint map of scars across Gennaro's chest and on the undersides of his arms. Then Gennaro and Frankie would steal downstairs to the basement, where Gennaro had been napping on sweat-dampened sheets, and Frankie would inhale Gennaro's musk and brush his lips along Gennaro's salty scars and down beneath the band of his boxers. Gennaro's breaths would deepen.

Sitting at the table with Big Vinny and Marie, Frankie thought:

Yes, Gennaro breathe, please breathe, deeper and deeper. He took another sip of coffee and nodded in agreement to whatever Marie said, and hoped that the DiCicos didn't notice the rise in his jeans through the glass-top kitchen table. *Don't break the glass.* He imagined Gennaro laughing.

"It's time for me to get back to the store," he said, and he offered to help Marie clear the table, but she frowned and shook her head. He stood, held his jacket in front of his crotch, and bent towards Marie and gave her a kiss on her cheek while she pulled a tissue from her sleeve and dapped at her tears. Big Vinny also stood; he removed a sheet of paper from a corkboard on the wall next to the kitchen door.

"Here, give Marie's grocery list to your father. Lena or Scungilli will be by later to pick up the groceries." Big Vinny pressed money into Frankie's hand and hugged him.

"An early birthday present," he said. "Something for your trip." Frankie didn't return his hug. Big Vinny patted Frankie's back and released him as if he understood.

Frankie's eyes followed cracks in the sidewalk, and he jiggled the change in his pocket as he walked home. *Step on the crack and break the devil's back.* He recalled the childhood jingle and flicked at the bills that Big Vinny had given him. He pulled his hand from his pocket and looked at the wad of crisp 100-dollar bills. For years he had ignored Lenny's rants about Big Vinny's blood money, but now he felt Gennaro's blood ooze through his fingers, more precious than all of Big Vinny's filthy money. He crumbled the bills, stuffed them back into his pocket, wiped his hand on his jeans, rubbed them together, balled them into tight fists, and when he finally got to the store, he took a deep breath and stretched out his fingers against the cool glass door and pushed.

"There you are, honey, we was just gonna leave."

Tootsie stood across the counter from Lenny while Tyrone pranced a toy unicorn with a long pink mane atop the bags of dry beans.

Lately, each time Frankie saw Tootsie she looked a little different —slightly thinner, maybe slow weight loss after having the baby. She also wore less makeup and silver had replaced her plastic bangles, as if she were taking beauty tips from Angie. But Tyrone contrasted his mother's new image with his pink nail polish, a red and yellow tam with matching scarf, and lime green rubber boots.

"Hey, buddy!" Frankie returned Tyrone's hug, which felt like a potion, and Frankie's hatred for Big Vinny abated. "Nice unicorn. Where did you get it?" Tyrone smiled, gave his head a little jerk, and he and his unicorn wandered back to the land of dried beans.

"How's Marie?" Lenny asked. Frankie shrugged his shoulders and handed Lenny the sheet of paper. "It's her list. Lena or Scungilli will come by later to pick up the groceries." When he pulled Marie's list from his pocket, Big Vinny's crumpled 100-dollar bills fell to the floor.

"You're throwing your money away," Tootsie said.

He picked up the wadded bills and tossed them on the counter. "A present from the Don."

Lenny's eyes flashed and he frowned. "Why don't you and Tootsie go inside the house and talk for a while? The store is slow and Tyrone looks like he's having fun." Tyrone sat on the floor, lining snails up behind his unicorn. "If he gets antsy, he knows where to find you."

Tootsie and Frankie went in the house, but first Frankie grabbed two Manhattan Specials from the cooler—Tootsie's favorite. They sat at the kitchen table, and Frankie handed her the espresso coffee soda and a glass, but she pushed the glass aside. "Don't dirty a glass on my account. I'm fine drinking out of a bottle." The bottle made a hissing sound when she twisted the cap. "Was it hard going over there?"

Another hissing sound as Frankie twisted the cap off of his soda. "Mrs. DiCico's a nice lady."

Tootsie nodded. "Yes, but it still took a lot of guts for you to do that."

Frankie's eyes wandered from Tootsie to his soda to the chief clock over the window to the small plastic holy water font next to the kitchen door that no one had filled since Filomena passed. Lenny used to tell Frankie that Grandma put priest piss in it. Now the little plastic font was just another empty knickknack. Frankie's eyes finally met Tootsie's. "Gennaro and I weren't just friends. I mean we were gay. I mean I'm still gay and being in his house made me miss him all over again, and I missed him when Dad and I were at Tucci's and I miss him right now. I miss him and I love him and I hate him and it's all mixed up and I'm all mixed up." Frankie's face felt as if it were on fire.

Tootsie shrugged her shoulders. "Messed up or not, you were strong enough to go over his house. That took balls."

Frankie slouched against the back of his chair as if he'd been punched. "I finally tell you that Gennaro and I were lovers, and all you say is that it took balls for me to go over his house."

"Honey, I always knew that you were in love with Gennaro, but I didn't know if you knew it. So now we both know it, or know that we both know it, or whatever." Tootsie took another swig of soda.

"You're the first person I've told this to. I kind of told my father, but not exactly, although I don't really know what I said to him. I was on a lot of medicine in the hospital, and there were times I was really upset. Maybe I said more than I remember."

"Whatever you said to your father, don't worry. He's an okay guy. Not like the rest of the macho cafones on your block." Tootsie belched. "Oops, sorry about that. I drank the soda too fast."

Frankie didn't expect Tootsie to be shocked or have a problem with his being gay, but he expected a little more than a shrug and a belch. They both laughed and he told her about the trip to Tucci's, and their moods turned somber as he described the house and how everywhere he looked he saw Gennaro.

"Was that a bad thing?" Tootsie said.

"Was what a bad thing?"

"Seeing Gennaro wherever you looked?"

He thought about that for a few moments. "No it wasn't bad ... it just was ... kind of hard, but at the same time comforting."

Tootsie wore a faint smile when he explained that something in the falls made him believe that everything would be okay. "I can't imagine how things will be okay," he said. "I'm not even sure that I want it to be okay, but it was like the falls took the choice away from me. Like it was saying whether you want it or not, all will get better. I know it sounds weird."

"Sounds like faith and hope," Tootsie said. "You know, believe something even though you don't know it yet."

Tootsie had a gift for making sense of nonsense. "You're too much," Frankie said.

She pressed the palms of her hands against her sides. "Too much! And here I thought I was losing weight."

Frankie laughed. "Actually, you have been looking thinner." He found his way back to talking about being gay and his relationship with Gennaro, beginning with how he thought that the gas can explosion had been an omen, showing him that his feelings for Gennaro were wrong. "But then I met you. You once said that the first time we met in church was no accident. Well, I agree. When we first met I was filled with guilt, and watching Tyrone with his pink fingernails and playing with a Barbie doll made me feel like God was giving me another message. Not a judgmental message but a loving message. I'm not saying that Tyrone is going to be gay or anything, but ..."

Tootsie smiled. "You don't have to explain to me. Tyrone is gonna be who he's gonna be."

"I guess it's a little new for me to talk about this stuff. Even with Gennaro, I didn't talk about this much. Especially with Gennaro. The first time we did anything, you know what I mean, was last August, and for the longest time he acted like nothing happened. Then when he finally came around to admitting that we weren't just friends, he still denied that he was gay, and we found these pictures of our great-grandfathers, and I tried to explain to him that maybe ... never mind. What difference does it all that make now? Anyway, has my dad told you about California?"

"Okay, honey, now you're confusing the hell out of me. I know that's not too hard to do, but how did we go from Gennaro denying that he was gay to pictures of your great-grandfather to you going to California?"

"I know, I'm sorry. But this is how my head works lately, or doesn't work. I'm all over the place." Frankie didn't explain about the cartoline postale, but he told Tootsie that Lenny bought him a plane ticket to Los Angeles. "I'm going stay with Vi and Ina."

"Wow!" Tootsie's eyes opened wide and she pressed her fingertips against her cheeks, making her lips pucker like a fish.

"Vi agreed to an open ended visit. You know, so I can see how I like it ... see how long I want to stay. When I'm ready to come home, Dad will buy me a ticket for the return flight."

"Well, I'm speechless."

"Good kind of speechless or bad?"

"Just speechless."

"I mean, do you think it's a good idea or a bad one?"

"I can't answer that one, honey, but I think it's good that you want to try something new. That's definitely a good sign."

"What do you mean?"

"It shows that you're healing. See, the waterfall was right."

Frankie finished his soda and fiddled with the empty bottle. "The funny thing about healing is that you don't really feel better, you just feel less."

They heard the door from the office to the dining room open and shut, and after the sound of shuffling rubber boots, Tyrone entered the kitchen. He went right to Frankie, threw his arms around him, and rested his head on Frankie's shoulder while the unicorn's horn jabbed Frankie's collarbone. Frankie didn't complain.

"I know someone who's going to miss you," Tootsie said.

Frankie pushed his chair back from the table so Tyrone could climb onto his lap. "Did you get tired of playing with snails?"

Tyrone laughed and gave his head a jerky nod. The corners of his mouth were smeared with chocolate. "Something tells me that my dad gave you candy."

Tootsie stood and placed the two empty soda bottles in the sink. She was definitely thinner.

"Tootsie, mind if I ask you a personal question?"

"Ask me anything. You know that, honey."

"Is there someone new in your life? I mean a guy."

She turned away from the sink, and her eyes shot up to the left and her lips scrunched over to the right as if she were searching her thoughts for the perfect answer, and she chuckled. "There's always a guy, honey."

"No, I mean a special guy. You look different lately."

"Oh that. I'm just trying on a new me. The old one didn't work so good. Hope I'll have better luck this time." She struck a pose with one hand on her hip and her head tossed back. Her silver hoop earrings flashed against her black hair. "What do you think?"

Tyrone jumped from Frankie's lap, struck the same pose, and they all burst out laughing.

"I think you're both beautiful, but Tyrone's green boots steal the show."

Tootsie glanced at the clock above the window. "Shit! Our bus will be here in a few minutes. Come on, Tyrone, or we'll have to ride your unicorn home."

They left the house through the front door and down the stoop, rather than walking back through the store.

"Tell your dad that I said goodbye," Tootsie said. She kissed Frankie on the cheek, grabbed Tyrone's hand, walked towards the bus stop, and called back over her shoulder, "See you soon."

"Don't forget. I'm leaving for California."

Tootsie stopped and turned around. "You mean soon?"

"Saturday."

"Oh no, no. That will never work." She dragged Tyrone back to where Frankie stood at the bottom of the stoop. "You didn't tell me this."

"But I just told you that I was …"

Tootsie shook her finger at Frankie and bopped her head back and forth like one of those bobble head dolls. "Don't even try to tell me that you …" Tyrone pulled on her arm as the bus drove up, stopped, and then drove away. "Cut it out, Tyrone. We'll catch the next one."

"Come on in the store," Frankie said. "My father will drive you home."

Lenny was writing a list of groceries from a phone order when they entered the store, and Tootsie ranted that Frankie hadn't given her fair warning about his California trip.

Lenny looked up from his pad.

"Just as I'm about to catch my bus, your son tells me that he's leaving for California on Saturday."

"That's not exactly what happened," Frankie said.

"How are you just going to leave without saying goodbye?"

Frankie rolled his eyes and shook his head. Lenny chuckled, put down his pencil, and asked Tootsie what she was doing Friday night.

"I don't know. Maybe I'll just go to Alaska without telling my friends," Tootsie said.

"Well, if you don't go to Alaska, we're having a little 18th birthday combined with a have-a-good-trip party. My family's coming. Why don't you join us?"

Tootsie flashed a look at Frankie. "Birthday! What else haven't you told me?"

Given that Frankie had just come out to Tootsie, he almost said not much, but instead, he explained to Lenny that Tootsie and Tyrone missed their bus and asked if he would drive her home before she drove them all crazy. They laughed, including Tyrone, who also jumped up and down and twirled his unicorn.

For the second time that day, Tootsie kissed Frankie goodbye and grabbed Tyrone's hand. "We'll see you on Friday."

A few customers shopped, purchasing mostly staples like milk, bread, eggs, and butter, but business was sporadic, and Frankie was alone with his thoughts most of the time while Lenny drove Tootsie and Tyrone home. He felt conflicted about leaving. Having lost Gennaro and also Filomena, the thought of being without Lenny frightened him, as did leaving his home, including the store, which was really just another room in their house—maybe the most important room.

There were the bedrooms, the kitchen, the living room, the dining room, the office, the breezeway, and the store and warehouse. All a part of home. Frankie wasn't only leaving his father and home, but also a way of life. He forced himself to look forward to Los Angeles and getting to know Ina, but then he felt guilty about leaving Lenny.

Just a little vacation. Stop being so dramatic. But he knew that it would be more than a vacation. It was a chance. The chance Lenny had lost. Lenny's insistence that Frankie go away to college had always irritated him, but now he felt differently. Staying here would feel as if he were living at the end of a story, an epilogue, especially with Gennaro gone. Life would amount to little more than a retelling of what used to be or imagining what might have been. He wondered if that had been what his father's life was like for all these years.

Frankie inhaled, looked at the walls of dry goods, the waxed cheeses hanging from iron hooks, the sawdust covered floorboards, and he knew that once he left he wouldn't come back, except as a visitor like his aunts and uncle and his father's high school friends.

When he was a small child, he had a recurring dream, one of those dreams where you feel as if you are being chased by something threatening. In the dream, Lenny tripped and fell and was unable to get up, but insisted that Frankie run off without him. Terrified for him and for himself, Frankie ran as fast as he could until he could no longer hear Lenny shout for him to keep running.

He stared out the window above the displays of canned tomatoes and olive oil and in between the faded sale signs, and he wondered if Big Vinny would reopen his club or if there would ever be another block party. He pictured Napolitano's stand at the curbside outside the store and tasted the sweet torrone they sold during the Feast of the Assumption, but he couldn't imagine a Feast without Gennaro's beautiful tenor voice or Filomena sitting at the head of the table under the grape arbor in the yard, orchestrating the Lasante assembly line of sandwich making. He didn't know how things would work out in Los Angeles, but he knew that he wouldn't come back here. Even if his stay with Vi and Ina turned out to be brief, he had already been accepted at several colleges, and he could travel until classes began. Lenny would not only agree to that, he would encourage it.

A snail slithered down the side of a bushel sack of dry lentils, and Frankie walked around the counter, across the front of the store, and picked up the stray snail, but instead of returning it to its bushel, he slipped it into his pocket. Without thinking, Frankie picked up the basket of snails. He locked the front door, carried the basket into the warehouse, left it there, and then retuned to the store. When Lenny came back from driving Tootsie and Tyrone home, Frankie dumped the basket of snails into a burlap sack, took his bike and the sack of snails from the warehouse without mentioning anything to Lenny. He hung the sack form his shoulders like a knapsack and rode his bike to Woodhaven Boulevard, and then onto to Crossbay Boulevard towards the beaches. He biked in the far right lane of an eight-lane boulevard—four lanes traveling east and four lanes west. Once Lenny biked the same route, and before him Vincenzo, but back then it was a gravel road that meandered through acres of marsh where ibis, osprey, heron, and egret enjoyed the vast wetlands. First two lanes were paved, wooden sidewalks became concrete, gas streetlights became electric, and

open land became rows of houses and stores and schools and churches and synagogues on a grid of streets that intersected avenues.

It was cool, but Frankie pedaled so quickly that sweat formed on
his brow and at the back of his neck. He turned into a place once called
Bare-ass Beach from the days when Lenny and Big Vinny and other
neighborhood boys swam there naked—a weedy area with several
lagoons.

Frankie emptied some of the sack into the weeds, which were
mostly brown with only hints of green. He walked a little further and
emptied it a little more, and he continued doing this until all of the
snails were free. He tossed the sack into the lagoon and watched it
float away and disappear into the bulrushes.

That night Frankie dreamt of Tucci's place. In his dream, he biked
along the path to the falls while carrying something very heavy, but
it was dark and he couldn't see what he was carrying, and it felt as if
no matter how fast he pedaled he was making very little progress.
Finally he reached the end of the path, exhausted and breathless, but
instead of the falls there was a meadow of buttercups washed in sun-
shine, and whatever weight Frankie carried had vanished.

34

Frankie didn't want a birthday party, but Angie insisted. "At least a little dinner and cake," she said. Since Frankie was leaving for Los Angeles and more than likely wouldn't return for graduation—the idea of graduating without Gennaro felt unbearable, he yielded. Angie invited the DiCicos, but explained that Frankie understood if they didn't attend. Fortunately only Lena came. Frankie's aunts, uncles and cousins, a few of his friends, including Johnny Pickle, were also there, and of course Tootsie and Tyrone. A little dinner and cake turned into a small banquet. There were too many guests to sit around the dining room table, even with the young ones eating in the kitchen, so Angie, Amelia, and Irish served buffet style, beginning with antipasto, followed by homemade gnocchi, and then roast beef and fresh ham with multiple side dishes. The antipasto was served at 2 p.m., and it was dusk before Lenny carried Frankie's birthday cake into the dining room—cassata from Panisi's. This was the first time since Filomena's funeral that the Lasante house was filled with people. The chatter, laughter, and even the occasional tears felt like a long overdue sigh of relief.

Tyrone had a difficult time with so many people in such confined spaces, so he spent most of the afternoon and evening watching television in Lenny's bedroom. Frankie carried each course upstairs to him and sat with him while he ate, enjoying the little breaks from the chaos downstairs, but eventually Tyrone went down to the dining room with Frankie for cake.

That morning while stuffing artichokes, Angie had mentioned that lit candles and singing Happy Birthday might be difficult, but that Mama believed that if you don't celebrate birthdays—cake, candles, and all—it was bad luck. "For Grandma's sake," she told Frankie. But when Frankie told Lenny what she said, he laughed.

"Maybe your Aunt Professor shares a few of Grandma's superstitions?"

Lenny carried the cassata, lit with 19 candles, one for good luck, into the crowded dining room, and everyone sang Happy Birthday. Despite the few cracking voices, the family celebrated life as always. Tony and his wife held on to the twins so they wouldn't dive into the cake while Amelia and Irish cut pieces for the children first and told them to go eat in the kitchen where Angie poured them glasses of milk. Even Tootsie pitched in and poured cups of coffee.

Folks milled about the kitchen, dining room, and living room. Some sat at the dining room table, some on the living room couch, easy chairs, and folding chairs that Lenny had opened earlier along with snack tables. Frankie and his friends sat on the steps between the living room and second floor. Tyrone nudged himself between Frankie and the staircase balusters.

Lenny handed Frankie his cellphone. "For you," he said. "I'll keep an eye on Tyrone."

It was Ina, but Frankie could barely hear her above the noise, so he brought the phone upstairs to his room.

"Hold on and listen," Ina said, giggling, and Frankie heard two voices sing Happy Birthday.

He kicked off his shoes and lay down on his bed, and the singing ended with Ina cheering and a barrage of questions. "Yes, I liked your birthday card and the picture," he told her. And: "Yes, I am excited to be going to Los Angeles." And: "Yes, I can't wait until I see you tomorrow," even though that wasn't completely true. Finally, Ina asked if Frankie wanted to talk to Mommy. She didn't wait for his answer.

"Hello." Vi's voice sounded small, almost apologetic. Her "Happy birthday, Frankie" sounded like a question, but he understood why her wishing him a happy birthday was awkward. He felt a little sorry for her. Not a lot, but enough to not cut their conversation short.

"Thank you," he said. He didn't try to fill the silence that followed. He just listened to their breathing

"Eighteen," she finally said.

"Yes." He was curt, and it felt a bit cruel—like an accusation. That moment meant more to her, or disturbed her more than it did him, or brought up more ghosts for her than it did for him, but she had already said she was sorry when she visited him in the hospital. Maybe his curt "yes" was an attempt to sabotage the visit. If he made her uncomfortable, she might change her mind, or maybe talking to her on his birthday hurt him more than he was willing to admit, but everything hurt. One hurt just bled into another. He thought of the falls at Tucci's place and as always, Gennaro. He imagined Gennaro saying: *You loved me Francesco and I fucked up plenty. We all do things that we're sorry for. Stop being a prick.*

"Thank you for letting me come stay with you," he said.

"Would you mind terribly if we celebrated your birthday again tomorrow night? Ina has the whole party planned—decorations and all."

"MOMMY!" He heard Ina whine in the background.

"I would actually like that," Frankie said.

"We'll see you tomorrow ... at the airport."

"I'm looking forward to it," he said, and Ina took the phone. They talked a bit longer, until he heard Vi tell her to let him get back to his guests.

"Yes, I also can't wait until tomorrow," he told Ina and pressed end. He rested his head on the pillows against the headboard, closed his eyes, heard the roar of Tucci's falls, and smelled its pepper spray. Rainbows flashed behind his eyelids until he saw Gennaro standing at the top of the falls and calling out: "Veni qua, Francesco." Frankie jumped when he felt a hand take his. Tyrone stood next to his bed.

"What's up, buddy?" He propped himself up on one elbow.

Tyrone climbed onto the bed and curled himself against Frankie's chest. "Iss ooo," he repeated several times, and Frankie was astonished, even though he couldn't make out what Tyrone was saying. Tyrone repeated it again, and Frankie understood: "Miss you."

He hugged Tyrone, but felt too overwhelmed to speak. He understood what it meant to miss someone. To miss someone so much that, even though you sit and stand and laugh and cry and eat and shit, every cell in your brain is screaming. *Where the fuck are you? Please come back! Please!*

He tried to respond to Tyrone several times before he was finally able to say: "I'll miss you too, but only for a little while. Not forever." And the word forever tasted like blood on his tongue. A few more seconds passed before Frankie stood and took Tyrone by the hand and led him from the bed to his desk where he opened his laptop. He sat, and Tyrone rested his head against Frankie's shoulder.

He clicked on the video of Gennaro and the waterfalls at Tucci's, and then pressed pause. Gennaro appeared suspended above the shimmering spray of the falls with his arms stretched out like angel's wings. "He was very important to me," Frankie said. "I loved him, but you reminded me that there are also other people I love very much."

Tyrone's head jerked just a little. Frankie closed his laptop.

Frankie held Tyrone's pink-finger-nailed hands. "You will always, always be very special to me. I love you very much. You are the bravest person I know. Do you understand?"

Tyrone laughed and gave his head a jerky nod. They joined the rest of the party downstairs, and Tyrone sat on Frankie's lap at the dining room table as Frankie finished eating his piece of cake. He hung close to Frankie for the rest of the evening.

Tootsie stayed later than the other guests and helped Lenny and Angie clean up. When she was about to leave, Frankie mentioned what had happened upstairs.

"See, I told you he could talk," Tootsie said. "He just hasn't had anything important to say for a while, until now." She gave Tyrone a hug, and his little curly head all but disappeared between her bosoms. She drew Frankie into their embrace, reminding him of the night of the block party when Big Vinny embraced him while holding Gennaro, but unlike that night, this was a joyous embrace.

"You and Tyrone are making my mascara run. Honey, hand me that purse," Tootsie said to Angie. "I'm sure I got some tissues in there."

Frankie promised that he'd come back from L.A. soon, though he knew that he wouldn't, and he assumed that Tootsie also knew.

While Lenny drove Tootsie and Tyrone home, Angie unloaded and reloaded the dishwasher, and Frankie finished packing. It didn't take him long. He took the Coney Island photograph from Lenny's dresser and placed it between his folded t-shirts.

"All packed?" Angie stood at his bedroom door.

"Just about."

"I'm going to bed. We have to get up early. How about a kiss for your aunt."

Frankie hugged Angie and planted a kiss on her cheek. "Thank you."

"For what?"

"For tonight. And for always being there. No one can replace that. You and Grandma were always there for me. You were my moms. I'll never forget that."

Angie's eyes filled. She gave Frankie a tight embrace then turned away and left his room.

Later, when Frankie went downstairs for a glass of juice, he found Lenny sitting at the kitchen table reading the newspaper. The overhead light exaggerated the gray in Lenny's hair and the lines around his mouth and eyes.

"I didn't hear you come home," Frankie said.

Lenny closed the paper. Frankie poured the juice in a glass and joined his father at the table.

"Are you all packed?"

"Yep."

"Tyrone saying 'miss you' was really something. Tootsie talked about it all the way home. She swears that he used to talk but suddenly stopped. She didn't mention anything about any seizures or fever. It's curious that he'd just stop talking."

Frankie shrugged his shoulders.

"He's not the only one who will miss you," Lenny said.

"I know that." Frankie drank the juice, stood and propped up his glass in the already packed dishwasher.

"Don't hurt her, Dad."

Lenny's brow wrinkled.

"I've been noticing little changes in Tootsie," Frankie said. "Losing weight and dressing more like ... well like a cross between Aunt Angie and Vi, like she went to a seminar on how to dress like a college professor. I thought that there might be some guy that she was trying to impress. Tonight I realized who he was. She's in love with you, Dad."

"In love? Don't you think that's an exaggeration?"

"No, I don't. She looks at you the way you look at Vi."

Lenny's eyes shifted downward as if he were searching for a response.

"And don't tell me I'm reading into things. Gennaro always told me that. I know about hurt. So do you. So does Tootsie. All I'm saying is she's not as tough as she acts."

Lenny stood up and hugged Frankie. "And you're really something," he said, but then he stepped back. Frankie could barely see Lenny's tears through his own.

"This is a good choice you're making," Lenny said. "You're going to be okay—more than okay."

He took the newspaper from the table and folded it under his arm. "I'm going up to bed. By the way ..." He took his wallet out of his back pocket and removed Big Vinny's money. "I think this is yours."

Frankie's stomach tensed, and he shook his head. "I don't want it."

Lenny returned the money to his wallet. "Your choice." He paused for a few moments. "One more thing. When I arrived at the hospital that night, a nurse handed me a plastic bag with your wallet and cellphone in it." Lenny slipped his hand into his pocket." I didn't recognize this, and with everything going on, I forgot about it until this morning."

Lenny pulled his hand from his pocket and held up a gold medal of Saint Francis hanging from a thin chain. It reflected the kitchen light the way it once reflected Christmas tree lights.

Frankie took the medal from Lenny's hand and kneaded it between his thumb and fingers. He closed his hand around the medal and threw his arms around Lenny. "Gennaro gave this to me on Christmas Eve. I thought it was lost."

"I'm so sorry about all of this, Frankie. I wish I could undo it all."

They talked for a while, leaning against the counter, and Frankie looked around the kitchen as if trying to memorize everything. They spoke about Gennaro and about going to Los Angeles. Eventually Lenny went up to bed, but Frankie remained in the kitchen, leaning against the counter and thinking about everything and nothing. He opened his hand and stared at the St. Francis medal. He slipped the chain over his head.

Lenny's footsteps faded. The house was quiet except for the hum of the refrigerator and the sound of water flushing down a pipe within one of the kitchen walls. Frankie removed the cartoline postale of the great-grandfathers from his pants pocket—he had shown them to Lena earlier—and spread the few pictures out on the kitchen table. No stories came to mind.

The kitchen light was too bright, so he gathered the photos, went up to his room for the rest of the cartoline postale and took them into the office where, under the single light bulb, he sat on the floor cross-legged and fanned them across the threadbare oriental carpet as he had done when he first discovered them. He heard Gennaro laugh and say: *The apple, or in this case the zucchini, doesn't fall far from the tree.* Followed by: *I love you, Francesco, but I'll never be who you want me to be.* And finally: *Don't expect too much from me. You'll be disappointed, but I do love you.* This time Gennaro's words didn't end with the sound of gunshots.

Frankie dialed the safe's combination and opened its iron door. He thought to keep at least one of the cartoline postale, the one of the lone boy with two diminutive horns poking out through his thick curly mane—the boy who resembled Gennaro. But instead he gathered all the photos, returned them to the safe, shut the door, and recalled the two small iron and leaded glass coffers containing the relics of Saint Padre Pio in a church he had visited several times with Filomena when he was very young. He remembered Filomena's euphoric expression as she brought her fingertips to the coffers, as if she were touching something sacred. His fingers lingered on the safe's iron door as Filomena's once had on the coffers. He spun the dial to lock the safe and went up to bed.

35

"**Y**ou have your tickets and money? It's amazing to think that you'll be in Los Angeles in a few hours. One day I'll fly in one of those tin cans. Who knows, maybe I'll be flying out to visit you at UCLA or maybe Berkeley." Lenny was babbling as if he had downed a dozen cups of espresso.

"I didn't apply to either of those colleges," Frankie said.

"There's still time."

"We'll see."

"Give L.A. a chance, Frankie. And Vi. We all make mistakes."

"I will. I promise."

Frankie hugged Lenny and Angie.

Before he disappeared into the crowd at Kennedy Airport, his eyes locked with Lenny's and he mouthed: "I love you, Dad." Lenny was too choked up to respond. He was also concerned that Frankie's black curly hair would invite suspicion, since he had heard about darker Italians having trouble with security in airports, but those were international flights. If nothing else, what had happened Christmas Eve reminded Lenny how little control he had over protecting Frankie, a lesson he should have learned the day Vi left. *He'll be okay,* he told himself, *with security, with Vi and Ina, and in time with having lost Gennaro.* Catching another glimpse of Frankie's hair and backpack set on the shoulders of the leather jacket Lena had given him just before they left for the airport—another gift from Big Vinny, Lenny felt incredibly grateful. *He'll be okay. I'll miss him like crazy, but, thank God, he's going to be okay.* Angie squeezed Lenny's hand. "It's only a little vacation, Lenny."

"I hope not," Lenny said.

As they left the airport they argued about how Angie would get home. She insisted that she should take the air train from Kennedy to the subway, and the subway back into the city. "I always do this when I travel for work," she said, but Lenny argued that he wasn't going to open the store anyway, so he may as well drive her into the city.

They compromised. Lenny drove Angie to the nearest subway station. Once in the car, Lenny again tried to convince her to let him drive her all the way into Manhattan, but she changed the subject.

"Tootsie looked different last night," she said. "Less garish. Oh, and in case you haven't noticed, she has a crush on you. But I've already told you that."

"Yes, you have, and Tootsie was never garish."

"Oops. Guess I struck a nerve. You better watch out, Lenny, unless you also have a thing for her."

"And how's your love life going?" Lenny asked. "Or have you already met all three of the sensitive guys in Manhattan?"

"Very funny … Frankie's going to be okay, you know."

"I hope so."

"I think Vi's changed for the better. Although that's not difficult considering she couldn't get any worse." Angie laughed. "Only kidding."

Lenny shook his head and parked at the curb next to the subway entrance. "Next time, I'll let you walk."

Angie leaned over and gave Lenny a kiss on the cheek. "You doing okay?"

"I'm fine, really."

Angie opened the door and stepped out of the car. Before she closed it, she ducked her head back down. "I'll see you Friday or Saturday."

"Unless a new Mr. Right, or should I say Mr. Left, sweeps you off your feet."

"Asshole!" She shut the car door.

Next, Lenny drove to the cemetery. He hadn't been there since before Christmas, and he was yet to visit Gennaro's grave. He stopped at the usual florist on Metropolitan Avenue, near one of the entrances to Saint John's Cemetery and bought sprays for the DiCico and Lasante graves. Inside the cemetery, he meandered through the curving roads, past gravestones and monuments softened by tree canopies and shrubs that showed a faint promise of spring. Maple trees were tinged red with tiny buds.

Scungilli's Buick was in the spot where Lenny usually parked. He sat in the car. Smoke billowed from the open windows. Lenny parked behind him, walked to the driver's side of the Buick, and found Scungilli ogling a girlie magazine with a De Nobili hanging from a corner of his bulldog lips.

"Good place to look at porn," Lenny said.

"Hey, if you gotta go, what better way? You know what I mean?"

"What else are you doing here aside from catching up on your reading?"

He nodded towards the gravestones. "Waiting for Big Vinny. I've been driving him here every day since Gennaro's funeral. He don't want nobody to know that he comes here, so we go in my car. He's hurting bad, Lenny. He don't let on none, but I never seen Big Vinny like this. It's a terrible thing."

Lenny looked over the top of Scungilli's Buick and saw Big Vinny sitting in one of those stadium-folding chairs. His back was to the road and he was facing the DiCico gravestone. There was an empty folding chair next to him.

When Lenny's shadow stretched across the grave, Big Vinny looked up and nodded as if he were expecting him. The sun reflected off the pink DiCico gravestone and Big Vinny's sunglasses, and he pointed to the empty chair. "I figured you'd show up today."

"Why's that?" Lenny said.

"It's the anniversary of your old man's death."

"Shit, I forgot all about it." He sat next to Big Vinny.

"You've had a lot on your mind, so I remembered for both of us." Big Vinny pointed to the spray he had placed on the Lasante grave — large enough to cover the names on the stone. "How could I forget? My mother had just left your store. Ten minutes later your father is dead. She hadn't even put the groceries away when my old man yells in the door that there's an ambulance in front of Lasante's store." Big Vinny extended his hands, one towards the Lasante stone and one towards the DiCico stone. "Shit happens that we never in a fuckin million years thought would happen."

Lenny placed both of the sprays he bought on the DiCico grave, sat back in the folding chair, and read the newest addition to the DiCico stone: Gennaro DiCico 1988-2008 — the dash between the dates much too scant to represent a life, no matter how short the life was. "I'm so sorry, Vinny. There are no words."

Big Vinny took two sandwiches out of a paper bag and handed Lenny one. "Marie made these. At least she still cooks for me. I guess that's something."

"Give her time, Vinny."

"Time. I got a lot of that. Too much." Big Vinny unwrapped his sandwich and handed Lenny a soda. "Looks like peppers and eggs. Remember when your father used to take us to Tucci's and your mother would pack enough food for a feast. Those were the days. Early on, my old man would also go, and all us kids piled on each other's laps in your old man's Buick. That was before they came up with those fucking seatbelts. Now you can't fit nobody in a car without the cops stopping you."

"Yes. I remember."

Big Vinny took a bite of his sandwich. A few sparrows perched on the pink tombstone. He broke small pieces of Italian bread and tossed them on the ground. The birds flew to Big Vinny's feet and pecked at the bread as if they were accustomed to him feeding them. "So what do you think, Lenny? Is Filomena cooking for my Gennaro now?"

Lenny chewed a mouthful of sandwich.

"I know you don't believe in that heaven nonsense," Big Vinny said. "Neither do I, but the women believe in it. Who knows, maybe they're right." Big Vinny looked at his watch. "I wonder if Frankie's plane took off yet? With all his black curly hair, they'll probably take him for a goddamn terrorist."

"Funny, I was thinking the same thing at the airport."

"Speaking of terrorists, you're okay with him living with Vi?"

"I'm okay with him getting as far away from 91st Avenue and 104th Street as possible. I wouldn't care if he were living with bin Laden."

"I hear you. I should have done that with my boys." Big Vinny nodded towards the pink gravestone. "Especially Gennaro. I should have made him a singer. I should have sent him to L.A. like you did with Frankie. I know people there. Instead I gave him to the fuckin worms. Maybe he's singing to Filomena. Who knows? Maybe the women know something we don't. Won't be the first time."

Lenny remained silent. Chewing his sandwich provided him with a good excuse to not respond to Big Vinny's comments.

More birds gathered around Big Vinny's feet. "You make a creepy Saint Francis," Lenny said. He thought of Frankie's medal. Big Vinny laughed, broke up the rest of his bread, and threw it for the birds.

"Remember old Mr. Bucci with the bum leg? He used to always throw food for the birds. Not just bread. He even threw pasta fagoli in his yard. My mother used to scold him over the fence. 'You're bringing rats,' she'd say. He'd answer: 'But, Rosa, they gotta eat too.' Crazy old bastard." Big Vinny laughed and stuffed the foil from the sandwiches back into the paper bag.

They sat quietly drinking their sodas. Lenny thought it strange to sit with Big Vinny in silence. Silence and Big Vinny were an incongruous mix.

"Tell Marie thank you for the sandwich," Lenny said.

"You tell her yourself. She won't hear it from me. So how long have you been shtupping Margherita Cartoloni?"

"Who?"

"Tootsie! You know the girl with the big tits who used to work in Panisi's."

"Who said I'm shtupping anyone?"

"These birds told me. Who the hell cares who told me? You know that kid of hers is half black."

That was Lenny's cue to leave, before Big Vinny and he wound up punching each other on the family graves. Fortunately, Scungilli appeared. "Hey, Big Vinny, where's my sandwich. Marie said she made peppers and eggs."

"I gave it to Lenny."

"What for?"

"Because you're getting too fat. I'm worried about your health."

"Then when are we gonna leave? I'm hungry."

Big Vinny stood, handed Scungilli the paper bag with the garbage in it and folded his chair. "Come on, Lenny, I gotta feed Scungilli, and I can see you've had enough of me."

Lenny stood without answering and folded his chair while Big Vinny made the sign of the cross, kissed his fingertips and pressed them against Gennaro's name on the stone. They walked back towards the cars while Big Vinny and Lenny carried the folding chairs, and Scungilli carried the bag of garbage.

"Son of a bitch," Scungilli shouted. "I just stepped in dog crap."

With the hand holding the garbage bag, Scungilli leaned on a gravestone. With his free hand he removed his shoe, and Big Vinny and Lenny laughed.

"That's good luck," Big Vinny said.

"To step in dog crap in a *summertery*?" Scungilli whined. "I don't think so."

Big Vinny scolded Scungilli for wiping his shoe on the edge of the gravestone.

"What do you want me to do, get in the car smelling like dog crap? Look, the name on the stone is an Irish name. Nobody's gonna come visit this grave anyway, or if they do they'll be too drunk to smell the dog crap."

"That reminds me, I was just gonna tell Lenny about those Sicilians who were hung in New Orleans for killing a mick cop," Big Vinny said.

"When was that, Big Vinny?" Scungilli asked. He stuffed his foot back in his shoe.

"I don't know, a long time ago."

"Oh. I thought you meant it just happened. Like at Mardi Gras or something."

Lenny tried to conceal his smile. If crime hadn't been so profitable, Big Vinny and Scungilli could have made a living doing standup.

"Did you know about that, Lenny?" Scungilli said as he unlocked the car and they put the folding chairs in the trunk.

"Sure Lenny knows about it, but he don't like to talk about it because he only talks about bad things that happen to coloreds and Puerto Ricans and stuff. Not Italians. It was this big mass lynching. As I was saying, some mick cop got killed and of course they blamed the Sicilians even though they didn't do it, and a bunch of punks got them out of jail and strung them up. They hung 11 of them."

"Where did you hear this, Big Vinny?" Scungilli said.

"They had it on that show about Italians on television."

"Did you know about this, Lenny?" Scungilli asked.

"Yes, a lot of Italians were lynched back then. That was before we convinced the rest of America that we were white."

"We are white," Big Vinny snapped.

"If you say so," Lenny said.

"I don't know, Big Vinny," Scungilli said. "Have you ever seen my cousin Louisa? And there are a lot of singers today who look Italian to me, but they say they're black. Like what's her name. I don't know her first name, but her last name is Keyes. And remember Lena Horne. Nice looking woman. In fact, she looked like my cousin Louisa."

"Point well taken, Scungilli," Lenny said. "A lot of hanky-panky went on for centuries crossing the Mediterranean."

"Yeah, yeah. You're a fucking anthropologist, Scungilli," Big Vinny said, and then he gave Lenny a hug. "I know you want Frankie to stay in L.A., but you're gonna miss him. Believe me."

"I already miss him, but, yes, I hope he stays in L.A." Lenny returned Big Vinny's hug.

After Lenny got in his car, Big Vinny motioned for him to lower the passenger side window. "So you still looking to sell the store?"

Lenny had no idea how Big Vinny knew about that, but he nodded. "There are these brothers, new from the old country. They were interested, but I don't know if they can come up with the money. Not sure if they can get a bank to give them a mortgage. We'll see."

"Yeah, Pulumbo is their last name," Big Vinny said. "Neapolitan. I know who you mean."

Of course he knew. He was Big Vinny.

"By the way, Frankie appreciated the jacket," Lenny said. "He wore it today."

"He wanted Gennaro's, but ... well you know. I bought the exact same jacket from a guy I know in Canarsie. That was the best I can do."

"Can't do more than that," Lenny said.

"Give Tootsie one for me. I told you all Marie will do for me now is cook. What are you gonna do? Maybe Tootsie's got a friend and we can go out on a double date."

Lenny shook his head and waved as he drove away. Scungilli scraped his shoe along the curb and Big Vinny waved his hands at him. "Googootza!"

Before driving home there was one more stop Lenny wanted to make. Traffic was light. It took him about a half an hour to find the house he was looking for—a small two-family with iron grates on the first-floor windows. A statue of the Blessed Mother looked over the front patch of dirt, while a tricycle lay across the sidewalk and a naked Barbie doll lay on the front stoop.

Lenny rummaged through his glove compartment for an envelope until he found one containing his auto insurance cards. He removed the cards and placed them back in the glove compartment. Next, he took the money that Big Vinny had given to Frankie from his wallet and slipped it into the envelope, along with an extra hundred-dollar bill of his own. No one was around, so he walked up the front stoop, read the name on the mailbox to make sure it matched the cabdriver's surname and left the envelope with the money in the mailbox. Small compensation for how the DiCicos destroyed the family.

Traffic picked up, so the drive home took a little longer. When Lenny got home, Doug Turner was just leaving the auto repair shop next to Big Vinny's club. Doug yelled across the avenue: "Hey, Lenny how did things go?"

"Good," Lenny said and looked at his watch. "His plane will be landing in less than an hour."

A delivery truck briefly blocked their view of each other. Once it passed, Doug crossed the avenue. He zipped up his jacket. "California sounds awfully good to me."

Lenny wanted to get inside before someone asked him to open the store.

"Do you want to come in?" Lenny asked.

"Okay, for a minute. I gotta pick up my kid soon."

Inside, Lenny offered Doug a glass of Sambuca. Doug passed on that, but accepted a beer, and they sat at the kitchen table. Doug apologized for coming in the house smelling of oil and gasoline.

"Better than stinking of provolone," Lenny said.

"I guess both our jobs give us an aroma," Doug said.

"Yeah, we should bottle it. Call it stink of workingmen."

They laughed. Doug opened his bottle of beer and Lenny poured himself a drink. Usually they spoke of politics, sometimes a little of sports, but that afternoon their conversation was more personal. Doug talked about growing up in Bedford Stuyvesant until his mom sent him to live with his grandparents in South Carolina. "Best thing she could have done," he said. "My grandparents were no-nonsense coun-try folk. Not sure I'd be here today if not for them."

Lenny talked about his father's untimely death and the impact that it had on his life. Maybe it was the combination of the emotions of the day, and two shots of Sambuca, but Lenny did a lot of venting. He talked about how he wanted Frankie to have the life he missed. He talked about Vi. He even talked about selling the store.

"Well, here's to Frankie staying in L.A. and going to college." Doug raised his almost empty bottle of beer. Lenny poured another Sambuca and tapped Doug's bottle with his glass.

"There is one glitch that could sabotage everything," Lenny said.

"What's that?"

And Lenny broke his rule about not talking about the DiCicos, especially with someone outside of his family. He told Doug his fears about what might happen if Frankie was called to testify at the trial about the cabdriver's murder. "Who knows how a slick lawyer might twist Frankie's words and make it appear as if he knows more than he's saying?"

"Another beer?" Lenny asked. Doug held up his long fingers. Ma-chine oil stained his dark brown knuckles and fingernails black. He shook his head.

Lenny continued. "From what I understand, they're struggling to build a case. When Frankie was in the hospital, I felt as if some of the officer's questions were efforts to connect the shooting to the cabdriver's murder. I guess I was right about that, but they don't have much on Michael and Jimmy except that some unknown witness overheard them talking about getting even with the cabby. With such shabby evidence a tough lawyer will drag down anyone in this neighborhood to get a conviction."

Doug turned the empty bottle and it squeaked against the enamel-top table. He remained silent.

"Frankie might get hurt in this," Lenny said. "I don't know how, but when something involves the DiCicos, most anything could hap-pen. Look at what happened Christmas night."

Doug stared at his empty bottle. "Another?" Lenny said again.

"No, no, I'm good."

"Yeah, guess I had too much. And said too much." Lenny sighed.

"Frankie's a good kid," Doug said. "And, I think, so was Gennaro. You can't help who your father is. Lord knows mine wasn't worth much." Doug's expression turned thoughtful, as if he were seeing something that Lenny couldn't. His tongue licked at his chapped lips and he stared off to the side. "Whatever happened to the cabdriver, the DiCicos already paid a big price. Unfortunately, it was Gennaro who paid the biggest price. But they all paid, even Big Vinny. I don't like the guy and I know he ain't crazy about me. Or let's say he ain't too crazy about my color. But his son was murdered. I lost a brother that way."

Doug spoke slowly, as if selecting his words carefully. It was that all too familiar oblique way of talking about the DiCicos. Like speaking of the tip of the iceberg when everyone knows the real story hides beneath the surface. Lenny stared at Doug.

"Yes, the DiCicos have already suffered a lot. No sense in adding fuel to the fire," Doug said. "You might burn down a whole neighborhood for one condemned house."

Suddenly Lenny thought, *It's Doug who overheard Michael and Jimmy.*

"Okay, I gotta pick up my kid. Thanks for the beer." Doug stood up and pushed his chair back into the table.

"Sorry about your brother. I didn't know."

"Long ago, Lenny. It was after that my mother sent me to South Carolina."

Lenny thought about Salvatore DiCico sending Giacomo to America to live with his family. "Parents do what they have to do," he said.

"Good parents," Doug said.

Lenny walked Doug to the front door. Doug paused on the stoop and turned back towards Lenny. "Don't worry about Frankie. It'll be okay. I got a good feeling about this."

"Doug ..." Lenny wanted to say that this wasn't just about Frankie. If Doug testified he was also putting his life and his child's life at risk. Big Vinny did not forgive easily. But Lenny wasn't sure if in fact Doug was the one who spoke to the police, and he already had said much more than he should have. "Never mind," he said. "Thanks for listening."

Doug nodded and crossed the avenue, and Lenny noticed a text from Frankie. He had arrived safely, and Vi and Ina picked him up at the airport. Ina held a sign with the words: Here To Pick Up My Big Brother. Later that evening Frankie called. They talked about the flight, the birthday party Ina had planned, and a little about Frankie's misgivings about the trip.

"One day at a time, Frankie," Lenny said. "After you give it a week or so, if you don't like being there, I'll buy your ticket to come back." Lenny almost said to come home, but he stopped himself.

"We'll see. It's all so different. I've never traveled this far."

The longest Lenny ever closed the store was when Frankie was in the hospital. Vacations were the occasional Sunday through Tuesday, and the furthest they ever traveled was to Washington, D.C. Lenny hoped that Frankie would stay in Los Angeles, but he also understood that Frankie was grieving and fragile, and Lenny would accept whatever Frankie chose to do.

He tried to lighten the conversation by asking Frankie if Vi had made him a cassata. Frankie chuckled and said they had an ice cream cake. Lenny didn't mention that he left Big Vinny's money at the cabdriver's house. Some things are better left unsaid, but he knew that Frankie would like the idea.

The following evening, Marie DiCico called Lenny. She was very talkative, asking about Frankie and his trip to California. She sounded much more upbeat than when they had last talked, and Lenny was a little confused by her phone call and her rambling. She wasn't in the habit of calling him, but then she said: "Lenny, I have some good news." And Lenny immediately thought of Doug's words: "Don't worry about Frankie. It'll be okay. I got a good feeling about this."

"The good news is that the murder charges against Michael and Jimmy have been dropped," Marie said. "Let me put Lena on the phone. She can explain it better."

"Hello." Lena sounded annoyed. "I don't know why my mother can't explain this. It's not difficult to understand. Our lawyer called. He said that whoever said that he had overheard my brothers say that they were going to get even with the cabdriver recanted. That's all the D.A. had. They've been trying all these months to build a case, questioning a whole bunch of people, but they couldn't find shit. Except for that one witness, the D.A. had nothing. And if you ask me, the witness they had was a phony. I don't believe he even existed."

Oh, he's real, Lenny wanted to say, just as he would have loved to tell Lena to put Big Vinny on the phone, and tell Big Vinny to kiss Doug Turner's feet because he just saved your sons' fat asses. Of course by saying that he would also be telling Big Vinny that Doug was the person who had informed the police in the first place. No telling what Big Vinny might do. "Good news, Lena. Please tell your mother that I'm very happy for her."

In the distance, Lenny heard Lena say: "Talk to him. I'm tired of being everyone's fucking carrier pigeon."

"You still there, Lenny?"

"Yes, Marie, I'm still here."

"I just wanted you to hear the news from us first. At least there's something I can be grateful for. Too much, Lenny. I couldn't take anymore."

"I understand, Marie. Believe me, I understand."

Lenny was just about to close the store when Marie had called, so he slipped his cellphone back into his pocket, locked the front door, and turned out the lights. No trial, Lenny thought. "Thank you ... thank you," he said as he walked up the three steps from the store to the breezeway. He wasn't sure who he was thanking—Doug, fate, Filomena, God?—but he was immensely grateful. He also felt remorse. There would be no justice for the cabdriver's family, but then Lenny thought justice was little more than lofty ideals on paper or in movies. In real life justice looked a lot like revenge. He knew that, had Doug testified, he would have placed his own child and himself at terrible risk. He thought of Lena's words, the D.A. had nothing. What if Doug had testified and there was no conviction? Then Big Vinny would want his justice. Doug would be a dead man. *Peace is more important than justice*, Lenny told himself while he stood in the middle of his office and scanned the walls of sour expressions. "What if this? What if that?" he said, and threw up his hands. "Too much. There will be no trial, and right now that's all I care about." He fell to his knees. "Mama, if you can hear me, and Gennaro if you loved him half as much as he loved you, please help him to heal. Basta!"

36

The day the sale closed on the Lasante's store and house, Big Vinny and Scungilli stopped in the store with a bottle of grappa for Lenny, which Marie wrapped in gold paper and tied with a red ribbon. Somehow, the Pulumbo brothers had secured a mortgage from a bank or through a personal loan. Lenny didn't ask any questions, but he suspected that Big Vinny had something to do with it.

"A few years later than you wanted," Big Vinny said, "but you're finally getting out of the neighborhood, and so are Scungilli and me. For a little while anyway."

The next day, the DiCico men and Scungilli began their sentences in an Upstate prison. Through plea bargains, Michael and Jimmy were sentenced to one to two years with probation; Scungilli, three to five years with probation; and Big Vinny, five to seven years with probation.

"With time off for good behavior," Big Vinny said, "we'll all be home for Christmas. The Pulumbos better sell baccalà if they know what's good for them."

Scungilli excused himself and left the store. Something Big Vinny must have told him to do so he could talk with Lenny privately. He leaned on the counter as if he were about to confide a secret. "Do me two favors, Lenny."

"What's that, Vinny?" Lenny feared that Big Vinny was about to hand him another envelope stuffed with cash.

"Look in on the girls. Lena's tough, but Marie is having a hard time. She's probably glad to get rid of me, but still … it won't be easy. I don't know that she'll ever get over losing Gennaro. My mother never got over losing Sal, but then neither did my old man."

Big Vinny pushed himself up and away from the counter. "It's a lousy thing to bury your kid. Bad enough to bury a parent or God forbid a wife, but never your kid. Marie likes you. She should have married you. She would have been better off, but you were too busy being Father Lasante until Vi woke your pecker up."

"I promise I'll keep an eye on Lena and Marie," Lenny said and waited for the second request.

"One more thing, Lenny. Take care of the grave. Don't let it look like nobody goes to see him."

"Of course," Lenny said. Big Vinny had this way of turning Lenny's stomach and breaking his heart at the same time.

"We're better than blood, Lenny, whether you like it or not. One time, last year—it was at the Feast. Seems like 100 years ago. The night before Filomena died. God rest her soul. I said that you were no better than us. I lied ... you shoulda left 104th Street a long time ago, but you did right by your family. You're a good man, Lenny Lasante. There's no better."

Lenny said thank you, but there was no sense in returning the compliment. Big Vinny could smell bullshit a mile away.

"Ciao," Big Vinny said and left the store.

Big Vinny and Lenny had had more fights than Lenny could remember. Lenny carried a scar over his left eyebrow from Big Vinny's diamond pinky ring, and Big Vinny tossed out more than a few white shirts that Lenny had bloodied. Since the last Feast of The Assumption there was a lot of loss, but not only loss. Frankie had also begun coursework at UCLA, and soon Lenny would move from Glenhaven into the basement apartment in Angie's house, which in gentrified Manhattan neighborhoods were called brownstone garden apartments. Lenny called it the cellar in Angie's attached house, which was good enough for him.

Tootsie seemed disappointed when Lenny first told her that he was selling the store and the house and moving into the city, but she understood—at least that's what she said. They saw each other often after Frankie left. Lenny even spent a few nights at her place when Tyrone was at his grandmother's. The night before Lenny moved to Angie's, Tootsie and he went to Russo's On The Bay for dinner.

They lifted their wine glasses for a toast.

"I get it, Lenny," she said. "You don't have to explain. You were seventeen when you started taking care of people, and you just got done. You need a break. Here's to a new beginning."

They each took a sip of their wine and placed their glasses back on the linen tablecloth.

"You also still got a thing for Vi," she said.

It was an upscale restaurant, dim lighting, good food, and Tootsie looked very pretty, but yes, Lenny still had a thing for Vi, or at least the idea of Vi. Tootsie reminded him too much of the neighborhood and of the folks who never considered leaving, but he couldn't tell her that. Letting Tootsie think that he was still in love with Vi was a kinder way of letting Tootsie down.

A waiter wearing a white dinner jacket and a black bowtie placed a plate of chicken cacciatore on the table before Tootsie and mussels fra diavolo over linguini before Lenny.

"Do me one favor, Lenny."

"What's that?"

"Tonight, instead of going back to my place, let's spend the night at your house."

It seemed like a silly idea, but Lenny agreed.

Most of the furniture was gone. Angie, Amelia, Irish, and Tony had divvied up some of the antiques. Lenny didn't want anything except for a few photographs and the cartoline postale for Frankie, which as it turned out had some monetary value, but Lenny doubted that Frankie would ever sell them, at least not the ones of the great-grandfathers.

Lenny didn't know why Tootsie wanted to spend their last evening together in the almost empty house, but the sex was great — slow and deliberate until their bodies could no longer hold back, and Lenny bit his lip not to call out Vi's name.

Afterwards, Tootsie gathered her clothes. "Aren't you spending the night?" Lenny said.

"Why? Vi's the only woman that you made love to in this house. So tonight I was Vi. I know that. If you ever change your mind, you know how to reach me."

Tootsie carried her clothes from the bedroom to the bathroom off the hallway.

After the front door closed downstairs, the house was silent—no creaks, no water running or toilets flushing, no voices, no fragrance of Jean Nate or sauce simmering or coffee perking. It was already someone else's house.

The next day, the smell of low tide wafted in from Jamaica Bay as the Pulumbo brothers removed the Lasante's Italian-American Groceries sign. They were Calabrese, not Neapolitan as Big Vinny had said. Very short and dark, and the neighbors called them the hardhead twins. Being hardheaded or stubborn was the hackneyed belief about people from Calabria, and they were called twins because they resembled each other, not because they were in fact twins.

The older brother held the ladder while the younger brother tottered near the top rung, struggling to reach the sign. Onlookers lost count of the number of times that the brother at the top of the ladder dropped whatever he was holding, several times bopping his brother's bald head, who let go of a barrage of curse words in dialect each time he was hit.

Quite an audience gathered before the brothers were done with their Southern Italian version of a Laurel and Hardy. Elders pulled little ones away from the ladder fearing that falling tools or worse, a falling sign might injure them. When not laughing, old women took tissues from the bosom or sleeve of their housedresses and dabbed at their eyes as if watching a cortege. Old men shook their heads in clouds of cigar smoke. "The end of an era," Lou Romano from Romano's Funeral home said as the sign came down.

Lenny waited for the crowd in front of the store to disperse before he left the house to sneak across the avenue and have lunch with Doug. When he entered the garage, Doug was scrubbing motor oil from his hands in a large rusty slop sink.

"Just in time," Doug said.

Lenny had never thanked Doug for recanting on what he had initially told the police, assuming he was in fact the sole witness that Big Vinny's lawyer spoke of. Lenny was pretty sure that he was—as sure as he could be of anything that had to do with Big Vinny. Given that the DiCico men were in jail, and no one else was in the garage except for the two of them, maybe now was the time to talk. But there was always the chance that someone might overhear them, and if it got back to Big Vinny that Doug was the D.A.'s witness, Doug would be a dead man and Lenny would be a hero. After all, he was the one who persuaded Doug to recant. At least that's how Big Vinny might see things.

Doug opened two weather-beaten lawn chairs and an equally worn card table behind an old Cadillac on a hydraulic lift. Next he took several Tupperware and two beers from a cooler, plastic and paperware from a shopping bag, and set everything on the card table.

"This is nice of you, Doug."

"Well, I figured you've been making me lunch all these years."

"Not exactly the same thing. This is a lot more than a sandwich, and you paid for your lunches."

Doug opened the Tupperware. "I can't take credit for all of it. One of the women from my church made the fried chicken, mac and cheese, and corn bread, but I made the collard greens. I figured you should finally taste what I've been doing with all those hambones."

Both men filled their plates and shook hot sauce on their collards. Doug also shook hot sauce on his chicken.

"Delicious, Doug. Especially the collards."

They talked about the new owners of the grocery store and how the Pulumbos planned to sell more cooked food.

"Maybe I'll teach them how to make greens," Doug said, and Lenny recalled Big Vinny's slur about Doug that evening during the Feast of The Assumption.

They talked about their kids, how well Doug's daughter was doing in middle school and how Frankie was doing in California. "He seems okay," Lenny said. "It's going to take time."

Doug bit into a chicken leg and nodded.

Lenny also spoke about Tootsie. Not in great detail, but that he liked her and appreciated all that she had done for Frankie. He admitted feeling guilty about the way things turned out.

Doug talked about a woman from church he was dating, the woman who had cooked much of their lunch.

What they didn't talk about was Big Vinny, his sons, or the cabdriver.

After they finished eating and folded the lawn chairs and card table, Doug handed Lenny a bottle of Sambuca.

"I remember you drank this that day in your house when we talked about a lot of stuff, and I told you not to worry about Frankie. I said he'd be okay. Look how good things turned out."

Lenny took the bottle from Doug, and their eyes locked. "You were right." Lenny held up his gift. "Thank you. You have no idea how grateful I am." They shook hands.

"You're welcome, Lenny. It was my pleasure. Don't be a stranger."

As Lenny crossed 91st Avenue, he thought: *Even if Big Vinny had his ear to the garage, he would have no idea what Doug and I were just talking about.* Lenny smiled and glanced at the new sign over the grocery store—Pulumbo Brothers.

37 ఒ Six Years Later

After Lenny moved into Angie's brownstone, he volunteered at The Good Samaritan Kitchen. First he volunteered during breakfast one or two days a week, then breakfasts and dinners, and then five days a week became seven days a week, until the program manager of the Kitchen retired, and Father Perez offered Lenny the job. Lenny said yes, as long as he wasn't required to attend Mass. Father laughed and called Lenny Saint Skeptic, which Lenny saw as an improvement over Hard Luck Lenny.

The Good Samaritan Kitchen was in Saint John the Baptist Church, where Filomena and Frankie once lit candles before a bust of Padre Pio, as Lenny had also done on the day he gave Big Vinny's envelope to a stranger at the Lefferts Boulevard Station. The volunteer staff called the people who dined at the Kitchen guests, and some of the guests bore a confidence and swagger that said this is only a temporary setback, just a hard-luck glitch, but others looked defeated — their eyes either vigilant or vacant, arms pocked with needle marks, breath reeking of alcohol. Mental illness, addiction, poverty, or some calamity had claimed their lives.

When Frankie visited Lenny in Manhattan, he often volunteered at the Kitchen, and on this Christmas day, six years after the cab-driver's son had revenged his father's murder, Frankie spotted a guest who reminded him of Gennaro—something in the way he smirked when Frankie asked him if he wanted ham or chicken, as if his question were silly, but Frankie often saw Gennaro in strangers. Not so much when he was in California, but always in New York City. It was more about attitude than physical appearance. The Gennaros Frankie noticed were tall or short, dark or light, maybe a boy climbing a jungle gym in Central Park, or an old man sitting on park bench feeding pigeons. Each time Frankie came East not a day passed without spotting at least one Gennaro. In California, he occasionally forgot, but in New York City all he did was remember.

"Can I have a little of both?" the young man asked.

Frankie stared at him as if not understanding his request.

"Some ham and some chicken."

He had black eyes under heavy black lashes, perfectly arched eyebrows, and a shadow of a beard. One of those men who might shave in the morning, again at noon, and still have a 5 o'clock shadow. The name Sam was printed above the brim of his red cap. Frankie placed a slice of ham and two chicken thighs on a plate, and he handed the plate to the server next to him wearing a yarmulke. The man added a scoop of mashed potatoes. Then a woman added vegetables. She was a rabbi, and most of the Christmas dinner volunteers were from her synagogue—a long-standing Christmas tradition at the Good Samaritan Kitchen.

Gennaro with the red cap that read Sam selected chocolate cake for dessert, and he glanced back at Frankie as if for approval. Frankie would have picked the apple pie, but he smiled. Chocolate cake was a fine choice.

Sam sat at one of the long folding tables where Lenny chatted with men as easily as he had once done with customers in Lasante's. Angie often complained that Lenny was too chummy with the guests.

"Things can get testy," she confided in Frankie during their cellphone conversations. "For the most part, your father is good at easing tensions, but sometimes he should call the police. Pushing 60, and he still thinks he's 20."

Frankie didn't like it when Angie exaggerated Lenny's age. Since Gennaro's death he especially feared losing Lenny but, at 56, Lenny felt and looked better than he had when he sold the store. His hair was grayer, but he joined a Y and either walked or took subways. He had sold his car when he moved to Manhattan. He also grew a beard and resembled an Italian Ernest Hemingway. Lenny patted Sam's shoulder, and Sam wished him a Merry Christmas.

Manhattan agreed with Lenny. He worked a lot but, when he wasn't working or at the Y, he frequented the places that he shared years ago with Frankie. Los Angeles, however, didn't agree with Frankie, but in his sophomore year at UCLA he began writing, and his stories took him far away from California—mostly to New York City, sometimes Purling in the Catskills, and sometimes Sicily.

Angie collected the trays, plates, and silverware after guests finished eating, and her boyfriend, Dan, worked the dishwasher. They'd been together for nearly three years and lately they talked of marriage—at least Dan did. He was Angie's first Republican. A large man, balding, and a genius with his hands— adept at carpentry, electrical work, and plumbing. For the most part, Lenny and Dan avoided talking politics, but sometimes conversations got pretty heated. However, Lenny liked Dan better than any of Angie's past boyfriends and definitely better than Angie's ex-husband.

The food line soon became shorter, and most of the seats in the dining area were taken. An undernourished Santa Claus made his way up and down the aisles and handed out gloves and scarfs to the guests. There were wrapped presents for the children.

Sam stuffed his gloves and scarf into his already bulging backpack. He talked to everyone at his table, though some of the men seemed distracted or more interested in their food than anything Sam had to say, but he didn't let that stop him. Frankie wondered if Sam could sing like Mario Lanza, or if there were tiny scars that lined his chest and biceps.

"Ham, please!" A heavy woman with wild salt and pepper hair glared at Frankie. Frankie apologized, placed several slices of ham on her plate, and chicken on the next two plates. He recognized some of the guests from past Christmas dinners and other New York visits, but he had never seen Sam. He would have remembered if he had. He would have written about him as he wrote about many people who, or incidents that, reminded him of Gennaro.

Angie tapped Frankie's shoulder. "I'll take over here. Your dad wants you to meet someone. Over there." Angie pointed towards an exit sign. Under it, Lenny talked with a woman.

Sam didn't seem to notice when Frankie passed his table even though Frankie paused behind Sam's chair, picked up stray sugar packets, and pretended to straighten the other chairs. Sam's backpack was covered with buttons. One was the size of a silver dollar with a picture of an ancient Greek theater before the smoldering Mt. Etna—the setting for many of the cartoline postale. Taormina was written across the bottom, and Frankie looked in disbelief from the button to Sam, back to the button, back to Sam, but Sam didn't notice. He held his fork like a trowel and scooped up a meld of mashed potatoes and vegetables. His knuckles were as chafed and grimy as were von Gloeden's Sicilian boys', including the great-grandfathers'.

Lenny waved to get Frankie's attention. Dazed, Frankie walked towards the exit sign, but rather than stop and talk with Lenny and his woman friend, Frankie passed them and continued out the door into the slip of alley. Lenny excused himself and followed him.

"Are you alright?" Lenny asked. They both wore aprons as they once had in Lasante's, but these aprons were stenciled with the quote: "And who is my neighbor?"

Frankie leaned against the stone wall. The cold air soothed him as he tried to answer Lenny, but he couldn't—not yet. Gennaro would have told him to stop reading into things. *It's just a fuckin button*, he would have said. Or would he? Maybe Gennaro might have finally agreed that not everything is random. There's much we don't know? So much so that we don't even know what we don't know until something as simple as a button on a backpack reminds us that life is more than chance.

"I'm okay, just a little woozy from standing over the steam table."

"Should I get you a folding chair?" Lenny asked.

"No. I'm really okay. Really. Let's go back inside. I'll be fine. I just needed some air."

Lenny's friend waited for them just inside the door. She looked to be in her fifties—bohemian Manhattan, a full-figured woman draped in black crepe. Her hair was piled atop her head, though stray winglets of her curly mane and beaded earrings brushed her shoulders as she bobbed her head as she spoke, which she seemed to do a lot.

"Frankie, this is Hannah Rosen. She's here to help with cleanup, but first I want to introduce you two. We met at an author series at the 92nd Street Y where she teaches fiction. I figured you'd have a lot in common, both being writers."

Frankie and Hannah shook hands, smiled, and exchanged the preliminary nice to meet you, and Frankie wondered if he should say something about having read her work, assuming that she was published. He didn't recognize her name, and he was much too distracted by thoughts of the Taormina button and Sam to exchange small talk with Hannah, even if she were Atwood or Morrison.

"Your father tells me that you're reading at Bluestockings Bookstore tomorrow evening."

"Yes. Not sure what kind of turnout there will be, given that it's the night after Christmas." *Can I go now*, he thought.

"Well, let's hope for a good showing. Not everyone celebrates Christmas."

He was about to excuse himself and get back to work and watching Sam, but Lenny beat him to it by saying that he had to collect trays.

Hannah reminded Frankie of Vi's friends, or colleagues as she called them, and of more than a few of his undergraduate and graduate professors—her elocution slow and affected, as if she were struggling to dumb down her thoughts.

"So you'll be reading from a collection of your short stories?" she asked.

Frankie assumed that Lenny had explained all of this to her, but he played along. "Yes, most of the stories have already been published individually, but this is my first collection."

"And so young. Very impressive."

Not so impressive, he thought, and he was much more interested in Sam than Lenny's latest squeeze. Who else might she be, and why else would she come to help clean up the Kitchen dressed as if she were going to a café on Madison Ave? She was also a little on the chubby side. *Just the way Dad likes his women*, Frankie thought.

"Thank you. I think Dad needs help collecting trays. Most of the guests have finished eating."

"Yes, I'll help. That's why I'm here. Just tell me what to do."

You can start by changing that dress, Frankie thought, but he smiled, nodded, and tried not to roll his eyes.

Unfortunately Sam was gone, unlike Hannah, who followed Frankie to the kitchen where he handed her an apron.

38

Lenny's apartment had its own entrance behind a wrought-iron gate to the right of the brownstone stoop and down three steps. The apartment, which had been renovated just before Lenny moved in, included a single, sleek open space (kitchen, dining, and sitting area), a bedroom, and a bathroom. The only furniture Lenny moved from the old house was the enamel-top kitchen table and its two chairs, his bed, and one dresser. The rest of the apartment was furnished with pieces that Angie picked out at IKEA—very utilitarian, except for framed posters that Lenny bought at the Metropolitan Museum of Art—Modigliani, Gauguin, Picasso. Bright, bold images.

Aside from a few cards, there was nothing Christmassy about Lenny's apartment. Since moving, he never decorated for holidays. Frankie once asked him if it was because of what had happened that night at Most Precious Blood, and Lenny shrugged his shoulders. "I was never big on Christmas," he said.

Last night they ate Christmas Eve dinner upstairs in Angie's apartment with Angie and Dan, where there was a small artificial tree with lights, and also several of the antiques from the old house including the mother bear and cubs humidor and pipe tray. Mama bear held a Christmas cactus in bloom on the tray above her head. The pipes, along with many other small items and furniture, had been donated to a local charity.

Frankie and Lenny sat at the enamel-top table and ate Christmas Eve leftovers. Lenny poured a glass of wine for Frankie and for himself. He raised his glass and said: "Boun Natale."

"What's Sam's story?" Frankie said nonchalantly, as if he were just making small talk, but not particularly curious about Sam. He stabbed a calamari ring with his fork and twirled several strands of linguini.

"Sam?"

"Yeah. A guy at the Kitchen. Around my age. Maybe a little older. Kind of nice looking. Looks as if he could use a shave."

"A lot of guys there look like they can use a shave."

"No. I mean he has a heavy beard. You know, like he always looks as if he needs a shave—even after he shaves."

"Sorry, but I don't know any guy named Sam. Maybe if I saw him. I don't know everyone's name. Some folks come and go." Lenny grated more Romano cheese onto his linguini. He held the chunk of cheese and grater out to Frankie.

"No, I'm good," Frankie said. "But you were talking to him today. He carried a backpack covered with buttons."

Lenny put down his fork, squinted at Frankie and twisted his mouth to one side as if confused by Frankie's interest.

"He wore a red baseball cap with his name on it. Sam."

"Oh, you mean Angel. I don't know where he got that cap, but his name is Angel, not Sam." Lenny finished his wine and took a deep breath. "His story? Iraq ... Assholes in Washington like Cheney ... Halliburton making big money off war ... Just pick one. That's Sam's story, just like it's the story of a lot of the guys at the Kitchen." Lenny raised his eyebrows. "Why so interested?"

Frankie shrugged, again feigning disinterest. "No reason. He had a button on his backpack that said Taormina. It just seemed odd."

"He has a lot of buttons that say a lot of things," Lenny said, as if he were channeling Gennaro.

"True, but it caught my eye."

"You doing okay?"

Frankie nodded.

Later, as he lay on the futon beneath a poster of Gauguin's *The Siesta*, but not able to sleep and rethinking which of his short stories he'd read tomorrow night at Bluestockings, Frankie heard Lenny in the bathroom. He called out to him. "Dad, I'll help out at breakfast in the morning."

"I leave at five," Lenny said.

Frankie set the alarm on his cellphone. He flinched when he heard Lenny drop something. He was used to flinching at loud noises, used to dreading Christmas, and used to missing Gennaro. He accepted missing Gennaro. It was simply a part of who Frankie was. Like an amputee, Frankie didn't cease moving forward, but his steps were more deliberate, always aware that something, or in Frankie's case someone, was missing. Stumbling, even falling, and then getting back up had become routine. He wondered what ghosts haunted Angel.

Come morning, it was an eight-block walk from Lenny's apartment to the Good Samaritan Kitchen, and though the seven blocks along 8th Avenue were short before they turned up 31st Street to Saint John the Baptist Church, it was icy cold, and Frankie was barely able to keep up with Lenny.

Lenny pierced the dark like a locomotive as steam rose from the scarf covering his mouth. Angie often complained about him walking alone every morning in the dark, again citing his age as her concern. Lenny dismissed Angie's concern with: "Most of the guys on the street know me. If I run into someone new, I'll invite him to breakfast or introduce him to you in case things go south with your Republican."

Two volunteer cooks, Earl and Cindy, met Lenny and Frankie in front of the church. They were an elderly couple who knew how to handle the temperamental ovens and had volunteered at the Kitchen longer than Frankie had been on the planet—at least that's what they said.

"Good morning, Lenny. I see you've brought the pup," Earl said. He was bald with a ring of gray hair, but he had a smooth boyish face and sky-blue eyes. Cindy's face, on the other hand, was a cushion of wrinkles, but her smile made her appear as ageless as Earl.

She asked about yesterday's Christmas dinner, and as Lenny answered, his voice rose and fell while he moved through the church basement like an automaton—switching on lights and turning up the thermostat. He left the ovens to Earl and Cindy and told Frankie that they were serving French toast today, and to fill small plastic cups with syrup—something Frankie had done many times before.

Frankie rolled out sheets of wax paper on a table, lined up the plastic cups in tidy rows, and carefully poured syrup from a large bottle into the tiny cups. More volunteers arrived, and soon the kitchen and dining area were filled with friendly chatter, opening folding chairs, making coffee, and pouring water into the steam-table trays.

The volunteers Frankie knew asked how he was doing. One woman he had never met joined him at the table and snapped lids on the cups Frankie had already filled. Her name was Tanya, and she spoke with a Jamaican accent.

It finally warmed up enough for the volunteers to remove their coats and put on aprons, while the hall outside the dining area filled with guests waiting for breakfast to be served.

Lenny assigned Frankie to coffee, which Frankie preferred rather than standing behind the steam tables or closed off in the kitchen or dishwasher room. If Angel showed up, Frankie was sure to see him. Lenny removed the rope separating the hallway from the dining area, and most of the guests lined up for coffee before they picked up their food trays.

Frankie handed out the Styrofoam cups filled with hot coffee and was moved, as always, by the guests' show of gratitude: "Thank you … God Bless." Some people barely made eye contact with him and others appeared to struggle with invisible demons, but most of the guests were friendly and polite. Once a guest had threatened to throw coffee at Frankie because Frankie had held his hand over the top of the cup, but when the short, emaciated man came back for seconds, scratching his gray matted head of hair, he smiled a mostly toothless smile and told Frankie to have a blessed day as if they were the best of friends.

The breakfast line was short when Angel finally appeared. At first it seemed that Angel was going to skip coffee but, after he placed his tray of food on a table, he walked towards Frankie.

"Coffee, please."

His breath smelled of cigarette smoke and something sweet like fermentation. He looked tired or hung-over—maybe both.

"Good morning," Frankie said with a bit too much enthusiasm.

"Thank you," Angel said and returned to his table.

It was 8:25 and they stopped serving at 8:30. A woman rushed in with a baby in one arm and pulling a toddler behind her, while her coat fanned open and the bottom of her sweater struggled to reach the top of her sweat pants, exposing a small paunch with stretch marks.

"Slow down, Diana," Lenny said. "You have plenty of time. I won't throw you out for at least another five minutes."

Diana laughed and handed the baby to an older woman already eating breakfast. She picked up a tray with one hand and held the toddler's arm with the other. He squirmed, but Diana meant business.

At 8:35 Frankie stopped serving coffee, picked up a stack of trays, and carried them to the room where two older men ran the dishwasher. One man with bushy gray eyebrows and a yellow Mets baseball cap asked Frankie about school, but Frankie kept his answers brief so he could get back to the dining area before Angel left.

He meandered around tables close to where Angel sat, gathering trays, talking to guests, and trying not to appear obvious. He approached Angel, smiled and made some mundane comment about the weather. Angel's breakfast plates sat on the table in front of him, and his empty tray was pushed to the side. Frankie pointed to the tray. "If you're done with that, I can take it for you."

Angel spooned cereal into his mouth. "Sure, thanks," he said. Milk dribbled from his spoon and caught in the stubble on his chin. He wiped his hand across his mouth.

His backpack was under his chair, so Frankie couldn't pretend to notice the Taormina button and comment about it.

He took a few steps away from Angel, but then retraced his steps as if he'd forgotten something.

"Didn't I notice yesterday that you had a backpack with a button of Taormina?"

Angel looked up from mixing jelly in his eggs. "Yesterday?" he said.

"Yes, I worked Christmas dinner." Frankie had never seen eyes as large and dark as Angel's.

Angel's pouty lips spread into a broad grin. "I remember. You're ham or chicken." He pulled his backpack out from under his chair. "Oh yeah. This big one says Taormina. I got it at some feast downtown."

"San Gennaro," Frankie said. He just about shouted *San* but *Gennaro* was barely audible.

"Yeah, that's it."

Still holding the tray, Frankie slumped onto the chair across from Angel.

"Are you okay?' Angel said. Several men at the table glanced at Frankie, but then returned to their food.

Angel was older than the boys in the cartoline postale and a bit older than Frankie, but there was something familiar about him, and Frankie imagined Gennaro rolling his eyes, and sighing. *There you go, Francesco, making something out of nothing. Even if he's hot and his name is Angel, he's still a drunk in a soup kitchen.* But Frankie dismissed thoughts of Gennaro.

"My great-grandfather was from Taormina," Frankie said. "In fact I wrote a story about it ... in a way, about him ... but fiction ... well, you know ..."

Angel interrupted Frankie's rambling. "You're a writer?"

"Yes ... kind of ... mostly short stories."

It was difficult to ignore the volunteers cleaning up around them, which is what Frankie should have been doing. Angel finished his coffee and wiped his mouth—this time with a napkin. He nodded. The corners of his mouth turned down and he stroked the bristles on his chin as if he were about to critique Frankie's writing. A tattoo crawled up his forearm where his flannel shirt was rolled up and his thermal undershirt was pushed back. Another tattoo climbed up his neck, and Frankie wondered what else was beneath Angel's flannel and thermal shirts. Maybe some tattoos resembled scars that traversed his chest and biceps. Angel leaned forward, took his tray back, and loaded it with his dirty dishes and silverware. Frankie didn't want him to leave.

"Do you like feasts?" Frankie asked, feeling like an idiot.

"I guess so."

Only a few people, aside from Diana and her toddler, were still eating. The older woman sitting next to Diana fed the baby from a bottle. Gray hair peeked out from under her black wig. Her face was ebony and deeply lined.

Frankie couldn't think of anything witty or clever to say and started to feel as if he were being ridiculous. *This is a soup kitchen, not a gay bar*, he thought.

"I should get back to work. Nice talking to you. I can take your tray." He stood, but as he reached for the tray, his fingertips brushed

Angel's, and Angel looked down at their hands. Frankie caught a flash of the parched Sicilian landscape, dark eyes, pouty lips, and a strong, heavily shadowed jaw. His breath quickened.

"You live in Manhattan?" Angel asked.

If only, Frankie thought, but he said California.

"You're dedicated."

At first Frankie was confused, but then he realized that Angel was joking about Frankie traveling from California to New York City just to volunteer at the Kitchen. His humor made him more appealing and reminded Frankie more of Gennaro.

"I see you met Angel." Lenny was standing next to them with a bucket of soapy water and a cloth. "I'll take that tray. You can start on the tables." Lenny plopped the bucket in front of Frankie. Some of the soapy water splashed on the table. "See you tomorrow, Angel," Lenny said, and walked back towards the kitchen.

"Lenny's a great guy," Angel said. "Does a lot of things for people here that no one knows about. He's helped me out a couple of times."

Frankie didn't mention that Lenny was his dad. Instead, he repeated that Taormina was the setting for one of his stories.

"Yes, the one about your great-grandfather."

"In a way," Frankie said. "Let's say it was inspired by some pictures of him and some letters and ... well anyway."

Frankie wondered what Angel did after he left the Kitchen. Did he spend his day drinking? Riding the subway for hours? Sleeping in a library? Maybe he worked? Lenny said that a lot of the guests have jobs that don't pay a fair enough wage. Or maybe Angel comes to the Kitchen for the company—something to quiet his ghosts.

Meeting Angel felt fated, like discovering the cartoline postale and that maybe, of all people, Gennaro had something to do with it. *Frankie meet Angel. You've both seen hell.*

"Do you know where Bluestockings Bookstore is?"

"Yes," Angel said. "I read a poem there a couple of years ago."

Hearing this, Frankie felt ashamed for thinking that Angel drank all day, or rode the subways for hours, or slept in a library, as if reading poetry set him above such behaviors.

"You can close your mouth," Angel said, laughing. "I was in a PTSD therapy group, and the shrink introduced us to an editor who wanted to publish a collection of stories and poems written by vets who had been to Iraq or Afghanistan. I agreed to give it a try."

"That's great," Frankie said, concerned that he sounded like Hannah or one of his professors.

"Maybe not that great, but they had a good spread at the bookstore, and I made a couple of bucks, and maybe helped some people see how the bottom one percent are being fucked over by the top one percent."

"You sound like my father."

Angel smiled. "I thought Lenny might be your father. You look like him, except for your pretty eyes."

The blood rushed to Frankie's ears and other places.

"Don't you have tables to wash? How about I see you tomorrow at breakfast?" Angel stood and picked up his backpack.

Frankie also stood. By now volunteers were washing tables and folding chairs. "How about I see you tonight?" Frankie asked, startled by his own words.

Angel's black eyes narrowed. "Tonight?"

"I mean, I'm reading some of my stories tonight at Bluestockings —7 pm. Why don't you come?"

"We'll see. I have to check my busy calendar." He smiled, put on his jacket, threw his backpack over his shoulder, and Frankie watched him leave. He liked the way he walked away.

Frankie scrubbed tables and thought of his years in therapy. After he had almost flunked out of his first semester at UCLA, Vi convinced him to seek help. A therapist said that Frankie was suffering from a form of PTSD. She said that his trouble sleeping, recurring night-mares, and phobias were the result of what had happened that night in Most Precious Blood. Frankie knew that the only reason he didn't wind up like some of the guys at the Kitchen was because Lenny came to Los Angeles. They moved into an apartment together and Lenny stayed until Frankie was back on his feet. Frankie also knew that some credit went to Vi, who cared enough to know that he was in trouble and pushed him to do something about it.

But for the grace of my father, Frankie thought, and carried the soapy bucket back to the kitchen.

39

Frankie's short stories spoke of life on 91st Avenue and 104th Street: browning garlic, simmering sauce, colored lights, arbors heavy with grapevines, lush gardens where roses and hydrangeas shared beds with ripening tomatoes and peppers, and of course the people with their admirable but deleterious sense of loyalty. Scratch through the veneer of fiction and you found real people, places, and events. But given Frankie's imagination and sense of whimsy, reality was relative.

An independent press published his collection, and his editor scheduled the reading at Bluestockings to coincide with Frankie's Christmas visit with Lenny. This was his second reading in the East. His first was in Provincetown. He had introduced the collection at a literary festival in New Orleans last April, and since then he had read at colleges and bookstores in Los Angeles and San Francisco.

Fortunately Hannah was right, and the turnout at Bluestockings was much better than Frankie had expected. He stood at a small podium, and folks sat on the floor cross-legged, making a u-shape around him. Behind them, every folding chair was taken. Lenny, Hannah, Angie, and Dan sat in the first row. Vi and Ina sat three rows behind them. They drove into Manhattan from Queens where they spent Christmas with Vi's mother, who Frankie now called Bobute—grandma in Lithuanian.

He met her four years ago after Vi's father died. Vi didn't offer an explanation for why she had postponed introductions until her father passed away, and Frankie didn't ask. Bobute was a nice enough woman—short, stout, and spoke with a very heavy accent. Her face was heavily lined. Frankie assumed lined skin would be Vi's fate, but hoped his Sicilian blood might spare him. Sometimes, Ina traveled East with him, and she either stayed with Bobute or Angie. At some point, Ina stopped asking Frankie to call Vi mom. Calling their grandmother Bobute was the unspoken compromise.

Behind Vi and Ina sat Gennaro's sister, Lena, and Johnny Pickle. They married soon after Big Vinny was released from prison. At their wedding, Big Vinny whispered to Frankie that he should have married Lena. "But Johnny's a Jew and Jews make good husbands," Big Vinny said. "And no Italian man would put up with Lena's attitude anyway." Frankie didn't mention that Big Vinny had always put up with Lena's attitude. She got away with saying things to her father that Michael and Jimmy could never. Only Gennaro had been favored more than Lena, but then Big Vinny was not the only one who favored Gennaro.

Lena appeared as if she might give birth before Frankie finished reading, but Johnny was the one who looked exhausted. He had grown into his large ears, and was a nice looking young man who just happened to be in dire need of a vacation from the DiCicos, including Lena.

Frankie didn't recognize anyone else in the audience. There was no Angel. The first story he read was titled "The Feast of The Assumption," and when he finished reading it, many in the audience wiped away tears. He followed with a light piece about snails. Now the reaction was smiles and occasional laughter. He read sections from two more stories. No yawns or rolling eyes. So far rapport with his audience was excellent, but he was nervous about the final story. It was the most revealing.

He thanked everyone for coming and said: "The title of the last piece I'll read to you this evening is 'Leaving Taormina,' which as you'll notice is also the title of my collection." Frankie held up his book to show the cover. Several people already had copies in their hands or resting on their laps.

"It's the story of a man who is about to emigrate from his small town in Sicily to America at a time when same-sex love was rarely spoken of or even acknowledged."

Frankie began to read his tale of Great-Grandfather Leonardo leaving Salvatore DiCico, although he changed their names, and when he neared the part where the lovers sought the shade of the citrus grove to share their last supper together, he looked up. Angel, his dark eyes framed by long lashes, the shadow of a beard accentuating his strong jawline, stood behind the final row of chairs. No cap, and at first Frankie barely recognized him with his tight curls trimmed close to his scalp, not much longer than the shadow of his beard.

It was warm and Angel had removed his coat. Fastened to his olive green t-shirt was a button about the size of a silver dollar. His forearms were sinewy and heavily tattooed, his black eyes smiled, as did his full lips, and Frankie continued to read the part of his story that he had dreamt not long after Most Precious Blood—more discovery than creation.

"Their hands were calloused and they led a donkey along rocky cliffs, down a dirt road, where they paused and shot stones from a precipice. Above them were buildings thirsting for whitewash and stacked like children's blocks precariously clinging to a lush, sun-bathed mountainside. A tremble and they would come tumbling down."

He looked up, and Angel smiled knowingly.

"They resumed their walk, coming upon a fork in the road where they bore left, away from the cliffs and down a steep slope until they entered the shade of a citrus grove, thick with the heady fragrance of lemon and orange blossoms. One man tethered the donkey to a tree and removed a burlap sack from off the donkey's back. On the earth beneath wizened limbs, the other spread a modest feast of bread, cheese, olives, and a bottle of wine. They leaned against the trunk of a lemon tree; their shoulders kissed as they ate and drank and spoke in soft fatalistic intonations—*Do this in memory of me.*"

Again Frankie looked up as if he were reading only to Angel, as if he were reminding Angel of the picnic they once shared. Angel nodded. Somehow Frankie was able to control the heaviness of his breaths, and he continued to read.

"In this faraway place, to the distant, mythical sound of Pan's flute, their tattered rags fell away, exposing their scars and bruises and their glistening bronze. One man licked the pearls of sweat from the hallow of his lover's neck and they ... "

When he finished reading, he scanned the audience, which he had all but forgotten, and they appeared stunned. *It can't be my words*, he thought. *I've read this story many times.* Though erotic, there were few explicit or gratuitous details. *I've never had this response*, he thought and felt embarrassed and exposed.

A few people turned to Angel, including Lenny, as if they understood that Frankie had been reading to him. Then the applause began and the audience gave Frankie a standing ovation. His neck and face burned in appreciation, embarrassment, and longing.

Angel also applauded. Frankie hadn't felt as drawn to another person since Gennaro. And he couldn't shake the feeling that somehow Gennaro willed this. He remembered his last visit to Tucci's and how he felt while watching the falls, as if Gennaro had given him permission. For what? Frankie didn't know. At the time, Lenny had suggested, *permission to go on living.*

Permission to go on living, Frankie thought as he watched Angel applaud.

40

While Lenny waited for Frankie to read, he skimmed through a book titled *The Italian Left: A History of Socialist and Communist Parties,* and he told Angie that he might buy it as a belated Christmas gift for Big Vinny. She rolled her eyes. Books were categorized under labels such as Race and Racism, Class and Labor, and Activist Strategies. The stacks were on wheels and had been pushed aside, maximizing the limited space for the ten rows of folding chairs, which curved before a battered podium. Bluestockings was about 30' by 30', and the good turnout in such a small space made for a cozy reading.

One street over from the bookstore was Orchard Street, where Vincenzo once argued with merchants about the price of Lenny's Easter suit and the material for Filomena to sew the girls' Easter dresses. Filomena told the children to stop fidgeting as the shop owner tickled them with a tape measure. This was before Tony was born. After he was born, Filomena had enough of sewing and they purchased all the children's Easter outfits in Sears.

Lenny reminded Angie of this bit of Lasante trivia and also mentioned that Bluestockings rents its space for community events. "You and Dan, your fiscally conservative boyfriend, should have your wedding reception here. It will be like old times. You can buy your dress on Orchard Street and walk around the corner for your wedding."

Angie poked Lenny in the ribs and told him to be quiet as a young man who looked as if he were held together with industrial staples introduced Frankie. Someone turned off what sounded to Lenny more like Beelzebub scolding his minions than music.

After introductions, Frankie began to read, and Lenny was transfixed. Frankie's voice was confident and soothing, and though Lenny had read and reread these stories many times, this was the first he had heard Frankie read aloud. Frankie made frequent and lingering eye contact with the audience, which gave his prose the intimacy of a bedtime story. Occasionally his eyes wandered to the front door as if he were expecting another guest, and Lenny couldn't help but think that Frankie was hoping for the resurrected Gennaro to appear.

As he read "Leaving Taormina," Lenny noticed Frankie's glance towards the door turn soft as if eyes could sigh, and Lenny looked back to see Angel standing behind the last row of folding chairs.

Each time Frankie's eyes rose from his book, they met Angel's, and the rest of the audience became voyeurs, an experience that felt oddly familiar to Lenny, like a memory without images or sounds—just a sense of déjà vu. The look in Frankie's eyes and the longing in his voice were reminiscent of Frankie's expression when Gennaro sang at The Feast of The Assumption and the sound of Frankie's voice when they talked about the falls at Tucci's, but there was something else, a memory Lenny couldn't quite locate as if it had been misplaced, or even dismissed long ago.

Frankie finished reading and looked at the audience. First silence, then one person and another and another applauded, until everyone applauded and stood. Some heads turned towards Angel as if he should also take a bow. And through all of this, the obscure memory sat on Lenny's shoulder and whispered in his ear like one of those pesky devils that the nuns once warned him about. For the most part, he tried to ignore it.

A woman with a shaved head, but for a small crown of dreadlocks, directed the audience to a table where Frankie was to autograph copies of his book. People lined up, but first Frankie excused himself and approached Angel. They spoke briefly, Angel nodded, and Frankie returned to the book table.

He appeared comfortable greeting his would-be fans, engaging in small talk, and signing his autograph—as comfortable as he was reading. This was his turf, and Lenny thought Frankie looked older, more mature—not the anxious boy who last night had inquired about Angel. Certainly not the boy he drove to the airport six years ago.

Hannah and Angie stood in line to purchase books. Angie already

had several copies, but she bought more to give to her university colleagues. Dan stood off by himself, jiggling keys in his pocket and glancing at the front door as if he were concerned about being spotted by
the RNC.

Johnny Pickle helped Lena on with her coat while Lena told Lenny about the condominium her father was buying for them in Forest
Hills. Johnny struggled to get her coat up over her shoulders. "I'll do
that," she snapped. "Just go get the car." Johnny gave Lenny a sheepish
grin and left.

"I knew they were lovers," Lena said.

Lenny looked at Lena without answering.

"My brother and Frankie. I knew they were lovers." She fastened
the top two buttons of her coat. Fastening the rest would have been
impossible.

"I knew it before I read Frankie's stories. In fact, I probably knew
that they would become lovers before they knew it. Of course Gennaro never mentioned anything to me, but neither did Frankie."

Lena slipped on her gloves and tucked her blond hair up into her
hat as she continued talking. "Well not in so many words he didn't,
but I didn't have to be a detective to read between what Frankie did
tell me, and once his stories were published, well, you'd have to be an
idiot not to figure things out."

"Your parents?" Lenny asked.

"Who knows? My mother is the queen of denial. How else could
she have stayed with my father? And my father? Well, he's Big Vinny.
He makes his own truth. I don't know if either one of them have ever
read Frankie's stories. If they have, they've never mentioned it to me.
But his stories are fiction, right? And you know how we DiCicos are
good about not looking too closely."

Lenny never went to see Big Vinny while he was in prison, but
he kept his promise and was in frequent contact with Marie and looked
after the DiCico grave, bringing flowers on holidays, birthdays, and
anniversaries. After Big Vinny was released from prison—early, as he
had predicted—Lenny first saw him at Lena's wedding and since then
at the cemetery. Scungilli was rarely with him. In prison, his diabetes
worsened, and he now required regular kidney dialysis. However, Big

Vinny always brought an extra chair and sandwich, just in case Lenny showed up.

They talked about a lot of things during their cemetery tête-à-têtes, but Big Vinny never suggested that Gennaro and Frankie were anything but, *like brothers*. "Like our grandfathers and fathers," Big Vinny said, "Only you and me weren't like brothers. Poor Scungilli had to stand in for you." Lenny just nodded when Big Vinny said this.

They didn't fight anymore. Even when Big Vinny complained about Muslims and Mexicans or whomever and whatever he happened to be angry about, Lenny just remained quiet, and Big Vinny eventually changed the subject. Once Lenny brought Doug with him to the cemetery, and after that, at least for a while, Big Vinny brought a third chair and sandwich, just in case.

Lenny told Lena that he saw Big Vinny at the cemetery a few days before Christmas. She nodded and kissed Lenny's cheek.

"I'm gonna wait by the door. I'll tell my parents you were asking for them. Tell Frankie that I said he did a great job, and it's time for him to get over Gennaro. Shit happens, and you have to move on. That guy over there ain't half bad." Lena nodded towards Angel who was sitting on a bench along the front window, reading Frankie's stories. His tattooed forearms rested against his knees. Lena waddled towards the front door. "Ciao," she said and wriggled her fingertips over her shoulder. The four karat diamond in her engagement ring caught the light from the overhead florescent, and Lenny thought, *Poor Johnny*.

Hannah approached. She was wearing her coat and slipped Frankie's book into her purse. "Well I guess I got what I came for," she said. "I already said goodbye to Angie and Dan. Please tell Vi that it was nice meeting her. Frankie's sister is lovely. As pretty as their mother."

"You're leaving?" Lenny asked. He hadn't introduced Vi as Frankie's mother, but assumed that Angie must have mentioned it.

"Yes, I have an early meeting tomorrow. You know how to reach me."

Lenny thought of Tootsie. Though Frankie kept in touch with her and Tyrone, Lenny hadn't seen Tootsie since the night they spent together in the old house.

Hannah's departure was abrupt, and Lenny wondered if he had said something wrong or if his behavior around Vi spoke of more than anything he might have said, but he regretted only that he might have been rude, not that Hannah left.

"Woman trouble, Lenny?"

Lenny sat next to Angel. "I thought you were reading."

"So that's where Frankie gets his green eyes." Angel looked at Vi, who was at the reception table filling a ceramic mug with chai. "Not bad. I didn't know there was a missus."

"There isn't," Lenny said. "We divorced years ago. She lives in California."

"And you still have a thing for her."

"Who said I still have the thing for her?"

"The lady who just walked out of here with her panties in a knot."

There was no smell of alcohol on Angel's breath. *He's a good guy*, Lenny thought.

Angel often helped other guests at the Kitchen. Little things like carrying someone's tray if they were in rough shape or calming someone who started running off at the mouth. Lenny tried not to make too much of Frankie's interest in Angel, or wonder if it was reciprocated. He told himself he was done with worrying. *Bottom line is, Frankie is 24.*

"What do you think of Frankie's writing?" Lenny asked.

"Good. I think it's good, but what do I know?"

"You know that I still have a thing for his mother." Angel cleared his throat and gave his head a little nod. Lenny turned to find Vi standing next to him holding a mug of chai with the words *Actively Offensive To Patriarchy* stenciled across the mug.

Angel whispered to Lenny: "I'm gonna find the crapper." And Lenny smiled up at Vi. No sense worrying about whether or not she overheard him. What difference did it make anyway.

"Did you choose that mug?" he asked.

Vi read it and laughed. "No, I didn't notice, but now I might buy one. Mind if I join you?"

She sat where Angel had and crossed her legs. Her skirt rose above her knees, and she smelled of something light, like a spring shower. "So what's with gypsy eyes?" she asked.

Lenny thought of the Jimi Hendrix song they once made love to in the warehouse. They played a lot of Hendrix and Janice Joplin though both performers were long gone by the time he met Vi.

"Who?" Lenny said.

"The guy you were talking to."

"That's Angel. He's one of the guys who comes to the Kitchen."

"He doesn't look like a homeless man," Vi said.

Lenny was irked by Vi's comment and felt somewhat defensive. "Angel's okay. Still healing from Iraq. That's all. He has a one-room flat, not too far from the Kitchen. Mostly vets live in his building."

"It seems as if Frankie is taken with him."

"Seems that way."

Vi sipped her tea and glanced at Ina, who was taller and thinner than Vi had been when she was a girl, but Ina clearly resembled her mom. She talked with the staple boy. "Maybe both of our kids have found love," Vi said.

Over the years, Lenny had grown very fond of Ina. They spent a lot of time together when Frankie was depressed and Lenny stayed with him in Los Angeles, and during her frequent visits to New York. But he was surprised to hear Vi say *our kids*. *Now I'm the one reading into things*, he thought.

"Ina's a bit young for him," Lenny said, but then he thought of the age difference between Vi and him and quickly qualified his comment. "What I mean is she's only 14."

"I know what you mean, Lenny."

Vi looked at Lenny and laughed, and he saw a glimpse of the girl he had met years ago.

They talked about the kids, about Vi's mother's failing health, about Vi's work, and Lenny's job at the Kitchen.

"Manhattan life certainly agrees with you," Vi said. "Ina's already talking about Columbia, maybe NYU. I'm sure Frankie will move back East after he completes his masters. That will give Ina more reason to come here for college. She and Frankie have become very close. I'll miss her. I'll miss both of them."

Lenny recalled his being accepted at Columbia years ago, but quickly dismissed those thoughts. "Maybe Angie could find you a job teaching in New Your City," he said, surprising himself.

"Maybe," Vi said, but Lenny assumed she was joking.

There were little more than a dozen folks remaining in Bluestockings, and Lenny noticed Dan holding several books as Angie put on her coat. Dan followed her to where Vi and Lenny sat. Over the years Angie and Vi had become friendly. Ina had often stayed with Angie, and given that Angie and Vi were professors, conversation between them came easily.

"How about dinner this week?" Angie asked. "I didn't get to talk much with Ina. Unless you're returning soon to L.A."

"No, we're here for another week." Vi glanced at Lenny. "Yes, dinner would be fun."

"Good. I'll call you tomorrow. I'll cook. Ina likes my lasagna."

They exchanged hugs, and Angie and Dan left the bookstore. Lenny thought about Vi coming to dinner, but then noticed Frankie and Angel sitting alone at the table where only a few books remained. Lenny's nascent but persistent memory returned. This time it was more than just the feeling of watching something that he shouldn't, but images were unclear, distant and dark, so remote that he was unsure if he was remembering or imagining. He was very young, and with one hand he pushed aside a lace curtain and looked through a small pane of glass. With his other hand he felt the cool of the glass doorknob. It was the French door between the dining room and office. Leonardo sat in the swivel desk chair and he leaned forward with his elbows resting on his knees and his chin pressed into his chest as if he were asleep. Slowly young Lenny turned the doorknob and opened the door just enough to poke his head into the office and inhale its musty smell. He wondered if he should wake his Nonno, but Leonardo wasn't asleep, and he removed his glasses and turned. Lenny saw the small puckered indentations on the sides of Leonardo's nose. They glistened pink and moist and he wondered if they hurt as his Nonno Leonardo extended one hand. Young Lenny climbed onto his lap. With his other hand, Leonardo tossed photographs on the desk. Lenny couldn't make out their images, but the photographs were thick, like cardboard. Leonardo smiled at Lenny, but a tear that pooled where a nose pad once pressed ran down the creases in the old man's face.

Vi's voice and the touch of her hand on his startled Lenny. "Are you okay?"

He looked at her hand and then into her eyes. "I was just remembering something. At least I think it was a memory. Yes, yes, I'm okay."

"Ina and I have to leave. Why don't I first drop you off?" Vi asked.

"I'm okay, really. I'll wait for Frankie."

"Are you sure?" Vi seemed unconvinced, but Lenny assured her that he was fine. By now, Ina, Frankie, Angel, and staple boy were clearing the folding chairs. Vi brought Ina her coat. "We'll see you at Angie's," Vi said to Lenny and Frankie. "I'm looking forward to it."

But Lenny, still lost in his memories, barely responded to Vi's comment.

After Vi and Ina left, Lenny helped push the stacks back into place. Staple boy, whose name turned out to be Tristan, was very appreciative. Frankie and Angel invited Lenny to join them for something to eat. "We're going to Chinatown," Frankie said.

"Thanks, but I have an early morning. By the way, I like your Taormina button," he said to Angel.

Frankie walked Lenny to the door while Angel helped Tristan push the last stack into place.

The cold roused Lenny from his fog. "Excellent job tonight. You're very talented."

"Thanks, Dad."

"Vi and Ina are coming to Aunt Angie's for dinner this week. When we know the day, maybe you'd like to invite Angel."

Frankie paused. His green eyes searched for an answer. "Yes. I would like that," he said. "In fact, I'd like that a lot."

Lenny gave Frankie a hug.

"I love you, Dad."

"I love you too, son," Lenny said.

Riding the subway home, Lenny recalled his memory of Leonardo looking at what Lenny assumed were the cartoline postale. The lights flashed on and off as the train rocked through the tunnel, and Lenny wondered why he hadn't remembered sooner. Had seeing Frankie and Angel together jarred his memory? *Frankie would make much of that,* Lenny thought, and the subway snaked from one stop to the next while he thought about Vi and Ina coming to dinner, and maybe Angel, and that Vi said she looked forward to it. Finally the train arrived at his station.

✎ Acknowledgments

Thank you Guernica Editions, especially Michael Mirolla, Editor-In-Chief, and David Moratto, book designer. It's been a pleasure and an honor to work with you. And thank you to all those who encouraged me along the way: friend and poet Amy Zamkoff—you were there when I first turned the ideas for my manuscript into words on paper; Hawley Green Writers (Robin Butler, Jeffrey Gorney, Mary Ellen Marusa)—you welcomed me into your group despite my critique parameters; initial draft readers—Kathy Effler and Susan Lansing. When I took an extended break from working on my manuscript, friend and author Ari Lev encouraged and supported my efforts writing creative nonfiction, and Francine Ringold, Senior Advisory Editor, and Elis O'Neal, Editor-in-chief, of *Nimrod International Journal of Prose and Poetry* were the first to publish one of my short stories. Paul Willis and Amie Evans of Saints and Sinners Literary Festival also supported and encouraged my work, and, when I finally revisited and revised *Most Precious Blood*, Amie Evans' insight and advice was invaluable. Len Fonte checked my Italian, as my Rosetta Stone remains in its box, unopened. Sue Weiss and Anne Marie Voutsinas read for edits and typos before I sent *Most Precious Blood* out in search of a publisher. Finally, thank you to my family for making the kitchen, dining room, and most any table an altar where story was revered: my parents Millie and Tony Sgambati who taught me that love means you show up despite differences or disagreements; my son Jesse Sgambati who teaches me through example that art is 10 percent inspiration and 90 percent hard work; Jack Stevens, you were my greatest cheerleader and always my better-half—more precious than blood.

About the Author

Vince Sgambati's family owned and operated an Italian-American grocery store similar to Lasante's. Though a work of fiction, the soul of *Most Precious Blood* is drawn from Vince's experiences, and like most of Lenny Lasante's childhood friends and siblings, Vince moved on, but often returned to reclaim some lost flavor of ethnicity. His short stories and creative nonfiction have appeared in journals and anthologies and have been recognized by the *Nimrod* Literary Awards: the Katherine Anne Porter Prize for Fiction and the *Saints and Sinners* Short Fiction Contest (2013 & 2016). *Most Precious Blood* is his first novel. Vince makes his home in the Finger Lakes area of Central New York and in Manhattan.